T0061560

HOMEWARD FROM HEAVEN

RUSSIAN LIBRARY

R

The Russian Library at Columbia University Press publishes an expansive selection of Russian literature in English translation, concentrating on works previously unavailable in English and those ripe for new translations. Works of premodern, modern, and contemporary literature are featured, including recent writing. The series seeks to demonstrate the breadth, surprising variety, and global importance of the Russian literary tradition and includes not only novels but also short stories, plays, poetry, memoirs, creative nonfiction, and works of mixed or fluid genre.

Editorial Board:

Vsevolod Bagno

Dmitry Bak

Rosamund Bartlett

Caryl Emerson

Peter B. Kaufman

Mark Lipovetsky

Oliver Ready

Stephanie Sandler

■ □ ■

For a list of books in the series, see page 269

HOMEWARD FROM HEAVEN

BORIS POPLAVSKY

Translated by Bryan Karetnyk

Columbia University Press   New York

Published with the support of Read Russia, Inc.,
    and the Institute of Literary Translation, Russia
Columbia University Press
Publishers Since 1893
New York   Chichester, West Sussex
cup.columbia.edu

Translation copyright © 2022 Bryan Karetnyk
All rights reserved

Library of Congress Cataloging-in-Publication Data
Names: Poplavskiĭ, Boris, 1903–1935, author. | Karetnyk, Bryan,
    translator.
Title: Homeward from heaven / Boris Poplavsky; translated by
    Bryan Karetnyk.
Other titles: Domoĭ s nebes. English
Description: New York : Columbia University Press, [2022] |
    Series: Russian library
Identifiers: LCCN 2021043777 (print) | LCCN 2021043778 (ebook) |
    ISBN 9780231199308 (hardback) | ISBN 9780231199315 (trade
    paperback) | ISBN 9780231553049 (ebook) Subjects: LCGFT:
Novels.
Classification: LCC PG3476.P633 D6613 2022 (print) |
    LCC PG3476.P633 (ebook) | DDC 891.73/42—dc23
LC record available at https://lccn.loc.gov/2021043777
LC ebook record available at https://lccn.loc.gov/2021043778

Cover design: Roberto de Vicq de Cumptich

CONTENTS

INTRODUCTION

BRYAN KARETNYK

"How did I live my life?" asked Proust in the twilight of his years. *"Ma vie qui semblait devoir être brève comme un jour d'hiver."*

▶ Boris Poplavsky, "On the subject of..." (1931)

T he final years of Boris Poplavsky's life were, according to his father, "profoundly enigmatic."[1] His friend, the artist and writer Ilya Zdanevich, characterized them aphoristically and with a dash of foreboding: "Mysticism, poverty, dubious associations, perhaps despair."[2] Rumors that his death, from a fatal dose of heroin, had not been accidental only added to his mystique. And in the end, the mythos, the cult that was built up around him after he died—"almost having reached the age of Christ," as the editor Louis Allain so elegantly observed—effectively canonized him, not only as one of the twentieth century's great *poètes maudits*, but also as a mystic, a seer, an oracle, a God-seeker.[3]

Boris Poplavsky was the quintessential wild child of Russian Montparnasse. Born in Moscow in 1903, he was raised in the exquisite sophistication and *fin-de-siècle* decadence of Russia's Silver Age.

Like others of his generation, he suffered adolescence during the paroxysms and traumas of revolution and civil war, before reaching maturity, both personal and artistic, amid the destitution and deracination of exile. In Paris, where he made a home for himself in 1921, he fell in with a bohemian group of expatriate artists, writers, philosophers, and idlers who haunted the cafés of the Rive Gauche during those now-legendary years between the two world wars.

Whether by design or by immutable nature, Poplavsky's life in exile was characterized by paradox and scandal. He was a poet and a pugilist, a dandy and a drifter, an ascetic and a debauchee, a weight-lifter and a morphinist. He was a Russian writer whose mature art owed perhaps more to Louis Aragon, Charles Baudelaire, André Breton, and Arthur Rimbaud than it did to any of the Russian classics. He was a gifted art critic who provocatively declared the absence of art to be more beautiful than art itself.[4] And he was a thinker who was just as at home discoursing on the spiritualism of Helena Blavatsky and Jiddu Krishnamurti as he was extolling the physical prowess of Primo Carnera and the centuries-old history of boxing, which, with typical perversity, he dubbed the most metaphysical of sports.[5] Indeed, Georgy Adamovich, the chief critic of the Paris school and an early champion of Poplavsky's, recalled of his many faces:

You could never know what Poplavsky would bring on any given day, who he would be on any given night: a monarchist, a communist, a mystic, a rationalist, a Nietzschean, a Marxist, a Christian, a Buddhist, or simply an athletic young man who detested every last bit of that abstract wisdom and believed that all one needed was a good night's sleep, a hearty meal, and access to a gym in which to build up one's muscles, whereas everything else was born of evil.[6]

For so seemingly elusive a figure, he was also, conspicuously, the one writer about whom nobody in the emigration was equivocal. His admirers, drawn mostly from artists of his own generation, displayed an almost fanatical devotion to him, seeing in him a luminary whose creative hybridization would rescue émigré letters from sterility and death. By contrast, his detractors, those venerable stalwarts who had attained fame back in prerevolutionary Russia, were not only mystified by the man and his work, but even disturbed by his "dangerous" writing, which dealt in surrealism, spiritual eclecticism, and sexuality so explicit as to rival the best of D.H. Lawrence and Henry Miller. Reviews of his verses ranged from the bewildered to the outraged, and after an extract of his first novel, *Apollon Bezobrazoff*, was published in 1931, the illustrious Dmitry Merezhkovsky was reportedly "unable to forgive himself for having given a chapter of his latest book, *The Unknown Jesus*, to [the literary journal] *Chisla*, where it appeared alongside Poplavsky's decadent novel with its sacrilegious filth."[7]

Misunderstood, marginalized, impoverished even by the abject standards of Montparnasse, Poplavsky cut a tragic, if defiant, figure. He would often find himself, nevertheless, at the mercy of chance acquaintances who exhibited a startling degree of callousness. "I would see him in the evenings at the library where he studied German philosophy," Zdanevich recollected. "Some wealthy friends of his, who saw him as entertainment, would drag him off to the bars. One day he asked them for help. They refused. But they did suggest that he try heroin."[8] On October 8, 1935, fate pushed him in the way of one Sergei Yarkho, a shady character who reputedly "persuaded Boris . . . to try a powder of illusions."[9] Plausible cases are still made for accident, suicide, and murder, but, whatever the true cause, when his lifeless body was discovered the following day, the news came as a sobering rebuke to those who had mistreated him, looked upon his plight, and turned away.

Cliché though it may be, it was in death that Poplavsky received his due. By the time that his life met its abrupt end, he had published only a single collection of poetry, *Flags* (1931), as well as a handful of fragments, essays, and reviews. Unbeknownst to many, however, he had also left behind one of the most significant collections of unpublished writing since Franz Kafka. The swift posthumous appearance of two more collections of his verses, *Snowy Hour* (1936) and *In a Wreath of Wax* (1938), brought about such a rapid reappraisal of his work that it was held up, now with unprecedented unanimity, to be not only among the finest produced by young writers of the emigration, but even, by Merezhkovsky no less, a vindication of the diaspora itself.[10] The years also brought with them greater understanding of and compassion for Poplavsky's life, transfigured in the eyes of his contemporaries, who now readily placed him in the prophetic tradition of Russian writers. Indeed, when extracts of his diaries appeared in 1938, the religious philosopher Nikolai Berdiaev took special note, describing them as "a document of a contemporary soul, a young Russian soul in emigration," and hailing Poplavsky as "a true martyr, a victim of his striving toward sainthood."[11]

■ □ ■

Composed in 1934 and 1935, *Homeward from Heaven* was Poplavsky's last major opus. He completed work on the novel only a matter of weeks before his death, and, basking in the satisfaction of its completion, even noted in his diary: "Now the dream is to buy a new gray notebook and to carry on with my licentious scribblings."[12] It was conceived of as the second part in a trilogy, the first book of which was *Apollon Bezobrazoff*, and the last of which was the planned but never-realized *Apocalypse of Thérèse*. Those wishing to take these works in order may consult John Kopper's fine translation, which was published in 2015; however, owing to the vast gulf that divides these two works thematically and stylistically, they may also be read independently without impediment or detriment to the reader. Indeed, as Poplavsky makes clear in the opening pages, the action of *Homeward from Heaven* takes place six years after the closing events of the first novel, and, with the sole exception of Bezobrazoff, the cast of characters has been changed by the passage of "many-winged time."

The novel opens in the summer of 1932 and closes precisely two years later. In view of the unfamiliarity that many readers will have with the period and milieu in which Poplavsky was writing, a few words are in order to aid the reader's orientation. As the sun rises on that first page, the French president, Paul Doumer, has just been assassinated by the émigré poet and madman Paul Gorgouloff, provoking a wave of anti-Russian sentiment across France. Those two ensuing years will see a number of momentous political events take place in Europe: Nazism will triumph in Germany, sending Hitler to power and emboldening fascist movements across the Continent; and in the Soviet Union, the completion of the first five-year plan will be hailed as a victory of socialism, while much of Ukraine and the Russian south will be plunged into the hell of a man-made famine that will end the lives of millions. In France, 10 francs are worth just less than 10 dollars today: a loaf of bread costs 2 francs, a decent meal at the Rotonde is around 20 francs, Bezobrazoff's beloved

Paris-Midi is priced at 25 centimes, and cocaine is sold illegally for 40 francs per gram. Oleg's unemployment benefit is paid out at a rate of 7 francs per day—all of which should give the reader some indication as to the real value of the 50 francs at which he is willing to set aside his own morals. The Russians of Paris, by now resigned to the fact of Soviet rule, though still longing for their lost homeland, range from the Maecenases to the mendicants, although wealthy men such as Katia's dapper, gray-haired, absent father are sooner the exception to the rule of poverty. Among the destitute, Oleg himself ranks with the humiliated and insulted, yet, like Poplavsky, he too ultimately manages to find in these dire circumstances "a tragic pauper's paradise for poets, dreamers, and romantics."[13]

When extracts of *Homeward from Heaven* began to appear in 1936, readers who had known Poplavsky took the novel initially to be a straightforward *roman à clef*, a chronicle of those last "enigmatic" years, constructed around his tempestuous affair with Natalia Stolyarova, his lover and muse, whom he first met in 1931. The romance brought him, as one commentator remarked, "radiant minutes of happiness, and endless hours of great torment,"[14] but it was broken off when Stolyarova returned to the Soviet Union in December 1934.[15] Two trips taken by Poplavsky to Stolyarova's *gîte* at La Favière in the summers of 1932 and 1934 provide much of the material for the opening chapters, a fact made all the more readily apparent by the occasional authorial slip, wherein Poplavsky erroneously refers to the Riviera setting not as Saint-Tropez, as it ought to be, but as La Favière and its environs. When the action removes to Paris in the ensuing chapters, the reader may also discern in Oleg's "band of poetic souls" several recognizable portraits of émigré artists and writers who numbered among Poplavsky's close friends, including the poet Lidia Chervinskaya, the novelist Yuri Felsen, and the poet and painter Serge Charchoune. Like Poplavsky himself, Oleg is "a zealot and a skeptic, a born mystic and a mystifier," and bears a pronounced resemblance to his author in habits, prejudices, and outlook. The domestic squalor of the place d'Italie, the perennial disdain for manual labor, the entrenched, almost comical reluctance to qualify as a taxi driver, the life of dissipation in the bars and cafés of Montparnasse, and the continual impassioned attempts to transcend the immediate reality of this abject existence through meditation, prayer, love, beauty, art, even weightlifting—all this shared life and experience binds Poplavsky and Oleg together profoundly and inextricably.

To write a novel with such stark and immediate autobiographical parallels was in keeping with the literary vogue of the day. Borrowing from their French counterparts, the Paris school of Russian writers was fast developing a taste for the so-called "human document" in fiction. Confessional, plotless, and deeply psychological, the genre reworked the traditions of the French naturalist school and came to be looked upon as the perfect creative vehicle through which to explore this new age of anxiety amid the despair of exile. In this pursuit, it encouraged émigré writers to eschew imagination and instead to draw bountifully on autobiography in an attempt to articulate the precise combination of existential malaise, social marginality, and spiritual *angoisse* that they experienced. "What kind of mug would barge in on art with imagination?"[16] Poplavsky himself exclaimed in a remarkable essay on James Joyce.

But is Oleg, then, a simple avatar of Poplavsky? Is Tania merely a thinly veiled portrait of Stolyarova? Not quite. For Poplavsky, the truth was always more ambivalent, more arcane. "The characters in both of my novels, every last one of them, are my own inventions," he recorded in his diary,

> but I have truly experienced their discordance and their struggle. Did I take them from life, copy them, develop them, exaggerate them to the point of monstrosity? No, I found them ready-made within myself, for they are my multiple personalities, and their struggle is the struggle in my heart, the struggle between compassion and severity, between a love of life and a love of death; they are all me, but who am I, really? I among them am nobody, nothing, the field upon which they do battle, a spectator. A spectator also because each of them and many others have sprung from the darkness of my soul to meet the people who have loved me.[17]

Participant and yet spectator, inscribed and yet effaced: such were the paradoxes of Poplavsky's life and writing, as both attempted to transcend convention. As an artist, Poplavsky could never have been satisfied to adhere to the strict anti-aesthetic code of the "human document," which traduced stylistic and rhetorical embellishment as hallmarks of the false and inauthentic. Instead, he opted for an orgy of collage and contrast: he set the spiritual amid the profane, the metaphysical alongside the carnal; he overlayered the bright, glaring light of realism with the surreal patina of dream; and into the prosaic documentary he introduced all manner of poetry, mysticism, and mythology, drawn from across the ages—for all this, in his reckoning, was every bit as real as the tangible world around.

Perhaps Adamovich, that great arbiter of Montparnasse, resolved the paradox best when he observed that Poplavsky's art was not the writer per se, but rather "a commentary to him, a supplement to his dreams, his thoughts, his doubts, and impulses."[18] *Homeward from*

Heaven is indeed such a commentary: to the final chapter of Poplavsky's foreshortened life. Yet the life that emerges from the pages that follow is not obscure or enigmatic, as so many claimed, but richly, radiantly, enduringly luminous. Truly, these are the years of "a life dominated by the sun," with all its magnificence, horror, wonder, and divinity.

NOTES

1. Iu. Poplavskii, "Boris Poplavskii," in *Boris Poplavskii v otsenkakh i vospominaniiakh sovremennikov*, ed. Lui Allen [Louis Allain] and Ol'ga Gris (St. Petersburg: Logos, 1995), 80.
2. Il'ia Zdanevich, "Boris Poplavskii," *Sintaksis* 16 (1986): 169.
3. Lui Allen [Louis Allain], "Predislovie," in *Boris Poplavskii v otsenkakh i vospominaniiakh sovremennikov*, 5.
4. Boris Poplavskii, *Sobranie sochinenii v trekh tomakh* (Moscow: Soglasie, 2000–2009) 3: 45.
5. Poplavskii, *Sobranie sochinenii*, 3: 71.
6. Georgii Adamovich, *Odinochestvo i svoboda*, (St Petersburg: Azbuka, 2006), 259.
7. Zinaida Gippius, quoted at A. Bem, "Chisla," *Rul'*, July 30, 1931.
8. Zdanevich, "Boris Poplavskii," 169.
9. Poplavskii, "Boris Poplavskii," 81.
10. Adamovich, *Odinochestvo i svoboda*, 254.
11. Nikolai Berdiaev, "Po povodu 'Dnevnikov' B. Poplavskogo," *Sovremennye zapiski* 68 (1939): 441–6, 441 and 443.
12. Poplavskii, *Sobranie sochinenii*, 3: 447.
13. Poplavskii, *Sobranie sochinenii*, 3: 50.
14. Allen, "Predislovie," 6.
15. Stolyarova figured among the small number of Russian émigrés who opted to return to the Soviet Union in the 1920s and 1930s, many of whom, upon return, found themselves under suspicion in the darkening political atmosphere of those years. Shortly after Stolyarova's arrival, her father was arrested and shot, and in 1937, at the start of the Great Terror, she was arrested for alleged participation in an "anti-Soviet organization" and sent to the Gulag until 1945. Before her departure from Paris, Poplavsky had promised that if she did not return within a year and if he received favorable news from her, he would go to Russia to be with her.
16. Poplavskii, *Sobranie sochinenii*, 3: 78.
17. Poplavskii, *Sobranie sochinenii*, 3: 444.
18. Adamovich, *Odinochestvo i svoboda*, 255.

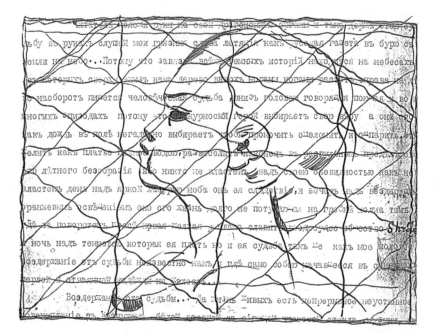

Detail of a deleted passage in the author's typescript.

A NOTE ON THE TEXT

As it did for so much of his writing, Boris Poplavsky's untimely death precluded the publication of any definitive authorized version of *Homeward from Heaven*. Thus, the question necessarily begs itself: How did the novel make its way into print, and on which edition is this translation based?

There is evidence to suggest that Poplavsky prepared at least one preliminary draft of *Homeward from Heaven* in manuscript, although only a single folio from that version survives today, held in the archives of the State Literary Museum in Moscow. The only extant copy of the complete text to have been produced during Poplavsky's lifetime is a later typescript, to which he made a substantial number of corrections, revisions, and additions, mostly by hand. This, we may reasonably surmise, is the finished version that he mentions in his diary entry for September 15, 1935.

After the author's death, his archive, including that typescript, was entrusted to his friend and literary executor, Nikolai Tatishchev, who, together with his wife Dina (née Schreibman)—Poplavsky's former lover and muse, and the prototype of Thérèse—corrected and lightly edited the typescript, preparing three extracts of the novel for print. These extracts were published between 1936 and 1938 in each issue of the short-lived émigré literary almanac *Krug*. However, owing to the subsequent decline of émigré publishing and the continued prohibition on printing émigré works in the Soviet Union, the *Krug* publications marked the extent of the novel's appearance in print for more than half a century.

In the decades after the war, Nikolai's son Stepan Tatishchev undertook to prepare a new typescript. The reasons for and precise date of this undertaking are not entirely clear, but this second typescript was based on the author's original one and took into account the edits made by Poplavsky and the senior Tatishchevs, with one important exception: it retained the passages that Poplavsky himself had marked for deletion. This typescript was eventually subjected to further revisions by Natalia Stolyarova and Alexander Bogoslovsky before going on to serve as the textual basis for the two ostensibly complete editions. The first of these was published by Logos in 1993, under the editorship of the French Slavist Louis Allain, while the latter was published by Soglasie in 2000 as part of Poplavsky's three-volume collected works. Despite being based on the same "new" typescript, the two published versions of the text exhibit a number of significant discrepancies. The Logos edition, while being in many respects the more polished of the two publications, makes cuts and frequent editorial interventions in an attempt to refine and bring clarity to Poplavsky's difficult, at times opaque, prose. The Soglasie edition, by contrast, makes fewer such interventions, yet incorporates a number of those passages that Poplavsky marked to be struck from the final version. Both editions, furthermore, contain errors of transcription, and their editors were forced to censor many of the text's more explicit moments.

Faced thus with these not entirely reliable editions, I have, in preparing the translation that follows, elected to work from a copy of Poplavsky's original typescript, which was provided to me from a private collection in France. By restoring to the text those previously censored passages and relegating those others marked for deletion to the endnotes, I hope to have produced what may be termed, with all the necessary provisos, a version of the text free from censorship and most closely resembling Poplavsky's intended artistic vision, albeit one transposed into a foreign idiom.

A NOTE ON TRANSLITERATION

T he very nature of emigration meant that every Russian in exile underwent various reincarnations in foreign languages and scripts. As such, any transliteration system imposed on a work of this period invariably requires that certain concessions be made.

French transliterations and conventions appropriate to the era have been used throughout the main body of text to reflect most closely the styles and usage preferred by émigrés living in France at the time. Elsewhere, for the reader's ease, I have used a simplified version of the common BGN/PCGN system, with names, places, and Russian words rendered further according to the most commonly recognizable and readable style (e.g., Lidia rather than Lidiya). Accepted and preferred spellings of historical figures, where they exist, have been also used (e.g., Serge Charchoune rather than Sergei Sharshun). Bibliographical entries detailing original publications, however, have been rendered uniformly according to the more scholarly Library of Congress system.

HOMEWARD FROM HEAVEN

Je rêvais que j'étais ineffablement heureux, mais sans aucune forme,
sans univers, sans Moi, et ma filière même était le Moi.*

▶ Jean Paul[1]

The sun was rising over the city. Serenely and independently, it lit up the empty streets and the upper stories of the buildings; determinedly and steadily it went about its business, penetrating every detail of the metalwork on the rooftops, illuminating the poplars' innumerable leaves, drying out the drenched sidewalks; and, behind the Gare Montparnasse, through the white steam rising over locomotives on a viaduct, it played with a radiant, rose-tinted cloud. There was no life at this hour; life was still sunk in slumber, where the sun could not penetrate; only aslant, through curtains, did it illuminate sleeping bodies, their lips pouting, their magnificent heads unrecognizable; sunk in slumber, where

---

* I dreamt that I was indescribably happy, but without form, without universe, without my Self, and my path alone was my Self (*French*).

the ignominious chaos of physiological mythology teems with yesterday's insults, crushed arms, comestible atrocities, splayed bodies,
and suppliant fears. Serenely and tranquilly the sun took charge of
the street, for, despite the chaos and neurasthenia of the cosmos,
summer was once again returning, serene and blinding. Many-
winged time has swept over our group of melodeclaimers, familiar
from the previous act.[2] Each of them has changed, all except Apollon
Bezobrazoff, who, not alive, ergo, not aging, not suffering, ergo, not
partaking in anything, archaic and aloof, has continued to journey
from one end of the city to another, like a serpent, slithering his way
unhurriedly across the railway tracks. In more recent times, this serpent has taken to passing the hours with the *Paris-Midi* and Fichte's
philosophy of science, in the margins of which he keeps his unpre-
tentious monastic diary.[3]

■ □ ■

"Almost warm today—or, rather, altogether warm already. How
quickly the city empties, how majestically it unwinds in the sun.
Ever since I began my studies at the faculty of theology, I have found
myself delighted more and more by the physical proximity to that
from which, in moral terms, I am farthest removed . . . The days
again pass without note (*sans histoires*), between dormitory (devi-
ous, melancholy eyes, clandestine toasts to Satan, insufferably shambolic singing and the inevitable 'hilarity' that goes with it . . . Russia,
blessed Mother Russia), lectures (where I, of course, am top of the
class), and library, crossing the length and breadth of the city on
foot, on the sunny side of the street . . . By which I mean to say that
each individual is utterly in thrall to his own dream of God . . .[4]

"But enough of all that. For now, my life is perfectly comfortable. The only thing I have not quite learned yet is how to stand through the entire service; then again, mastering the physically unendurable has always been a kind of Holy Grail for me, like eating without salt or writing with my left hand or, come to think of it, joining the clergy (as opposed to the army or the ranks of rakes and reprobates) . . . But what, exactly, does the devil—he who cares nothing for people or the State—busy himself with, if not God? The devil is the most religious being on earth, for he never doubts, has never doubted the existence of God, staring Him, as he does, in the eye all day long; he is doubt incarnate when it comes to the motives behind all this creation, however . . . Could He not have created . . . Or did that elementary indulgence in sexual fantasy force Him to . . . At what price, though . . . But enough of all that. Won't this lecture ever begin?

"May 1932."

(The years pass, while A. B. remains the same.)

■ □ ■

Oleg and God were playing a duet on a sizzling piano made up of the city's terracotta roof tiles. He was first to weary, but God went on playing for a long time yet, never tiring amid the storm clouds, whereas Oleg merely listened, scratching his head, narrowing his eyes, pulling a wry face at the white, but so excruciatingly white sky, so painful to behold even without the sun.

A hot, gray day, rain falling through a haze, but once again the pavement dries out, and over the rooftops, now and then, there comes the sound of distant thunder. Hot and damp, a summer without sun . . . How morose you are, Oleg . . . You too, like every passerby, have on your weary, perspiring face that constant, pointed, inevitable look of summertime sadness, the one shared by all those who stay or are left behind in the city . . . Why not go and seek out this summer by the beach, the one whose photographs fill the pages of illustrated magazines, the very ones you eye upon the walls of the kiosk with that air of studied indifference. A great many hang there, each cover boasting happy, rude faces and happy, suntanned bodies beside the dazzling water . . . Why not go there, to this thousand-visaged sea? Aren't you ashamed of dreaming idly, or are you a dreamer, a masturbator of the imagination? . . . Again, the rain drums down on the warm asphalt and the glossy, freshly washed leaves of the chestnut trees . . . Rain, rain, rain . . .

■ □ ■

Today you sit alone in a café. All your friends have either left or abandoned you because of your callousness, but now it is you who need them, for you are human too, and that is why it hurts so . . . So why not take off? Haven't you already accomplished what you set out to achieve? Doesn't it fill you with pride? . . . You haven't wanted so desperately to get away from this warm, rainy, urban torment in a long while. To go there, to the wild, wanton, spirited sea, to the hopelessly beautiful women lying on the sand . . . Your exams are over . . . After all, he had no qualms about going: not him, the student, the boy scout. And he felt better for it immediately, as if a burden had been lifted from his soul. As he left, he even began to take pleasure in everything around him in a condescending sort of way, for how good it is suddenly to deliver oneself from forced, insincere sympathy for others . . .

■ □ ■

"Now that I have the six hundred francs, I find myself no longer minded to go to this holiday camp . . .[5] I think I'll take a train to Toulon and try my luck alone. I'll head down to the sea somewhere in the Bandol, where Katherine Mansfield so elegantly died.[6] As I write on board this train, I am subjected to the unremitting, wretched, idle chatter of my fellow students, countrymen and women who all of a sudden grow exceptionally boisterous the moment the train begins to pull into a station. The rain let up some time ago, and so now people crowd the platforms, people who will remain here unfathomably all their lives, selling local news and coffee in paper cups . . . When I awaken, I'll see the sunrise over the Rhône and something resembling mountains . . . I don't feel like sleeping, though . . . My heart is empty, and it's all so tedious that I'm grateful for any distraction afforded by my surroundings. With avid eyes, I take in my classmates' ungainly, youthful, effeminate faces and the girls' infinitely more mature, antique profiles—all this jaundiced, lumpen, ravishing, disgusting, Russian flesh . . . After all their whooping and shrieking, they grew tired and morose and began to croon, interrupting one another, out of tune and time. Then, after amiably ensconcing themselves (and gallantly crushing the women), they nodded off. Having claimed a spot for myself, I stepped into the corridor and poked my head out into the darkness, reveling in the speeding whirlwind of coal and steam, while occasionally, in the distance up ahead, I could make out the locomotive; a brilliant glow would burst forth from its chimney, momentarily and splendidly illuminating the trees, the telegraph poles, and the plume of smoke above the train . . .

"When I returned to my berth, I found the lamp already extinguished and opposite me, in the reflected light of the corridor, a pair of French newlyweds grunting and writhing, emboldened by the darkness to this touching intimacy. Isolated among Russians, they have spent the entire journey eating and gazing out the window, continually unfastening and refastening the buckles on their brand-new suitcases. During these long, dark hours, I went about clandestinely observing my old, original foe, which had so uninhibitedly possessed the couple together with slumber ... I recall once having read in a newspaper somewhere that an old acrobat, whose signature act was the flying trapeze, lamented how difficult it was to find a partner, since only man and wife or a father and child of the same blood are able to understand each other implicitly, for they breathe with the same breath, are a single phrase within a great sea of bodily, carnal music; and I alone among them, like a cadaver among the living, a monster of suppressed sexuality, revel in this and perish from the freedom, the light, the chastity.

"The sleeping newlyweds continue to take on an ever more vegetative form, so that now I cannot even distinguish where either of them begins or ends; they are conjoined, glued, fused to one another, and, having renounced their individual independence, are rewarded with a warm and rich life, while I, like the devil on the rock, regard with enormous eyes of wonderment the first human couple in an earthly paradise, for they have money, and where there is money, there is life.

"As I reflected on all this, I fell asleep and awoke in the bright light of day, as the train skimmed along the low-running bank of a broad river. To our right towered mountains, nestled among which were whole desolate towns half-hewn from the rockface, complete with crumbling castles. I caught my first glimpse of the sea ere long . . .

"Thus encountering the sea, I felt as if I were turning away from the earth, away from man with his crude, formless weight, toward woman in all her dazzling, dubious, diabolical composure, redolent of nothing, reflective of everything. The train slowly snaked its way along the shore of the Étang de Berre's smooth mirrorlike lagoon, from which, like doves from the shoulders of Aphrodite, seaplanes took steadily and gracefully to the air; there was something radiant, something abominably archaic and implacably splendid about its dazed azure dormancy, and I realized that I should have to wrestle with the luster of the sea as I once did with woman, with the luster of her body amid the dark of night, only now in the blaze of day, for, as congress with the sun is to a lustful woman, bringing her to hot perspiration and the point of exhaustion, so a love of the sea is to me, monster of suppressed lust that I am.

"We fellow travelers had long grown used to each other, and in daylight the carriage seemed so cozy and familiar, like a cottage that one must vacate the very next morning. The sky had been shining an immaculate pale blue for so long, but there it was at last, between the rose-colored factory buildings, like a sparkling ray of sapphire, like a magnificent nude set amid antique burlap, and beside it, in enormous lettering: Briqueterie Centrale de Marseille.* With sudden respectability, the newlyweds set about packing their cases, flaunting with every fiber of their being that they had somewhere to go; the fug of spilled vitality that hung in the carriage was replaced by the fragrance of eau de cologne, which reeked of morning, youth,

---

* Marseilles Central Brick Factory (*French*).

and happiness. An irresistible frisson of anticipation quivered in my temples as everything outside burned, with a brightness that was almost unbearable, into my night-weary eyes, which were particularly photosensitive on account of a lack of sleep, and irritated by the endless tunnels, cuttings, back gardens, front gardens, and suburban stations that obscured the sea. At last, the train came to a halt at a cumbersome-looking station full of suntanned gentlemen wearing white trousers of a prewar cut. There we had to wait another half-hour, but as soon as the train started moving again, I made a run for it, locked myself in the lavatory, where the sky's brilliance came streaming in through the frosted glass, and, stripping off, nervously set about examining myself in the shuddering mirror—was I in good enough shape to exhibit myself on the beach without any sense of shame?"

■ □ ■

"The world cannot only have been thought up by God, for thought lacks duration, its essence consisting in the ecstasy of revelation. Yet nor can the world only be God's imagining, for the imagined must be subordinate to the imaginer, and in that case, there would be no sin, no freedom, no redemption . . . No, the world must be God's dream, one that burgeoned and blossomed precisely at that moment when His imagination ceased to obey Him. He must have fallen asleep and dreamed it, losing His dominion, renouncing it. There was something of a heavenly fall from grace in this, the starry sky imagining itself a man—and, of course, it was none other than the devil who had taught asceticism to this man, because love is that self-same dream of life, which so dulcetly lulled God to sleep, whereas awakening spells the death of solitude and knowledge, while life itself is a hypnosis taken lachrymally seriously. Thus, here again, high above the shore, over the radiant music of the sea, I find myself wrestling with you, O happiness of mine, my dream, my love, my life; but how strange and sweet it would be to give in, once more to be a man, to suffer again . . . How sublimely cold and outrageously clever are those who manage to break, for an instant or a while, the fiery circle of the heart's unceasing congress with life—but not for monstrous dreams of unsated lust, like the cabbalistic debauchery of Adam's mind prior to Eve's creation, debauchery that spawned every evil under the moon, not for sleepless Eros, but for a blinding, painfully bright light, for the stark awakening of Luciferian virginity, in which diabolical frenzy I look down from here, from this lofty precipice, onto a narrow strip of beach by the glassiest, most poisonously blue sea, whence the strains of an electric gramophone drift up to me so unmistakably amid the brilliant noonday still. There, among the tents and their gaily colored parasols, around an upturned canoe, bronzed figures dance in the water, half-naked virgins, the suntanned, strong-legged she-devils of these parts, splash and frolic about, while white clouds cover the distant horizon."

■ □ ■

Oleg's journey to the sea passed in a sense of wonder and alarm, which made its dazzling novelty almost unbearable. Neither he nor Bezobrazoff yet imagined that they could sleep in the middle of the forest on a mattress of pine needles, wrapped in their blankets like Indians, or on the beach, or wherever indeed they pleased, for there was no rain, nothing at all to remind them of France on this strange emerald shore, where, with one blithe and one heavy heart, each for his own reasons, they now rode a little steam engine from Toulon right along the coast, among the rocks, the *gîtes*, the cactuses, and the stripped cork oaks. Oleg talked the night away in the corridor of the carriage—such was he plagued by anxiety, a horror of the unusual and unforeseen, and also by a childish fear of loneliness. It was strange . . . This whole trip had come about so unexpectedly, as though it were some merry twist of fate, and yet his weak heart was troubled. With uncharacteristic agitation, he had spent a humiliating night trying to latch on to someone, but everybody as always maintained a suspicious, dismal distance from him, and it was only Bezobrazoff who patiently—like the rain—heard out his disjointed speech, for Oleg was unable, at times shamefully so, to dissemble. It all gushed forth from his tongue, like a drunkard's piss, colorless and bland. For his part, he suffered terribly, embarrassed by his own loquaciousness, but it was a direct consequence, a facet even, of his terror, the inability to abide himself and his life, to bear the precious burden, the furtive, elephantine strain of loneliness. And so, before long, without wishing it himself, Bezobrazoff had heard the whole backstory to the trip: about the spiritualist circle, about Kumareff's suicide, about the New Year's Eve party in a half-lit atelier, where in a single night Oleg's old life had been shattered and this new one begun, one that was unfamiliar, too real for a man who for so many years had sat at a grimy marble table, like a pale-faced fortune-teller over some cold coffee grounds, in the early stages of melancholy— the decline of one yet to live. But in vain did Oleg, having spoken at such length, look to Bezobrazoff for any glimmer of an answer, for judgment, damnation, a reaction of any kind. Apollon, who listened, as it just so happened, with great professional interest, could give no answer, for, according to his habit, he pondered slowly, refusing to think, to judge, to intervene, and yet he had that easy, forthright, good-natured consideration in spades—he would light up, pull his cap down over his eyes, hook his thumbs around his waistband, and, in his cheap *marinière*, his thick arms bared to the shoulders, listen without so much as looking at his vis-à-vis, rocking on his heels in the corridor with such a calm, thievish, proletarian look about him—one that would not have been out of place in the circus—that everybody on the train kept looking his way with a kind of hostile respect. By the time they left Paris, Apollon was already completely black from the sun and had taken a notion to speak only in French, which he enjoyed doing, chewing his words and drawling in such first-rate Parisian argot that his newly acquired and much-beloved title—"student of theology"—would utterly baffle the chance acquaintance with whom he had only just been discussing boxing, swimming, and aviation at great length. In distinction to Oleg, the novelty of the situation, in a somewhat drearily restrained manner, secretly intoxicated Bezobrazoff. He had leapt at the opportunity to go on this trip, as though diving into water, muscles strained and nostrils flared, as though entering into a fight with an opponent that he could not yet see but sensed immediately—the dazzling majesty of the world, the south, a gay holiday. But even he needed a *copain*, a partner in crime, for they were both of them young men of the city, having grown up amid the smoke-filled poverty of émigré cafés, for whom this trip was, by all accounts, an extraordinary event. Bezobrazoff, however, was finding his bearings quicker than Oleg; as Thérèse had been wont to say of him (sorrowfully, scornfully smiling all the while): "If that one takes it into his head to apply himself to life, he'll never be hard up."

Now, at a small connecting station, they sat amid the midday splendor and, like soldiers, chain-smoked beside their belongings— a suitcase and a little knapsack, which Bezobrazoff, prison-fashion, had tethered to his belt. With a porter's flourish he flung one of them over his shoulder and balanced it there, much to the chagrin of the locals, who, having come to look upon visitors as their own lawful property, watched him with undisguised malevolence. But Bezobrazoff turned around in his own malevolence, like a fish in water, and even took off his cap, which together with his jacket he thrust into his suitcase, leaving him, like a convict, in nothing but his striped vest.

The single-story station was sunk in a daze of sunshine; all its windows were covered by shutters, so that it seemed deserted, and only the clocks there led the forbiddingly efficient life of the railway. Around it there were some dreary flowerbeds and tracks overgrown with wild grass. The noonday silence was so distinct that it seemed almost visible, almost tangible, especially after the roar of the city, to which one so easily accustoms oneself, as to the sound of a neighboring waterfall in Finland—so much, in fact, that during your first days in the countryside you seem to be going deaf. Meanwhile, beyond the silence, slowly and steadily punctuating it, a little locomotive puffed away, unseen, with its head in the clouds, while under the sun, amid perfect stillness, a water tower, a "castle of water," displayed its empty windows.[7] The invisible sea already permeated everything, from the gnarled pines to the rose-colored gravel on the platform, at the end of which, rippling gently, a sailor collar slept. The dazzling, roaring sea was somewhere nearby, and Apollon Bezobrazoff was looking forward to it, grinning as he rolled his shoulders, whereas Oleg thought anxiously of Tania, and of how he would look in a bathing costume.

Oleg recalled that first encounter with his sovereign, whom he had found at long last and recognized immediately. For so long at that wretched New Year's Eve party she had stared silently and unflinchingly at him from behind the half-lowered lashes of her Tartar eyes. Having installed himself in an armchair by her side, and pressing, lifting her heavy, antique, sallow hands, he had recounted to her his life story—a pursuit that was in no way new to him—but on this occasion he met his match: his tale garnered no especial sympathy from her, and he was stunned into silence by the brute and agonizing force of those narrow, avid eyes with their contemptuous gaze. Thus, it had been a novelty for him, who had grown so accustomed to the morbid, motherly tenderness of Jewish women, so much so that he suddenly realized that his weak soul, unconscious of this, had all his life secretly idolized the power of restraint, silence, pride, destiny, the judge and arbiter in a beloved, and that Tania, to his woe, combined all of this and more: soft, heavy, feminine shoulders, the terrible, latent potential of life, a hidden infinity of warmth and cruelty.

As they approached Le Lavandou on that screeching, shuddering little engine, Oleg suddenly recalled the curious and unfamiliar sense of doubt that he had experienced as he peered into those unflinching Tartar eyes, and while the pain in his heart now grew and grew, what had seemed only a second ago the embodiment of kindness, warmth, and life, suddenly became a physical manifestation of coldness, vanity, and mockery; then the urge to kiss her transformed momentarily almost into hatred and very nearly into a desire to strike that grossly exquisite, so mysteriously bestial face.

02

Tania met Oleg, nostrils aflare with curiosity. Six years ago, in Thérèse's days, he had been a hunched-over youth in a grubby collar, a boy who seemed younger than his years; something backward and immature, something childish and distracted had glimmered in him back then, something that was liable to wander off and hang its head, but after neurasthenia and a thousand neuroses, the earthly and corporeal had prevailed, and so he had grown up, grown heavier—he had become a man.[1] That resounding nocturnal despair, the one that had prevented him from accepting life and entering into it, had soon grown repugnant to him, like a disease of the skin; suddenly he had discovered within himself another being, much cruder, funnier, more decisive, more devout, in the sense that this being, having learned to bear its own cross, hesitated now to judge or make a high-handed show of sympathy for another's burden, ignorant as it was of the joys of others and those blessed, mysterious things that go on between them and God, things that are like the unseen nocturnal caresses of man and wife. Since then, since he, like Bezobrazoff, had become more withdrawn, colder, happier, his dealings with others had improved, much to his surprise; instead of those continual insults of old, he had in fact forged relationships, for severity, reticence and detachment are the true markers of civility in Iron Age man, who recognizes the rightful and immeasurable solitude of his individualism and shies above all else from the molestations of sentimentalism. Knowing deep down, though, that true relations can exist only between man and wife, between man and God, between men belonging to the same regiment or the same profession, knowing that this risibly austere human fellowship makes no pretension to absolute intimate knowledge, the very possibility of which (along with the continual rebukes of those who do allow for it) Oleg deemed blindness and an insult to man's heart of stone, scorched as it is by original sin, believing that it was better simply to admit that the heart is a stone and, in this candor, to find some stoical truth—knowing all this, he held himself erect, squared his shoulders, and sprouted forth luxuriant hair, which, untamed and bleached by the sun, had begun to curl. Oleg was even entertaining the idea of growing a beard in imitation of Bezobrazoff, who would scratch his own and stroke it with an inimitable, atavistic, peasantlike gesture. Standing there naked, he seemed broader and heavier than Bezobrazoff, although Bezobrazoff was stronger and showed the effects of more consistent training. Oleg was sullen and impulsive, bitterly melancholic, and after a little wine he liked to sing and would even go looking for a fight—but somehow it never quite got to that. Having once despaired in rebellious, sacrilegious anguish for everyone and for life itself, he now reached out to it ardently, to this unfamiliar life, homeward from heaven, headlong into a hot, pungent, seething mist. In recent months, for reasons unknown, he had even begun to look for work and set himself the task of memorizing the city streets with the aid of a taxi-driver's manual. It was thus, as he changed physically, that Tania had come to his attention. A different person now, he had for so long failed to notice her, having been mixed up with Ira and her torments, forever humiliated and beleaguered by her mawkish, morbid concern for him, which he himself did nothing to inspire. When at last, not without Tania's inadvertent participation, Ira prized herself away from Oleg and went her inscrutable, empyrean way, he regained, after the initial headrush of solitude, his rich, undivided anguish in full, was filled to the brim with restless, weighty, Slavic despair, and, with this almost unbearable burden in his heart, came to Saint-Tropez. The encounter with Bezobrazoff momentarily took him back six years. He told Bezobrazoff everything, but had no time to be angry with him: so striking, so captivating, so unlike anything else was this new life of his in the forest.

For these were, after all, his first days there. His short-lived restless happiness began on the seventh of August, at a long, uncovered table where, in varying states of undress, the whole company sat: Tania, in long sailor's trousers; Nadia, an extraordinarily beautiful if somewhat clumsy girl, who had literally nothing on but a pair of palm-sized bathing accoutrements; Nika Bloudoff, a tawny ape-man whose modesty was barely disguised; and another tall, sullen youth in soccer shorts. There were also some robust-looking old-timers, bearded and solemn, who had contrived somehow to keep afloat in life—and yet, but for a vague fear of them, Oleg scarcely noticed their presence.

The evening marched on toward sunset, slowly blushing pink, but it was so bright, so replete with the relentless chirring of cicadas and so thick with the aroma of pine trees that the heat lingered on, incandescent after the endless day. The perfectly still air weighed on the flat surface of the sea like a viscous rose oil. Since morning, not a single ripple had blemished the sky's azure complexion, not a single gust of wind had disturbed the torpid sultriness of the forest, whose outlying pines, tortured by hibernal winds, came to an end upon the sand itself, bestrewing it with pine needles. Flushing red, fading into the vermilion haze of twilight, everything was shrouded in a fairy-tale silence, entranced by the plenitude of terrestrial life, so much so that it all seemed suddenly like a film set, a hallucination, an evil spell, and Oleg recalled what Apollon had told him about the world being God's sinful dream. Yes, he thought, a fathomless, truly leaden dream.

■ □ ■

"High up in the mountains, with my back to a wall of granite, I sit in the comfortable pose of the ancient ascetics, next to a rose-colored pine tree that had been gnarled by the wind. Down below, the shrub-decked hills that were so difficult to reach descend one spur after another. A maroon auto is meandering farther and farther down the lilac road, sounding its horn at the bend. That is where the vineyards begin, stretching out as far as the artificial pink and yellow of the first bathing huts—hastily knocked together, looking quite toylike beside the aquamarine sea, which itself seems static and miniature from such a height. The hush here is pristine, ancient, chaste, and broken only by the barely audible, uninterrupted call of the invisible cicadas. It is still summer, and the days are endlessly long, but August is around the corner—and then they will fall silent.

"Thus ensconced, I try to think of nothing. But sure enough, that familiar anguish, the thought of having lost something, of having renounced evil once and for all, rears its head again. Yes, it's true,

I lost a friend, I lost a comrade, I lost God. How did I manage it? I mocked Him . . . I do not deny His existence, for He is too much in evidence, and as I gaze upon the world, I find myself forever gazing at Him. But nevermore shall I say to Him 'Thou'; I shall say only 'He.'

"Silence, silence, a monstrous silence hangs over the ocean of life. Whether a pale azure or a deep turquoise, the ocean remains immaculately black, pitch-dark in its very depths. Albescent rays slowly pierce the clouds' majestic hands, and a faint, feeble birdsong reaches the farthest corners of the world. But its bursts are broken by silences, as though at times the bird were plagued by profound doubt. The sounds grow fainter and fainter until at last they vanish entirely. Yet here the bird is, beside me, sheltered between two rocks, as its little breast is crushed by the dazzling melancholy of a summer's day. And now a stopping train, with its fiery engine spitting out steam from every linchpin, encroaches on the landscape, en route from Italy. It seems to be running from a thunderstorm. Already half the sky behind it has darkened to a black streaked with violet. Low on the horizon little bolts of lightning strike, visible but without making a single sound to break the leaden flow of universal silence, while the flow of images is now broken, divided now into two worlds, a heaven and a hell. Likewise fleeing the scene, a ponderous flock of airplanes, a crooked triangle in precarious equilibrium, creeps low overhead with a heavy mechanical roar. Five unwieldy, hulking crates of wood and steel seem to battle the wind, which has finally picked up and through which an almost indistinguishable hawk, like a minnow in a great wave, glides melancholily, defying the elements with a humiliating perfection of flight."

■ □ ■

The evening ended strangely. After tea and having washed the dishes in a clay chamber pot, where the ubiquitous wasps, dead and alive, clung to everything, they all, with obligatory cheer, made their way down to the rocks beneath the cliffs. There, having arrayed them-selves any old how, they immediately discovered that they had noth-ing to talk about together, since not one of them was possessed of genuine insight, that tragic and poisonous insight that is the preserve of Russian Europeans like Bezobrazoff, who, like little Hamlets, so love to soliloquize on all manner of trifles. Dispossessed children that they were, they had left behind long ago those time-honored Russian intellectual debates (so turgid and indelicate), and, fortu-nately or unfortunately, their paths were never to cross again. The Russian soul took its course, however: lacking wit, cracking woeful, puerile jokes, they pulled mirthless faces until eventually they fell silent, bewitched at last by the languorous, deathly wiles of a nature so deeply alien to them. Like schoolchildren having fallen asleep over the *Odyssey*, they found themselves, before they knew it, wad-ing in and out of its terrifying black rocky shores, dumbstruck as they huddled there together, dimly aware of strange and powerful deities lurking at every turn. The moon was slowly rising, and for some time they had been surrounded by that treacherous rose-fingered mist in which every contour is lost, and every sound becomes alarmingly distinct. The shallow waters plashed at their feet in a way that was somehow abhorrent, squalid even, and somewhere an altogether different kind of grasshopper, not the one found during the day, chirred away dismally, piercingly, periodically falling silent. But now the last astral glimmer of the late sunset had been extinguished, and from the colossal moon there stretched a vast, rudely gilded path, one that none of them cared to tread. Smoldering cigarettes glowed rhythmically, the sea was as black as pitch, and the cliffs towered up like patches of pale fog. Suddenly, faint though unmistakable strains of music reached them from the far side of the rocks, from across the underbrush and the sandbar; it was coming from the casino, whose jaundiced lights shimmered on the invisible water. An electric gramophone was piping out the redoubtably popular "Tango Plegaria." The slow, guttural refrain of that summer, its dark, muffled melody reverberated joylessly, deep in the youngsters' hearts, which sank in horror and dismay. Truly, there was something burned-out, crushing, dead, foreign about that majestic scenery, devoid as it was of any softness, like the set of an opera, or a nightmare in which everything from the outset is suspiciously bright and stark. In the end, it was Apollon who was first to stir from this collective pathological stupor, and Oleg was even glad of it, for it put an end to that awkward mix of intimacy and estrangement that he felt whenever he was with Tania in the presence of others. But then, how pleasant it was to wrap himself in a blanket for the first time, like a boy scout, and to go, stumbling in the Cimmerian dark of the forest, searching among the bushes for a convenient spot to bed down for the night, wondering, marveling at the open void, at the peaceful murk, at the silence, and the absence of policemen. But again now, the moonlight blue flooded the path between the pine trees, and for a long while he and Bezobrazoff lay there on the earth, discussing provisions, watermelons, milk, macaroni, the tent, until in the end Apollon tired of responding, and Oleg gloomily resigned himself to his solitary hopes and fears. But Oleg fell asleep and lapsed into a thousand nightmares of lost tickets, of being late, of perpetual searching for Tania among far-fetched, dismal backstreets. Those dreams, so lurid, so unnaturally bright, crushed and strangled him, until in the end everything vanished in the bottomless, welcome stupor of complete and utter exhaustion.[2]

■ □ ■

Oleg remembered well those first awakenings in La Favière . . .[3] What struck him at first was how he could possibly see high overhead, instead of a yellowed ceiling, the fresh, as though always newly washed, boughs of pine trees, finer specimens of which you could never imagine, and, among them and above them, such an immaculately blue sky in all its indescribable matinal tenderness, constancy, and serenity . . . How could it be possible to live, to sleep under the open sky, and for no one, no policeman to harass you? The absence of any need to dress or to make a bed made getting up even more pleasurable . . . All was still asleep in that cottage closest to the beach; and though its windows were open, everything was consumed by a dangerous, thriving, hostile life that was steeped in slumber, like a jolly strongman whose strength preserves him even in his dreams.

Having performed their ablutions in a wooden basin filled with water and combed their wet heads without the aid of a mirror, the two bandits strolled into town. Whenever they entered a shop, Oleg would beg Bezobrazoff not to steal anything, but each time they did, with astounding sangfroid and deftness of execution, Bezobrazoff would pinch enormous slabs of chocolate, all the while, with inimitable bravado, carrying on his conversation with the shop girl as she disappeared into the storeroom for bread. They walked past still-sleeping hotels that had been painted a far-fetched shade of pink, making them look like fairground booths, and there, at a vacant lot at the end of the boulevard, they sat themselves down on a little stone wall that encompassed a deserted beach and, dangling their legs, drank milk so cold that it made their noses ache. Bloated now, they proceeded unhurriedly to make their way back through the bushes, behind which they found scarlet figures opening tins of food with comical solemnity outside their sophisticated, modern tents, the very sight of which immediately, abominably returned the soul to the city, to the display window of a department store. For, newcomers though they were, Oleg and Bezobrazoff were true wanderers at heart, having unconsciously cast off their urban appearance the moment they arrived. Farther ahead, the path skirted a deserted beach with thousands of colorful rocks and stones, over which the unaccountably azure water lapped lazily, anointing them and conferring on them a fabulous iridescence.

Those mornings with Apollon were a happy time. It was only then, or so it seemed, before Tania awoke, that Oleg could truly appreciate the nature surrounding him. Whenever she appeared at the far end of the beach, with her affectedly nonchalant way of walking, everything around would suddenly lose its significance for Oleg, and be reduced to a mere backdrop for the torture that was taking place.

It was dazzlingly still that morning. To their left, above the distant cape, towered ever-receding mountains, while up ahead, amber-colored pine trees stood motionless atop the cliffs. They found themselves walking along a carpet of needles: baked by the sun, their fragrance was warm and piquant amid the chirring of cicadas. Having made their way back up to the clifftop, passing again on their way the cottage, where somebody was noisily washing himself, they descended to their secluded beach, where there was not another living soul. Overnight the water had removed every trace of their naked feet, and now the sand, laden with moisture, was so smooth that the beach seemed pristine—so pristine, in fact, that they felt almost ashamed to spoil it with their footprints. "There are those who defile the sea, pollute it; not only do they sully it so that their fresh, glossy excrement floats up beside them as they hasten away, but they splash around and call to one another, befouling the horizon with their soft bodies," Bezobrazoff would say, recalling his favorite words by Konstantin Leontiev, which spoke of nature's perfection and its rude tainting—by a city type with spindly legs . . .[4] But while they were alone, and while Bezobrazoff practiced his gymnastics using a kerosene can that the sea had spat out and that he had filled with wet sand and gravel (lying on his back, he would hold it aloft with the tips of his fingers, raising and lowering it behind his head), a glowering Oleg scratched his shame and sagely gave himself over to indolence under the sun. City type that he was, the sea had a devastating effect on him, like that of liquor on an Eskimo; he would literally lose himself, disappear amid its brilliance, unable to think or speak. Having made up his mind at last, he waded into the water. It was warm, but still the initial shock sent an unpleasant chill through his scorching body; he found a deep spot and, squeezing his eyes tightly shut, launched himself forward into a front crawl, propelling himself with five or six strokes, all the while keeping his face below the water's surface. A bubbling sound surrounded him as the water seethed—and as his arms plied, rent, cleft the water, their tumultuous movement rang deafeningly in his ears. Even louder, though, was the roar of his breathing when, having gulped down a breath of air, he would roll from side to side, exhaling it forcefully underwater in a firework of bubbles. His weaker left arm struck the water listlessly, while his stronger right would resurface with the corner of his elbow like a shark's fin and hammer the water as he cut the waves with his palm. Dazed by the noise and almost unable to see anything up ahead, Oleg swam on in fits and starts; Apollon was too lazy to keep pace with him, so he swam behind in a comfortable overarm stroke, but in the end, he overtook Oleg, who had exhausted and overexerted himself. They delayed turning back for so long that when at last they did look round, the beach suddenly seemed to have vanished somewhere, while its pines were nothing more than little flecks of jade; but Apollon swam farther and farther out, changing his stroke often . . .

O joy of man's pure, physical estate, having broken free, joy of exertion, joy of verdant noise, joy of submitting to waters that forever converge behind the body in a tempest of light and bubble before the eyes! O happy hand, especially the right, that gets up to all kinds of mischief, that brawls with the water in spite of every law that bids the palm glide through it smoothly, like a fish, without angles—but then there would be none of that spume and merry uproar, and so Oleg would disturb the water extravagantly, inelegantly, and the maelstrom that it provoked would always impede his movement, while Bezobrazoff would slip on and on, silently, inconspicuously, like a swarthy dolphin. O happy foot, having tired of doing its tap dance and now plying the water any old how! . . . O happy face and comical, unhappy eyes, stinging from the salt! . . . Suddenly, though, it became "a little bit frightening." After all, they had swum out so very far. But Bezobrazoff was keeping track of the precise distance they had covered by the far-off sight of Saint-Tropez as it slowly, house by house, appeared from behind a nearby rocky promontory, at the tip of which Tania's cottage glinted like a watchtower in the sun . . . "Hang on!" cried Bezobrazoff. "Help's on its way!" And sure enough, a boat with a hulking great sail very nearly drowned Bezobrazoff, for they had been in the sea a good hour and a half, during which time the beach had filled up with faint-hearted vacationers. The locals were almost superstitious about not going in the water, but often, at the insistence of their pitiful concerns, they would take a boat and make their sullen way out to rescue the drowning. Bezobrazoff was only too pleased to let them draw near, and, when they cried out from the boat, "*Tiens bon, mon brave, on arrive!*"* he swam away, ostentatiously plowing the waves, while an overwrought Oleg floundered in the water, shouting at them: "*Alors! Plus possible de circuler là-dedans. Bande d'impotents!*"+ Having swum out quite a considerable distance, there, where the one-time transparent sea seemed a dark, inky blue beneath them, they lay out triumphantly on their backs and thrived. Above and below were two azure expanses of equal warmth, while the shoreline, a thin strip of green, stretched out to infinity (it was impossible to know where their beach ended and the neighboring one began), and over that strip the mountains towered in all their crushing weight. Jittery and afraid, Oleg had in fact long wanted to turn back—at times, his chest was wrenched by acute bouts of anxiety and terror—but then Bezobrazoff came about, and they paddled as best they could— sidewise, without any of their usual antics—toward the shore. They were so exhausted that they seemed rooted to the spot, too weak to clamber out amid the rush of the breakers, and every oncoming wave seemed poised to drag them back out to sea. Floundering there in distress for a second time, they very nearly drowned in the shallows. Once again the beach was deserted, for the roguishly kempt young things had finished playing catch and, having dipped their weary

---

* Hang on, lads, help's on the way! (*French*)
+ Damn it! There's hardly any space to move here as it is, you bunch of cretins! (*French*)

limbs in the water, had now retired, quite satisfied with themselves, to their luncheons at home. For Oleg and Bezobrazoff, however, luncheon was a much trickier affair: they had to creep into the kitchen, trying to go unnoticed as they passed the long table in the garden, and there, on a tripod in the antediluvian hearth, boil their macaroni with smoky tomatoes, so that, having munched that down, they could sink their teeth greedily into the sweet, coral flesh of a watermelon, burying their faces in it and spitting out the seeds.

After this midday repast, Bezobrazoff disappeared with a book that he never read but always carried with him, absorbing its contents through osmosis. He ventured into the mountains, where he climbed the rocks until he was drenched in sweat so that, far from all creation, he might sleep in some sort of aerie. There, as he drifted off, he thought his gilded Buddhist thoughts—of that revolving celestial wheel, of the oneness of freedom and necessity, of the lightness of a world that can be blown away in a single breath of air, like a golden postprandial drowsiness—while several miles down below, with unbearable speed, cruelty, and trepidation, Oleg's brief happiness began, like a thunderstorm soon to give way to a long and arduous deluge of tears.

■ □ ■

From the opposite end of the beach, perched confidently atop strong, ample legs, deliberately, for a surfeit of sensuality, trying not to move her hips, Tania, in all her malicious majesty, made her slow approach. For all his near-sightedness, Oleg immediately recognized her provocatively inconspicuous figure and, desperate now with joy, froze in a painfully awkward pose. Slowly still, not quickening her pace for anything, Tania walked up to him and greeted him in an affectedly nonchalant voice, one that was so at odds with the cruel Tartar fire in her eyes. Her gaze, so fraught, so inscrutable, tormented Oleg, who now found himself drawn irresistibly to those eyes, eyes that revealed only what she wanted him to see. This forever-guarded gaze so abashed Oleg that he preferred to walk a little behind her, for that way, unseen, he could look at her to his heart's content, delighting in the expressive, swaying triangle made by her broad tawny back, and finally at her narrow hips in their sun-bleached cornflower cotton. Tania was not tall, but she was so well proportioned and solidly built that she seemed colossal, like the Parthenon of Athens, a sublime four stories tall, with shoulders like its columns, curving up inwardly under the weight of her muscles. Oleg recalled an occasion when Bezobrazoff had sunk into thought and, as though remembering something, puffed out his lips disdainfully, sorrowfully, before declaring: "If you want to know for certain whether you love a person or not, watch them from behind as they walk down a street alone and unawares. There's something astoundingly unique in the way a person walks and in the expressiveness of the back—in its weakness or strength, in particular—and if that doesn't melt your heart, then nothing will ever make you fall in love with them."

As he trailed behind her, Oleg did watch her back to his heart's content and, without getting too worked up—perish the thought!— though with a quiver of excitement, he perceived the sunny logic of her body's impeccable poise against the apricot-and-azure backdrop of the sea and cliffs—and for someone who thirsted after the golden reality of Laforgue's and Proust's theological melancholy, all this was a kind of revelation, one so beautiful as to be almost brazen.[5] It told of the nature of incarnation and of the objective discovery of the soul, not of its fall into materiality but of its dazzling exterioriza-tion, wherein it found glory; it told of antiquity, of the happiness of the fortunate races, of the irreparable shame of everything that has betrayed life and is born without love, joy, or virtue. There was, even for him, something serenely destructive about this chaste, nervous mechanism; it engendered an inimical fear, an archaic terror, rap-ture before the gods—the same rapture that allowed those deities to identify mortals unerringly before turning their backs on them with a smile. Oleg and Tania went up into the mountains: she, mirthful, serene, noticing everything, remarking on everything as she went; he, mirthless, agitated, answering her rhapsodically, ramblingly, irrelevantly. Indefatigably surefooted, Tania jumped from rock to rock, climbing higher and higher up the mountain, flaunting her fearlessness and reveling in the terror, until a vista of another beach just like theirs, only more pristine, opened up on the other side of the ridge, and at last she relented, seeing that beyond the next, even loftier mountain encompassing that beach, barricading it, the sea was kissing the shore upon the white sand, in perfect seclusion, and that nothing could disturb it.

At this point, they installed themselves among the scorching rocks and, as they sat there, had their first proper conversation. During the course of this, Oleg agreed so readily to everything Tania said that he found himself suddenly plunged into an abyss of unfamiliar truths that were quite the opposite to those on which he had for so long and forever unhappily subsisted. Behind the impetuosity of this descent and apostasy, however, lurked fear, an ever-present terror of the unknown and the irreparable, one that wrenched his innards horribly.

What was it, really, that he saw in this fleshy, brazen woman? That she could bear children? That she could bear him, with his blackened ears and craven mouth? She would like to have a child by me, but I do not want to be born. When I was born anew, I didn't consent to giving birth again. No sooner was I born than I had to vie for awakening and chastity . . . at the cost of life.

What a vulpine, canine scent she trails, though her tail sweeps away the tracks she leaves behind . . . The fat vixen Patrikeyevna with her Tartar eyes . . . All the better to see me with . . . How quickly in her presence, how instantaneously Oleg forswore his autonomy, his dignity, his courage, his humor. How his face changes when she appears with that inscrutable look, with that spring in her step, arching her back, conscious of her sex as she walks. Apropos of which, just how do women experience their sex? . . . As a treasure between their legs? . . . How often do they quiver at a shrill, rasping sound or convulse hideously, doubling over with a sharp pain there as they use their sex alone, as though it were the center of their very being, to evaluate, to explore, almost to probe the world? . . . They take care of it, wash it, carry it with them wherever they go, even to church—especially to church. The male member is a thing apart . . . it just hangs there, while theirs is hidden away, concealed, intimately confined, and the chief gesture to protect this treasure is to cover it with a hand. Meanwhile, they shy nervously from the male sex, fearing it, for to them a man, with all his ideas, is but a walking, talking, erect phallus.

■ □ ■

Just look, Apollon, how infinitely unexpected, how unexpectedly rich the shape of each stone. Weigh it. Take it in your hands. Don't be afraid of the effort. See now how ardently the earth loves it, not for a moment letting it be torn from its belly. Isn't that why you cherish your heavy arms and train them so, only to separate a lover from his beloved, like Gilgamesh, who incurred the wrath of the gods for separating lovers in order to have them build the walls of his imperishable cities.[6]

Press your face to the ground's piney warmth and listen—you will hear nothing, but down there, the subterranean heat labors away and fiery rivers flow. If you strain your ears and forget yourself, perhaps you will hear a stubborn little birdie busily, mournfully, cheerfully, insistently calling out, revealing all its secrets. Once again you will perceive that the essence of everything is to be found on the surface, not beyond, for there is nowhere beyond it. Lay open your palm and kiss it. It is not within, between the bones and blood, that the body is discovered, but in the skin's golden honesty. The skin is the revelation of the body, of languor, joy, health, terror, sin, and lust, for nothing is more profound than the skin. Kiss the burning skin of the earth, caress it, sniff it, taste it. It is not under the skin but in its nakedness that the soul of the earth is bared, that it draws breath, for nothing is more profound than the surface. But what would the skin be without eyes to behold it? Does the old maid who has never known a man not claw herself in disgust? All the beauty of the world rejoices in your vision, just as your vision does in it. Just look, Apollon, the earth can bear you easily, just as an enormous tree can easily bear a bird that situates, exposes, punctuates its magnitude with the fantastic remoteness of its noonday song. You and the earth understand each other well, and that is why your chest breathes so evenly, as if there were no breath whatsoever; that is why your heart beats so steadily, as if it were not there at all. The earth sees itself in you and finds itself beautiful. You are a mirror of its warmth made manifest, and steadily, evenly, without mist or haze, that warmth spreads out before you, as if it had been set before the azure face of the world. The mirror's virtue is your virtue: to reflect everything, to be everywhere, to lose oneself, to be lost in the mirror of vision, to face unflinchingly those dazzling, blinding human eyes. Thus were you met and thus, almost without flinching, did you reflect Tania's heavy eyes, and only for the briefest moment was there a ripple on the surface, spreading out in scarcely visible circles, ribbons and rays before dying away again. No, Apollon, you won't find God in man until you love the man in God. Everything individual seems indecent to you, doggedly attached to itself, destined above all for itself, bound by the nobility of the game to defend its own uniqueness. That is why it is indecent to fear death. The vision of one noonday spectator is the continuation of another's, if that vision is good and he can forget himself, lose himself in the absolute perfection of what he sees. But you're tired, Apollon. Though you don't realize it, you're deathly tired of this rejoicing, you're tired of seeing, tired of being seen. Thus, the brightest hour isn't so very far from the first flush of evening, while at night both the spectator and what he sees vanish, and only the stars and ardent, beating hearts go on burning in their insatiable thirst for happiness. In losing that thirst, you also lost that ever-present nocturnal life, and now you, Apollon, are the most superficial man in all creation, for thirst and pain are its depth, and you do not feel pain.

Softly, slowly, like a great wave of sunshine, through a thousand forms and torments, the world arrives at a clear proof of itself, although it cannot bear to see it. For a long while, it just gazes upon itself from a lofty mountain, bidding farewell in a sunny stupor, startled by the futility of its own beauty . . . Your strength, Bezobrazoff, in renouncing all part in this, in renouncing insult and injury, in renouncing triumph and condemnation, lies in this—your brittle, gilded, deathly detachment from everything that lives. But why was it so terribly painful? Why did the sun-drenched ringing from those scorching stones inspire nothing but pain?

How often, after receiving an unanticipated snub, have you peered into the face of your adversary in dumb spiritual wonder, telling yourself over and over again: this individual is free to prefer his wickedness to my good? As if suddenly waking and sensing for the first time all the irreparable finality of that freedom and vaguely recalling that long-forgotten cosmic moment, when the sky with its thousands of dazzling eyes froze in terror . . . Whatever is he doing? Is a man's life and happiness not enough? O stop, stop . . . After all, there is only one freedom in the world, and now it is yours entirely, but there will come a time when it will be yours and his for evermore . . . But the golden dreamer was not following, as in a daze of resolution he watched the man, who, like an athletic vegetable, understood nothing and looked to God in his naked innocence; and suddenly a fiery arrow shot from God's mouth, racing out, and the whole sky gasped, while the man imperceptibly but curiously changed color, and the angels saw that even his Creator had changed, for earlier He had no face at all—and with fire on their lips, having turned their backs on him respectfully, the angels told of this . . . And suddenly, from a fiery cloud there emerged a splendid, heavily masculine, Titianesque figure heading toward the man, and nobody died as they beheld it in their inexpressible, calm awareness of rapture.

■ □ ■

Beyond the mountains circumscribing the landscape, others soon drew into view, dwarfing those first ones. But their foothills were so far away that they could not be reached that day, or even that night. Turn from them, O soul, sense their rocky unattainability at your back and cast your gaze toward the sea, for you have already ventured far enough and need not stray too far from these inhabited parts. Thus did Tania and Oleg not climb very high above the littoral world; there, where that first ridge ended among sparse pine trees gnarled by a wind blown once upon a time, they paused in a rocky hollow and squinted as they looked down at the sea below. But out in the distance, over the horizon, a remote white strip of remote bad weather was sending forth row upon row of waves to blacken the water. The sun was at its zenith, and August had only just begun.

"'Fear those who have failed in life: for they shall be thine own undoing, and thou shalt never help them.' These breath-taking words were uttered by a certain practitioner of the dark arts . . . The earth should belong to the healthy, well-begotten races—it isn't an alms-house, after all. This sentiment is born of true compassion for the weak; they ought to be wiped from the face of the earth."

"But what are they guilty of, really?"

"Nothing at all . . . It isn't the chair's fault if it doesn't stand on its legs, nor the mirror if its reflection is crooked. But they should be destroyed all the same, insofar as their creators are to blame."

"Hence, the unfit should forgo the right to have children."

"What arrant rubbish . . . It isn't the parents who go on living, embodied in the child, but their love; that's why pure-blooded fathers often beget wretched, stillborn offspring, whereas even the most neurotic and fragile of individuals can produce a strapping son with tanned little legs, because it is not they who become flesh, but their love . . . Every inherently successful, innately happy person is, after all, a well of the mysterious purity given over by dozens of generations, their countless sacrifices for the sake of life itself, and they, like honey, are spilled in this person's body . . . It isn't the weak I pity, but the stillborn, those inanimate young corpses. Though I blush at this pity, for only rapture can bind me . . . I can be moved to pity despite myself, but when I love, I'm steadfast and without mercy, and I shudder in disgust whenever a grown man demands pity . . ."

Tania was speaking in general terms. She had just read her first banned books and, in all the novelty of her newly acquired intellectual freedom, delighted in her cruelty, as only children can delight in evil—that is to say, with all their heart, torturing living creatures with complete and utter abandon . . . In that moment, Oleg seemed to her like a hot, heavy body, one that was physically incapable of crying but that could cause her pain, an excruciatingly sweet pain, about which she, having never experienced it, wrote in her diary: "How wondrously God has arranged it, so that a woman does not suffer from the weight of a man's body on her."

Struck disagreeably, Oleg held his tongue as he looked up to find her golden-chestnut hair blowing against the dazzlingly lifeless azure of the sky . . . Then they slowly made their way down . . .

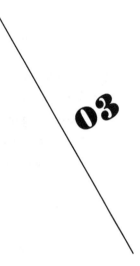

03

Tu peux sortir en robe de cristal,
Ta beauté continue.*
▶ Paul Eluard[1]

"**O** sea, O sea, how often I have come to you, cried, called and asked of you, and you have answered me without answering, comforted me without knowing, forever singing steadily of beauty and the innocence of all things, O sea, *O mer, amour.*[2]

"O sea, most voluptuous and most chaste of all divinities, you array yourself identically for me and for your wealthy suitor who dangles his arm over the white side of his motorboat—always just as freshly washed, just as resplendent before a thousand artists, as before a desolate cliff-lined shore where a poor lone fisherman reads yesteryear's newspaper. Perfectly still in your farthest depths, you eternally flirt, glitter, and play in the sunlight, reflecting its rays

---

* You may step out in a crystal gown, / Your beauty continues. (*French*)

like a second sun, like a heart flirting with God, while I am bathed from head to toe in your aquamarine rays, so that the page on which I am writing shows a pale blue. The finest sand settles upon the page, and over it inclines a sprig of mint, which with equal indifference for the viewer has already shed its blossom; for August is passing, a strange month—neither summer nor fall, both summer and fall, like my thirty years of age.

"Godspeed, little bird, Godspeed, as you take wing to a call in the reeds, for tomorrow comes September; there the sky and the blood are colder, and there will not be a soul on the sands of this desolate beach, and gently the mint, as tall as a book, will sway. *O mer, amour.*

"Sorceress, how often you change your attire in a day, how well I know your many dresses of azures and aquamarines, emeralds, dark noonday lilacs that roar so splendidly in the wind, dark evening grays bespread with white lace, and matinal roses and whites, so smooth that, like the Savior's robe, they seem to have been fashioned without a single stich. But above all I love your first morning dresses, that glitter so, graced with sequins, rays, and swirls, in which you meet the triumphant August day. *O mer, amour.*

"Quietly in the noonday azure, between the rocks suffused with heat, with uninterrupted clarity, the cicadas chirr melodiously, and suddenly everything stops altogether, in accordance with some secret, unwritten rhythm, and then once again the air simmers in the sun with a thousand uniform voices. There are no ripples in the sea, no shadows of fish in the water, not a single bird in the lofty air.

"O sea, how I love you. Soon I shall throw myself at you and kiss your salty lips, and you, insensible to that kiss, will answer it, through the roar in my ears, through the salty pain of my bitten lips. O sea, first and final love."

■ □ ■

Jumping from rock to rock, Tania and Oleg made their way down toward the water—she in front, playful, delighted by her own fearlessness, the precision of her movements, and the strength of her brown legs; he behind, stumbling clumsily, often falling and scraping his hands, overexcited, dumb with love, diffidence, and the torrid heat. At any other time, he would gladly have taken part in the race and made a show of his desperation, but now the blood was pounding so hard in his ears that he could hardly keep up with her; finally, after frightening off a whole colony of nudists, who like spindly red crayfish were hiding behind the rocks, the exhausted couple climbed down onto the flat boulders of the rocky cape, where they sat down and each breaking wave covered them with a fan of fresh sea spray. The wind was picking up; over the horizon hung a thin white strip— there, beyond the horizon, a storm was raging, sending hither column upon column of tall waves, which every so often in their haste lost their seething white crests.

Each wave as it drew near would dig before itself a dark-blue pit, at the bottom of which glistening stones would wash over one another noisily; the wave would rise up in a towering blue wall, and just on the point of breaking it would shoot up as it crashed against the rocks. Then the spume would spurt up high over their heads; in the cracks between the rocks the surging azure would rush forward, but as the waves retreated whole waterfalls would go sweeping back out to sea.

Not content just to sit there, however, Tania moved in closer and threw off her shoes. The water turned the broad hems of her faded beach pajamas dark, but even that was not enough; crazed, she clambered out onto the wet rocks, leaving Oleg, like an old man, to fret terribly—for under the dazzling sky the sea and the wind were becoming visibly, satanically fierce. Now a wave which from Oleg's vantage looked as tall as a house would approach, and in mock terror Tania would dash back, shouting inaudibly. With a wild freshness, water would pour down from the sky, covering their faces and chests; their clothes and hair clung to their faces. Squinting and snorting, they would dry themselves, and in response the crystalline waves would advance, one after another, thundering theatrically down, drenching them from head to toe. One especially powerful wave all but dragged Oleg out to sea, so that, clinging to the sand with all four limbs, he barely managed to hold his ground and was given a thorough fright. The spectacle before them was now awe-inspiring and the danger considerable, for in such a cauldron the ability to swim would be rendered useless, and Tania, as is so often the case with those who are naturally strong, understood nothing of sports and was a poor swimmer.

Amid the endless fountains and the constant joyous thunder, they were now laughing uncontrollably, emboldened to the point of recklessness, clambering through the waves right into the inferno itself. Tania would throw out her arms and with her eyes tightly closed turn her face to the water; with all her roistering and revelry, she at last managed to reassure Oleg and get him to join in.

Finally, having had their fill of enjoyment, exhausted, happily worn out, as wet as puppies, they clambered back, found their shoes, and clumsily set about putting them on their wet seashell-pink feet;

they ran their fingers cursorily through their hair, and set off homeward along the mountain path. Soon, as they emerged from the rocky chaos, they came across a pale-faced group of bored Russian vacationers, who sat with their cigarettes and their *Latest News*, gawping at them in a kind of superstitious bewilderment.[3]

Once again, Tania's broad sallow back, no longer as formidable and hostile as before, swayed from side to side in front of Oleg, and he was almost happy—for a whole month of these escapades lay in store. But soon enough, by the garden gate, they had to part; the time had come for Tania to crawl through the window into her room, since the entire bourgeois company of adults had long been assembled at the table on the patio. And Oleg, finding himself alone in the woods, resigned once again to his lower-class status, took to wandering wherever his eyes led him, searching for Bezobrazoff so that the two of them could steal, like Indians, into the kitchen and munch their everlasting rice with tomatoes and oil, which they now cooked four days in advance on the brazier; they had appetites like wolves, though, and to eat after having been in the sea was a great pleasure.

After dinner, Tania cloistered herself away to study, but no sooner would the jalousie be shut than she would fall asleep in the oppressive heat, her shoulder and face always resting on the same page which was worn by the weight of her slumber. In the noonday wilderness, Oleg wandered wild and solitary, his sun-bleached hair appearing here and there at random on the rocks. Time passed slowly as he waited, and everything around him seemed dreary—too unremittingly bright, too threatening, alien, inimically, dazzlingly indifferent. Just as slowly and softly as ever, the waves broke over the sand, and the water seemed to doze there for half a minute before stirring again, not in the least quickening its habitual rhythm just because Oleg, as he frowned malevolently into the deep-blue expanse, was sitting, waiting on the beach. He would have liked for everything to speed up, as it sometimes does in the movies, and rush headlong toward six o'clock. And at six, amid a deathly silence, listening to the crunch of his own footsteps across the gravel, he would approach the cottage as if it were a lion's cage and knock on the window. Receiving no answer, he would carefully draw back the jalousie, and Tania, awakened by the bright light, embarrassed, her face saturated with sleep and as red as a scullery maid's, would leap up and set about fixing her hair.

Soon Nadia, a broad-faced girl of unusually doll-like, athletic beauty, would come in—also by means of the window. In contrast to Tania, she was prone to laughter in a spontaneous, naïvely coquettish sort of way, and regarded everything with those huge, defiant lapis eyes of hers, although like Tania she, too, could be instinctively, ferociously silent and reserved. After Nadia, her thug of a boyfriend would barge in—her tall, somber, good-looking guardian, a man of political convictions who spoke a strange Parisian-Russian patois, a mélange of Gallicisms and garbled Soviet jargon. Nadia and Tania never uttered a word when they were together—Tania maliciously, intelligently, keenly awaiting, seizing, critiquing every word; Nadia naïvely, crudely laughing deep down, her enormous, protruding, totally vacant sky-blue eyes wide open. Pliant and as elusive as a wild beast, she was a magnificent specimen of Russian sexual creativity.

It was a beautiful gathering of young athletic bodies which had been piled into a small, whitewashed room, whose window had neither frames nor glass, but only one half of an antique green Italian shutter. But floating, hanging over them was that everlasting torment, that hereditary, prudish Russian ennui of Chekhov's grandiloquent heroes, which does not deign to speak of anything earthly or intimate, and does not know how to speak of anything exalted without listlessness: the spirit wrestling with the body. A rather crude, affected camaraderie on the surface; an austere, tense romantic struggle beneath. The everlasting, joyless, agonizingly familiar atmosphere of a Russian schoolhouse.

Sometimes an ape-man would join the group (perhaps even walking on his hands)—a taciturn, swarthy figure composed entirely of muscles, with the beautiful, striking, thick-lipped face of a Spanish criminal-cum-artist-cum-aristocrat. And finally, out of nowhere, Apollon Bezobrazoff would appear (through the door, like an old man), met by a somber, significant look from Tania's suddenly darkened eyes, and with him a Georgian-looking young lady who was thoroughly exhausted by the heat.

Conversation flagged, because inwardly Oleg, as the eldest, thought himself above the rest, while outwardly he groveled ineptly, trying desperately on Tania's account to buoy the group; he compromised his dignity and sincerity and chastised himself for doing so, all the while maliciously mimicking to himself their semi-Russian turns of phrase.

Accordingly, everybody liked to dance. For one thing, it put an end to conversation, and for another it meant sexual liberation, a covert sexual-aesthetic release from the tedium oppressing their youthful hearts. They liked to drink, too, but were wary of this, for somewhere nearby lived and walked a terrible bearded creator, their patron—a glitter-eyed, gold-spectacled former revolutionary, now a learned chemist and a real man of business.

The gramophone's mechanical voice sounded odd amid the sun-drenched hush of the garden on the rocky cape. It was a melancholy sound, cracked, as if coming from afar, from Paris, as if heard on the telephone, barely audible. Outside, the dazzling noonday heat was now replaced by the tranquil, radiant warmth of evening. The chirring of the cicadas was growing louder, but already the garden was bathed in the peach-colored light of clouds at sunset, and beyond them the sea below was already taking on that strange, heavy, leaden, oily shine, which immediately made everything threatening and a tad unreal; it seemed that any second now, between two branches, strangely dreamlike and with an astral clarity, there would appear in the distance a black Aegean ship, its auburn sail hanging motionless over the mirrorlike surface.

Slow and serene, mournfully insistent, like a bee, the gramophone wailed, and everything continued to bask in the reflected reddish brilliance of the sky.

Suddenly understanding, suddenly catching sight of something new, alien, and inescapably tormenting in Tania, Oleg could no longer quite believe that it was she who had spent the morning ambling and horsing around with him. Flirting sullenly with Bezobrazoff, she was once again her majestic, stony, overbearing self.

Several times already Oleg had tried to get up to invite Tania to dance, but his heart would begin beating so excruciatingly and he would seem to himself so awkward, so ugly and narrow-shouldered that, with a psychopathic fear of rejection, he could not make up his mind. But in the end, he stood up anyway, and, barely conscious, barely touching Tania, he placed his arm around her. The gramophone struck up "Jalousie," a slow, eternally memorable tzigane tango of that summer, and so, barely brushing against her, barely daring to move, he floated across the room with her, and the room floated before them in the sultry rose-tinged twilight of a still August evening.[4] They were dancing; suddenly Oleg's heart was discovering, realizing, understanding that together they were floating into one infinitely long abyss of pain, into humiliation, defeat, injury, and separation; yet the sheer force of floating off, of breaking away, of casting off from land and their old life was so overpowering, so new, so compelling, that Oleg, transported, neglecting to protect himself, bared himself to pain and proceeded inexorably toward that force as if marching into battle—melting, perishing irrevocably, selling himself into slavery amid the hot, flushed, still, evening air.

Ringing softly as they came to life, muffled sounds slowly made their way through the heavy air, and were now destroying Oleg, literally tearing him apart; with a sweetness that was painful, and a pain that was sweet, they were entering into, rushing into, slicing into his heart. It was as if tremendous distances, mountains, frescoes, fabulous accounts of cities and voyages were unfolding somewhere on the other side of the window, yet even with the tips of his fingers he did not dare to touch, did not dare to feel the extraordinary, formidable body of this deity that was dancing with him. The dance ended, but Oleg knew now that his heart had opened, awakened for a long time to come. He knew also that Tania did not love him and perhaps never would. Within him the twilight faded to darkness, so palpably that it suffocated him; something threatening like a thunderstorm in summer, something never to be repeated tortured him and slashed voluptuously at his soul. And for a long time afterwards, he and Bezobrazoff, like a pair of escaped convicts, sat in their forest facing each other by two tree stumps, munching on their insipid rice and tomatoes, topping it off with sweet, unpeeled cucumbers, calmed by the distinct presence of something irreparable.

The infinitely long summer's day was finally over. The fainthearted, hysterical housekeeper was laying the table for dinner. In her strange, sullen way, Tania agreed to meet Oleg after saying good-bye to Ivan Gerasimovich, who was staying in the cottage next door. Both girls had agreed to return home to sleep, but there and then, just past the garden gate, without a word to one another, they parted, disappearing into the darkness to go about their dark affairs. Sitting awkwardly on a pile of pine needles by the side of the path, Oleg waited. The darkness in the forest was impenetrable. On weekdays there was no music in Saint-Tropez, and somewhere far, far away, beyond the mountains, the engines of military aircraft droned as they made their night flights. Sometimes one of the colossal stars would begin to move between the black branches, or on occasion two or three in synchronized symmetry, but having crossed the sky they would vanish amid a dull rumbling, and the surrounding night would once again be rendered beautiful, impenetrable, hostile. In the midst of all this Oleg was like a prehistoric hunter—lost, tense, all ears. For him, a city youth, a child of the cafés, a young émigré who had grown up in the rain, all this preserved its sense of wonder, and the silence was so powerful, so terrifying, so perfect that Oleg could hear the blood coursing continually through his ears. From far, far in the distance, Oleg could hear Tania's approach; he heard the last words that she had laughingly cast in Nadia's direction ("You ought to be more careful with him"), and the soft, distinct, approaching crunch of gravel under her strong little feet and the snapping of twigs beneath them. Then at last, faintly hovering between the trees, there appeared a soft, silent fairy-tale disk of white light from an electric torch. Concealing himself, Oleg remained silent; the white light drew nearer, completely masking the figure behind it, and suddenly Oleg felt himself to be the object of an electric eye. With the look of a captured beast, he stared into it wildly.

On that star-filled night, heavy with the scent of pine needles, among the rocks that despite the darkness were still warm with their memory of the sun, they quarreled for the first time, and in a crazed fit of bravado Oleg tore himself away from Tania and went off to wander the shore in the ominous light of the late-rising waning moon, humming to himself as he went his favorite crude strains of the wedding march from *Lohengrin*; and then suddenly, all at once, something snuffed out the emotion, his heart physically contracted with a presentiment of the irreparable, and he rushed off in search of her but could not find her.[5] O horrible, horrible, primeval bewilderment, the ancient despair among the giants of fate and nature . . . With wild suffering in his heart, he ran back toward the cottages and stopped in confusion at a crossing of several roads. The moon had risen higher now, and the entire forest was gashed with white strips— but where among them was Tania? . . . Where had she gone? . . . She was not at home—Oleg had already looked in her low window . . . Where, whither, in which direction had she set off in this threatening chaos of trees, moonlight, and rocks? Despair, despair . . . I'll never see her again, all is lost. Above him, carved out in black silhouettes against a theatrically blue-tinted sky, terrific needle-clothed monsters loomed—as if their swaying boughs were reaching out in the moon's motionless storm, a silent storm of moonlight, like gargantuan black hairs lashed by the silent wind—and at their feet, Oleg literally wrung and gnawed his hands in suspense and anxiety, while everything once again reminded him of a theater; all this was only pretending to be the sky, the trees, the moon, all the better to crush and destroy him. To destroy his soul, which had soared too high, which had ascended in its solitude, and so, like a mad dog, had been condemned by nature itself.

On that star-filled night, they shared their first kiss, for several hours completely losing all sense of reality in a frenzy of sensuality. But it was not with peace, not with sweet reconciliation and new life that their lips met, but with something fiercely, mercilessly hostile. Twisted all awry in his strong paws, Tania lay frozen on the ground, as if in a cataleptic fit, while he, in a lunacy devoid of pleasure, in an uneasy, oppressive delirium of unexpected good fortune and expected foul play, kneaded, wrung and kissed this taut, burning flesh, until, exhausted, sated with suffering and pleasure, in the grip of some kind of remorse, she told him: "No, I can't love you. There's a man I'm bound to, promised to . . . I'm tired, sick of lying, and I haven't the strength now to brace my spiritual muscles and bare my heart to you . . ." "So you don't want to play for real money, just for small change—well, I can do without your sordid change . . . So long and farewell . . ." All aflame, all riled up by Tania's wanton caresses, Oleg tore himself away from her and, suddenly going berserk, suddenly growing cruel from all the passion of his love, hardening toward her, consumed, convulsed by the belligerent madness of his rancor, he disappeared in the darkness. Thinking that he would return, Tania buttoned up her dress and waited; sullenly, scornfully, bitterly she got up and made her surefooted way down the slope through the underbrush, and soon reached slumbering Saint-Tropez. Like some athletic apparition, she roamed the streets and unexpectedly ran into the whole almost-adult gang of Oleg's enemies. She drank and danced with them till morning, while all that night Oleg searched for her, watching for her, wandering about in a flood of tears, terrified, repentant, naïvely imagining even that she might have fallen off a cliff. He himself had visions of throwing himself from somewhere even higher than that, until the pale blue of morning began to glimmer and he, wincing as if from a blow and shielding his eyes with his hands, crawled into his tent, collapsing into heavy, sweet oblivion. From that day, from that night, Oleg's torments began.

■ □ ■

And another dazzling August day rose over Saint-Tropez. It may even have been more flawless, more radiant, and more peaceful, because the cicadas, having roared out their sunrise service, suddenly fell quiet, fading away to complete silence, as if they had never been there at all.

Opening his eyes, Oleg, not instantly but only a heartbeat later, remembered what had happened. At first, when again he saw those vivid, exquisite new boughs amid the blue expanse above him, he wanted to laugh out loud, to rouse Bezobrazoff from his slumber, but precisely one second later the consciousness of something urgent and irreparable jolted and squeezed his heart so that he first opened his eyes painfully wide and then immediately winced; at that very moment the irreparable began to come true, and Oleg's hell began.

That morning Tania had gone off to the market in Saint-Tropez with the housekeeper; to run after them in search of her would have been ludicrous, senseless, for in public Tania could master herself splendidly and, with especial callousness, utter words through clenched teeth to those with whom she wanted to have it out in private. In a climate of peace, this stood to make any happiness more acute, for it introduced a patch of hostility into the fabric of love, commemorating, underscoring the distance traveled, or else a patch of love's beginning into its continuation. How pleasant it is on occasion, at a ball, to greet someone one loves ceremoniously, as though from a distance, when they, decked out in their finery and in full possession of their charms, appear to us in that same enigmatic aura of fleeting formality and embarrassment or affected stiffness in which, once upon a time, they first appeared to our wonder-stricken eyes. But in times of quarrel this feigned aloofness can seem real—so much so that Tania's politeness now made Oleg literally suffer.

And so there was little to do but while away the hours until after dinner, and in Oleg's tortured, anxious state of mind this proved hellishly difficult. Again Oleg swam out almost beyond the horizon, and, returning with no little difficulty to a completely deserted beach, which all those Franco-Russian youths had leggily abandoned in favor of their respective cottages, he suddenly stumbled upon the object of his long-held and impotent desire—a white canoe that belonged to a certain toupee-wearing aristocrat, who always looked at Oleg with particular malevolence.

That morning for the last time the sea shone for Oleg with its dazzling blue calm. He did not know then that it was for the last time; he did not yet believe in separation—just as a living person does not, cannot for a long time, in spite of all obviousness, believe in death. Tossing about, the unwieldy boat was drifting rapidly away from the shore. Here was the point to which Oleg would ordinarily swim, just to spite the vacationers. Shouldn't you turn back? After all, the swim tired you out, and your hands ache from rowing. No, keep going, farther into the deep blue, out toward where you can glimpse the abandoned lighthouse in the distance, like a white tuffet, or a bark, a buoy, a shooting target—it's hard to make out.

Once again Oleg turned his back on the shore, very nearly capsizing the canoe. The boundless aquamarine of the sea, the unembraceable azure of the sky opened out before him . . . On and on into the distance. Now, after he rounded the cape, the waves became long, tall, deep, uniform mountains of blue. As they advanced toward the shore, they slowed the boat, which no longer seemed to be moving. The scorching sun blazed overhead, but in spite of his worry that he was far from both the shore and the little island, Oleg now and then forgot about everything, set down his oar and gazed into the distance, immersing himself in the chaste pleasure of contemplation. It was wondrously beautiful, especially down in the great depths below. Through the dark-lilac crystal some black strips were still visible against the lighter sand on the seabed. Behind him the towns of Saint-Tropez and Sainte-Maxime vanished, and everything collapsed into a narrow strip of sand under a green strip of pine trees. But the mountains instead shot up and closed in, while the lofty billows of white cloud above them magnified their height still more. To the left and right appeared an unfamiliar shoreline; the sea's violent rocking forced Oleg to his senses and, despite his blistered hands, to row with all his might. Suddenly the islet emerged from the water— big, rocky, almost totally obscured by a colony of birds—and as Oleg drew closer, the waves of the open sea pounded so hard and raised the boat up so high that it filled almost to the top with water; yet it did not sink, for both its covered bow and stern were impervious to water. But it was climbing out that proved to be the hardest part. Without gradation, the rocks plunged sheer into the water's depths. Between the rocks water and spume seethed, and everything around was covered with jagged seashells. Oleg looked back in terror, but to return without resting was utterly unthinkable. Having at last made up his mind, he discarded the oar onto the rocks, climbed down into the water, pushed and dragged the boat out to a spot where he could secure it and, covered in scratches, with a terrific pain in his back, unsteady with fatigue, excitement and exultation, he climbed up onto the hot rocks amidst a cloud of startled birds.

How far away from everything he was. His heart was bursting from loneliness and a fear of the sea's vast azure. Going back was torture. For two hours he drifted, weak with exhaustion and borne away by the current, until at last he moored half a mile from where he had set out. Then, with the pitiful, exhausted look of a man expecting to be congratulated, he made his way back along the shore toward the beach and immediately caught sight of Tania, who was squinting and watching him with idle malevolence as she talked in a slow undertone with his enemies; he had already summoned up the courage to go over to her, when a narrow-shouldered, Arabian-looking young man, as gaunt as a skeleton, marched right up to them, and, judging by the abrupt movement with which Tania got to her feet, and the fact that they immediately, without saying goodbye to anyone, headed off into the forest at the other end of the beach, Oleg understood that this was her fiancé.

The sun set over the black shoreline; this is how I imagined the rocks where a shackled convict wrestles with his fate. My love, promise me that you won't leave me, let me bid you farewell once more. The sun set, and again the day blazed forth, the mountains concealed themselves in wings of stone, the green plumage of the hills burned in the sunlight. High, high above, the primordial being, the everlastingly new, peerless azure was reflected in the water. And far off in the sea, scarcely visible amid the noonday silence, motionless in that same pose, lay the islands whither once a day a dark-brown launch set out from Le Lavandou in the white-hot stillness; its antediluvian motor would knock and rattle endlessly on, until finally it faded away, and the cicadas would resume their clamor, although their voices were now fainter.

The white air, a searing white liquid fire, filled and isolated every object; everything was concealed, consumed, and combined by it, as if by the real presence of some indifferent, all-pervading deity.

O incandescent happiness, summer, world without happiness, how beautiful, merciless, dazzlingly perfect you are over my world of torment; for it is over the wilderness, over the cyclopean fortresses where prisoners gasp for air, over the stone quarries filled with the dry, hollow clanging of convicts' hammers, over Rio de Janeiro, over Caledonia, over Guiana that such a dazzlingly flawless sun hangs suspended.

Oleg's torments had begun. Now meeting Tania was no longer a possibility, and only at dinner time, as he loitered waiflike by the kitchen, would he catch a glimpse of her faded blue culottes before she vanished off again until nightfall with her curly-haired gypsy fiancé, with his so delicate, so painfully refined, never-sunburnt, biblical face. And just as Oleg had once smugly marveled at her boldness and facility in going off with him, in spite of all circumstances and without giving herself away, endlessly to wander, swim, clamber about on the rocks, so too, with that same perfection of feline technique, she now disappeared with her narrow-shouldered victim; and Oleg, his tireless surveillance notwithstanding, never once encountered them, never glimpsed them anywhere—not on the beach by the languid water, not in the forest where her degenerate suitor's tent appeared to be entirely uninhabited, not in the mountains, not on the road. She disappeared, she ceased to be. Oleg tried to read (he had brought so many books with him that he had scarcely been able

to carry his suitcase), but thus far he had not read a single page—
it all seemed to him such deathly, inane nonsense. Sometimes he
would fly into a black rage and, straining every muscle, prowl around
the rocks, searching for them; but that too was futile, for they had
seemingly left La Favière.

Black from the sun, muscular, disheveled, wearing the tight-fitting
faded *marinière* that was the uniform of his exile, he would wander
about Le Lavandou, met and followed by surprised and hostile looks.
He would sit on the jetty past which no ships sailed, or in churches
where there were no worshippers. He had grown to like the polluted
water of the port, the bottles and tins on the seabed, the newspaper kiosk. Mortally humiliated, in a humiliating rage of jealousy, he
would make his appearance here and there; he no longer swam and
even stopped practicing his calisthenics. As for the mountain wastelands, the rocks, the clouds, the sea vistas—he did not even think
about those anymore; it all seemed like a clownish stage set now,
a crudely painted backdrop for a ballet. It's all crude, crude, crude,
he would spitefully tell himself over and again, what truly primitive
tastes in art the Creator has, and only once in a while, as he rounded
a bend in a path, a microscopic inlet would come into view between
two rocks and astound him with its useless perfection, unnoticed by
anyone—there he would lie down, his stomach on the sand and his
face to the water, humming thoughtlessly, lifelessly, examining the
stones and the gravel on the seabed. Sun-baked tawny stone walls
would surround him on all sides; everything would lose its sense of
proportion, and the variegated gravel on the bottom would seem to
be an inertly joyous world of its own. Microscopic waves would lap
at his hands, warming them . . . The pain would abate . . . He would
fall asleep face-down in the sand, slumber for an hour or two, lost to

the world, and then suddenly jump up, look around with blood-shot eyes and, wringing his hands, set off again on his futile search.

O torment, prison of jealousy under this blinding sky, why had he come here, given in, yielded to temptation, renounced Apollon's way of life—staunchly, proudly athletic, devoid of happiness, nature, destiny. For all the ardor that had amassed over the years in this solitary individual, who had reached heights that he should never have known, was now unleashed upon the earth and gushed forth toward Tania.

He did not see her, but still he saw her wherever he looked—and she seemed to grow even more beautiful. Her gentle and evil face with its startlingly tender, flawless, malign lips, her knitted brow, and such perfect, precise, animal-like movements, struck directly at heart. In the noonday still she was everywhere, she was nowhere.

Everything was now repugnant to Oleg: the sea no longer beckoned him to swim, the mountains no longer called him to tramp about, walking on the sand was as arduous as wading through glue, he no longer had an appetite, and at night only the savior of repose would grace his presence. After dinner, everyone but Tania and her insolent brute would now gather together and, having all lapsed into the gloomy black melancholy of an abortive summer, sit down on a blanket under a tree and play cards, or on a mattress in the tent which, when drenched in sunlight, bore the pink-and-yellow stripes of an Arabian camp. Nadia and her athletic Slavophile quarreled; coarsely, as though her lord and master, he railed at her for her mistakes at cards . . . "What do you know anyway? Well, fine then, deal . . . Fine." The Orthodox young lady could not bear the heat and was making ready to leave, watching everything with her prodigious eyes that brimmed with bewildered sorrow. The ape-man was engrossed in his inscrutable Spanish thoughts; he now wore his hair up like an Indian and had ribbons dangling from his wrists—thus did he reveal a wild, primordial elegance in adorning his completely naked body. Apollon Bezobrazoff, wizened and with an overgrowth of beard, was vying in immobility with the rocks: as he reclined on a rock, he would turn to rock; he would absent himself and, to everybody's surprise, could be found reading the tomes that Oleg had with such effort and so vainly carried there on his back.

And where had Oleg's thought-laden books all vanished without a trace, all his thick notebooks crisscrossed over with scribblings? Oleg had left them all in Paris. For a whole month now he had not read, nor written, nor prayed. A wild freedom from God and a fear of God accompanied him everywhere. Thus, it seemed, face to face with the world, defenseless and disconsolate, he could meet this unfamiliar life more cleanly—but life, like the unendurable sun, sparing him nothing, was striking him full in the face.

Both friends ceased to understand each other completely. Apollon ridiculed Tania, while Oleg, despairing, sought protection in the shadow of his friend's soul. But having rested awhile, having managed to anesthetize the pain momentarily, he leaped up, as he had done from slumbering on the sand, and with a heavy head took up his search for Tania. He no longer prayed, as had been his habit for so long, and fear hung over his head like a falling stone. He wrested himself free of God's grasp, ran off into the primeval forests, stalked, disheveled, the scorched deadfall, and with ever-increasing abandon, ever-increasing vulnerability his heart dissolved, broke, seethed, tore itself away from him. At times the pain would grow unbearable, everything inside him seemed to burst, his eyes, fingers, hair, lips, and shoulders ached; he howled, wept, prostrated himself on the earth, but for the most part he was subdued by the stupor of his bewilderment. His arms and legs felt enormous, gorged with blood, inflamed by the sun, and impossible to lift. The torrid heat drained the color from everything; now everything was gray, black, and pale blueish. To eat was almost impossible, but then there was nothing to eat. Oleg lost his skill in cooking and ate only what Bezobrazoff gave him, devouring it without so much as glancing at what was on the plate, or else, having lost all sense of shame, he would finish off leftovers in the kitchen, where the housekeeper, guessing at his state of mind, would feed him with a disdainful sorrow.

The housekeeper, still young and with the tumid face of a religious icon, spoke of Tania and Nadia with a kind of morbid dramatism. She had nurtured them but had failed to cultivate them, and they, like two Slavonic ducklings hatched by a Jewish hen, had slipped out of her hands, like two eels, into the murky swamp of a French lycée and sequestered themselves away in hostile secrecy early on. Exuberant and unmarried, she came to resent them with the unhealthy passion of a childless creature and was ever quick to attribute all Tania's past history simply to "carnality," and on her lips this shameful term embarrassed Oleg to the point of loathing, but, crippled as he was by the pain of his love, he agreed with everything she said, sat there on the bed, eating up the scraps, and found a strange feminine pleasure in settling himself in the kitchen, shelling peas and listening endlessly to pathologically inflated tales of Tania's early acts of cruelty. But one thing surprised him all the same: namely, the story of how Tania, so as to test her strength, spitefully and with her own hand, crushed and strangled a dove that she often liked to hold, delighting in its elegant frailty . . . The sorrows of his own captive infancy stirred in him, his old love of nightlights, cupboards, the outhouses, the kitchen, the maid, the back yard, the streets, the evening, the snow that lay about when he, in a wreath of wax, renounced his life.[6]

The nights were drawing in. Of an evening Oleg and Apollon Bezobrazoff would spend hours sitting on the parapet over the embankment, silently watching as under the sycamores, which were garlanded in little variegated lamps like electric stars, a monstrously carefree crowd slow-danced among white wicker chairs. The pair would return after dark and, emerging suddenly from the underbrush as they headed toward the sea, stop in bewilderment. Lighting up the water like a torch, a large boat would glide past, filled with people frozen in various attitudes. Dripping fiery droplets into the sea, a golden flame burned brightly, and the rays of light emanating from it dispersed below the surface, illuminating the water's depths. The bushes along the shoreline were bathed in orange.

Slowly, without a word, without a splash of the oars, the boat would glide past and vanish behind the rocks, while they continued to stand there, perplexed (and with good reason), frightened, as if it had been the Lethean ferryman in his barge, garbed in the tattered trappings of a fisherman and aiming at an octopus with a harpoon.[7]

A strange shoreline, thought Oleg, I can't see a single bird or fish on the sand, no crabs, no seashells, what a godforsaken place. The cicadas had fallen silent for good—September was setting in, and at night the water looked like cold black oil.

One morning Oleg was awoken by a sound that he had not heard in a long time: the distinctive patter of rain. Beyond the innumerable branches he could see no clouds, but still a gust of rain struck his face, and everything around glistened under the white sky, calling to mind the countryside near Moscow. No one could be bothered to wrap up; sitting there in their damp gray tent with the cards outspread, they smoked and smoked. Tania was also there, because her feeble betrothed, whom she no longer loved, had already packed his bags and headed home—a naked, hairy dragonfly on a shabby bicycle. But soon enough they tired of cards and lay them aside to get wet and cleave together; only one of them, trampled under Tania's foot, would be taken back by Oleg—a single card from a whole new and extravagantly short-lived summer's game; and although there was money left, yet departure fluttered in the gray sky.

Ivan Gerasimovich left, and so of course that evening the whole group, enlivened by this event, assembled in Le Lavandou for a drink. Oleg remembered how, with peculiar energy, they extracted from their suitcases, from that pleasant chaos of soiled underwear, letters, and ubiquitous sand, their cherished pressed trousers, how, trading smiles, they shaved with seawater, combed their hair, capering in front of the microscopic mirror, sprinkled themselves with eau de cologne, and rolled up the already short sleeves of their *marinières* as far as they would go. Around his wrist, like a convict, Oleg fixed a strap that Tania had given him—Tania, who was so grasping and miserly when it came to gifts—and with which he would not be parted, even in the farthest reaches of the swimming barrier.

Having smartened themselves up at last, and now filled with the inane excitement of anticipation, they all made their brisk, surefooted way in the dark, down familiar rocks, past the airstrip and through the wilderness to Le Lavandou.

Beneath the bright stars, on wires, electric lamps were burning, whitely lighting dead cactuses and the ice cream vendor's kiosk. Electric gramophones were playing in both casinos, but they could go there only to dance, whereas to drink—well, they knew another place, cheap, right at the end of the embankment, where under a white lamp brightly lighting bare legs, the locals would sit sprawled out and, with the look of connoisseurs, silently observe the boules cast by sedate players. It was rather like a game of skittles, only without any skittles.

They sat on the sidelines, on the edge of darkness, and, while the proprietor dashed off to fetch some rosé wine, Oleg motionlessly, strangerlike, examined a strange, motionless Tania in her city dress.

In a daze of suddenly ebbing pain, in the quiescence of a life that suddenly forgot itself, smitten, driven from himself by another's existence, Oleg watched Tania, but she seemed not to sense his gaze and looked off somewhere in the other direction. Because of this inattention, he could look to his heart's content, recalling and comparing her many different faces.

Dressed up, looking extraordinarily grand all of a sudden, squaring her shoulders and feeling the embrace of her pale-blue dress (a curiously pleasant sensation, like armor), she sat there in a wicker chair, brightly, sharply lit in profile, with only her head turned as she stubbornly, grimly looked out toward the sea, which was invisible and indicated only by a few yellow lamplights dotted along the quay. There was something of winter in this unmoving figure, something sober, something that had woken entirely from these summer antics, something morose, stoical, almost masculine. Her lips pouted wearily, scornfully; her face, never having tanned, showed pale, and her extraordinarily straight, neatly hewn nose cut clean the gloom, almost threateningly. But in her eyes, which since childhood had been encircled by creases, there glinted a weariness that was totally unfamiliar to Oleg; excruciatingly delicious to see, it was a sadness of sorts, an unexpected detachment from the world, and behind it lurked the shadow of some lofty, nebulous, melancholy humanity, the sort one finds in very gifted and very depraved cold people. Oleg quite literally forgot himself; how unexpected it all was, the very image of Thérèse's ascetic, celestial beauty, just as it had been on her antique, almost bovine face, only now without that dreadful pre-Hellenic look of consumptive emaciation. The bitter, intelligent, living mass of Tania's body unflinchingly, stubbornly gazed out to sea, understanding, sensing, gleaning something on the border of two faiths, two infinities, summer and snow, Oleg and her soul. Like an ancient shepherd, Oleg watched this servant of mystery from across the table with an ecstasy and fear that was tantamount to sacrilege. He drank, and slowly his fingers and eyes filled with invisible lead, his body grew abnormally heavy, sounds became muffled, the people around him seemed to be talking at a remove, images lost their anchoring in space, night entered his heart.

Tania drank little but soon grew drunk; and though it did not show, she seemed more amiable somehow. Something good-natured, almost jealously maternal now shone in her slanting greenish eyes, with which she laughingly surveyed the group. The Slavophile wavered between broodiness and laughter, dismissing and denying everything. As he played with the tassel on his wrist-band, the ape-man listened with vacant surprise to the bumptious ravings of the wide-eyed young lady. Nadia laughed, flashing her thirty-two teeth that might have driven a dentist to despair. Tipsy, though resisting inebriation, Bezobrazoff scratched his beard Russianly and pulled it into a fist as he followed the game of boules. But the tables were emptying, and at this late hour the proprietor, with little teetering steps, carried them inside; and so the group was soon left alone under the white lamplight.

Making a dismal nuisance of themselves, they made their way back, singing coarsely and out of tune. They overturned a bathing hut and shouted obscenities at one of the of the locals, who, to the surprise and relief of all, ventured nothing in reply. Boisterously jostling with one another, they crammed into the white-winged Goéland,* a bar modeled on a submarine, decorated and finished after the latest cubist fashion. There, lounging on green divans, they struck drunken attitudes and deplorably, indiscreetly set about haranguing one another on private matters. As they danced, they again clashed, cast aside all restraint, clamoring with threatening gaiety and looking impudently at outsiders, so that again they were soon left alone. Their mood began to darken; they grew tired and, reluctantly settling up, set off homeward, soon straying from one another, losing one another in the black wilderness.

Oleg found himself walking beside Tania, wonderstruck, uplifted, emboldened by the alcohol, crooning a French gypsy romance which he had only just learned: *"Poursuivant le néant d'amours sans lendemain, sans amis, sans tendresse, je poursuis mon chemin. Et la nuit m'envahit. Tout est brume, tout est bruit."*[†8]

And he listened to his own voice, for usually, because of nerves or pride, he could not bring himself to sing—a persecution complex would choke him, but now it had let go of his throat. Then suddenly, seizing the initiative, he took her arm and hugged her shoulder. Tania put up no resistance; on the contrary, she yielded to him and waited, longing for other, more decisive actions, because, despite her

---

* Seagull (*French*)

† Pursuing the emptiness of loves without tomorrow, without friendship, without tenderness, I continue on my way. And the night engulfs me. All is mist, all is noise. (*French*)

soul, which oppressed and humiliated this statuesque body, she had always been subliminally drawn to him, had always wanted, always thrilled at his warm, dry touch; but much to his own distress, Oleg quickly sobered up and, as they neared the cottage, resumed his submissive, wary, inhibited, injured role. "How tiresome," thought Tania, "again with this overthinking of things; even when he's drunk, he can't find it in him to forget himself, to stop intellectualizing and standing in awe of everything on earth . . ." Worse still, losing all grasp on reality, Oleg now wept, compounding his misfortune: staggering, stumbling, shedding tears, he sniveled theatrically from a sense of self-pity. "How physically repulsive I find men who weep. They make my skin crawl," Tania would later inscribe in her diary. Fear and juvenile indecision tormented him, for there was not long to go, and their fleeting drunken intimacy was ebbing away with every step; then right there, by the garden fence, Oleg broke. Resting his head on the cold wire mesh, he flatly, with a schoolboy's naïveté, demanded a decisive answer: "No, you've got to tell me now, once and for all: do you love me, or don't you, won't you ever love anyone?"

04

Comment se fait-il que le public du monde n'ait pas encore crié
"Au rideau," n'ait pas demandé l'acte suivant avec d'autres êtres que
l'homme, d'autres femmes, d'autres fêtes.[*]

▶ Guy de Maupassant[1]

"**N**o," said Tania, suddenly breaking free and steeling
herself. "No, I don't love you. I don't love you and
I won't ever love you. I like you. I'm attracted to you,
and I find you intriguing, as a man, but I don't love you," she said,
pleased with herself. Gone was that cool, detached, grown-up tone,
arrayed in snow beneath a white lamp. Together with the wine and
darkness, with this senseless body that had strayed from life and
could not understand itself, she rushed now to the opposite extreme.
There was a buzzing in her ears, as if the hot, wild wind of freedom
and solitude were blowing across an ancient forest where her fate, like

---

[*] How is it that the worldly audience has not yet called out, "Curtain," has not yet demanded
the next act, with other beings than mankind, other women, other pleasures? (*French*)

that of the ancient, hallowed satyrs, was filled until the dawn, until the reckoning, with a peculiar loneliness, the earth's cruelty and sin.

Now she reveled in her cruelty, her words, her broad, high-borne shoulders. But all of a sudden, she saw that she had in fact gone too far, for her words had an instantly sobering effect on Oleg. In the blink of an eye, he had grown up and become a man. A wrathful, spiteful, irrepressible, retaliatory spark glinted in his eyes. He looked at her for a second, as though he were seeing for the first time all those days they had spent together, all those nights on a blanket in the forest with sand between their teeth, all those desperately happy kisses they had shared. All this flashed momentarily before his eyes, and then, in all earnestness, in all fearlessness, he struck her with the back of his hand.

Tania went reeling and had to prop herself up against the fence. Her eyes were wide open.

"Goodbye," he said. "You've had your fun, you wretch."

Turning sharply, he set off down the path with sudden determination. But where was he heading? . . . For the rocks, and from there, in a final pageant of youthful strength and despair, amid the black milk of night, he would dive into the water, scattering spume in all directions, and then, to the muffled sound of continually chattering teeth, he would swim for hours, no longer tormented by the need to conserve his energy for the return. A one-way trip, then, out there, into the open sea, where, black and broad, the black-maned wave roars; then finally, without impediment or restraint, he would swim past the six-mile mark and, completely exhausted, lie out on his back, his face to the slowly twinkling stars, at which point, perhaps no longer over the sea but over the Elysian fields, a uniquely, wondrously beautiful sun would rise.

Tania hurried after him, stumbling and cradling her cheek, suddenly awake and having succumbed to his decisiveness, to his belated and ludicrously desperate show of heroism: "No, Oleg, you can't do this," she insisted, howling louder and louder.

In an instant, their roles had been reversed. The ever-electric current, sparking and flowing in the opposite direction, dragged her inexorably, shamefully, mechanically along behind Oleg. And she, Tania, the Lucifer of Saint-Michel, was forced now to go after him, to forgo her composure, to babble, to flounder, to weep.[2] But, novice that he was to life and apprentice to affairs of the heart, Oleg could not maintain the upper hand for long, could not hold on to this magical advantage, for which he had unwittingly and so dearly paid, or was about to pay. Slowly, in silence now, they walked beside one another, down into the reeds. A colossal moon cast sharp, black shadows that strode on ahead of them, while the bamboo glinted and before them lay a white carpet of finest dust, pulverized by the sun, deadening their footsteps. Once again Oleg began to falter, and amid the silence, shame and finality swelled. Tania's footsteps grew angrier, more distinct, and, as she walked, her hips began to sway again—freely, naturally, almost imperceptibly.

"For God's sake, leave me alone. What do you want from me? It's over."

"Oleg, don't be like that. Better, go, think it over. After all, I scarcely know myself, and I know you even less. I don't know what kind of a person you are. One minute you act like a man, then the next you're a baby. Snap out of it! You should be ashamed of yourself!"

"Leave off! Don't you pretend you give a damn about this! No one will find out. So, a drunkard's gone and got himself drowned. Serves him right. They all meet a bad end."

"Enough of this childishness, Oleg. Get a grip of yourself."

"Just go, leave me alone!" Suddenly an elusive string snapped in him, and all at once he lost everything that he had won with such difficulty. "Go! Go on, you bitch! You know that's what you are, don't you? You'd have to be an imbecile not to realize it."

As she was subjected to this invective, Tania held herself erect. She drifted off and lost herself before finally returning to her senses: "Is that so? . . ." She was like stone. She turned away, in a sudden diabolical rage, and hardly noticed the climax of Oleg's resolve. As she walked off, she held her face to the moon and, beholding herself thus, bathed in her own light, like an antique silver statue with high cheekbones. Bewildered, plainly, palpably sensing his loss, sensing that he would lose this final gamble, Oleg set off in the opposite direction and did not look back. With every step he took, he lifted his legs as though they were kettlebells, and, as he pressed on, he squirmed, tormented by unbearable shame, cowardice, and despair. With his back, his nape, with every inch of his skin, he watched, heard, absorbed each of Tania's footsteps, so that his spine momentarily ached from the strain as it swelled with blood. But Tania's barely audible steps continued to fade into the distance, and he realized that she had reached the crossroads and disappeared from sight behind the wall of rushes. Suddenly a howl, a cry, a roar escaped his mouth; it was labored and truly unbearable to hear, like a fit, like retching: "Tania! . . ." (Hearing this, Tania stopped dead in her tracks, as silent and cunning as a wolf.) "Tania! . . ." He turned around. Stomping, staggering, he began to run, searching high and low . . . There was nobody in sight . . . He cried out again: "Tania!" And then right beside him, from an inky patch of shadow, there suddenly came a harsh, proud, evil: "What?" He very nearly jumped out of his skin and, in a lunacy, bursting into tears, threw himself at her feet, prostrating himself like a Russian, like a schismatic, like an Arab, with all his might, with all his tears. Delighting bitterly, he buried his face in the dust, eating, chewing, clawing at it, howling, cowering, feigning, aping, repeating, resolving—all in an epileptic fit of tears.

This fathomless Russian blood, this monastic Tartar fanaticism momentarily sparked something feminine, hysterical, murky, ancient even, in Tania's heart. Barely conscious of it, she did not see what she was doing as she repeated those thousand-year-old gestures of her people. She sat down beside him and clasped his wet head to her breast, and then, as he bawled and mumbled incoherently with his mouth full of sand, she stroked and kissed his hair, pressing it to her warm, smooth, sun-tanned, living belly.

Having found at last the warmth, taste, and smell of her body, he imbibed it all with his nostrils, his eyes, his entire face, this aroma of hay, sweat, sunshine, and urine. It calmed him as he prattled there, still shaking. And they both let themselves be carried away, lost in the moment, their hearts suddenly and truly warmed. Like a wounded soldier, like a miscreant with a malady, like Svetlana of Sorrows having found at last her young Vasia, Tania whimpered, purred over him—for how long, he lost track—until eventually, despite herself, her deceitful, deathly, urban nature came into its own. It all looked so ridiculous; ashamed to sit on the road like that, they stood up, dusted themselves down and, beneath a paling sky, around and across the fields, hauled themselves home. As they walked, they said nothing, but could both of them sense now that Oleg's overwhelming defeat, thanks namely to his Russian fanaticism and its irreparability, had shattered some mature, Occidental sense of aloofness forever and created a new platonic bond between them, making some kind of love possible, even though tomorrow she would be ferociously, slavishly uninhibited again. For now, however, he belonged to Tania, for she had gloomily, reluctantly taken charge of him. They parted in silence and in sorrow. Tania's melancholy eyes, like an Eskimo's, looked off to the side, while tirelessly she received Oleg's long and, to her regret, unforgettable kisses.

■ □ ■

Soon, the day after their moonlit confrontation, the first gale of autumn swept in over the shore. It lashed the forest, disheveled their hair and, with a wild, melancholy freshness, stuck their clothes to their bodies; it blustered, ran riot, laid waste to the tents and bathing huts, and carried a number of boats out to sea. The beach emptied and was transformed. With unrelenting regularity, terrific gray waves crashed and roared, washing up all manner of troublesome, foul debris that seethed and danced in them—pieces of bark, corks, jerricans, driftwood, boards.

Suddenly Tania turned to Oleg with an excruciating kindness that disarmed him completely. She demanded unequivocally that he leave, "because Yasha's coming back, and, if you go, I'll be able to figure it all out." (This was said in the crassly naïve certainty that everything in the world revolved around her.) And through the utter humiliation of his lovelorn enslavement, a feeling of profound resentment flooded Oleg's heart. Did she not realize that he had not left Paris for ten years and that the opportunity may not present itself again for another decade?

Drearily, gloomily, the thirty-year-old adolescent bid farewell to his colossal friend—his one and only. Since the small hours, he had thrown himself into its embrace, and in a delirium of sorrow he swam without end, battling the waves with a melancholy joy. Before long, the shore had disappeared from view altogether. As he splashed about for the last time, he would scramble up onto the ridge as fast as he could, only then to be swept off its other side, carried down into the glittering abyss by the swell; and this solitary but so desperately happy battle with the waves stayed with him for evermore, like the smack of a salty kiss that stung his lips. Rain was falling now on the waves, every one of which, in its deep agitation, was strewn with gray specks, as if gooseflesh had appeared on the sea's sparkling silver skin. Oleg was worn out, swimming now on his side like a turtle and sitting low in the water like a frog. By the time he reached the shore again, he had drunk what seemed like half the sea and was barely able to crawl out—for the breakers kept sweeping him literally off his feet. Yet as he lay there upon the wet sand, he almost fell asleep in exhaustion, almost wept with fatigue and sorrow. But he got up and left, shaved, quickly threw his beggarly belongings into his suitcase, which was full of sand—the same sand that in each of his pockets and in the turn-ups of his trousers he would carry back with him to Paris, where he would spend the many melancholy months afterwards shaking it out, sniffing it, fingering it. He appeared before Tania like a sacrificial bull, and with humiliating condescension she led him to the bus at Saint-Tropez. By the rocks she kissed his lips tenderly, with a good-natured sense of territoriality, but now, in front of the crowd waiting for the bus, she knitted her brow and practically turned away, fearing that he would kiss her goodbye in full view of everyone. It hurt Oleg, but he was so accustomed to hurt that no sooner had the maroon omnibus swung out onto the lilac road, gaining speed, than he was gripped by an aching, reckless, childish love of speed and of the journey's finality. He thrust his head out of the window, whistled and sang, relishing his neighbor's horror as the Russian driver sped along with death-defying agility, swerving about and overtaking private autos—one last authentic slice of the uniquely Russian Côte d'Azur.

Thus, Oleg left, and the sea, before all others, forgot him. Colossal and thousand-hued, it calmed the very next morning, having scattered bathing cabins and altered the contours of the dunes along the shore. Now it shone dazzlingly radiant before its myriad new September worshippers. Past them plodded heavy mythological horses along the sand, sunk mightily to their ankles, hauling antediluvian carts from which, like the crimson blood of a dying summer, flowed the sweet nectar of crushed grapes. Never, but never would Oleg see this rocky lilac shore again, where so untimely though entirely, if only for a short while, did he awaken to life.

His return to Paris was somehow a painfully morose and joyous affair. When he went out early in the morning, everybody would gaze at his sun-tanned ebony-black head with its perfectly bleached flaxen hair. It was hot there, too, but it was a different kind of heat; the air was thick and muggy, as it so wearyingly is in autumn, and all the while pale, squinting figures trudged the streets in sandals. But Oleg did not forget the sea, he would never forget it, although after Tania's betrayal, it no longer sung to him of happiness and life, yet sing it did, unrelenting and unembraceable, without words, the blinding witness to so many summer dramas and pointless confrontations. The footprints that Oleg left on the sand were washed away before all the others. Only at the end of October did Tania return to Paris, and only in the middle of November did she write him a letter, informing him of the fact.

PROSE D'OUTRE-TOMBE[*]

Question: What is your greatest regret in life?

Answer: That I surrendered my virginity.

Q: But what is the suffering that it causes you?

A: A dying man comes to know the heart of woman. A dying woman comes to know the slavery of man. Each of them, lost, seeks himself vainly, without a way out in the other, hence this *perpetuum mobile* of hellish torments.

Q: But what *exactly* is the suffering that it causes you?

A: It's hard for the living to understand . . . impossible . . . Oh . . . Oh, ugh . . . I'm M. I'm F. I'm M . . . I'm F . . .

Q: Are you able to pray?

A: No . . . Life is a photograph. Death is a phonograph's record of life. But nothing new comes this way . . . Only more of the same: I'm M. I'm F. I'm M. I'm F.

SOMMEIL-APPRENTISSAGE DE LA MORT[†]

A room, dimly lit with a jaundiced electric light . . . Oleg knows that he hasn't seen such lightbulbs—dusky amber in color, with an incandescent filament shaped in a figure of eight—for a long time . . . Not since . . . So, the unendurable lives on . . . The room has grimy brick walls, and everything combines to give the impression of a cellar, abandonment, the servitude of an engine room, factories, and

---

* Prose from beyond the Grave (*French*)

† Dream-Rehearsal of Death (*French*)

backyards. But that isn't what matters; what matters is something somewhere else, feigning invisibility for the present moment. At first, everything seems normal, but a terrible, dreamy ennui weighs on the heart, while the body is in a daze—unable to stand or stir. Gradually it becomes clear that *it all has to do with the chair,* and now Oleg looks at it, unable to avert his eyes. But a curious thing: the longer this goes on—*and it has already been going on for so long,* for years perhaps—the weaker he grows, as though he were losing his very substantiality, as though it were flowing out through his eyes and into the chair, while the chair, keeping its distance, evidently absorbs it, gaining weight as it stands there, motionless, in its corner... Time limps languidly on, and Oleg senses now that almost no power on earth will tear that chair away from the filthy concrete floor, that the chair has sprouted deep roots in it, and suddenly he sees... Of course. It's because the chair is *slowly swelling with blood* . . . Now he realizes that before, when he was free, he was a man, he was M, whereas the chair was a woman, a thing, an object, while here, "in captivity," some kind of magical polarity has been reversed, and the chair, which he always carried within him, as he did his weakness, his shame, his sin, has come to life and become the master over its creator; while he becomes more and more paralyzed and loses his very essence, the chair grows and comes astonishingly, disgustingly to life, swelling with borrowed vitality, never stirring from its spot. Everything around, as though caught in the beam of a magic lantern whose focus keeps shifting, has shifted, slipped, retreated into the irreversible petrifaction of everlasting slavery. "I'm M. I'm F." The words ring in his head. "I'm M. I'm F." Desperate all of a sudden, he writhes, straining to break free of the ground, resisting valiantly, as though an invisible hand were stopping him, but, gnashing his teeth—as the chair gnashes its own—he prevails. Every so often, one of the chair's legs manages to raise itself up off the concrete, and then—O horrors!—it transpires that this leg is attached to the floor by thick, lumpish, blue-and-red veins, engorged with blood. (Oleg is reminded of his gleaming, red member, as, between thrusts, it is drawn halfway out a vagina.) Then the leg firmly reattaches itself to the floor . . . The chair crouches, gnashes, triumphs; it is utterly impossible to uproot it. Oleg languishes, wasting away, while the chair, with its abiding and firm-rooted servitude, slowly strikes at his chest. Another minute, another hour, and it will all be over, for the chair, with its four legs, with its four pumps, was draining the life-blood from him. And suddenly, a juvenile prayer surfaces, awakens in his forsaken heart: "O Lord, protect and save . . ."—and suddenly, the draining action seems to slow, or rather it migrates into another dimension, weakened, as though in a picture, and some white day-light, the dawn in the window freshens his face. Then—O joy!—people are beginning to talk, and with such happiness does he listen to their babbling. Morning has truly broken, and someone, looking at the mercury thermometer, says in his father's voice: "There won't be any school today."

■ □ ■

Dear reader! Between the first and second acts of this piece of occult pulp fiction, a whole year has passed. Now it is having returned not from the sea, but from the ocean, with brown legs, that Oleg again awaits Tania at the Passy Métro station. It was a year of humiliations for Oleg, in one café after another, where Tania broke every record of tardiness, a year of deathly boredom by the sea and the ocean, on a filthy, down-at-heel beach, by the cold water, beneath a pale sky. Lest he run into the group from the cottage, he would walk for miles and miles to go for a swim, and there, among the thorns, like a mangy wolf-pup, he would howl away his hurt that Tania had simply not taken him with her to the south—naturally, so that he should not interfere with her ability to have it out. All the same, Oleg had the good sense to acquire a tan, to run wild, to swell in all his rude, rustic beauty. Dear reader, etc.[3]

■ □ ■

Once again, the mercury had climbed up from the burning bush that was the Eiffel Tower, rising to fifteen like some crimson creature from the depths, while the electric clock seemed to have ground to a halt at twenty minutes past nine.[4] It was too late even for the cinema now. Oleg mused how everything in the city changed, cut off at a quarter past nine. Those with places to be, or simply with places they wanted to be, had already reached their destinations, gone in and exchanged greetings, while those with nowhere to go and whom no one had come to visit suddenly realized that there was nothing more to wait for; yet still they persevered, fidgeting from resentment and apathy, and for the first time they looked about themselves soberly and deliberated what was left for them to do that evening—or rather, not that evening but that night—and, with a pitiful, exaggeratedly stoical gesture, they lit their cigarettes.

Much to his delight, Oleg found in his pocket whole half-cigarettes—"Heaven sent," he thought. He lit one but, in his absent-mindedness, set the entire pack alight; the flames, with their hot crackle, singed his eyebrows, but as the cigarette end continued to smoke, cold trickles of rain cooled his face and, squinting there in bitter pleasure, he inhaled the acrid tobacco smoke, that familiar stale aroma of an extinguished cigarette. Thus, frowning to the point of pain in his forehead, he walked up a dark rue Franklin and past the empty bandstand at the Trocadéro, where the greenish gas flames mingled with the crowd. Suddenly the rain let up and, having lost his bearings, he paused to inspect the photographs adorning the front of the Cinéma Les Miracles. He had spent what seemed like an eternity there, under the disdainful eye of the liveried doorman, when suddenly a colossal blow to the neck made him gasp for breath: *"Alors, vieille chaude-pisse, on ne reconnaît plus les potes?"** Standing before him was Bezobrazoff, handsome and tanned, evidently having just returned from work in the fields. He carried on cursing Oleg: "What's got into you? I've been following you and calling out your name for a whole ten minutes already, and all you do, you swine, is cross the road!" And for the very first time, the old friends kissed each other warmly.

■ □ ■

O city, city, as the night wears on, after the setting sun has burned itself out and only the laurel reflection of its eternal trail glimmers in the west, and the air, not yet recovered from its scorching presence, is still stifling, the walls are still warmed through, and above them, like incandescent iron, the red lines of neon lights burst into mysterious, bright life, their ruby glow falling on leaves and faces, while from an open window the invisible jazz of a radio station disperses

---

* Well, you clap-riddled old codger, don't you recognize your pals anymore? (*French*)

through the air distinctly and ethereally. The moon over the dappled water looks warm and inviting—as if you could reach out and touch it. The recesses of an iron viaduct fade to a dark lilac, and there above them, dim rows of little electric lamps have already lit up, indicating in perspective the station looming over the suspension railway.

There was nothing to do. Overwhelmed suddenly by his useless strength and the sultriness of the urban evening, having been knocked out of the rhythm of his self-defense, the sun-tanned youth sat on the platform while it emptied periodically. Then something of the countryside would materialize, and once more the stoically hunched figure of a tramp would appear on the opposite side, soon to vanish again amid the many-legged crowd of passengers. In the meantime, the station seemed like a ship of iron, where the passengers and the ticket inspector, bloated from the monotony of it, were suspended somewhere above both the city and time—these silent, aimless travelers with no hope of return. But still, leave they must: how was it that they all had somewhere to go, while he, Oleg, essentially had nowhere? And so when he went down to the embankment, it was all the same to him whether he turned left or right or cut across the Pont de Passy.[5] Dragging his feet, he eventually crossed the bridge and passed that same bandstand at the Trocadéro, where again the decadent gas was burning. He reached the inhospitable avenue Kléber, slowed by the Arc de Triomphe (to defile or not the grave of the unknown soldier?), and idled his way down the Champs-Elysées.

Only yesterday evening had he returned from the ocean, and already the city oppressed him. There was something magisterially sultry in the familiar sorrow of a scorching evening on the cusp of autumn, on the cusp of night. Passersby crowded along the wide avenue; the people here were a little cleaner, but they lacked the easy-going familiarity of the French proletariat, who would jeer and jest beneath the trees, while others dragged along their sullen children and sat in Maupassantesque poses on yellow iron chairs.[6] Those masses, so beloved by Oleg, were a different breed than those at the station, where he, cursing himself vainly for his weakness, now awaited Tania once again. The people alighting there were drunk on the heavy, languid joy of a squandered Sunday: broad-shouldered adolescents were exchanging smiles with drowsy, golden-faced girls; fathers were returning from the suburbs with entire gardens of flowers in oilcloth shopping bags; there was a priest sweltering under his black tallith, fanning his bald head democratically with his medieval hat, which had left a crimson imprint around his forehead; last of all, a total inebriate slumped out of a carriage after being almost entrapped by the automatic doors, and, sidewise somehow, flouting every law of equilibrium, he advanced toward the exit as everybody else looked on in sympathy, concern, and secret envy, while he, also having been forced to wait an outrageous length of time in a café only for the person not to show, muttered something to the void and accompanied those dark words with erratic, heavy gestures.

Oleg surveyed anew his demesne with an unhealthy mix of sorrow and joy, for this city, and in particular these streets, was the very place where he, for the first time, had grown so utterly, lachrymally exasperated with his own loneliness and, having accepted it, embarked upon a new, solitary, stoical, spectatorial life. Today, however, he had found himself once again utterly defenseless; as he had done in the old days, he had gone somewhere and waited for something, and now, of course, he was being drawn unwittingly to Montparnasse, to see his comrades in literature. Before long, as he made his way about their usual haunts, he managed to shake off the gnawing pain of that eternal waiting by the Métro in Grenelle. He had waited for her almost until ten o'clock, breaking every record of chivalry and spinelessness, only to find himself plunged once again, alone, into that twilight hour, when everyone was happily ensconced wherever they needed to be, and outside, in the streets, only superfluous individuals, deceived lovers and out-of-work foreigners remained. Among them, the cry of newspaper-sellers echoed monotonously in the quiet city air, and in an unnatural bass, the radio was proclaiming the results of a bicycle race. They were tormented by work-weary boots and the wild desire if not to drown their sorrows, then to complain to someone older and all-powerful, or to pick a fight with the first person to come their way.

As Oleg strode through these districts, these worlds and the people themselves seemed to change, as though they belonged to different races, divided by deserted, sinister-looking alleyways. Thus, in Saint-Michel, without any transition, he suddenly found himself amid a crowded demonstration of adolescents, with their cacophonous voices, provocatively free movements, and jutting shoulders. They were all talking over one another loudly, making a nuisance of themselves and jostling passersby. Oleg squared his shoulders and sneered at them, but no one tried to bar his way; his face, wild and furrowed with exertion, provoked only surprise and hostility. Soon enough, his shoulders relaxed and, defeated without landing a single punch, he dragged his heels along the length of the wall, suddenly reduced by exhaustion to his customary station of a former youth. He had to cut across yet another boundary between two worlds on the avenue de l'Observatoire, that juncture of two physiologies, for, you see, a person from the boulevard du Montparnasse is of an entirely different breed—with a different style, a different mode of expression, a different voice. Here was France, faith in the living earth, from which, however much you pulled, you would always remain buried up to your waist in the healthy thousand-year mulch of your fathers' bones—and here was this naked man, torn from the earth like a mandrake, in all his morbid wit, in all his apocalyptic loneliness.

By now, the distant lights of Montparnasse were illuminating the evening. Oleg had livened up, and his heart had begun to beat quicker. Old friends and old scores, old egos and old humiliations— and, with each and every last one of them, Oleg's own ambiguous, dubious relationships. At one time or another, Oleg had either harangued them all or demeaned himself before them, been irate with some and ashamed before others, only then to lose sight of that other desire—to show off his tan, to parade his ruddy health and newly rediscovered joy in the wildness, the wilderness, the earth— and so now, momentarily forgetting the newspapers and cigarette ends floating in the cold water of that cheap vacation spot, he concocted an entire fantasy, an African epic in the style of Jack London.[7] There was a keen, distracted tension already simmering in him; he was on his way to see his friends, once again having fallen somehow into the tedious though all-too-familiar neurosis of "who is sleeping with whom," regretting already that he would open his mouth, talk over everyone and suddenly find himself the object of general reproach, bored and spurned, even though they would be sure to meet him, as one of their own, with great fanfare.

And indeed, no sooner had Oleg made his way around the terrace of the Rotonde, so renowned for its latest artistic failures, than he spotted up ahead, through the open windows of the Napoli,[8] his elegant crowd of miscreants—Tchernosvitoff, Okolichine, and Sve-tobaïeff.[9] They were truly glad to see him and, after he strode up to them with affected gaucherie and a banditlike swagger, mimicking some old American films he had seen, they met him magnanimously, plaintively, with questions about the sea. But Oleg hadn't the time to boast or take exception to anyone, for almost simultaneously, although from the other direction, Alla Rachkavadze, Gulja Bark, and Katia Muromtseff approached the table. These three were girl-friends, or, rather, two girlfriends, Gulja and Alla, a pair of slouching young women, catty but wittily so, dressed from head to toe in chic fashions from abroad, plus Katia, a recent addition, a bird of passage, a haughty, simple-minded merchant's daughter (the sort with large eyes and broad hips, the sort to hold fast to life).

They all stood up and began to kiss the ladies' hands gallantly, which Oleg, much too abashed, did not dare to do. He was pleased, however, to take Alla's cold, clammy hand in his own outsized mitt, which was attached to an arm bared all the way to the shoulder. Now there's a girl for you, he thought, slender arms, a look of jouissance on her face—sleepy Alla's half-bared slender arm. She's no Tania, with her bearlike paw . . .

They complained at first of the sultriness and their heartache at the impending storm. And sure enough, no sooner had they men-tioned it than a clap of thunder suddenly rolled over the roofs of the buildings.

"It's funny," said Gulja, "the thunder makes such a racket, as though it's actually doing something, but there's still no rain."

And, as though to answer her, infrequently to begin with but then continuously, great, heavy drops of rain began to strike the broad canopy, the road darkened instantly, and the waiters, wincing in their haste, began to carry the chairs in, while those seated too close to the windows moved farther toward the wall. Now the rain was making such a din that conversation proved difficult. Alla lit a cigarette as she gawped there in her malevolent Georgian way; suddenly, the night sky lit up with a wonderful, bright light, and, with a tremendous crack that assaulted their ears, a bolt of lightning struck nearby, somewhere toward the boulevard Raspail. Oleg leaped up from his chair and ran to take a look—at what, exactly, heaven only knew. By the time he returned, Alla and Katia had disappeared along with almost all the group, leaving behind only Gulja Bark, who carried on smoking grimly as she spoke to Tchernosvitoff in hushed tones. Without turning to face her, this sun-tanned forty-five-year-old Surrealist, with the face of an Indo-Spanish pastor and an old man's iron spectacles, nodded politely as he emitted some inarticulate sounds. Tchernosvitoff, this Hispano-Russo-Franco-Slovak schismatic-anthroposophical loner, was the group's latest discovery, and perhaps its most astounding. But soon, like a wise old wolf, hardened by the savagery of his apostate nobility, he got up and took his leave ceremoniously, in the old fashion, offering his hand flat out, perhaps because he sensed that he might be needed somewhere, or that Gulja, having fallen out with the group, had momentarily latched onto him. And so, despite themselves, Oleg and Gulja sat opposite one another, each angry at someone and something else; these old acquaintances groped now for something, anything to talk about, for appearances' sake, but they were both of them affected and irked by this feeling of embarrassment and bewilderment. In the end, it was Oleg who spoke first, but no sooner had he opened his mouth than Alla and Katia returned with the whole gang, all of them suddenly and suspiciously lively.

"Oleg, we're going to a *tapis-franc* to listen to some gypsies!"

"But why? They aren't real."

"They may not be real, but they sing better than the real ones."

As soon as they entered the establishment on the rue du Montparnasse, inexplicably and inappropriately named "Cabaret aux Fleurs," the quick-paced, muffled rhythms of the electric gramophone stirred in Oleg some forgotten, crude, happy sentiments.[10] "A-ha, and so it begins, *la vie parisienne*. Well, I'll be damned . . ." In the cramped premises with its carnivalesque lighting, young Frenchmen and women were jostling and carrying on as they crowded the passageway. Dressed up as sailors, they danced among themselves, imitating Negro gestures and movements, the focus of which, however, was banished to the background. Then the lights went out, a spotlight fired up, and in its white beam appeared the enchanting painted faces of the Russian singers. After a moment's pause, they launched, all at once, into the usual routine, crooning in their familiar, almost liturgical voices:

Dearest love, do stay awhile!
Will you, won't you stay awhile!

Oleg and Katia found themselves cast together between a window and a high counter. Their first glass renewed that familiar but always surprising electric contact between them and temporarily isolated them from the rest of the group, who, grinning like pimps—that is, in the pure Parnassian fashion—had turned the other way. Katia narrowed her broad, lashless gypsy eyes, and her cheeks burned brightly and irresistibly from the alcohol.

"It's expensive here," ventured Oleg in his unconvincing imitation of an apache. "We could always go and down one at a bistro, then come back to dance."

Against all expectation, Katia liked his style and agreed to go with him. In a dingy café on Edgar Quinet, some short, handsome French sailors—perfectly real ones this time—looked at Oleg conspiratorially, and, unbeknownst to Oleg and Katia, the sailors drank with them, knocking back five glasses each of some potent calvados. As they walked back, Oleg's ears were ringing so much that he could no longer hear his own footsteps, but still they went on talking over one another, about the summer, about Denmark, and about something else that they found extraordinarily funny. When they returned, the bar seemed different somehow, more cramped, brighter—at once brighter and darker—and they stepped inside as though coming home.

> Set the steamboat going.
> Unfurl and hoist the sails.
> That's what set me loving him,
> His curls and head of hair.
> Sing a song for me or don't,
> I'm gnawed by longing all the day.
> Braid the horse's mane or don't,
> It leads me ditchward all the same.

Now Oleg was breathing heavily and spoiling for a fight. Drunk as he was, though, he was incapacitated and there was nothing worth striking—not for a man of his sporting caliber. Pleasingly, as if in a fairground, the lighting changed once again: red lamps lit up, and Oleg and Katia began to dance, suddenly reconciled by this unusual fact to finding themselves in each other's arms, suddenly rejuvenated and, with every ounce of strength, tending to their contrived sense of decorum. Oleg, as he was sometimes struck by a particular cultivation of the mind, was now taken aback by the uncommon musical plasticity of this tall and beautiful young woman. As they made their quick turns, everything merged into a kaleidoscopic haze, everything became exceedingly and synchronously lovely, and utterly inconsequential through the sweet, almost cloying smell of Katia's hair.

O brilliant, brawny body, thought Oleg as he danced, I'm so glad to have you. You know instinctively whom you're meant to love, while the brain, no matter how much it thinks, will never know this and will tell you either everyone or no one. Like the music's living embodiment, you now pause for a fraction of a second, now glide backward, now turn at full tilt, sway and dip. And how much meaning there is in the forbidding radiance of your eyes! Oleg had once very nearly choked from astonishment and gratitude when he read in Hegel that the body is the manifestation, the incarnation of the soul: hence, it is neither a burden nor a veil, but the perfection and splendor of creation. The body is dangerous, it grins, it vibrates like a musical string when high above it, amid the flapping of flags and the roar of the crowd, comes the click and bang of a starting pistol; then, uncoiling in an instant, you find that you have to put your soul, your heart, your life into that first desperate sprint, to forge ahead with your chest, your teeth, your face, for everything in the race rests on that first dash—until that same body, panting lightly, heavily, uncontrollably, exhaling air underwater as, having grown used to the rhythm, it pushes away the arm in front of it with an habitual motion, with all its being, plowing ahead like a ribbon, like a fish, a swimming body, a dancing body, a loving body, its teeth clenched, no longer conserving, no longer sparing itself, joyously, savagely roaring, wrestling, vanquishing, frantically faltering, is suddenly delivered of the ordeal. How naïve are those who would have another body, failing to find themselves in themselves: truly they neither know their own beauty, nor suspect the hidden ugliness of their soul.

Having forgotten their individual existence, having forgotten themselves, Oleg and Katia danced, as though they really were a single entity. Oleg recalled the old circus custom that allowed only brother and sister or man and wife to perform several of the more daring acrobatic acts. As he hit upon this, something strange, a sweet, heavy terror, pierced his heart, and for a moment he even lost his footing. And so they returned to the counter, where they found Okolichine, well-shorn, well-heeled, much improved by the vodka he had drunk, and Okolichine, this Jewish lord without a farthing in his pocket, said to Oleg deftly and discreetly, with an air of complicity and patronage:

"My congratulations! Only I shouldn't celebrate too soon."

But Okolichine's words of caution fell on deaf ears, for Oleg's heart, with all its accumulated, unbearably heavy gold, was pining, bursting, spent suddenly on this new haughty figure who had appeared from heaven knew where—for better or for worse?—and was now dancing with some young *métèque* (which was to say, a Frenchman, in Oleg's use of the term).[11] Katia was holding her lustrous head stiffly, comically high, but elegantly so, and when she sobered all of a sudden, she came to herself in the arms of her disciplined admirer. Her black-winged, black-browed gypsy face with its bovine antiquity was now absolutely devoid of expression, and, as though in a dream, Oleg was suddenly taken aback by her beauty. As she extended back her beautiful, plump, slightly crooked leg ("Aha, so you too know how to play the game . . ."), which ended with so perfectly curved a foot in a slim slipper, the toe of which barely—not too much, not too little, but just as much as was necessary—grazed the amber floor behind it, Oleg could but marvel at her and her partner: "That military-drilled son of a bitch. *Comme j'aimerais lui casser quelque chose!*"* But at the same time, he vaguely, mutely, shamefully sensed how accustomed, how attuned, how natural Katia was in polite society, the sort that was utterly inaccessible to him, the sort filled with those regimented, restrained, anglified curs, the ones he so envied, and how difficult it would be for him, with that broad nature of his, which he so despised, not to fall in love with her (*c'était déjà fait*)† but to enter her life and stay near her. In that moment, he felt like a disheveled vagabond and had a desire either to pick a fight or to rouse himself, to go and open his copy of Hegel. Yes, Hegel, Oleg mused, realizing that Hegel would be of no help to him now, for he would only increase his frenzy, his diabolical fury, and his determination, which ordinarily reared its head so inopportunely and mostly to his detriment. These bitter thoughts were suddenly cut short, however, when Katia abandoned her admirer and sat down beside Oleg, taking him by the arm and saying: "Well, heavy head, are you in a sulk? You should sing something. They say you're a good singer." Blushing now, bereft of her feminine charms, though still managing to wink at the pink-flushed but ever-immaculate Okolichine ("They say you're drunk, my dear"), she

---

* How I'd like to break something of his. (*French*)
† it was already too late (*French*)

began to laugh, revealing her uneven teeth and covering them awkwardly with her fantastically white hand. All of a sudden, she was being so fraternally, maternally, intimately kind that Oleg realized: he was done for, not for a day, but for an awfully long time. Meanwhile, the revitalized chorus now sang:

Fine tumblers of cut crystal tumbled off the table-top,
The glasses did not break—alas, it was my life that broke.

Oleg was becoming ever more sullen and drunk. Suddenly, as if from nowhere, Alla appeared; svelte, serious-looking, and with eyes like pools of water, she looked every bit the hapless Georgian princess.

"Listen, Alik, you're drunk again, and sullen, and in love. And as if that weren't enough, I'll bet you're spoiling for a fight."

In no mood for badinage, Oleg said simply and matter-of-factly:

"Who is she, Alla? Where did she come from?"

"She's a merchant's daughter, from Denmark. She's perfect for you, only nothing will come of it, because you don't know how to 'put on airs,' as we used to say at the lycée."

Suddenly it seemed to Oleg that the gypsy chorus was singing about him:

Fare ye well for now, O friends,
For pastures new I must depart.
Spare me not your pity, friends,
Farewell, my camp, farewell, my art . . .

■ □ ■

"For one last time, for one last chance, how I should fain believe. Does it truly matter now? What will be will be. For love cannot be measured, nor can it be known, but there in blackest depths of soul, as in a whirlpool around it goes . . ."

What, indeed, did it matter now? Had that bright cloud, that memory of summer freedom not been swept out to sea long ago? . . . The stormy night gazed in through the window. There will come a time when you will forget the joy, the sorrow, the night, the rain, and what will it matter then that this was all so long ago?

Katia is sitting on the floor, the toes of her slippers hidden by the dark-green silk of her dress; she holds a guitar in her hands, in an old-fashioned way that fires the blood. Her lips hardly move, her voice hardly makes a sound . . . What is she singing, humming, saying, as she stares off into the distance, gazing wide-eyed at the wall of the empty room? There, on a rug, among the modish white furniture, the scattered books and empty bottles, the suitcases and stacks of paper, in this already-abandoned apartment, in this chaos of migration, calm, familiar, Russian through and through, Katia gently plies the guitar with her fingers.

"Nothing do I need—your belated sorrow, your indifferent words. The past, it cannot be returned. All I want is this: to fearless peer a moment more into the river's depths . . ."

Yes, Oleg, fearless. Dust curls over the hot earth, the boundless steppe has been extinguished, wearily, with softest yearning, the campfire song has been extinguished . . . The sun has scorched the earth with flames, everything has crumbled into dreams without joy, and a lone voice above the deathly embers sings in ancient harmony . . . Life gallops past, and there's no time to live. Well, let us take a guitar and pray. We'll drink, we'll wait, we'll sing a song of happiness, of a happiness going for a song . . .

Sounds coursed slowly through Oleg's drunken soul. Then all of a sudden, they faded, and for a long time they whispered of snow, of thick wooden walls, of night-lights, candles, and kerosene lamps, of window ledges, where children lie, propped up on their elbows, looking out forever and a day to see how early the sun sets in the north.

Amid the deep nocturnal silence of the faubourgs, the words sounded oddly solemn, with the surprising comeliness of simplicity, remorse, and recompense. At number thirteen, whither Katia, after much laughing and misbehaving, had invited Oleg (in inebriated seriousness, desperately, using her Russian wiles and looking him straight in the eye), not once did Oleg sidle up to her, flirt with her, lay a finger on her; instead, he sprawled out in an easy chair with a cigarette and drunkenly pontificated, sulked, listened . . .

"A dazzling ray of sun does impale the shuttered glass; intoxicated by the light, I'm struck by dizziness. Your lately uttered words do keep on ringing in my ears; expressions black as darkness found upon the riverbed . . ."

As though from afar, from another room, the air carried a voice, a whisper, a lament, a whimper, a refrain—as though from another world, another life, calmed by the Divine, free, familiar, absolutely devoid of its enduring power to disfigure, devoid of its intensity, its barbarity, its desperation, its terror . . . A life without religion—or, no, rather one keeping the church and the candles, but dispensing with that eternity of diabolical, mystical insanity, the torrid, desolate, Babylonian dust of unattainable sainthood . . .

Ah, forests, forests . . . Envelop me, calm my savage, wild soul with your sounds. Let me lie down in the darkness and hear the nightingale's languid song . . . Let me lose my soul amid a lofty paradise of pines . . . You have grown too close to the sky: the light is driving you mad. The blistering sun of the wilderness will burn your broad shoulders . . . A spruce darkness languishes over the marsh as the moon serenely rises . . . You have returned, you are asleep, near to the dawn, near to the earth . . . Ah, Katia, Katia, homeward from heaven, from the scorching hell of sainthood, savagery, sport, and books to the earth, to the humility of work, weariness, and physical love . . . Ah, Katia, how from the mountains of Babel the hermit-devil pines for the earth, the grass, and the round, heavy white breast of his homeland . . .

But suddenly the door opened, and in came barging Alla, Tchernosvitoff, Hayes, Okolichine, and Tcherepahodoff. Roused and riled, the couple got up. Then, crazed with love and malice, Oleg left.

■ □ ■

Righteousness . . . It means sitting on a chair that vanishes from under you every minute, as if termites were eating it from within. Then, in an instant, your behind hits the ground and the back of your head bangs against a coffee table . . . Peace in God: that is what the hermit hardly ever finds . . . And yet, sin also knows peace: take, for instance, the Assyrian peace of those almond-eyed women in the Café du Dôme, who spend all morning vainly anointing, dressing, and adorning their bodies, or else on the telephone, or else in bed with an English illustrated magazine. But these moments of peace, too, end in the disquiet of obesity, gonorrhea, ennui . . . Then there is your metallic peace, Bezobrazoff, the irrevocability of a glass angel atop a golden chariot . . .

Peace in God, peace in springtime . . . God makes His peace with man when man buys Him off with circumcision, marriage, and submission, with the emasculation that is mysticism, greatness, solitude, and virginity . . . For He Himself is the persecutor of virgins, tormenting them with His overwhelming love . . . "I pray Thee, O Lord, put an end to all this, withdraw, extinguish Thy light!" Tania had once howled in a mystical fit. "Otherwise, I'll die, I'll perish, I'll yield, and my soul will be rent from my body."

The causes of that eternal inner struggle, the shock of those greatest, bitterest falls, range from weariness, overexertion, and too zealous prayer to the ringing in your ears, the salt taste of blood in your mouth and the shards of glass and lead lodged in the bridge of your nose . . . The long white days lacking chivalry, happiness, strength, lacking any grace whatever, above the half-finished ruins of an outward life, forsaken, undervalued, underplayed, lost through negligence; the damnation of the scorched road; the lead in your hands and in your heart; asceticism—my thanks to each and every blessed one of you . . . When suddenly, unexpectedly, astoundingly, terrifyingly, a door opens in the depths of your heart, and you find there an unbearable, unendurable glory, deafening tears of joy, a presence, God's physical presence, belonging, devotion, destiny, betrayal, His mark—and you scarcely have time to cry out and close your eyes, for your heart is aching, burning, bursting, breaking, melting, gushing, trickling away amid a torrent of Divine love . . .

When his tear-stinging eyes opened at last, Oleg, dirty and disheveled, climbed off the divan, his heart pounding . . . Life at first seemed impossible to him, but then, after eating and shaving, he felt suddenly revived, ready to rejoin the garish, madcap life of Montparnasse. In his eyes, wide and sensitive to the light, the world seemed full of fire, every building a monster sleeping in the sun, feigning tameness, every corner, every sunset cloud, every streetlamp an animate being, a hidden angel or demon, a fiery butterfly blazing slowly amid the twilight. Whenever he met anyone, the wild, burning joy of sociability would erupt in his heart. He would talk so much, pay excessive compliments and attention, and cause such a fuss that his chance companion would be left feeling acutely embarrassed, so much that they would try to give him the slip as soon as possible . . . From one person to the next, from one table to the next, sometimes laughing till he keeled over, sometimes frightening to the point of monstrosity, he overtalked, overlaughed, overexcited himself, until, scarcely alive, his heart pounding as he climbed the stairs, he would arrive home, collapse onto the sunken divan (he, an athlete and a swimmer!) and, O horrors, find himself unable to sleep . . . Burning with a crazed, blistering brilliance, disjointed images would now race before his eyes, the cushion would be too low, his whole body would itch, and every other minute he would jump up, turn on the light and, with teeth chattering, try to locate invisible fleas . . . Then, at last, having gathered his strength, he would force his thoughts to stop and, body contracted, eyes fixed, he would freeze in the impenetrable dark, only to be set upon by a new foe—hallucinations and waking nightmares . . . The furniture would begin to move, clothes on a hanger would assume the silhouette of a hanged man, a shapeless mass of wood and paper would begin to crawl up the stairs, and so on until dawn, until he eventually lapsed into the incoherent humiliation of dreams.

05

Triste est le monde,
Le monde est triste,
La Belle Rosemonde
Embrasse son Christ.*,1

Oleg had not meditated for two days. A thick, bleary fog of happiness, wine, and Katia's physical presence had turned his life into a torrent of images and torments from which he could not awaken. He would find himself drifting away, borne by a hot current, forever agitated, in a rush to go somewhere, laundering his socks, shaving, kissing Katia's heavy head, hastily passing water but never quite managing to empty his bladder and tucking away his prick so quickly that, to his eternal fury, some would always dribble down his leg. Amid daydreaming of taxicabs and winning the national lottery, he would fall asleep, incapable of stirring, for hours at a time, or else he would suddenly jump to his feet, fearing that he had missed some appointment.

* Sad is the world, / The world is sad, / The fair Rosamund / Kisses her Christ. (*French*)

He had been driven mad by the objectivity that had entered his life, by that foreign presence intruding on his own, by that other touch for which he had cried out for so long and now almost regretted . . . Often as he returned home, he would glare at his gleaming boots, which would remind him that he had spent the whole day sprawled over the divan or in bed, kissing, sniffing, groping at that young, live, dangerous body. The architectural symmetry of his solitude had been completely shattered, and now he was forever hurrying somewhere with an odious, mistrustful, brazen look about him . . . "Oh, if only to stay at home," he would roar wildly all of a sudden, "and not have to shave and go out in unironed trousers." In the privy, he would brood, sing, and whistle (for that was his life, hidden away from everyone).

Finally, one free evening, with no plans to go anywhere, Oleg lay out on the divan and attempted to clarify his stance with regard to God (*prendre position devant Dieu*), to understand his place in the unrelenting evanescence of everything . . . Having been a student of this for many long years, he was still able to smile, giddy with life, anticipating the catharsis, the repose . . . First his muscular body would snap to attention. He would place his legs one over the other, right over left (just like the hanged man on the twelfth Tarot card). He would fold his arms across his chest and throw back his head on outstretched neck, almost without any support, as far as it would go. And automatically there would follow a heavy sigh of relief, stillness, death—and with it, a diabolical tension, one absent in those elongated stone figures that adorn sarcophagi.

In his left palm Oleg clutched a watch that was quickly heating up from the strain of these five minutes of internal silence.

He closed his eyes and beheld a monstrous though familiar sight, a gigantic steel hydraulic press with steam issuing from its nostrils. The slow motion of its jaws forced every living thing beyond the threshold of consciousness ... The press vanished ... There was a difference between thinking about "nothing" and not thinking about anything. A familiar tension in the bridge of his nose, the darkness, night, oblivion . . . Time was advancing at a hellishly slow pace; he could hear the beating of his heart, a ringing in his ears; his body was itching but it was forbidden to itch, and suddenly, like a magic lantern, like a blistering flood, there was a rush of images, associations, memories; his inner voice again began to growl, and in an instant Oleg found himself in Montparnasse, in Denmark, in a universe of stars, but then he came to his senses and, as though clinging desperately to the last carriage of a burning train, he tried to reverse the sequence of visions and make his way back to that original nothing. A distinct feeling of exertion, a dissociation from his own self, and the circle was complete, the original darkness restored, and only from the lingering tension did misshapen rings of fire float about in it.

At last, the five minutes passed, and Oleg, transformed by effort, a little aged and iconlike, awakens to the conscious Dark Night ...

Who am I?

Not who, but what.

Where are my limits?

They do not exist. You know that. In profound solitude, beneath his borrowed mask, man is left not with himself but with nothing, not even with everyone else. An ocean of zeros, and upon it, like the voice of a wireless on an icy mountain, the comical talking parrot of oblivion.

You are splendor's lackey, a slave to ambition, bondage, the body's black thirst, yet after the disappearance of a thousand women and a thousand spectators, you too shall vanish, for two empty mirrors cannot distinguish one from the other . . . Where are you now?

Only a moment ago I was everywhere, scattered throughout the universe, but more importantly I was on the Champs-Elysées and in Montparnasse, and my essence, like a sticky liquid fire, was spilled in the wake of ten perfumed, pure-blooded monsters, but soon it was gathered up in a gnashing fiat of will, and all at once I was nowhere, for everywhere else was forbidden me.

To remain on this border of two infinities, one has to integrate, to fix this point in the stream with the threads of real relationships, eternal memories of family and friendship, but how is this possible for me, if Katia's Oleg loathes Tania's, if Thérèse's Oleg is different again, and so, one after another, they collapse, drown, dissolve into nothing, while I am ἄπειρος,* the void, the dark night that gave birth to them and swallowed them whole, if I am a dark, fiery mirror, the fiery sea, a thousand metamorphoses with no recollection of any lineage, and how weary I am from the incessant carnival of a thousand tragedies—yet such are my dreams. Asceticism is a violent awakening from the cosmic slumber of an imaginary life, an awakening that is conscious, ampliative, instantaneous, involuntary, tremendous, an awakening from pain, as when in the stupefaction of parting a thousand-colored cloth is ripped off and in one fell stroke the universe collapses into nothing. "The cosmos dissolves in tears. And, like mascara, the cosmos dissolves in tears . . ."[2] Once again, as it did before the beginning of the world. From the sunken divan, with

---

* infinity (*Ancient Greek*)

human eyes, Nothing stared into the face of the Begetter of all ills, of life itself . . . Face to face, at a dizzying height . . .

Oleg was breathing heavily, his eyes closed, his brows knitted, frowning, bathed in sweat from the strain, again with his body outstretched and his lips pursed. Dark Lord of this magnificent tomb, where are you? . . . Nowhere . . . For Paris is somewhere, sometime between the heavens and the earth, where the day's snow falls slowly and then instantly melts upon the wet asphalt . . . What is the time, what the hour? . . . There is no hour. The time is never . . . It has lost its way amid the centuries, between Aegean mysteries, Stoicism, Hegel and Laforgue . . . The moon, the cosmic Nothing that sees everything but for itself, motionlessly looks through Oleg's eyes at the cosmic Everything that races before him, like a sea of storm clouds . . . The self-actualization of a transcendental subject is impossible; hence Nothing speaks to God . . . But why should God answer? . . . Being rent from his family, his people, his history, Oleg had soared headlong into that pure nonexistence from which God had endeavored in the beginning to create the heaven and the earth, but which ultimately He had failed to overcome at its core, and so, at first from pain, though later with the satanic, blinding courage of asceticism, it had cast Him off, awakened suddenly by all the contours of the heaven and the earth . . . Now Oleg felt, saw with his body, mimicked all the music of creation, all the mountains asleep under the sun, like the wrinkles on his face . . .

Oleg had no genuine intimate relationships with anyone. Clearly, Tania had been wrong to kiss him and to get mixed up with those ten nice blond chaps, whom she also kissed and with whom she corresponded and was forever having things out . . . Katia loved—although, perhaps she no longer loved—the heavy, violent, blood-spattered shadow of the bar, one that was, like an importunate musical leit-motif, so eager, so desperate to live, to take on all Katia's dreams of the good life in Russia, the taxicabs, the gypsy romances, the communism, the eternal derision of all and sundry . . . The singing, the fighting, the joking—was it not all the same to Oleg? Was it not all the same to him, this Nothing, who he would be today, tomorrow, this winter . . . And now this Nothing-Never-Nobody was wailing, howling, groaning, begging God to return him to time, to history, to his family, his memory, his life.

God in heaven . . . Prattling like a child, repeating the same words a thousand times over, Oleg whimpered inwardly: "Let me be someone, make me a man. After all, I don't love anyone. I don't know how to remember, how to take anything seriously. I love Thee, O Lord, Thou Memory Everlasting of the living." Tears suddenly sprang from his heart, carrying, spilling life from the fount of his heart and watering his soul; they welled in the corners of his eyes and silently their warm streams trickled to his ears . . . O Lord, Almighty, maker of heaven and earth . . . "I don't even need a future. In a moment, I'll wake up and disappear, I'll get up from my knees—reaching out my hands from the divan, but still with my eyes closed—and there You'll be. You'll be right there before me, and I'll love, dare to love You . . . Wretched Nothing, I worship You and I forgive You all my torments, my loneliness, my need, for I have behaved wrongly, I have blighted myself, I have renounced life . . ." Tears, tears. Oleg was weeping convulsively, while the sun that is love was still shining, still bathing him in its light . . . At last, he clumsily extricated himself from the divan and, on his knees, damp, filthy, and disheveled, pointed wildly to a spot on the wall: "There! You're here, You're here. Blessed be! It is I who shall bless You. May You live, live forever . . ."

Weariness, exhaustion, stinging eyes that deliciously tingled and itched. What was the time? ... On the divan once again, with his face to the wall ... As feeble as a child ... His face pressed into the cushion, as though into somebody's warm, black breast ... Slumber ... dream ... pain's annihilation.

■ □ ■

One day gives way to the next. They each have their dawn, which nobody sees but for the tramps and drunkards as they squint grudgingly up at the sky. They each have their evening, which begins subtly enough, in the color of the page that you are reading now, before slowly melting from buff into rose, azure, ash, and then black—yet it feels wrong somehow to switch on a light, lest you catch yourself, dying of sorrow, between two fires, as Oleg had once done between Apollon and Thérèse. Perfectly still, with a book in his hands, a dark figure gazes into space, pondering the complex and bitter geography of his loneliness, which, says he, he must find a way to cross, so that before long he can be forcibly and shamefully sent back, like one administratively exiled and now obliged to return to prison.[3]

All of a sudden, this tedious, so very familiar mountain landscape disappeared miraculously from Oleg's eyes, only to be replaced by eternal waiting, the relentless fear and anxiety of getting his days and times and places confused, a kind of airy nonchalance mixed with brooding concern whenever he spoke to friends, as if he had found some kind of employment or come into an inheritance. Particularly happy were those get-togethers when Oleg, having been jolted back to life and suddenly emerging from his books, during the course of reading which he had sprouted an ursine coat of hair, grown bloated and malodorous, brushed his eyebrows until they were practically bald, picked his ears and scratched his head, when suddenly, from the world of specters, from out of time, in one swift motion he would resurface into day itself, bathe his legs—which he rarely did, stoically preferring filth, the smell of perspiration, tobacco, and urine—wash and mend his socks, extract from under the mattress his discarded and still-warm trousers, shave, take a grubby flannel and wipe his face until it was red, and, now younger, better looking, tiptoe out of doors, square his shoulders to the autumnal damp and, still retaining those vestiges of summer, sun-tanned and alive, soar and stride, restraining himself all the while, as he made his way to find Katia. Had he allowed himself, he would have run all the way, and the only reason he did not do this was that he feared to break into an unseemly sweat and worried, because for him, someone so unnaturally energetic, someone who could become intoxicated without having touched a drop of wine, the date's most advantageous moment was the very first, when the face still retains that stillness that so suits wild characters, the iciness of the street, the cold, the eau de cologne, and nervous excitement. Katia lived in a hotel on the boulevard du Montparnasse, and along his way he would pass by two pairs of clocks—one in the depths of a garage on the avenue de l'Observatoire, the other over the public baths—both running eternally late, and so he would always have to pick up the pace, chasing those minutes through the *quartier*, which was no easy task. At last, Oleg would catch one final glimpse of himself in the mirror (a detrimental look over his shoulder, for well he knew that it would only intensify his inhibition) and, straining every one of his muscles, like a boxer rising from his stool, he would step off the street and into the vestibule. That strained look of desperation made him decidedly suspicious in the eyes of the owner, whom Oleg had to fight his way past every time, exerting what could almost be termed mental violence, before he would find himself on the staircase. What was more, the owner and his wife were wholly on the side of Solomon, who would always arrive in his motor car and who knew how to talk; only the other day, Oleg had been subjected to a typical example of their partiality. Katia had been detained somewhere and was running late. Oleg took a walk and lingered under the awning of a book shop, but when he returned, he saw, through the glass of the door, a note attached to the key hook. As he went in, he couldn't resist lifting it up with his finger and reading it: "*Mr. S. ne viendra pas ce soir.*"* Scarcely had Oleg even registered that this son of a bitch was referring to himself so grandly in the third person, when the owner swooped down on him with a threatening: "*Qu'est-ce qu'il y a?*"† Oleg gritted his teeth and left, but later Katia rewarded him, reading the note to him in the owner's presence, jokingly, in a stage voice, and just like that, continuing to laugh and wave the note about, she made her way upstairs.

At the time, he had failed to appreciate that evening, when Katia had dressed in front of him, but now that he no longer saw her, could no longer see her, its minutest details revived clearly, excruciatingly, before his eyes. He recalled how Katia had perfumed her lips and the lobes of her ears with the tip of her finger, all the while slyly, anxiously staring at him in the mirror, and how he had restrained himself with such helpless pride, or simply had not dared to take her

---

* Mr. S. cannot come this evening. (*French*)
† Can I help you? (*French*)

in his arms or kiss her, and instead shifted restlessly from one foot to the other, not realizing his power to make her late for Solomon. Still, late she was, by almost an hour, late because of the tears that suddenly began to stream, rolling from the corners of her enormous lashless eyes, making the kohl run down her cheeks, and so she had been obliged to begin everything over again.

All this posturing of Katia's had of course been done for Oleg's sake. (Hers was the attitude of a base person—the duplicitous tears, the tardiness, the thinly veiled mockery of the note, the fact that she had taken such cares to dress, to do her makeup, to perfume herself.) Just before they left, Katia had stood by the bedside table, laboriously gulping down handfuls of her cocoa cereal, the very sight of which gave Oleg heartache, and laughed, saying:

"How plaintively, how like a schoolboy you just said, 'Is it *really* time to go?' "

"Don't you like pathetic intonations?" said Oleg after a momentary frown, bracing himself for the rebuff.

"No, I do. There was a blond boy at university who had a voice like that, and I was in love with him . . ."

Oleg brightened up at this, but it was the last success of which he could boast. The torture of his impending separation from Katia was already fogging his mind, and only vaguely could he imagine why she needed to drag him to that Café du Dôme, or, more importantly, why he had to go in with her, even though he had already tried to say his goodbyes several times over. Perhaps back then he had yet to realize his greatest victory—namely, that Katia wanted Solomon to see him. She deliberately wanted to cast them together in that crowded place, to have Oleg protect her, to revel proudly in her delight.

Today, however, as Oleg climbed the stairs, another painfully vivid moment came back to him. He was, of course, being overly sensitive. Later on, he would lament: "*Par délicatesse j'ai perdu ma vie . . .*"[*,4] A dozen times Katia had expected him to lose his head, to kiss her, to embrace her with all his heavy warmth, but his acquaintance with Bezobrazoff and those days with Tania had left their mark. He alternated, now radiating a studiedly joyous, cool warmth, now truly experiencing the vague fear of something irreparable, the ascetic terror of falling into a seething whirlpool: it was unbecoming. Katia had suddenly unclenched her hands, and something savage, something coquettish and eunuchlike flashed in his clumsy grin, but then in his dreams the light of her body revealed itself to him entirely, and he had awakened, trembling all over with happiness, as if, having been exposed to the full blaze of the sun, he had suddenly found himself in a darkened room, almost totally unable to see or comprehend anything at first. He had dreamed of a little wooden house set amid sun-drenched sands, near to but not within view of the sea. He, Katia, and Tania had been examining some symbolic pictures, boxes, and cards, which were animated by their attention and began to move.

Then all three of them, gratified by their ability, had set off completely naked down a narrow umber path that was cut into the rock, laughing gaily and tenderly as they made their way down the rocky steps toward the shore, where Stavitsky's wedding party, with all those girls in attendance, was settling down aboard a paddle steamer made of some soft, cold, white material—silk, perhaps, or ice cream—sailing into an ocean of a thousand forms of existence.[5]

---

* It was sensitivity that cost me my life. (*French*)

Then, in a room decked in white, in the brilliant radiance of a garden, Katia had lain on top of Oleg, half of her still floating in the
air, while his entire body had drunk up, imbibed her presence. Then
more dreams had followed . . .

Oleg had awakened in a state of arousal and wistfully groped
his hot, frustrated girth. He had to wait for it to subside before he
crawled out of bed, for the sight of a drowsy, unshaven man with an
erection in the mirror would amuse him, arouse him, aggrieve him; it
would lure him to gaze in the mirror for long periods, it would draw
him to that solitary vice. But as for the act itself, as for taking Katia's
pubic hair in his outspread palm, neither could he imagine it, nor
had he felt any immediate conscious desire to do it; instead, everything had dissolved in the radiant surprise of happiness.

On the evening that Oleg recalled as he followed Katia upstairs,
avidly watching the heavy grace of her legs, how their muscles tensed
with each step and how, as they climbed the stairs, they exposed
themselves a little more than usual, like two laboring ancient
deities—on that evening they had sat together in each other's arms
for a long while, not quite daring to kiss each other openly on the
lips but, with fear and trepidation, taking pleasure in caressing one
another. By and by, Katia had removed her arm, leaned back and lit
a cigarette, tossing back her head and exhaling the smoke ceiling-
ward. Her navy hunting jacket had gone awry, become hitched up,
and between it and her old silk skirt there flashed a flawlessly white,
extraordinarily smooth strip of flesh. As Oleg's hand reached that
spot, it stopped, as if burned, but still it sent a wave of intense, searing pleasure directly through her body. Aware of this impossible
intimacy, Katia had frozen in alarm, hoping for, fearing his audacity.
Once again, however, Oleg had not dared to go any further, while

Katia, emboldened now, rearranged herself, arching her entire body and hanging her slightly parted legs over the side of the bed. She had turned her head away and said through her teeth, gypsy-fashion: "I really oughtn't to be like this with you"—alluding directly to the fact that they were wasting valuable time, but Oleg, who had led such a violently chaste life for so long, ran cold with surprise and, fearing that he would be unable to get properly aroused, really did, in his morbid anxiety, cool off completely.

Katia had then got up, suddenly aged and blushing—on the whole, she blushed too easily: joy, deceit, malice, they would all send the blood coursing through her delicate skin. She drank some water, gulped down her cocoa cereal, lit a cigarette, and narrowed her eyes.

There'll be time yet, he would try to reassure himself, unaware how often these are a couple's happiest days, neglecting them, taking them for granted as a child does, not knowing that soon, tomorrow, Tania would once again bare her claws and his happiness with Katia would find itself mired in quarrels.

■ ◻ ■

Another vision. Early one morning, his head wet from the rain, drops of which, mingling with eau de cologne, trickle down from his forehead onto his lips, Oleg gaily darts past the owner and, his heart pounding, races upstairs, annoyed at this pounding of his heart and consoling himself that it is not from weakness but from torment that it pounds. With all the restraint that he can muster, he knocks on the cherished door of No. 40 . . . Silence . . . He knocks louder . . . Silence again, almost unbearable this time, all the more so as he begins to feel his stomach start to churn with apprehension.

But the key, with its broad brass star ("So that people don't carry it around in their pockets . . ."), was sticking out of the door, impudently, occultly motionless ("Like a devil pretending to be a key . . ."), and so, plucking up his courage on the spur of the moment, Oleg opened the door and found himself standing before an empty bed with crumpled sheets ("She's given me the slip, hit the town, gone to do it with Solomon . . . How I'd like to give him one right in his scrawny face!"). But then he saw her lying face-down on the carpet between the mirror and a valise, fully dressed, still wearing her overcoat with its charming fur epaulets. Quickly closing the door, he threw off his coat and jacket, went over to her and lifted her effortlessly, apprehensively up off the ground, feeling in his arms the pliant, precious weight of her spine and hips. He laid her down on the bed and chastely fixed her skirt. Suddenly she stirred and mumbled something rapidly, indistinctly; she looked around blearily, absently, recognized Oleg and, suddenly reaching out her hand to him, pulled him toward her. Ordinarily so proud and forbiddingly calculating, she buried her head in his sweater and, desperately pressing herself to him, began to bawl.

For a long, long while she carried on mumbling, sniveling, and crying, but eventually this wore her out; she moved her head languidly and dozed off as she nuzzled Oleg, whose arm had grown numb, but who, despite the torment, did not dare to move it. From her mutterings he learned that she had met Solomon at the Café du Dôme the previous day, that he, sensing something untoward, had taken her for a drink, that, having had that drink, they at last had things out, and that for the first time she had been frank with him, whereupon he had suddenly dropped that boorish, vain act of his, shrinking, quailing, explaining that he was already thirty-five, that he did not wish to ruin her youth, turning her whole world upside down just like that, while she, who had underestimated her own power, had expected some foul spectacle, perhaps even a fight. Oleg learned also that he had amicably invited himself up to her room afterwards and that at first it had all been very nice, but that later it had gone back to the old ways, after which she had roared and screamed, stayed up until five o'clock in the morning and then dressed for work, when all of a sudden her head had begun to spin.

Time went by. Crying, sniveling, mumbling incoherently in her sleep, Katia clung to Oleg more and more tightly, nuzzling him like a bear cub, looking for protection. Meanwhile, Oleg's heart was melting, breaking, sniveling, mumbling with tenderness—but he was worried: what if she suddenly woke up in a rage, angry at both herself and him for this display of weakness? But the awakening was an altogether different affair . . . She laughed, put on her makeup, even poked fun at herself; she sent Oleg out to the delicatessen, but before all that there was a minor, though exquisitely joyous, verbal incident. Finding himself too warm by Katia's side, Oleg had taken off his sailor's sweater and, with all his sportsman's flirtatiousness, made sure to roll the sleeves of his vest all the way up to his naked shoulders, baring his over-developed arms. Closing her eyes, Katia buried her face in his arms and, after a brief pause, said: "You have such smooth tanned skin . . . I do so hate it when men have hairy arms and a black tangle of hair on the backs of their hands . . . Ugh . . ." Her whole body shuddered with disgust, but her eyes remained firmly shut. Then Oleg realized that it was Solomon who had this tangle of black hair on his pale and doubtless skeletal arms, and that it was he whom Katia was recalling with disgust as she pressed herself to him . . . In this moment, Oleg's victory over his rival was total, and, as always in impossible situations, he outwardly let the words wash over him, while in fact he guarded them jealously in his heart.

At the Italian delicatessen, Oleg bought some sausage, beer, sauerkraut, and lardo, knowing full well that he, vegetarian that he was, would not be partaking of all this slaughter, but that did not bother him, for the excitement made him forget about the food and his dreams entirely; there were even times when he would forget to piss for a whole day, and for so long that he, not daring to relieve himself in the toilet, would, because of the strain, dream only of going out, escaping, dashing madly to a pissotière and pissing, pissing in a rush of bliss, having at last cast off the torment of lovemaking and, in the freedom of his solitude, just letting go.

As he was paying up, Oleg made a pathetic attempt to flirt with the cashier, extracting Katia's hundred francs with an air of independence, for the gesture itself seemed to prove to him that in these fabled days, his and Katia's money was one and the same. Still, as he made his way back to Katia's room, he made the effort at least to buy some cigarettes with his own money, so that at first he would be less inclined to smoke, to poison Katia with his Lucky Strikes, even though he loved them with a passion. Yet it was around the subject of money, no less, the money that had vanished so suddenly, that their happiness began to deteriorate outwardly, for it was money and money alone that caused their last, most poisonous rows.

Carrying everything in his arms, Oleg returned to the hotel and destroyed the owner with his look of happy satisfaction. Upstairs, however, it transpired that there were no spoons or forks or chairs at all in the room. Katia laid out their repast on a newspaper directly on top of the valise. She sat on the floor beside it (she always loved to sit on the floor, cozily, covering the toes of her shoes with her skirt, like the lady of the manor) . . . Oleg sat awkwardly, uncomfortably on the other side (he was forever watching his own movements nervously, trying to stand up, to walk, to smoke in a striking and manly way, and so he would often seem ridiculously unnatural, comic even).

Having cried away her grief, Katia was now munching on sauerkraut, eating it with her bare hands and washing it down with a half-bottle of English beer and some carraway seeds. Her cheeks full, she was laughing with all that sweet, plump face of hers, which she had powdered so quickly and completely that even her eyelashes were now white. Like a hale and hearty person whose spiritual ailments are ultimately translated into a wild hunger, she ate almost like a wolf, devouring the food, practically flaunting her slovenliness, her peasant manner, while her hands, so fantastically white, trumpeted her high-born origins . . . Now she was overcome by an untrammeled good humor; she would tell anecdotes and continually try to speak with her mouth full, covering it with her hands lest she spit over Oleg in her mirthful haste, gorging herself until at last she could not utter a single word and only just managed to restrain herself enough to avoid hiccuping. As far as Oleg was concerned, there was something endearingly familiar, vulgar, bestial even, about this gluttony; love deprived him still of any hunger, and he was indifferent to everything except her . . . Having caught their breath, they sat down once again beside each other on the bed, facing the window, and surrounded themselves with clouds of tobacco smoke . . . Katia fell silent and just smiled at Oleg, her heavy, greasy eyes staring into the dim electric burner enswathed in worlds of smoke.

The corners of the room slowly vanished amid the darkness. The window was a perfect pale blue, and across the street golden specks appeared as lights in the neighboring building were switched on.

The people there lived a hard, plodding, steady life, the kind so usually despised by Oleg, but right now he seemed to have made his peace with both it and the rain. As he went over to the window, he saw dark, low-hanging clouds, a glittering street, the chartreuse light of the streetlamp at the corner, but this too now seemed essential and incapable of grieving his heart. The hours passed. They hardly spoke, too weary to live and be happy; in the dark, grateful for the peace and quiet, they exchanged the occasional word in profound astonishment. By now, Katia was lying on his lap, having settled herself, having buried her face into the dark black of his sweater with a familiar Slavonic canine gesture that Oleg loved so much, and once again he found himself yearning to return to Russia. That icy European nobility rolled off his shoulders, and he felt like the disheveled Russian student with contradictory beliefs that he was. In their seated silence in this foreign hotel room in this foreign country, there was something of the midnight blue of a Russian forest, something of the untold sorrow of late evening in Sokolniki, where often, having ventured too far on his skis and having lost the others, he (and his brother) would sit down on a frozen white snow cap on a bench and peer into the indescribable azure of the snow, which reached its end with a blackness of trees. High up, ravens would soar over the tops of pines, and their plangent, lingering cries would grip his heart; then suddenly, in the distance, glowing like a little house, a tram would approach through the snow with a ring of its bell, its two lamps bathing them in crimson light with a forlorn, fairy-tale, gingerbread melancholy.

Oleg's throat was parched from smoking. He drank some water, lit a match, and sat down again, making himself a little more comfortable, and once again those golden hours stretched out before him with fabulous largesse, the sort that comes only from financial security, youth, or despair. Occasionally the waiter would knock on the door, or the light would flicker. At one point, Katia went downstairs to take a telephone call, but she returned soon enough, telling Oleg how she had made up a story about having double-booked herself so as to remain at liberty.

As he made his way home later on, Oleg asked himself what the trouble really was and why time's continuity had been ruptured so violently that he had completely lost track of the past, having almost no thought for Tania. Where was she now, come to think of it? And he delighted in the fact that he did not care.

We each of us walk down the street, carrying our own solitary cell upon our shoulders, and, as soon as we stop to exchange a few words with an acquaintance, the bars, as if they were alive, take root in the ground before us. Around a table, as in an American penal colony, people talk behind bars, politely baring their gleaming white teeth like wolves. But how naïve they are who take this civility at face value, and how soon they bang their delicate features against the invisible bars. For every man has his price; for that sum he will sell any one of his comrades in an instant. (Truly, is there any friendship in the world that has the whip hand over a lovers' tryst? . . .) For me, that price is in the region of fifty francs, for another perhaps it is more, depending on his mode of life. At La Favière, Oleg had become well aware that he was living in a stone age, that beneath a thin layer of powder the glacial bestiality of life threatened to escape at any moment, that one could rely only on oneself, or a person fooled by love—and even then, for only as many days as the illusion lasted. Hence his recent fixation on physical strength, health, education, vanity, for bold aloofness seemed to him more honest,

more decent than impracticable urbanity, and in it he fancied that he
had found more than a sense of original sin, more than a measure of
candor vis-à-vis the natural impossibility of loving someone morally,
of treating someone attentively, with interest . . . That is why Oleg
knew, for instance, that one can associate only with people who have
the same amount of spare cash: if you have a little less, then you're
on your own, brothers, for you'll never be a part of the clique, you'll
automatically fall into a pitiful second place, when, breaking every
rule of decorum, breaking into a cold sweat from the humiliation,
you suddenly find that you have to ask: "Volodya, listen, I need to let
you in on a secret . . ." But this Volodya can already read it on your
face and, reluctant to cause a scene, has already agreed to cover you,
but not without first exchanging a few meaningful glances with the
others, as if to say, *here we go again.* Happy fellow, don't rub shoulders with the unfortunate; give them a wide berth. Unhappy fellow,
don't go near those whose luck is in; your every word shall be an
affliction and a rebuke, an insult and a blight . . . Oleg suddenly grew
up and came of age the very moment when he opened his eyes to
this beastly life in which each man, for the slightest amusement, a
game of bridge, the cinema or simply dinner at the house of some
wealthy philanthropist, willingly casts aside another with all his tragedies, a life in which the astonishing frequency of universal meetings
testifies only to the fact that so very often none of these opportun-
ists receive anything in the course of an evening other than a cup of
coffee. Oleg became a man and, O miracle of miracles! his relations
with his friends and acquaintances suddenly improved, for he was
able to renounce that long-held hidden reproach of others' callousness, having almost fully comprehended, at last, his own cruelty . . .
Now, hardened and steeling himself, he learned quickly, without

sentimentality, to say his goodbyes and leave, or not to join in the company altogether if he got so much as a whiff that they were getting ready to go out on a spree. He mastered the ways of the Stone Age and ceased putting others in awkward positions through a display or demand for pity, for at long last he had grasped the metaphysical impossibility of pitying another without causing injury, as well as the profound humiliation, not unlike gross insult, of appearing pitiful to oneself . . . Something arid, carefree, hard manifested in his social dealings, together with sleeveless sweaters, a monocle, and an "American" haircut—shorn clean around the sides, with an oasislike tuft on top.

I do not expect mercy and I blush to show it . . . Forever at war, forever in the woods, forever on guard and at the ready—then one day, in Katia's room, he had been filled with a profound calm and security; the eternal duel between them had ended in a flash, and Oleg, against all odds and expectations, had grown younger, relaxed his shoulders and begun to speak in a totally different voice, one that was artless and unselfconscious, instead of that forever tense, slightly rasping one with its feigned joviality—the voice of life's cruelties.

The room slowly darkened, drowning in the indigo of twilight and cigarette smoke. The remains of their cannibalistic feast lingered on the floor and on the valise: the half-eaten sauerkraut in a darkened carton, a pint of beer, cigarette ends. They were sitting low on the bed, beside each other . . . Katia's fit of unoccasioned, satiated gaiety had already passed, and now she was taciturn, still, gazing in profile over the bed's dusky copper railing out of the window, where a heavy and interminable spring rain was falling. The day was tailing away; the prostitutional squalor of the hotel room was almost invisible. They did not bother to switch on the light.

Calmly, vacantly, in a stupor of happiness, Oleg watched Katia, but she did not look around, although it was obvious that she could feel his gaze. Her face, with its straight, almost Greek nose, expressed a kind of contented, obscure humility before the twilight, the rain, idleness, and her own depravity. Over her slightly puffy eyelids, painted lashes, like black rays—straight, not curving—set off her large, somewhat bovine eyes. Her mouth was broad, and she had a strong jawline with a protruding chin, and her shiny, perfumed locks fell from her smooth, low brow with a perfectly Greek splendor . . . The cloying fragrance of this expensive perfume clung to everything, and later that night, as he came home and took off his shirt, he was surprised to find it on the shoulder and collar, wherever Katia's heavy head had touched him. Naked and chaste in his old monastic solitude, Oleg sniffed the shirt in a daze, as if he could not bring himself to believe that Katia truly existed.

Katia was not especially clever, at least not in conversation, but she was able to pass judgment on anything with surprising clarity and assurance, without the need for complicated arguments. In her particular kind of intelligence there was that precious quality, so rare among Russians, which may be termed a sense of proportion, as well as a rare dislike of exaggeration. For instance, despite her petty-mercantile habits and tremendous avarice (so great, in fact, that she did not hesitate to count out the change that Oleg brought back with him), Katia was a communist, and one without any fashionable Western agenda. "It's all so desperate and hopeless," she would say of Europe, while Oleg, with all his clever arguments, would lapse into a bewildered silence. On the whole, she reasoned the way she played the guitar: quietly, calmly, somberly, expertly, singing along barely audibly—without any particular voice, but with absolute pitch. She loved Tolstoy and Chekhov, had grown sick of Dostoevsky, which, as far as Oleg was concerned, was always the mark of a good head. "Have you ever noticed," she once said to him, "that Dostoevsky never describes nature? He talked his entire life away, so much that I doubt he ever saw a forest. And if it's a street that he's describing, then it's forever filthy and at night." Oleg laughed long and hard, struck by the subtlety of this observation. For Katia was, after all, a fallen woman.

The following morning, Oleg woke Katia at around eleven o'clock and dragged her out, laughing and all pink from the cold water, into the street. It was November 11, Armistice Day. They had agreed to go and watch the military parade, but by eleven o'clock it was long already over, and only as they walked down the boulevard du Montparnasse did they see a colonial regiment dressed in khaki greatcoats returning to its barracks, weary but in strict formation. As they marched, the first ranks looked dashing, but those toward the rear, with their typical French innocuousness and bonhomie (which stayed with them even in the army), were out of step, walking almost at random behind the machine-gun carts . . . In any event, a decision was taken to go to the Louvre or at very least to the neighboring Luxembourg museum, but as they were marching past, it occurred to Katia that they would soon have to eat, and so they plunged themselves into the curious daytime charm of a deserted café, one filled with the crimson sheen of velvet banquettes. After a hot chocolate and some toast, Katia suddenly ordered a "Manhattan" cocktail, then vermouth, then cassis, then Cointreau, and, just like that, they drank their way, heavily, pathetically, happily, through the broad light of day, getting plastered, laughing and arguing in this empty arena, much to the amazement of the waiters, in whose estimation Oleg had risen. It was Katia who paid for it all, however. Eventually, all that remained was for them to make their way home. Leaving Katia in the restaurant opposite her hotel—for she, having gone through the iron schooling of inebriation at Eton, could conduct herself immaculately when drunk—Oleg staggered home to eat, solely out of a sense of propriety and class struggle.[6] When he returned, though, he found Katia asleep on the bed in the already half-dark room, still dressed in her short cinnamon-colored fur coat. Even now, it was possible to read on Katia's face, illumined as it was by the last, fading blue of the rain, something squalid, sordid, too-soon squandered, perhaps even lost forever; then again, her face retained that antique appearance of scrupulous serenity, a proud, melancholic resignation to itself and to life, a serenity that, in Oleg's eyes, only lent significance to the movement of people and without which they seemed somehow like jumping mice of enlightenment. Then again . . . Did she not guess—or, worse yet, did she not see—how he vomited, disappearing supposedly for cigarettes and returning, of course, without them, and then again, as a ship caught in the wind, listing low to the water while it races on, how he sank, foundered, cast off, and made a run for it in a nervous frenzy of washing, shaving, and greasy food . . . "If I don't eat, I won't be able to get it up. I'll have her, though . . . I don't have the energy for all that endless joking, preening, posturing with phony youth, and dazzling her with my teeth, which I'll have to brush anyway. There's a smell of onion on my breath. I'll squeeze some toothpaste into my mouth along the way and eat it."

Now Oleg finds himself in the street, and all his filthy, hungover nobility has vanished without trace; once again the wheel of life has been spun by Yakîn-Boaz, once again there is a maelstrom of joy and terror, and Oleg, hurrying all the way, thinks: will last night's socks, which he had not yet had time to wash, make their presence known?[7] And suddenly a melancholy laugh erupts: "At school we used to call it 'coming in with a bouquet' . . ."

Once again the fiery wheel of life has been spun . . . Between shaving, walking, and their first happy kisses under the rain . . . Katia had such a monastic, Russian way about her, the origins of which were uncertain; whenever Oleg, with a deep bow, would kiss her hand, she would kiss his head like a bishop, or perhaps a nursemaid, and in the rain her pungent scent would seem unnatural, a spring miracle, like the fragrance of a garden that suddenly, once upon a snowy night, comes into bloom in December . . . The streetlamps brightly lit the snow . . . As the snow had swirled, large flakes of it had landed on Katia's long velvet gloves with their leather trim, like a fox's paw, which she wore, according to the latest fashion, in a size bigger than her hand; they would stay there for a long while without melting and adorn the fur epaulets of her simple English coat, which in the end her father himself had selected and bought for her—a dapper, gray-haired gentleman with a rosy face, gold teeth, and contrived good cheer, he liked to make a show of fawning over his daughter, miserly devil that he was, every bit like a tree around which nothing grows for several miles . . .

Day after day flew by in the tender, snowy charm of almost round-the-clock togetherness, during which, as though losing track of time, Katia lavished money on Oleg almost incessantly, with the desperate gypsylike generosity of youth and financial security, having suddenly vaulted over her own greedy, impetuous nature.

Neither of them knew any longer what time it was, whether it was evening or dead of night outside, whether they had eaten . . . Oleg wrote nothing. He did not even apply himself to his diary, or else, as soon as he opened it and glanced inside, his eyes falling on the innumerable "a warm, white day, like a horse in the mountains, in the sweat of sorrow," etc., etc., he would write across the pages while laughing: "I'm alive, alive . . . alive at last . . ."

■ □ ■

Now there was nothing left of Oleg's indomitable, roguish, forever squanderable health . . . Today, on a dazzling, white winter's day, he awoke a hundred miles from the surface of life . . . Last night he had gone to bed too late, talked too much, become too excited, and, when there was nobody left to talk to, he had carried on hysterically, causing a ruction at the bar of the Café du Dôme—whither, in the early hours of the morning, all the hopeless déclassés would crawl. There, at last, he had found himself some people to talk to, every one of whom had been barred by the proprietor several times over for failure to pay their bills, for disorderly conduct and mendicancy; later, after a time, all this would be forgotten, and the fat gloomy-looking garçon with his especially vacant air would replenish their glasses; they, in turn, would bow and scrape, put on airs, and demean themselves in every way imaginable—their ordinarily meek dispositions notwithstanding. There one could find paperless chauffeurs with no passports, a slightly stooping vagrant chiromancer, a six-fingered peddler with an imitation-gold chain, a long-haired artist who could hear voices, and, in front of the café, the sidewalk was plied by dross of an even bitterer breed—narrow-shouldered pederasts without any signs of underwear, Arabs and bushy-bearded old drunkards lost in thought, those who would not even dare approach the bar . . . By tacit agreement with the proprietor, nobody was taken to the constabulary, lest the café lose its license to open at night; only occasionally would somebody be dragged down the rue Delambre and given a good roughing-up, and the indescribable individual, having sobered up instantaneously, would then go down toward Edgar Quinet to hide, only then to circle round and, half an hour later, reappear on the boulevard. There, Oleg had made a thorough nuisance of himself with some pudgy-faced Slavic-looking unshaven Hamlet in broken spectacles; he had filled the air with youthful obscenities, without which, after a certain degree of weariness and woe, he could no longer join two sentences together (native Russian punctuation, appeasement, accusations, grievances about everything under the sun). He had spluttered until the point of exhaustion, until the belated and unwelcome winter's dawn, and, with spittle in his mouth, and with a ringing in his ears, he dragged himself home to the place d'Italie.

The fact of the matter was that he and Katia had had a terrible argument the previous morning; the subject of their quarrel had been Soviet literature, although, of course, the real issue had lain elsewhere. They did not see each other after luncheon, and in the evening, to spite him, Katia had sat down to a game of bridge with her cronies, who viciously welcomed her appearance as a portent of the imminent decline of Oleg's star, for that was how love affairs were supposed to end in their universe—that is to say, with one of the melodeclaimers playing a sullen, histrionic game of bridge, while the other kept a humiliating, ill-tempered vigil at the neighboring table, strenuously and thereby all the more unsuccessfully trying to behave as if nothing had happened . . . Only at one o'clock, by which time Oleg, utterly exhausted, having waited so long that he was black with disgust and positively seething with rage, having

sullenly, stubbornly smoked one cigarette after another, burning
his lips, though still managing to maintain his outward composure
and refusing to go downstairs, where the gamblers made a habit of
cretinizing—only then did she, like a mythological vision, high of
chest and white of arm, her eyes narrowed by laughter, suddenly
appear on the staircase and, swaying slightly and moving her hips
deliberately, enchantingly, pass between the tables, while after her,
like toads and other such slippery amphibia, crawled a number of
literary figures belonging to a rival aesthetic-Slavophilic set, one that
Oleg detested so . . . As he watched them, he took a wicked pleasure in contemplating how a person can turn crimson and disfigured
after a prolonged bout of laughter, how his clothes become skewed,
how his lips swell and his hands fill with blood . . . Moving her hips
airily, alluringly, abominably, Katia was making her way toward his
table . . . She was surrounded by toads, frogs, and salamanders, all
of them croaking, hissing, spitting, smoking, dissembling, straight-
ening out their misshapen trousers . . . For a moment Oleg's heart
stopped beating and everything turned into a desperate plea, a
prayer that she would notice him, stop, sit down beside him. But
when all seemed lost, she suddenly sat down, looking very demure,
on the very edge of the chair, while her mythological retinue reluctantly, under duress, began to greet him, seething, cringing, dumbstruck, having failed, after all, to keep this sorceress from her odious
captor . . . But no sooner had Katia granted Oleg's unspoken wish
than he recalled the iron law of their hostile relations, the lynch-law
of any Russian love. He froze, petrified, and turned aside, whither
some waiters were standing, and, borne by the unnatural courage
of his spite, he called one of them over, paid, handing over a tip for
all to see, and, without saying goodbye, as he so often did, swanned

off on legs that seemed like metallic springs, lamely comprehending their direction . . . He crossed over to the other side of the boulevard Raspail, and there, by a cheap-looking restaurant, he cowered in fear, in despair, in doubt and indecision, and began to roam aimlessly about the district, not knowing whether to return, but realizing in any event that he had completely forfeited the chance to go home . . .

■ □ ■

Oleg could not get up for a long time after he woke . . . The previous night's verbal frenzy had been replaced by a total physical breakdown and a certain fragility, a glassiness throughout his whole body, which he had not experienced in a long while . . . It was difficult to raise his arms, although, having grown numb on the hard bed, they ached and tingled . . . What was more, he did not quite understand where he was and why Bezobrazoff was not in the room—so much had everything that was current, coarse, vivid, and deeply shameful forsaken him, leaving him behind for far-distant lands. This long-forgotten fragile, glassy physiology, unbidden in his sick brain, corresponded to very different times, different years, different faces . . . His new life, so shameful and brutal, a reflection of his newfound full-bloodedness and health, had vanished somewhere, spirited away, washed clean by exhaustion. Just as during the excavations of a modern-day tin-can city another, older, medieval one is discovered, and under that a third, belonging to antiquity, then a fourth, Aegean, and a fifth, Neolithic, and as a conservator cleans away the primitive primary colors of a lubok icon and discovers beneath them the emeralds and violets of Rublev's Blessed Virgin, as a flood, washing away the sand, reveals cyclopean walls—so too, now, did he salvage within himself a former snowy soul, barely alive, duskily stiffening in a wreath of wax at the approach of that first sorrowful encounter with life, a soul for which there was no longer any room, which could not be reflected in his new, heavy physiology, drunk as it was on an accumulation of blood . . .[8] But how many of them, these souls, had there been? As Oleg lay in bed, smoking a cigarette, he tried to recall . . .

06

There was one standing motionless at a corner, without any friends, without a single acquaintance, without anything decent to wear, narrow-shouldered, gazing with ineffable submissiveness at the four o'clock winter sky, which was poised to crumble into snow, scatter off in all directions, and fall in a shower of snowflakes. There it stood in a wreath of wax, its feet wet, having just cut off all its friends and foes alike, having just climbed four flights of stairs only to find nobody at home. A soul with nowhere, absolutely nowhere to go . . . To go back to the Beauséjour, to that dusty yellow light hanging from the ceiling . . . He would rather have dashed his head against the pavement, rather have gone on walking all through the night. The entryways to the buildings loomed a dusky, winter blue; the people were in such a rush, guarding their bundles jealously. But Oleg had already gorged himself silly on chocolate, making himself sick, having spent all his money on it, having gone, out of grief, to the boulangerie again and again and bought confections costing forty centimes a piece . . . Cold, standing stock-still, drunk on loneliness, this soul, clutching its melting wreath of wax, grew numb as it watched the night fall slowly and clumsily, like

a pair of eyebrows, before turning its back on its pension. Through a
light dusting of snow, the now-retired No. 82 trams made their way,
brightly clanging with a near-festive melancholy...[1] The street emptied, and suddenly amid the darkness of despair came a bright idea:
"It's already gone seven. By the time I make it to the Russian canteen at Glacière, it'll be eight . . . I'll have some kasha and go to the
cinema . . ."[2]

■ □ ■

There was another soul that Oleg recollected. This one loved to get
up early, often before dawn . . . This one knew nothing of sports or
effort; hunched over and narrow in the shoulders, eyes agog, this
one loved to roam the clean and deserted city at sunrise, listening
to the nightingales as they freely and languidly warbled, chirped,
and cooed behind the high walls of a Catholic monastery, these tiny
and sublime birds that remained true to their rhythms of a hundred
millennia . . . The pavement glistened a misty blue, and in the distance the frameworks of buildings under construction seemed like
ancient fortresses made of rose-colored marble, over which, like a
little mother-of-pearl shell, the moon sank in the dawn azure of the
sky; there was something mysterious about this leisurely warbling,
something awash with the invigorating energy of forests, streams,
and caves . . . As the sun slowly rose, green trucks that washed the
streets would pass by with the hiss of broad, fanlike jets of water.
The first trams would set out, reflecting the sun's rays, and, having
just woken, make an almighty din with the feverish ringing of their
bells. Lorries carrying cement would raise clouds of dust, and now
one would have to go quite a way out, to the very edge of town, to

the city fortifications, in order to find that summer stillness, the slow hum of an airplane that seems to have stopped mid-air, a graveyard where a small, old-fashioned freight locomotive slowly shunts old goods wagons. This soul, hiding in the dawns, the outskirts, the sun-drenched wastelands, was no longer as defenseless as the first . . . There was now something of dolorous antiquity, of melancholic stoicism in the lean shoulders and large, static, dark-gray eyes, yet this one, too, had disappeared, yielding to the eternally radiant, the forbiddingly beautiful, the thoroughly masculine world of Apollon Bezobrazoff.

How long ago it all was. It almost seemed as though they were entirely different people, youths in a variety of *demi-saisons*, and yet each one of them was me: broad-shouldered and scrawny; with a face red and swollen from the heat, and with delicate, lily-white hands; covered in perspiration from physical exhaustion, and slumped over a piece of paper; with bulging arms, grimy and gorged with blood, crushed under the weight of dumbbells; with a broad, bony, unshaven face, looking to teach someone a lesson; and others still, ones who wept in church, who lay prone on the floor in a flood of tears, in a crisis of faith, ones who played cards, who examined their manhood in the mirror or puffed out their chest in the reflection of a shop window, ones who frowned and pouted, drunkards who bowed and scraped, proud men, silent men, talkative men, men driven mad by bitterness, men who quailed before a bus conductor—and every last one of them me . . . Me . . . Me . . . Truly, it was not I who lived, but these souls who lived in me, while I was but a store for old stage-props, words of diverse origins, all kinds of smiles, characters who had long since left the stage. But here comes yet another soul, quite different from the rest . . . With a monocle, with a tassel about his trousers, with a hole in his heart and an unholy heart, he walks, rejoicing devilishly, for Laforgue has bequeathed him the moon . . . The soul of 1925.[3]

The stagnant heat of an incarnadine urban sunset, the tedium, the perspiration, the pain in his heart, and at the street corner, with a chamber pot on his head, a stranger dancing, while all around, like birds of the night, pages of his verse flutter in the air . . .

Weakness, weakness in the mornings, grubby, weary arms, a polka-dot tie, rising late, scorning the park, the sunshine . . . By night, in a café, surrounded by tobacco smoke, through the icy window of a monocle: a brilliant, fateful madness of wit, tall tales and fables, a quadrille of genitalia with combed partings, a soldier relaxing in the shadow of his own phallus . . . The subversion of everything, the affirmation of anything, a grandiose show of contempt for order, and poetry from every corner . . . In the lavatory of the Rotonde, graffiti penciled on the door and drawn with fingers on the mirror, on telegraph slips at the post office and, with an illegible expression, on the back of a newspaper lying in the street, and always this wicked abandon, this flight, this soaring of sinister humor, this weariness in the morning, this unsavory fare, standing up or on the go, shoveling it in . . .

And the very next day again, toward evening, the tremendous, heavy summer moon would appear, floating low over the roofs, and along with it the heavy musical languor of an endless day, spilling into everything, gates flung open, crotches weary after a day in trousers with no underwear, the hoarse singing of drunken soldiers on a Sunday night, and in each light, behind each lamp, the smiling spirit of the underworld, a dead man, a skeleton, a half-woman half-policeman, a male phallus wearing a straw hat, an enormous bedbug playing the piano . . . From the aqueous black of night: white legs, the puce heads of drowned men, the clattering of a pianola, the stench of urine, and the first, early rustle of withered leaves under an old, worn-out boot . . . Heartache both subtle and exquisite, waves of perspiration, the urge to masturbate, to practice occultism, exhibitionism . . . Yes, to expose oneself, to expose oneself ironically from the window of a Métro carriage on the other side of the embankment, as in Egypt; the savor of beer, the aroma of incense, hay, churches, semen, a chop house, and above it all that same gigantic moon— goddess of water and madness, dazzling, physically palpable in the water, in one's body, on earth, in one's hands, everywhere. The unintelligible voice of the boulevard.

A blinding ray of light in the room. I'm no longer asleep, but what is there to get up for? I'm twenty-five years old . . . How long ago, how terribly long ago all this was, was, was . . .

Night. The streets are empty. A lead weight throughout my body . . . I hiccup . . . I rock back and forth. Ah, what does it matter? I've been had—had! (By whom, the whole world?) And suddenly— face-down on a bench . . . Let the grave punish me . . .[4]

■ □ ■

Why really had they argued? Of course it had nothing to do with Soviet literature. It was because of Slonohodoff . . . Slonohodoff, that broad-shouldered, dull-witted Adonis, that laid-back knight in shining armor, that Eurasian . . . He had told Oleg, as he rested his perfectly Greek chin in the broad palm of his hand, that Katia, after much hesitation, had proposed, recently, plainly, that she and he should have sex, and that he had been glad to take up her offer, but, in the middle of the act, her crooked yellow teeth and the general air of neuroses had made such an onerous impression on him that he, cutting short the affair, had cast her out to the mercy of fate. What had truly astonished Oleg, however, was not the fact itself, but rather what Katia had dropped into their conversation, as though in passing: "You know, Oleg is so passionately in love with me. I just don't know what to do with him."

■ □ ■

Since the dawn of time, the devil has gone in search of those who dwell in the wilderness: nine for a novice, ninety for a real monk . . . But so too do saints persecute sinners, just as a guilty conscience does mankind; yet is the attention of the very Lord of Untruth not more valuable? Thus, importunately, did Apollon Bezobrazoff dream heart-rending, celestial dreams. "God is persecuting me," he would tell Oleg one day, with the look of a lost soul . . .

Oleg had taken up with Bezobrazoff once more . . . The latter loved to arrange their meetings in new and different cafés, locales with unexpected mores. One Sunday evening in spring they met on the boulevard de Sébastopol in a lurid, brightly painted taphouse where a makeshift band was making the most deafening of rackets. As he stared straight into the mirror, stumbling across his own reflection and relishing its shabby appearance, his own eternal incognito, Apollon listened to an implausibly, extraordinarily, fantastically out-of-tune accordion. The other musicians were mediocre, but this accordion introduced into the jota an independent, off-beat musical phrase and rose to such a swinish, devilish, hellish shriek that it almost seemed to be doing it on purpose . . .[5] The accordionist, his face crimson and paralyzed with strain, shamanized over his shambolic squeezebox, droning, muttering, squawking, seemingly deaf to it all . . .

The accordion wailed . . . What was it wailing about? . . . The street hummed quietly . . . What was it humming about? . . . People were talking, moving their lips inaudibly . . . What were they arguing about? . . . Apollon Bezobrazoff was silent as he stared at his vis-à-vis, his reflection in the mirror. What was he thinking about? . . . Haughtily, sullenly, the reflection stared back at him, but what did it sight in its glass eyes, what did it distinguish without seeing? . . . Over the musical racket, through the piercing brilliance of the cheap lamps, Oleg, like some deaf-and-dumb demon, gesticulated spasmodically with his glass, his matches, his eyebrows, flexing his muscles, sniffing, flaring his nostrils . . . Next to him, Apollon looked as though he belonged to a difference race, and that they could communicate at all seemed astonishing.

Oleg told Bezobrazoff all about Tatiana, Katia, sex, class struggle, the lynch-law. But what was his mirror-image, reflected in the mirror's mirror, thinking about? As the mirror chatted away, it imitated his face, yet the face lost all meaning in the mirror as it searched for the latter therein . . . The mirror imitated the senselessness of the table, the lamp, the face as it searched in the mirror for sense, but it stopped short at imitating the music, and so the unimitated music became inimitable. The Apollon in the mirror and the Apollon beside the mirror seemed identical, but Oleg—that is, mirror-Oleg—differed from the Oleg who was speaking in the room, because the mirror did not reproduce the sound. Yet once again they proved identical, for the sound was utterly inaudible above the music. Oleg shouted himself hoarse amid the unremitting shriek of the accordion, but even he could not always hear himself speak, and so speaking-Oleg was made equal to unspeaking-Oleg, and they were both of them alike mirror-Oleg, who could not speak. But what was Bezobrazoff thinking about? . . . Exactly the same thing that the music was squalling about, about nothing and everything all at once, about any old thing, to be precise, with the sole difference that the music desperately missed the mark, whereas Apollon deliberately renounced it . . . And so Oleg spent the whole evening like that, gesticulating while the music wailed on . . . Silent, and yet talking . . . But the thundering music was beside the point, and Apollon kept on stalking his own reflection in the mirror . . .

The result, at the evening's end, was a kind of equilibrium: Oleg was exhausted and dissatisfied (Apollon had agreed with him on every point), Apollon was satisfied (Oleg had simply been unable to crush the satisfaction that he had brought in from the street), the musician was satisfied (people had listened to him), the audience was satisfied (it was over) . . . Oleg had talked about himself, Apollon had said "yes" and "of course" . . . All in all, they had talked their fill, talked too much, talked until there was nothing left to be said.

How Oleg frowned now . . . Oracular, baleful, on the verge of collapse . . . He staggered down the boulevard . . . We talked and talked and talked ad nauseam . . . Mind you, I did most of the talking . . . Yet again he's slipped through my fingers . . . Majestic yet monotonous, exasperatingly perfect . . . Hold on, some inquisitive old biddy's asking him something. "*Monsieur Personne cherche Madame Personne* . . ."* Is he indeed? . . . Oh, my soul, when will you at last be able to be like him—gargantuan, haughty, baleful, oracular—when will you at last see the inhumane grandeur of things? . . . Their curious

---

* Mr. So-and-So is looking for Mrs. So-and-So. (*French*)

finality, their sacred resignation to their once-given form, their holy foolishness and uselessness beyond it. Their absolute acceptance of their purpose.

Apollon made no reply, and yet, as far as Oleg was concerned, a conversation was taking place. Bezobrazoff was scarcely listening, which hurt Oleg, for his words, as they fell into the maelstrom of Bezobrazoffism, faded and lost their weight, until eventually they fell silent with a distinctly plaintive sound . . . They paled and dulled, lost their import and weight . . . No, they did not quite fall silent, for Apollon Bezobrazoff was not at all a damper, like so many humourists—dissipated, de-electrified half-men—no, sometimes the sound would even intensify, but it would become distorted as it entered the atmosphere around him, stretching out and swelling like a man in flight, one who metamorphoses in a dream and loses his head. As they flew, the meaning of the words changed: what had been funny and innocuous was rendered terrible and threatening (words about sex), what had been happy became melancholy (words about the sky, power, reason), what had been new became ancient (each and every word) . . . Apollon made no reply, and yet his answer was written across his brow . . . Suddenly Oleg fell silent, embarrassed, falling, ashamed of his indecent folly, the tragic triviality of his own words. The cruel and unusual punishment of being rendered motionless, as though he were caught in some magnetic anomaly, came upon him from all sides; everything was losing its strength, its color, so that even objects trapped in Bezobrazoff's field of vision appeared to be experiencing those first vague signs of weight, of tension, until at last they began to move unmistakably, squirming under his gaze . . . Take, for instance, the croissant in his basket: Oleg thought he saw it tremble the very moment Apollon fixed it in his gaze, and suddenly the pastry began to move convulsively, as though Apollon were squeezing the very life out of it with his eyes . . . You see through the living—that is, you see only skeletons . . . *Que faire?* Skeletons are always interesting: *l'homme est bavard—son squelette, toujours élégant.**

O loneliness, you are always with me, like a heart condition that you can never remember, never feel, and then one day, all of a sudden, your breathing stops, like the one-man cell that I carry with me everywhere . . . Deaf-muteness . . . Amnesia . . . Illiteracy . . . Alone on the boulevard, having forgotten my kin, I halt, blinded by my riches . . . Free, utterly free to go left or right, to stay and light a cigarette, to go home and sleep in the middle of the day, or to transform day into night in an instant by taking a trip to the cinema, to that underground kingdom of sound shadows. Hell, punishment, hard labor, paradise, bliss, reward . . . Once again Oleg mocked his people, who did not conceive of loneliness except as something underground, who suffered by it, were compelled to it against their will, who were incapable of individualization. Alone, alone, alone. As free as a lion (a vegetarian lion) in the wilderness. But who was he? . . . A student? . . . No, Oleg had failed at the very first exam and—O the shame!—in an essay on Gogol . . . A writer? . . . Yes, in the lavatory, applying his finger to the wall, in his dreams, his diaries, in fragments with neither head nor tail . . . A monk with muddy feet and a splash of eau de cologne. A proletarian, no; an unemployed bourgeois, no; an impoverished ideologue of the bourgeoisie . . . An idler? . . . No, Oleg busied himself the whole day with something or other . . . A philosopher? . . . But he had never in fact read a single book from

---

* It can't be helped . . . man is talkative—his skeleton, forever elegant. (*French*)

cover to cover . . . A fool? . . . No, because he always believed that he could have written the book himself . . . A nobody . . . A nonentity . . . A nothing . . . without a people . . . without a social background . . . without a political party or religious faith . . . And at the same time, what a uniquely Russian mug, with its crooked nose, puffy cheeks, and thick lips . . . But suddenly the nose grew narrower, the lips thinner, and a calm, sarcastic, disdainful, Bezobrazoffesque light fell on his face. There was something diabolical, distant, monastic, celestial shining through it . . . Suddenly, as though awakening, he peered at his surroundings with cold surprise, but already he was far removed from the miraculous, ascetic stillness of that metaphysical bandit. Apropos of which, where was he, that hero of no adventure? . . . Who could say? And if Bezobrazoff had indeed vanished, then, even if a whole army of his friends happened to be living right next door, not one of them would find him . . . For Bezobrazoff was everybody and no one, and perhaps he had already changed his surname and now truly considered himself to be a Frenchman.

As Oleg walked along the avenue de l'Observatoire, it shocked him to realize that all of this was alien to Katia . . . There was nothing otherworldly, nothing icy or incorruptible about her; like some beautiful white animal, filled with quiet heartache, Katia forever saw the ground behind everything . . . She marveled that Bezobrazoff did not work, that no one had any money, that Oleg had failed his exams to become a taxicab driver.

That's the kind of lifeline you have; you'll live till you're ninety years old, by which time you'll have written ninety books . . . She has money, but to her, work is bliss, a victory over sleep, over inebriation and melancholy . . . These days she dreams of opening some fashionable atelier.

We'll work, Oleg... We'll live, live, live... We'll bid farewell to the lot of them, we'll go to Russia, to somewhere in the Urals, to a factory with a forested wilderness and magnetic cliffs beyond... We'll go about ragged... Fine... Among the ragged... We'll learn to talk in thieves' cant, the language of spivs and Zoshchenko...[6] Ah, Russia, Russia... Homeward from Heaven... Homeward from books and words and the drunken arrogance of bars. And Oleg would say, "Yes, Katia..." And his eyes would light up, just as they did from everything else: from music, from wine, even from a fistfight in the street. Yet Bezobrazoff's distant, calm, ironic voice carried on speaking inside him.

■ □ ■

Oleg grew to feel sorry for Katia. He realized that he would be the first to fall out of love with her, to out-snub her, to spoil their relations. He realized that he was rubber, invulnerable, that nothing could harm him, that nothing was worth anything to him, that it would all of it be forgotten, and that it was precisely because it all hurt him so terribly that he was essentially numb, impervious to life itself. But Apollon, you corruptor of youth, where you have been, something hard, cheerful, malign, ironic, secretive, and wistful appears on people's faces, and I am beginning to understand why so often you loved to talk, that it was the devil, to spite the gods, who taught man asceticism.

Time and again Oleg would take a stand against Katia, her body, her warmth, her simplicity, calm, humor, submissiveness, comeliness, and all because Tatiana had once again managed to dig her claws into his defenseless heart. One day, as he had been making his way from one café to another, ambling along the pavement, among the automobiles, he had caught sight of her walking straight ahead, coolly, with that astoundingly dispassionate exterior of hers, her face full of feigned ennui and thundering menace . . .

Admiring her helplessly for half an instant, he had carried on, but suddenly he heard his name being called out. "Oleg! . . ." He turned and sped toward her, overjoyed, embarrassed, rejuvenated by the shock, the delight, the amazement, the pain . . . Together they strolled along the boulevards, and Oleg saw her up to her room.

■ □ ■

The exhaustion, the exhaustion of getting up late . . . Arms like lead . . . A ringing in your ears . . . A metallic taste in your mouth . . . The noise of the bar, the captivating, crude clanging of two pianos being played at once, had faded together with the happy, dull weight of alcohol poisoning . . . What had also faded was the haste, the concern, the urgency, the desperation of the dancing, and so too, together with the night's unintelligible, inebriated abandon, another desperate concern—the pressing need for Katia's presence . . .

In the afternoon, when Oleg scratched his head with his heavy paw, having just crawled out from under the duvet and in dire need of relieving himself (but lacking the resolve to don his old shoes or rush barefoot across the cold floor), Katia seemed far away, as if the distance from the place d'Italie to Montparnasse had suddenly grown by half a dozen miles . . . Why that struggle with the owner, that rush, that waste of money, that eternal humiliation of worn-out boots that stood out so patently on the shining glass floor of the bar? . . . Why that wild speculation, that wild exaltation, that profligacy of power, wit, and youth? . . . The white winter sky peered in through the window . . . Having at last made up his mind, Oleg picked his way over to the washstand on heels alone and relieved himself at great length in the basin, listening to the characteristic gurgling of the liquid, which for some unknown reason put him in mind of Finland. Then, leaning over like a dog, he lapped up water from the tap, delighting in its fresh abundance before pouring it over his head, snorting and rubbing his eyes and ears until they were red. Then, screwing up his eyes, he searched for a towel and wiped his face and eyes until they, too, were red. He then combed his hair down over his forehead, undoing his part with the broken end of a comb; the cold sensation of his glued-down hair gripped his head, and as he looked into the mirror, he decided that it was impossible for a man of his age to go out without having shaved.

Then, with comic despair, he began to tot up the money that he had spent the previous day, remembering even the littlest sums— for matches, a stamp, and so forth. Furious with himself: "Well, how much for yesterday's spree, then? Ten francs, shall we say? You ought to be ashamed of yourself. Come on, there were two pianos, after all—five francs each? . . . So then, save for the ten, you spent only eight, plus an additional three for beans and eggs . . ." Suddenly, deep in his soul there was a loud, heavy protestation at this disparity: "So I ate only three francs, while the other eighteen went to the tapster for his vomit-inducing dynamite, and practically with my compliments, too . . . It's nothing to her, the swine, she could have paid for me, but she just doesn't get it, she doesn't understand what it means to me—ten francs, five francs, one franc . . ." After drinking a liter of soured milk from a moldy churn, Oleg scratched his modesty and rummaged in his pockets, before eventually getting down on all fours and, flushed with exertion, peering into the dusty darkness under the divan, vainly looking for a cigarette end, a butt, a stub. Having found one, he cheered up a little. He stood up and lit it, grimacing and singeing his nose, and began exhaling thick clouds of smoke as he set about squeezing out any impurities on his face—the dull, age-old, humiliating occupation of many a hopeless, bewildering morning, but, damn it, there were no blackheads, and so this entertainment failed him.

Suddenly Oleg remembered the look on Katia's face as she, visible only in profile and down to the waist through the glass of a telephone booth, had been having it out in English—this much he could tell—with her poor, unsuspecting victim, Solomon, who had rung her up from London . . . Oh, the passionate class hatred he felt for her in those minutes, for the amoral ease she showed in ordering a taxi, in giving elaborate instructions to a porter, or in telephoning her sister in Denmark, simply out of a sense of evening ennui, to ask her about some once-cherished record, the name of which had slipped her mind. Yet, despite himself, he could not help admiring her plaintively, impassively inclining face, which had a look of seriousness even when it was crossed by a mute, mirthless smile, and when above her whispering lips only her brows moved, and bags swelled under her eyes . . . That face beside the receiver knew how to hurt him; it had awakened his love . . . That little prick had revived him, and all those recent rash decisions, made only to spite her as he scratched between his toes and sniffed his fingers—to go over his poems from 1924,[7] to start reading Hartmann's *Philosophy of the Unconscious*,[8] to wash his underwear, to attend an all-night vigil on the rue Pétel[9]—all that had vanished in an instant, receded into the distance, and now there came a flicker of concern in his heart.

Katia was a degenerate, but Oleg found ridiculous anybody who was unaware of his own monstrosity. She was on a sweeping downward path, but in full knowledge of the fact, and that was why she conducted herself with dignity, sometimes even with majesty, somberness, simplicity . . . For, in his opinion, people of every distinction sank, darkened, descended from heaven to earth and came to naught . . . They had all at one time or another come tearing into life in the naïve frenzy of youth, despising the failures, creating, inventing themselves, the things that they would do and would never permit themselves to do: thus the schoolboy in preparing for an exam, while lying in his bed in the morning, draws up a stringent program for the day ahead—but outside it just so happens to be much warmer than he expected; the summer sun and the heavy hum of bees play among the tea-things, and later on his classmates will arrive with the suggestion of a boat trip before lessons, after which, of course, he has to eat, and then after luncheon the sun will blaze on the grass so languorously, so unendurably that he cannot help falling asleep over his open book.

Katia, too, could not help falling asleep over the open book of life, partly because her wealthy, leisurely home life, the one that she had enjoyed since school, had accustomed her to rising late, inebriation, unmaidenly humor. And so it was that in those late awakenings to a heavy head Katia had hit upon the idea of communism; but communism was somewhere far away, and she could only pray for its coming. Practically speaking, however, she loved money, and she unconsciously both despised the poor and was drawn to them. Every time she found herself scandalized that nobody in Oleg's circle worked, that they were forever trying to take her for a ride, and that Oleg, with this habitual, foreign, cringing look, would avert his eyes whenever the bill came, expecting savior from her or indeed anybody else willing, and only if worst came to worst would he extract some small change and reluctantly be parted with it. Katia, that indestructible breed of merchant's daughter, having been accustomed since childhood to the patronizing, disdainful tone with which those has-beens who no longer belonged to the same milieu would be discussed around the table, was simply tactless in matters of money, and although the class struggle between her and Oleg had passed without remark thus far, it was precisely this woeful subject that ought to have served as the most excruciating indication that their friendship had fallen apart at the seams.

The previous day, he had bumped into Tania at the door as he was leaving the Grossmans' apartment, whereupon she suddenly, clumsily, with affected conviviality, forced him to accompany her back upstairs, for she was on her way to sit for her portrait . . .[10]

Tania sat down in an easy chair, while this household of painters set their sights on her. For a time, Oleg remained silent, just staring at her. In her obscenely revealing dress, suntanned and full-breasted, she looked, next to their narrow-shouldered pale-facedness, like a bear that had found its way into the Métro. While the tedious business of the painting dragged on, Oleg wandered off to another room, where he turned on the gramophone and, with nervous affectation, set about tap dancing—alone, to the music, for a full hour. In the end, they left together, but, having been driven to a cool frenzy by all this waiting, Oleg was no longer in any mood to be accommodating . . . Tania wanted to see him, but she hesitated, not daring to make any plans with him, pouting and watching him from under her brow. Outside the station, everything suddenly came out in a stream of meaningless yet essentially romantic and, at the same time, hateful terms. Oleg had the last word in profanity and stormed off, leaving her dazed and distressed in the middle of the sidewalk. He sped off in whichever direction his eyes led him; they were so filled with malice that passersby instinctively turned to look at him. He, too, would turn, ready for any eventuality . . . Just as a worker, having found new and better employment, pours scorn on his former exploiter in the coarsest, most humiliating of ways, slighting him in the street, indignantly, provocatively lighting a cigarette as he speaks to him, so too Oleg had sought out the most offensive expressions, such as "slave-owner," "generous nature," "enigmatic woman," and so forth—but now it was to Katia's hotel that he found himself rushing, for that was where he would surely triumph over Tania . . .

Now the window was completely black—the ceiling lamp had long since been casting its jaundiced light over the room, but still Katia and Oleg could not be parted. All of a sudden, the world had expanded too far around them and been filled with a quiet, heavy spring rain. They both lay there, perfectly still, saying nothing, in each other's embrace but not quite kissing, repenting of something, remembering something irreparable, raking over the past, as though arriving home at long last and turning around with the gloomy, almost solemn tranquility that comes with the ultimate realization that they had been wrong all along. They both related the story of their lives, asking endless questions about the smallest minutiae, as if there had just passed a relatively brief period of absence, prior to which they had known every last detail about each other . . . With the words "life" and "love for the flesh, the earth, and nature," they distanced themselves and their world from the frailty of Montparnasse. With the words "memory," "friendship," "gypsies," and "twilight," they distanced themselves from Tania and her leonine arrogance, which knew no kinship. Truly, Katia lived on her memories, in the profound way that only Russians do. She admitted to herself that she had an innate love of tormenting people, that she was forever quarreling with her friends, but that she could never cut ties with any of them for good, that each of them reserved certain rights to her, and that, were they to turn up that very instant, then, well, I'm awfully sorry Oleg, but you'd have to go . . . She admitted also that she had taken upon herself the unrelenting burden of several never-healed, never-forgotten, never-ended relationships, which now hung somewhere between heaven and earth by the unbearable rebuke of some unfulfilled heavenly decree. "With me, everything always begins in the space of four days, and goes on for four years . . ." Oleg sensed this especially, as he delved into her handbag, a bloated, shapeless tortoise, which looked odd on so elegant a woman.

Oleg recalled how slowly, each time pausing in silence and thinking, seeing countless faces, buildings, and meetings before her very eyes, she would produce from that bag business cards, memoranda, photographs, and notes scribbled down in restaurants. Each and every one of them was connected with some difficult event that she continued to carry in her heart, and, with a transcendental, melancholy smile in her puffy eyes, she would either tear them up or reread them, trying to tell their story but falling silent, grieving, humming something, and sometimes even stopping in bewilderment, clearly failing to recognize something, unable to recall a name, a face, a place.

They met like this for a whole month. December set in over the city. Some belated, one might even say unjustly fair weather rustled autumn's golden leaves. The sky turned from azure to black, filling with leaden thunder clouds, so that it was often too warm to wear an overcoat, but without one a storm could blow in and, in the blink of an eye, leave you standing under an awning, threatening to make you late for an appointment.

In the street, amid a torrential downpour, their wet cheeks would meet with a joyous, salty freshness, and so it was that often they took the wrong way to the Métro, gorged themselves on pastries in a patisserie, went without dinner, smoked, and traipsed endlessly about the shops, selecting but never purchasing some ladies' bauble, because Katia had arranged to spend Christmas with her parents in Copenhagen, and her impending departure imbued their lives with the exquisite torment of a spa romance.

Christmas was approaching. That winter was uncommonly warm, and there were days with heavy, almost springlike showers; only for a day or two did unyielding white snow blanket the Luxembourg Gardens, and Oleg, radiating the internal heat of his full-bloodedness, relished his imperviousness to catching cold. Without an overcoat, without a hat, squaring his shoulders, he would make his way across the city, red, like a crab, from the cold and his own good charity . . . Katia would rise late. He would spend the morning at the library, snubbing his neighbors as he gaily, gloomily prevailed over Hegel—and all this instead of mugging up on streets for his taxi-drivers' exam . . . "I'll manage it in the month when she's away," he would think. But essentially these were the same mornings, filled with the sunny, metaphysical Schadenfreude of insouciance and good health, that he had experienced with Tatiana . . . Later he ate, shaved, and, scattering his belongings in every direction, hurried to his meeting, suddenly changed, alive and radiant, with the sweet chill of accomplishment in his heart. Clean-shaven and wearing new trousers over his grubby, tanned legs, without any underpants, Oleg trudged to the kettlebell club, his heart palpitating with nervous anticipation. His idiotic heart: in the hour that he spent manhandling the weights, he would hear nothing, yet all it took was a single letter from Katia to make it beat like crazy . . . As he approached the place d'Italie, Oleg was amazed, as always, by the cleanliness of the area and the smartness of the green railings around the little square. ("No vandalism. Not like Russia . . .") Past the photographer's shop window. ("Perhaps I should have my picture taken in the nude, down to the waist, and show it to Katia . . .") Past the mirror of the hatter's shop. ("I'll never wear a cap again— it's cheaper and more modern . . .") Outside the linen-man's shop. ("Here I am, going about without underpants—and what of it? I'm so used to it that I no longer feel the chafing. Only, I must make sure to finish pissing, otherwise end up dribbling down my leg . . .") Past the cinema; he had not been in a long while and felt no inclination to go alone at midday. ("It's the height of wintertime boredom, the pinnacle of loneliness, to go to the pictures by oneself during the day . . .") Past the bakery. ("Perhaps I'll have a bite to eat after training, but no, it isn't worth it—white, dead bread, devoid of nutrients, like chalk, and all you can think about while you chew it is your missing teeth . . .") Past the pharmacy. ("Just how do people manage to buy condoms? I'd burn with shame and never have the courage . . .") Past the undertaker. ("Stuff and nonsense . . .") Past the music shop; lingering there, he contemplated buying a ten-valve radio, to make the era dance and spin . . . ("Katia and I could dance to some London jazz in my room . . . I could dance naked, sporting an erection, I could have sex, listening to jazz, or to something better—to a tango or a Boston waltz, not to Wagner or the 'Eroica' Symphony;[11] or, yes, better still: to Debussy's 'L'Après-midi d'un faune.'")[12] Past Hermès

("Screw the boxing machine, it's time for something serious . . .").[13] As he approached the alleyway near the Jean Dame Gymnasium ("Brace yourself, steady on now, don't dilly-dally, don't be nervous, don't look at anyone . . ."), Oleg drew in his shoulders and paid his three francs, looking utterly like an adolescent as he passed through the hall under the skeptical gaze of the enormous, fat cashier . . . The smell of sweat, the cavernousness, a bath-house light hanging from the ceiling, a broken wooden ring on the dais, to the left the parallel bars and a neat row of Indian clubs, to the right sandbags and enormous black barbells stacked like soldiers against the wall, great black bombs connected by a bar as tall as a man, several of which he was not strong enough even to move.

Oleg clumsily removed his jacket, but he did not undress completely, nor did he shower, partly because he was embarrassed, partly because the water made him weaker, partly because of the blind terror that his things might be stolen in the changing room . . . Twelve o'clock: luckily—but also to his secret regret—there was nobody there; only a lone, white, naked figure, jerking about like a madman, was practicing shadow-boxing, sparring with an imaginary opponent, and some hulking great strongmen, retired champions who were stuffing themselves with an air of condescension behind a glass wall . . . Well, then, time to get to work . . . An excursion over to the parallel bars . . . A handstand . . . A vault to the right . . . Ankle catching on the bar . . . Loss of balance . . . Tumbling head over heels to land on hands and knees . . . Confusion, looking around in every direction . . . The weights . . . Let's take the twenty-five and the thirty to begin with . . . On the right . . . On the left . . . Take a short bar from the wall and effortlessly, without a hitch . . . ("What a disgrace . . . no self-belief left . . . Why is your heart pounding like that? It must be your actor's soul . . ."). *Bon! ça va* . . . The thirty-five on the left . . . Keep it up, don't pause. ("Don't disgrace yourself! . . ."). Thirty-five on the shoulder, smoothly does it. ("See, you coward . . .") Straight onto the fifty-fives, no resting. ("That's over a hundred and twenty pounds . . .") As soon as Oleg picked them up, the terrific size of the iron globes made his chest clench. ("You'll never move those . . .") But, harnessing every ounce of self-pity and all the frenzied, unspent erotic torment of his *amour propre*, Oleg wrenched the weight up, and by some miracle—in a lightning flash of desperation, in an elephantine moment of fanaticism—it found its way to his shoulder, completely mangling, crushing his wrist in the process. Oleg squatted slightly and—O miracle of miracles!—conquered his own age, infirmity, poverty, and lucklessness: the kettlebell trembled, yielded, and shot up toward the filthy glass ceiling ("You're out of your mind, don't take your eye off it . . . it could kill you . . ."), shaking, almost collapsing, causing unbearable pain in his shoulder, flooding his heart with crazed pride . . . Then it went crashing to the floor . . . The noise of the impact caused a fat face to poke out from behind the partition, but, seeing with his professional eye that it was only fifty-five kilos, the man said nothing . . .

For a long while afterwards, Oleg curled, carried, and tossed about the familiar thirty-kilo weights . . . They were nothing to him, it felt almost like holding a book in his hand, and he manipulated them without looking, which recklessness threatened mortal danger from above, below, behind, and in front. Then, much to the surprise of the man with the face, a twenty-kilo ingot came to a perfect rest as it hung from Oleg's outstretched arm. Now, swollen like an ox, Oleg triumphantly edged his way into the shower, knowing inwardly, however, and chiding himself for having done it, that training in full view of everybody, his heart pounding with vanity, did him no good. While he had been wontedly waving around a seventy-pound cast-iron ball, the gymnasium had gradually begun to fill with people: two fat red men, undoubtedly drunk, had come to settle an argument with kettlebells; a lanky youth had arrived on doctor's orders; and a tawny Adonis was plying the rings. But Oleg had already gripped, curled, pushed, and wrestled his way through his forty minutes. From under the warm soapy shower, scalded and still with soap in his ears, exhausted, happy, overwrought but victorious, he bundled himself out into the street.

07

That morning, Lucifer bared his horns. They quarreled the whole day, proud like barbarians, doubting the body and its simple deep attraction. In a diabolical fury, amid plumes of smoke, they cursed each other cruelly in that cramped hotel room. Proud and playing at abandonment, they suddenly turned on each other, like foes, all the while inwardly, at their own peril, refusing to believe that any of this could possibly spell the end . . .

O what an unholy pleasure it is to quarrel, to tear up the precious past and, giddy with malevolence, to utter irrevocable words. All the delicate, rainy enchantment of those days suddenly seemed hollow and unreal, and later on, Oleg remembered how Thérèse would tell him that people are like stones, stones that slowly and clumsily become entangled in a golden web spun by the heavenly insect of friendship, so that one day the thousand-threaded fabric becomes so strong that everyone together can be lifted up, as in a fisherman's net, and dredged from the riverbed of impermanence. But at the slightest provocation, she said, the stones will suddenly begin to jerk about convulsively, casting off their splendid attire because it hampers their morbid, wild freedom not to exist—and yet, as soon as that flash of wickedness subsides, the golden insect of memory will carry on.

"If you love me, why won't you work? Why won't you take your taxi-driver's exam?"

"Why don't *you* study the streets and look for work?"

"If people truly want to, they can always find work or pass an exam."

"I do not work because that is how I live, because that is how I have learned to live: to swindle, to screw out every last centime out of the state, to buy boots at the flea market (and not without a measure of pride). Because I have eked out a life for thirty years without ever having to work, and I am used to the freedom that it affords me."

"Receiving state benefits . . . As though you're some kind of invalid, someone who's been injured at work, a has-been. But where, the question begs itself, and what exactly were you? What have you ever actively taken part in? What did you even do during the Civil War?"[1]

"I've never participated in anything. Amid the hurly-burly of retreat, I read. Wrapped in a goat's-skin jacket, I discovered Nietzsche in Novorossiysk. I was on the moon—and am proud of the fact. I've always lived outside of history, like Lucifer, in kid-gloves, somewhere between India and Hegel. (*Emulating Bezobrazoff more and more.*) I labored over my studies until I finally learned to limit my needs. I quit smoking. Now I do my own laundry and don't even go to the cinema anymore. I find myself forever spinning in some ascetic triangle, between bed, the library, a café, and church, like some demon that has taken holy orders . . ."

Suddenly, with genuine unabashed grief, so much in fact that tears welled in her eyes, Katia said:

"But that isn't a life . . . It's no life, I tell you!"

Oleg was dumbstricken. Everything that he had spent so long searching for, learning, everything that he was so proud of, suddenly melted away in that deep internal groan, that full-blooded cry, that wail . . . Truly it was no life, no life at all. Some terrible, utterly naïve error that he had made in respect to life, Katia, and Russia, had suddenly revealed itself in the elemental plashing of her tears—underneath a leaden sky, exhausted by its precious burden, the burden of their happiness and grief . . . And once again Katia broke down, dissolving heavily, happily, hysterically in tears, like earth amid rain, while Oleg tried to comfort her, taking her in his arms and unexpectedly losing his head, squeezing her firm thighs, touching them, feeling their soft, heavy elasticity. Suddenly, plucking the courage from seemingly nowhere, he parted them, although Katia seemed oblivious to it, and unbuttoned himself, freeing his swollen length, which had long since been straining in his trousers. Then, in the blink of an eye, he moved Katia's skirt aside, searching for the entrance to her body, and there, beneath her skirt, as though she had purposely worn nothing, he found her stockings held in place by elasticated bands that cut off the blood, and now her hot, tormenting alabaster body, which had also gone to pieces because of all the tears, sensitivity, sorrow, and surprise, yielded, parting to meet him. At long last, Oleg touched her living warmth, which seemed almost to scorch him; another brief effort and her soft, wet heat enfolded him to the root. Now, with heart pounding from the success and rejoicing that his worst fears had not been realized (he had not gone limp), he no longer hesitated to penetrate as deeply as possible. Katia shuddered and instinctively moved her legs wider apart, returning his embrace and pressing him closer to her . . . But still she would not open her eyes, and both the savor of tears and the familiar itch of eyelids weary from all that crying mingled deliciously with the gargantuan weight of the pent-up body now straddling her.

Causing exquisite pain with his powerful, lumbering movements inside her—there, in the depths of her belly, almost up to her chest—he moved back and forth, engorged, splitting her asunder . . . Katia gripped Oleg even more tightly as she rocked her hips in spasmodic ecstasy, but then, clumsily, they parted, and Katia wantonly spread her legs as wide as they would go. Oleg, his member wet and glistening, adjusted his stance and immersed himself in the warm dough of her body. He had yet to climax, but Katia clung to him convulsively and all of a sudden grew weak—sweetly, lingeringly weak—but even so, wearily and with gratitude, she still received his hot presence inside her.

At last, with a mighty heave, as though for the first time in his life, Oleg unburdened himself completely, without pulling out. But Katia grew aroused again, and so Oleg carried on thrusting his now semi-erect member. It recovered its stiffness before long, and, delighting at this, like a schoolboy, Oleg despoiled her once more, slowly, heavily, determinedly. Having opened her eyes wide, Katia now half-closed them again, and, as she mumbled something indistinctly, she submitted to him in sweet, languorous ecstasy, almost fainting with bliss, but then she climaxed for a second time, and a terrible, beatific weariness stole her away from Oleg. Observing all this, Oleg, who, although yet to finish for a second time, was enjoying a healthy sense of satisfaction, disengaged himself from her and, after a ungainly, unmentionable moment of self-extrication, lay down alongside her. In embarrassed surprise, they both remained perfectly silent as they buried their heads into the pillow. Katia fretted but did not dare to go to the bathroom. Having got what he wanted, again, alas, inopportunely, half-heartedly, in a bitter struggle with pride and power, Oleg laughed as he hid his face in the pillow, seething, pondering how many concessions, how much money, how many records and libations he would get out of her yet . . . By now, the room was quite warm, but still they spoke not a word to each other. Sleep slowly overcame them, and now Katia, having had her fill of crying, shouting, and loving, drifted off, while Oleg pretended to slumber . . .

■ □ ■

I did it . . . The release was painful, though, and now my glands ache. It's been a while . . . But still, I did it, as simple as that: the end of an era. I did it, I conquered and planted my seed in a new land. But it was no vice. Come to think of it, though, maybe the solitary vice *is* more pleasant, especially if you do it in front of a mirror and with a soapy hand . . . Maybe I should do her again and really give her something to remember? But what a pity that would be. No, let her sleep. I've practically done her in . . . A revolver, a steel prick with lead sperm, violating, penetrating her as I pleased . . . Hunting down an adulteress with two pricks—one red, the other made of steel in my back pocket . . . No, I've worn her out down there; she was wincing in pain toward the end, but then that only made her submit to me all the more . . . My length, my tool, my weapon . . . It was like losing my virginity. After all, for a long time, for two years, I haven't laid a finger on anyone, let alone ravished anyone. In fact, my greatest pleasure—and a totally remorseless one, at that—has come from emptying my bladder in the most desperate of situations.

This could cause havoc, though. Every day I'll have to . . . No, thank God, she's leaving tomorrow . . . What more is there to discuss? The meaning of creation? Everything? But then, it's always more pleasant to be in the audience. The whole world is one pornographic picture house. But then, who is the viewer? A white cow, serene, heavy, alive . . . It's a pity that I'm not a woman. Maybe I just don't understand . . . First, it's at arm's length, then it's inside you, in the pit of your stomach, near your heart. As dear Boris is fond of saying, women don't like to look at the male member because, for them, a man with all his ideas is a phallus.[2] There's something going on down there . . . I need to clean myself up . . . No, not on the trousers, you swine! It always leaves a mark when it dries . . . a white patch at the fly. O manhood, manhood! There are men who battle their way through life, wielding their manhood, hardly ever sleeping . . . If only I could have some milk . . . She's crushing my arm . . . How long has it been? Two years that I've gone without, but no more, and all thanks to the whore of Tsargrad . . .[3] What more can you do with a woman after you've done her in? . . . Take her money? Piss all over her? . . . Ah, to piss on another human being, like in Lermontov's "The Uhlan Girl" . . .[4] That must be nice. Tomorrow I'll see that lumpen wretch Tania. She'll be able to tell in an instant, of course, and she'll be sore. But so what? Let her be sore. Maybe she'll appreciate how agonizing it was for me. Who am I kidding? Anyway, I've done it now, that's what matters. I've well and truly done it . . . All this is setting my heart at ease, but now life seems debased somehow . . . But then pride, too, is base . . . Now see here, you're a man like any other, you have your needs. Everybody does it, except for God . . . But is that really true? Creation, after all, is like having sex with Nothing, with nature; prayer is sex with the soul. Isn't that why God persecutes me so? Talk and sing you may, but you have a vagina, a gash, a nothing. But why did it have to finish like that? . . . If only I hadn't spilled that vitality. I could have worn her out without coming . . .

■ □ ■

Uncertain how to extricate herself from the situation, Katia carried on sleeping, waking, and feigning sleep . . . Realizing this, Oleg suddenly felt a sense of freedom . . . He hurriedly combed his hair and went to the bathroom, where he pulled out and examined his member in surprise. Just the same as before, only the smell was different. He sniffed his hand, and O! what a comic, perverse, smug look he had . . . And what of it? The monk, sinning with worldly passions, resumes his reading of the *Great Lives of Saints*,[5] and so tomorrow he would return to work, to the weights—ah, my dumbbell, my ship of the desert, my Bactrian of iron, how I love thee . . .

Oleg walked quickly, enjoying the cold air pricking his ears. It was a desolate night, and the streetlamps were glowing serenely amid the snow. The clear and iron world of Monsieur Nonentity was once again all around. His soul had taken on a serious demeanor, as was fitting, and his face had filled out, matured, and acquired a melancholy attractiveness. The winter chill took him back to those distant years. He recalled Thérèse and Bezobrazoff, the howl of the wind in that boarded-up house and the demon in the attic playing his nightly exercises on the piano. Everything pertaining to today and yesterday seemed bestial to him—a garish, gloomy chaos of splayed organs. Having possessed Katia, he found himself, as it were, delivered from her. Her heavy, beautiful young body lay somewhere far away, like marble, upon the snow. Having had his way with her, he had set out on unclean legs. And once again Thérèse, slight though broad of shoulder, with her enormous gray owl's eyes, appeared fleetingly before him. Ah, if only to kiss those eyes—he would renounce Katia and Tania and maybe even life itself into the bargain. He no longer understood why he had done it, just as in ancient times a Catholic bishop, drawn into conflict by the spread of in-fighting, may not see, in the wake of victorious battle, what all that blood had and had still to do with his holy vows. The tranquility of spring was long since over. The snow now fell thicker, and everything around was white. One had to walk on virgin ground, leaving behind a never-ending ribbon of footsteps beneath the streetlamps. Suddenly Oleg felt a wild pang of regret: why, oh, why had he kissed the ground so irredeemably, forsaking in an instant not only his own vitality, but also memories of his homeland and his comrades in their crystalline incorruptibility? Tears of some treachery welled in his eyes, and, exposing his face to the snow and dying of repentance and a childish fear of the police, he knelt and prostrated himself several times while reciting the prayer "O Heavenly King."[6]

■ □ ■

The stones were talking among themselves . . . "How ancient we are, how hot the sun's rays, how quickly time passes . . . Only the other day, here and around, a city was raised; today, its ruins form a part of the ground, while half my right side is not yet worn away . . . As for the people, what can they be thinking in their mosquito age? Our conversation began when we all emerged from the blackened glacier, where for a millennium, in a crater, we were tossed from right to left to right to left . . . A thousand years for a rejoinder, it could have been worse . . ."

The second stone . . . "For a thousand years the sun has risen to my right, for a thousand years I've lain at the foot of this door, enchanted, covered in graffiti, with the door turning on me. Before that, for ten thousand years I lay in a shallow spot on the seabed . . . How young we seem. I'll make a study of the clouds, for stones are clouds sunk beneath the waves, and how changeable they are . . . The sea roars all around, nature wanly caresses its wet, stony hair, and another thousand years have gone by . . ."

Katia dreaming . . . "How heavily he weighed on me and entered me, thrusting decisively, uncontrollably—he, ordinarily so helpless. And how much cleverer that head down there than the one up on top: two glands, two brows with hair, two cerebral hemispheres with their convolutions . . . And tomorrow I'm leaving. He's driven me away, worn me down. It hurts to walk. But his eyes were calm, more concerned with what was going on around. A melancholy sex fiend with vacant eyes."

Music in the air . . . "I'm dying away, dying away. I'm nearing the final note, while they have only just begun. All this is but a competition of talking machines, a prick in a vagina, the sobbing and blubbing of a hidden radio. I'm dying away, dying away, and how far to go until the serenity of spring."

Isadora Duncan,[7] in a panopticon, in a waxen voice . . .[8] "I, too, lived, and I, too, did it, but with whom, how many times, and in which positions—even God himself cannot recall. I did it when I was drunk, happy, young, old, standing up, reading a newspaper. I did it in church. My whole life, like an organ hanging upon an organ. Whereas now, I've been dismembered, my parts were torn apart by an underground night, and only the dance, with the inertia of gold, in a wreath of wax, now contemplates God."

The gods of ancient mysteries, locked in the backroom of a restaurant . . . "Will I, won't I, evil eye, Jap's eye . . . We were, and have been forgotten, but we listen—there, behind the door, life is at it . . . We count and we sing . . . One, two—the heaven and the earth . . . One, two, three—bright light from heaven down to earth . . . Four—man awakens and dismally rubs . . . Four, five—ah, forget it, to hell with all these secrets."

Oleg dreaming . . . "Why did I come? My glands ache. To do it is to die, having buried your head in the earth. And meanwhile, high above, clouds pass through your room, and the washbasin is full of Pilate's blood. And how irrevocable it all is—like rain in the desert, like a ship at sea."

Katia . . . "But tomorrow I leave."

The dawn from the courtyard, loudly and with reticence: "Oh, all right, then, wake up. That's quite enough fooling around, enveloping yourselves in clouds of excrement."

■ □ ■

On the following morning, they began to argue once again. Oleg, secretly angry with Katia because of her incorrigible agreeability. Katia, berating him for being sullen and not grateful enough, now that she had given him everything she had to offer, and attempting to exact punishment on his pocket by refusing to pay for him any longer. Sleet had been falling heavily since the early hours. The day had dawned with its impenetrable yellow twilight. The streetlamps glowed. In the taxicab, through the snow, they were cheered by an unfamiliar, fanciful sense of excitement for the approaching holidays.

Piles of sweetmeats had been hauled out into the streets, while shop assistants and loudspeakers sang hoarsely and without cease.

Only those first moments had been ones of happiness. After waiting for what seemed like an eternity, after enduring the owner's torments as every minute he poked his head into the drawing room, Oleg at last set eyes on Katia. Hiding their happiness and embarrassment, the two of them greeted each other politely and with genteel civility. Oleg relished the fact that Katia had dressed up, although he would soon find out that she had done so not for him, but for the city. The whole day they quarreled monosyllabically, "atmospherically," failing to find a common language, lashing out at each other all the while. What had bound them irrevocably now failed to unite them in any meaningful way and rather only underscored their differences in upbringing, which, having briefly been eclipsed by love, were once again plain for all to see.

He was a loner—the child forever beaten by half-crazed parents, the narrow-shouldered schoolboy, who at an early age had learned to powder his face, to steal money, to sniff cocaine and to pray, who at an early age had collided with the ice sheet of life . . .[9] She was the pampered, spoiled only daughter of two families and had grown used to the attention that was lavished on her . . . He was an outcast, a bohemian . . . She was a merchant's daughter, a bourgeoise . . . He was proud in spite of everything: he had survived, without hanging himself, without masturbating . . . She, too, was proud: she lived in comfort, like an ordinary human being, with all her icons and name-day celebrations; she studied, drank, had as much sex as she pleased, and led her life like a pig in clover . . . There was a difference in their sense of humor, too, for he was in the habit of mocking the middle classes, whereas she liked to poke fun at has-beens, the bohemian way of life, former Russians, and whatnot. Having given Oleg her all (vaguely sensing that she would rue it one day), and having lost, having forfeited love, Katia tried to wipe yesterday's union from the face of the earth through her outward demeanor . . . She addressed him formally, she sat in profile the whole time, and for a moment she truly managed to pique Oleg, to rouse and revive in him the memory of that pure and distant figure that he had once loved. But in the airline's ticket office she could not resist savoring, openly reveling in drawing out her conversation in English with the handsome clerk, who himself, in his bright uniform and manner, recalled an aviator. She pronounced the word "Copenhagen"—the only one that Oleg could understand amid their birdlike telegraphese—with such triumphantly proud aspiration. And so before long, in the department store Aux Trois Quartiers, there came one final blow-out, although essentially not a single unrepeatable word was spoken.[10]

Unable to restrain himself, wanting desperately to participate, Oleg sidled up to Katia with unbidden advice about a handbag that she had picked out. "It's far too expensive," he ventured with an absurd, knowing air, and so maladroitly that the professionally discriminating shopgirl instantly detected a certain tension between them. The girl sneered so brazenly that Katia immediately blushed and grew angry with Oleg. In the end, she chose to buy the bag, and the shopgirl suggested having it monogrammed in oxide with modern cubist initials. The bag itself cost fifty francs, the lettering an additional twenty. Oleg, who like a beggar knew the value of money and economized to a comical degree, grew neurotically incensed and began to insist, whereupon Katia, no longer able to contain herself, exploded:

"What, you're counting my money now, are you?"

Oleg was flabbergasted by this. Having lost his sense of composure, he merely repeated under his breath: "You cow, you utter, utter cow . . ." Resentment robbed him of his sense of orientation, and he fell foul of the glass doors as they were leaving. But there was still an awfully long time to go before the flight, and Katia, perhaps sensing that she had overstepped the mark, blushed often and flirted obtusely, grimly, cringing in embarrassment.

Oleg now found himself in a patisserie, in a daze of resentment, weariness and physical anguish at the irreparability of it all. Outside, snow continued to fall in large flakes. Being well fed under the family roof, Katia spent thriftily on food whenever she went out, as children of wealthy parents are wont to do, regarding it as something tedious and tiresome, something that has already been provided once and for all. With the unwitting rudeness of her class, she selected and sedately sampled candied chestnuts for her trip to Denmark—a delicacy that Oleg would never have dared to touch, nor ever would have been offered. Wishing to show off (look at me, see how strong I am!), he ate a pastry and despairingly paid the one franc and seventy-five centimes for it, once again completely humiliating himself in the eyes of a shopgirl. He paid up front, humbly, slyly, without waiting (aha, so he eats on his own money . . .), and thereby cut himself off completely from Katia (he's got no reason to eye up somebody else's purse then) . . . "Screw you, you cow, you utter, utter cow," he carried on muttering almost aloud. And there, in a café near the Opéra itself, their last parting commenced, only this time it was real—and for a brief moment amid this wicked stupor, with such ineffably profound, desperate sorrow, flashed the memory of their recent but already so irretrievably bygone past.

Oleg and Katia sat right by the window on either side of a narrow table. They had both turned away from the other patrons and were looking out at the street in parallel. The jaundiced day, having fought belatedly for its spectral existence, was now clearly giving way to night. Heavy worlds of snow were falling right in front of the windows of the Opéra. The neon advertisements were ablaze, and their liquid fire reflected a fantastic violet flame upon the wet pillars. Passersby materialized and vanished again, each with a unique dusting of snow on his head and shoulders. Some were completely immaculate, clearly having just left their apartments, and now went trudging past, wearing intent frowns on their well-groomed faces. Others carried piles of snow that towered up on their hats and collars like great white edifices . . . As they peered in, they each took the measure of Oleg, estimating his social station and sexual worth, scoffing at him or else humbly conceding in an unequal fight. These figures, whose kindly demeanor belied their bestial nature, would appear wherever his gaze came to rest, and, as when a swimmer suddenly hits his leg against a piece of driftwood, they would immediately attract his wolfish, downtrodden, arrogant, demonically pugilistic, histrionically cold gaze. "A *maquereau-souteneur*˙ of convictions . . ." They scrutinized Katia with interest, too. A dozen times Oleg wanted to run outside and punch one of them in the face, but then another thought prevailed: "You can't fight them all... Plus, they'd throw you out . . . And anyway, you can't very well hide the fact that she's the one paying for these libations . . ." Automobiles glided past in their snowy blankets, time marched on, and their conversation, having been rekindled for the dozenth time, now came

---

* pimp (*French*)

to an end for the dozenth time—but beneath it all, the despair of those two creatures, who had so early and irreparably come down in the world and gone astray in life, grew and grew, having suddenly awakened to the finality of their tiff. But strong lies the spiteful spirit. "Why don't you just piss off before I smack that fat face of yours and give you something to remember . . ." But as Oleg peered into that well-sated face, he was horrified to distinguish there Ophelia's lofty fatigue, the wondrous Greek sorrow of a great mouth, lips pursed in unconcealed revulsion . . . Her eyelashes, like a pair of black velvet scissors, snipped unceasingly at threads in the air, the shadows of memory. Those living, moving, beating lashes, like a swift's jet wings, were doing battle with an invisible adversary. Her perfectly straight nose told of her race, her poise, her childish sense of resignation, as well as her claim to family, land, and maturity. Her high brow, devoid of any thought, was consumed in listening, feeling, groping for some precious, fateful balance of life and strength, herself and others, frailty and courage, like some white marble disk from which a hanging balance is suspended. And her hair—her hair was like an enormous tawny bird perched atop her head . . .

Katia smoked one cigarette after another and, with the puerile stubbornness of a sore loser, toyed spitefully with Oleg. He so loved the bovine stillness of her profile, its antique blankness, and while he recalled the white-horned cattle, those daughters of Apollo devoured by Laërtes' men, for which every last one of them paid with his life, the mirage in the street, like flayed hides, crept and lowed with menacing alarm before his soul.[11] Once again this lost woman, this class alien, this bourgeois whore who was surely about to leave, about to fly off, seemed to him like a statue molded from hot wax, a figure from an ancient fresco come to life, just as in times past, in the beginning, he had likened her to Demeter of Eleusis[12] as she suddenly straightened up ceiling high, as she suddenly, in her rage, forgot her incognito, her old woman's disguise—terrific, high-breasted, golden-haired, wrathful, suddenly letting fall the baby that she burned, whispering over the fire of the hearth, and, in a deep, heavy, thundering voice, ordering the stunned princesses, Cadmus' daughters,[13] to erect a temple and observe the mysteries of autumn . . . Oleg was well aware of the occult trait whereby a person will suddenly grow more beautiful in anger and awaken, full of bitter resentment, to the cruel mystery of their beauty—a trait shared by souls who have long abased themselves before others.

Raising her chin and eyebrows, at a sudden loss for words, Katia, with antique majesty, stared blankly at the swirling sleet outside.

■ □ ■

Oleg returned home. As he entered his room, racked by happiness, blood, victory over blood, victory over happiness, he sat down, sprawled out and pressed his face to his only friend—to a steel surface. Slowly the cold entered his tormented, scratched skin . . . His friend remained perfectly still, and only rhythmically, from time to time, did the steam gurgle and hiss inside it before floating off, a transparent cloud into stillest azure tinged with green, while the mechanism of its steel flywheels and pistons stood at rest. Closing his eyes, Oleg visualized his iron friend, his old cyclopean helicopter, his hoist to a fourth dimension, to his meditation, his entire life's work. Closing his eyes, he stroked his friend. With will alone, this steam press would be roused from its immobility and crush Katia's duskily radiant face and all manner of life. And once again Monsieur Nonentity, that aristocratic denizen, the first Lord of the Magnificent Sepulcher, would awaken in that cramped, woebegone place. Oleg had been raging passionately, hopelessly, irreparably, well and truly upset, it seemed, having cried, drunk, and fought, yet as he returned home under the rain, he had calmed down and, as soon as he stepped into his chaotic atelier and switched on the light, he immediately felt as if he were half an inch from a monastery and *The Imitation of Christ*, which was seemingly the only book that he deigned to read slowly, leisurely, gritting his teeth and declining to devour its pages, pausing at almost every line in amazement and, out of a sense of respect, not even daring to write down his great occult thoughts in the margins.[14] Pressing himself to the cold surface of the iron man, like a lonely inventor in the depths of his potting-shed laboratory, pressing himself to his clumsy, homemade, flightless airplane, Oleg finally heaved a sigh of relief. Slowly the tremendous machine's innards gurgled and hissed, while a scorching, viridescent cloud appeared amid the underwater turquoise of the room, and once again the two comrades fell silent as they listened to their fate . . . On the previous day, he had told Katia as he said goodbye: "I'm a religious man, you see, I've suffered so much because of churches and books . . . The only sign whereby I can recognize a comrade in my ascetic happiness and misfortune, either in the street or during a conversation, is the wicked, merciless, bitter smirk they have during any discussion of a religious topic, for only they know . . . how evident God is, and how unattainable He is, how every horizon is filled by Him, but how not a single one of His rays of light pierces the heart . . . For millennia, the devil has peered into the face of God, as Mercury does the face of the Sun, knowing its littlest feature. An astonishing serenity rests with him, but they do not see each other.

"A magic crystal, the center of the invisible source of cosmic sex, this face—like an agonizing summer's sky in which the sun is hidden, but at which it still hurts to look amid the heavy languor— is filled with the radiance of strength, poise, and compassion, as well as all the austerity of life and death, good and evil . . . The devil stands at arm's length, but gazes at it from another dimension, craning his neck intently, exhaustingly. He sees eyes, but apprehends no gaze; he almost touches a nose, but feels no breath . . . The metaphysical ugliness, the meditation, the steam issuing from his nostrils—it all carries him to the very surface of God, to the emerald-and-azure sky, this grandiose profile from which the scales of the Last Judgment are hung, this perfect stillness, this dazzling, baleful languor of a Pyrrhic victory. The inhuman beauty of life and reason are held in equilibrium: the right eye azure, the left black, like the Ephesian Diana, the austerity and compassion of the masculine and feminine, the antique corners of a steel mouth, and above all this, above the dazzlingly white hair, parted exactly down the middle (the path of the righteous), a crown of absolute indifference toward everything . . .[15] The devil sees all at arm's length from the face of the Divine, having been raised, by the madness of will alone, in a time machine made incandescent by that will, to an incredible height, where no mortal can reach without losing his life, where death alone, ruddy-faced, ascetic, athletic, rises up 'on wings of cruelty' to meet himself, on the hoist of asceticism, while reproachfully, threateningly, motionlessly, the thousand eyes of the Sentinels of the Threshold observe this brave soul, waiting for the slightest weakness, the slightest misstep, to punish what is hateful, for it was the devil who taught man asceticism."

■ □ ■

On the other side of the misted windows, snow was slowly falling . . . The time had come to part, to break the trance, to pay up, get up, and begin moving toward the exit. Those final, most offensive words had been spoken, and, what was more, Oleg and Katia's happiness, stunned at last by the manifest finality of their separation, stunned to the point of physical frailty, a lamentable weakness in the legs—this happiness had perhaps never felt so torn, snatched away by necessity, had perhaps never throbbed, never wept so much anywhere between heaven and earth, among the electric lamps that shone over their drinks (the payment of which was an involved affair), or there, outside, where, like dolphins with glaring headlamps, motor cars would draw into view before vanishing again. Now everything disappeared and melted behind an impenetrable blizzard, and so, too, in a few hours' time, according to the inexorable schedule, a hulking, great Imperial Airways airplane would take off and instantly vanish. Blinded by the snow, unable to see anything ahead, quietly and unerringly it would navigate by a continuous—now weakening, now intensifying—transmission from a radio beacon. The blizzard . . . Despite the obtuse indifference that is a mark of happiness in the average Frenchman, many of the ruddy-faced bartenders were staring out of the window, feeling a little subdued. The regulars were exchanging pleasantries with the owner, but their voices broke off somehow and fell into the void, and now it was only the new arrivals who cracked jokes forcefully and cheerfully, turning down their collars and stamping their enormous feet. Oleg and Katia did not turn around, however. Each had definitively vanquished the other, both of them victorious, both of them defeated. Stock-still, their hearts listened carefully: in the snow above them, their intimacy was straining and groaning, declining to be severed. Oleg was the first to get up. Once again, it was the heavy stupor of their love that tore him away, whispering in his ear: "Only having hurt her as much as possible right now, only having been able to do that, will you ever see her again . . ."

Scarcely had Oleg finished paying with Katia's money than she came out with her final, savage words of reproach: that he, Oleg, to spite them both, had failed to learn the value of life, that he had muddied their friendship, malignly driven it to a cruel lover's feud, that he had never once in his life brought her money or a country, and that the world was unsparing of those who were drunken, wayward, and self-pitying. While he listened to this stream of fantastically cruel, malicious words, while she upbraided him for having dared to give the waiter one franc and fifty centimes of her money as a tip when she had distinctly indicated a one-franc tip with her fingers in response to the questioning look that he gave her, Oleg thought to himself: "We've sat here for three fucking hours. The waiter could have earned ten francs from this table alone . . ."

The tirade stopped just as suddenly as it began. As far as Oleg was concerned, it was one further proof of her love for him, and in the midst of all her harsh, monstrously rude behavior, he could just make out the thwarted, vanishing fever of their never-realized kisses. He stood up.

"I've arranged to meet Tania. I'll see you around."

"If you go now, I'll never see you again." (Meaning: You've hurt me, and if you go now, I'll be sore all the way and won't write to you, but rest assured I'll come back all the sooner, and I'll make certain, without your knowing it, to see you in order to exact my revenge, to return the pain in kind, to suffer these unrepeatable torments all over again.)

In a fury of courage, Oleg held his nerve and took to the door. A gust of snowflakes flew into the café . . . Once again, he stepped out into the mirage created by the ghostly light of the streetlamp, and instantly disappeared from sight.

I f clocks about the city stop, they still tell the correct time twice a day: come to rest on twelve, at midday and midnight. Then, little by little, they grow late, they begin to lie, they deceive, they rave, until at last, toward evening, they ineptly, statically, steal up on the truth once again. Thus, for a whole day, Oleg would dwell somewhere between Aristotle and Hartmann, beyond time and space, but every evening, having made a dizzying loop, he would plunge from eternity back into time, on time, never late, and with beating heart he would fly to Katia's front door; just like a devil on one's shoulder, a vampire, a traveler, who at the third crow of the cockerel is transformed into a table or a chair, albeit not at the first attempt—for blood would first flow through the air, and, in an iridescent cloud, little arms and legs form—but then stably enough for one to sit on it, and only occasionally, from either abstraction or insult, would the chair burst into flames before vanishing into a fourth dimension, and then Oleg's love would heavily, comically hit the ground backward. He took great pains to maintain the pretense of being a person whenever he was with Katia. She suspected nothing of Monsieur Nonentity, into whom he would frequently metamorphose at the library or on the divan, his face to the wall, his head toward God . . . And only by accident would slip-ups and mistakes occur, after which their tenderness, like a fish in a tank suddenly drained of water, would desperately, clumsily bang into the icy glass . . . Such had been the case when Oleg told Katia about Bezobrazoff . . . (She did not care for him.) Or again when he got carried away, indulging in his Gnostic, Buddhist theories of creation, and the Fall of God: he had tried in vain to talk Him out of it, but was unable to guard against cold reason—he, Lucifer, the Great Ascetic, the first teacher of all ascetics. That was when their relationship had begun to cool, and Oleg's voice, like a gear whose teeth have all but worn down, had screeched away in the emptiness—all the more so, since it was then, because of him, that Katia had plucked up the courage to treat Solomon so rudely, vying with him for her Orthodox sense of happiness. Morally beaten and half-inebriated, she needed somebody who was able to listen, to indulge her in her never-ending complaints; she also needed two enormous eyes, in which, as in the still water of a pond, her hapless black-winged head might be reflected; but Oleg was utterly incapable of listening and was almost congenitally lacking this gift, this grace. But alas, there now came another situation to muddy these dark waters:—

Tania suddenly staked her claim . . .

■ □ ■

One day, by chance or design, Oleg and Tania had bumped into each other on the boulevard Raspail. Oleg agreed to call on her, at first reluctantly, as though out of politeness. But she, in her bestial astonishment—how could it be that her toy, her slave, her robot suddenly hesitated to obey her?—laid on her charms. For a brief moment, Oleg attempted to resist inwardly, but then, realizing his good fortune, he changed tack and at great length played the happy and independent free agent. He played the part almost without any self-interest, for in the time that he had spent with Katia, he had simply forgotten all about his ignominious dependency on her. When they met later, he was markedly jolly. Rudely radiant and availing himself of that special aura that always surrounds those blessed by good fortune, he stood before Tania as he had essentially always been, but as she had never known him to be: an obscenely healthy and discerning know-it-all, an obnoxiously happy tramp-cum-athlete. There was something aristocratic and debonair about him now, something outwardly agreeable, like sunlight on water; something different, which rendered him momentarily incapable of fawning or being rude, incapable of cutting someone down to size or giving them a beating—that blunt Russian show of generosity and indifference, his sportsman's swarthy veneer, the cheery and studied presumption of poverty—and all this, only after he had kicked his only vice (that of loving her too much), all this rang and rioted in his words, while despite herself, Tania gazed at him in secret admiration. There was no longer any trace of that old, humiliated, vindictive, pinched, beggarly look that he had once worn. But now, when Oleg bared himself to Tania again, astonished by his good fortune and memories of their long-fought battle, bewildered by this unexpected total victory, he clung to his new style all the more easily, because in her eyes he truly was a new man. Like one who had risen from the dead, but not before learning that it was not all so bad on the other side. Devilishly empowered by this knowledge, Oleg knew beyond all doubt that he could get by without her. No longer a mythical creature, she was, he suddenly saw, young and broad-shouldered, quick to take offense, and vain, although unexpectedly kinder and more candid than he had supposed in those bygone times, when he had so passionately yearned to know her "private life" at any cost, while she, sensing the acutely inflated price of this exposure, had been all the more careful to conceal it from him.

And so once again they began to meet . . .

■ □ ■

That evening, Oleg visited Tania after dinner, and in that building, which usually teemed with relatives of hers, there was nobody except for the two of them.

It was strange—the sweet, curious strangeness of something ordinarily impossible. They could talk at full volume, go raking through the kitchen cupboards in search of jam, cheese and biscuits, and eat while they stood there, washing it all down with cold tea drunk from cups with broken handles—for Tania's apartment was chaotic, slovenly, bacheloresque even, since she had no mother, and droves of her tiresome relatives would fill the place so often that it was never entirely clear to whom it belonged. Tania and Oleg wandered about the rooms and made telephone calls, having decided that they would stay in that evening. Oleg now found particular pleasure in being able to say that on Tuesday and Wednesday he was busy, and on Thursday too, that, in point of fact, he was busy for the foreseeable, whereas previously he had always been mortifyingly free, and that same woeful dialogue had ensued between them eternally: with a frown, Tania would ask when they would see each other again, and he would always fume and flush, answering that it would be whenever she wanted, knowing that she herself knew perfectly well that he was always free for her.

In the callousness of good fortune, Oleg recognized neither himself nor Tania's apartment. For how often, literally shaking, like a lamb being led to the slaughter, had he stepped through the front door as though through the very gates of hell and discreetly crossed himself right there in the vestibule. So servile had he looked that the concierge, even though she knew him by sight, once asked him to take the service stairs—one of the ultimate humiliations of Parisian life.

Now, however, Oleg delighted in his newfound ability to examine the furniture and photographs without the need to keep an eye on Tania's expression all the while, or else to look in the mirror—his favorite artistic, masturbatory pastime. He liked this cheerful and wicked version of himself, to whom Tania, approaching from behind and suddenly appearing over his shoulder, said in a shy, sly voice while she combed her hair:

"Just think, we have this whole apartment all to ourselves."

Ensconced, at ease on the divan, having removed his jacket, Oleg flirted while he smoked a cigarette, flexing his brawny arm, and, as he fooled around, he scrutinized the symmetrically horned, thoughtful heads that, despite himself, the designer of this cubist wallpaper had fashioned from triangles of dark and light cobalt. He had noticed them long ago, and though they had horns, these heads looked melancholy somehow, wistfully tilting to one side, gazing blindly somewhere high above the room. Oleg experienced a feeling of serenity, as if he had taken a seat in a lion's den after the lions had been whisked away to the zoo. After striking languid poses in front of the mirror and perfuming her earlobes, lips, and heavy bosom, Tania migrated over to the divan and, drawing her legs up and settling them in that typically Russian way, began to purr softly behind clouds of smoke.

Flirting, flaunting his strength, secure in his mastery over himself and her, Oleg, in his collarless black mariner's vest, broadened his shoulders and made himself comfortable at the other end of the divan. Their talk, as always, began with acquaintances, few though they were, as was common in émigré circles, having been stripped to the bone by the same old mockery . . . Their outward congeniality masked an internal tension and wariness . . . What was going to happen? . . . Tania's glinting, wicked gaze escaped from under her brows. Oleg set the gramophone going, squinting from the smoke curling up from the cigarette that he held in in his mouth, grimacing and humming, before returning to his spot on the divan . . . Silence. For Tania the tension was unbearable, however. She stood up and crossed the room, showing off her chest coquettishly, and then she proceeded to comb her hair in front of the mirror once again, making eyes at herself, before returning to the divan directly, with a sway of the hips . . . Oleg waited . . . Propping herself up on one knee, Tania leaned over him, resting her tawny arms on the cushion. Suddenly, looking him straight in the eyes, asked point-blank:

"Are you living with her?"

"No, but I ought to have been."

"Why?" she asked with a smirk.

"There would have been no going back then. You know how it is: we spare ourselves, we fear to get our hands dirty, lest the sky come falling down."

Tania carried on staring at him in silence. Her hair, golden, leonine, low hanging, grazed his face, smelling of cheap eau de cologne, soap, health, jam, and tobacco . . . Oleg no longer recalled Katia.

He was gripped, captivated by the thought of when and how he might begin to kiss Tania, how he might take in his hand her heavy full breasts, which right now, like fruit from the tree of knowledge, were hanging over him. Tania sat down beside him, and suddenly her shoulders and head appeared in his lap. Instinctively, impulsively, he took her in his arms and their lips met. At last Oleg felt their moist, warm chill, that particular taste, the unique combination of saliva, lipstick, scent and tobacco—then all of a sudden there came a sweet, sharp, stinging pain. Oleg pulled away and, playing the cad, said: "She-devil! You bit me . . ." Now Oleg caressed and manipulated her face with its high cheekbones, as though molding it—he had always regretted not becoming a sculptor—and Tania closed her eyes in spontaneous bliss . . . This was a habit of his. Even before, Tania had loved it, but now his heavy, dry palms brought her wild pleasure. Slowly, as though working blue clay, Oleg, with profound, ancient satisfaction, fingered each bump and ridge of this precious face that had once inspired such terror in him, but was now smiling like a tame lion, peacefully, lazily, menacingly. Oleg stroked the back of her head gently, carefully, grazing her large masculine ears with sweet surprise. "I adore you physically," he said almost without knowing it, with the warmth of rapture in his voice, which surprised even him . . . "Not sexually, you understand—though, who knows, perhaps I adore you in that way too—but physically . . . You see, I could go on forever, looking at you, caressing you. I could draw you, I could contemplate you while you move about the room unawares, while you comb your hair and lift your heavy arms . . . O joy, whole days in a shuttered room, among the rose-colored reflections of the sun and the sea, without a single thought, immersing, dissolving in the natural stillness. From His living concealment, God spies on his beloved creation, listening as it purrs, splashes, sighs, snaps its fingers, cuts the pages of a book or sleeps, suddenly exposed, suddenly robbed of His dreadful, protective gaze and confined to the defenseless beauty of nature, of unknowing existence, like a forest that knows not the noise of its own verdant slumber . . ." For a long, infinitely long time, in the frozen stupor of astonishment and happiness, as though transfixed by the sound of something, Oleg examined Tania's strong yet slender clammy palm, always like a mother's cooling salve. He detested the cold, clammy palms of others, palms that would so remarkably, almost providentially interlace with his own forever hot, dry hand, but the damp chill of Tania's spread over his face an extraordinary tranquility, the coolness of caves on a seashore, the freshness of leaves at dawn, snow.

Just as slowly, Oleg continued to caress and mold Tania's shoulders, breasts, and thighs. He clasped them, unable to believe his luck. He would barely touch her breasts, then, delighting in the firmness of the flesh, he would squeeze them in his powerful paw, and Tania would shudder in exquisite pain as she closed her eyes, absolutely still, and pretended to sleep. This repose beneath his tender touch reminded him of the sun-drenched serenity of sand and mountains, the majestic architecture of the clouds . . . How Oleg loved the body! The powerful, languid Michelangelesque freedom of a body *en plein air*; the baleful, unshakable, sleepy expression of colossi, who know of their nakedness but do not deign to notice it; but, most importantly, the profound, unhurried caresses, as leisurely as a sunny day, the love not for forbidden parts, but for the whole body, a love repressed for so long and, like the sweet honey of sunshine, radiating in the heavy languor of touch.

Tania continued to lie there almost motionless, while he continued to sculpt, rejoicing almost blindly at the touch, as though he were studying her body, as a blind Michelangelo might have studied his own statues, feeling them, fondling them in the torrid darkness of his impairment . . . It was as though Tania herself were not there, but just when doubt overcame him and he pulled away, her hand would emerge from the stillness and, stroking his hair, return him, press him to her. Oleg realized that it was for him that Tania was completely naked under her dress, with no fancy, frilly nonsense, least of all those garters for which he fostered a neurotic hatred; naked, as she had been back then, in the south, and that pure, sleek nakedness, still bearing the mark of summer, that nudity, over which the fabric slid with such tormenting, arousing ease, united both parts of their happiness: that first fleeting encounter and the confidence of the present. Without realizing it, Tania tensed beneath Oleg's hands, and now her whole body, smooth, tawny, as taut as a drum, arching almost like a bridge, terrified him with its flawless perfection. He wished that she were softer, that she lacked that antique immaculacy with those thighs and the almost flat stomach of Artemis. There was something menacing and disdainful of weakness in this strong tawny perfection . . .

Slowly, with an almost morose sense of idolatry, Oleg kissed her thighs, her stomach, and her firm mound of Venus, the freshly washed hairs on which smelled of that constant, ubiquitous Cadum soap, and also of the human body, a subtle feminine smell, redolent of hay, of which she smelled all over, a patch of blossoming summer meadow on the barren soil of the city, a patch of high-crested Russian earth, made bitter by its own fertility amid the frozen hell of deathly, weary, corpselike white bodies.

Oleg was becoming aroused, but he managed not to lose his head. His length, like a strong, heavy bough, strained toward Tania. She could feel it through her dress, but Oleg held back, lost in that mysterious feeling wherein sensuality, in its abundance, no longer recognizes itself and transforms into an elaborate and passionate ravishment of sight, touch, and art, containing a glimmer of his finest Grecian dreams. This was the reward for his ascetic life, which had been so hard-won, for his athletic training, for his abstinence from masturbation, for the luxury of his new, calmer health . . . Forgetting herself, Tania instinctively moved one thigh away, but Oleg knew that as soon as he climbed on top of her, she, in a nervous frenzy of belated virginity, would clasp them tightly shut again, bringing them together with such force that, were his head to be caught between them, she would have smothered him to death—and herein lay the fear of life and the fear of the death of life, of blasphemy and waste, and the fear of God, which was poisoning her overripe days.

"You know, Oleg, I could never bring myself to use any of those contraptions people use to avoid falling pregnant, or, as others do, to pull away at the last second. I simply wouldn't dare . . . As far as I'm concerned, to live with you is to conceive a child at once . . ."

Oleg mused how even a spineless ass such as he could be disgusted by the sight of spilled semen; it made his heart clench. For he held this hot and heavy occult liquid to be, in a sense, life itself, and he understood the Jews who forbade it to be spilled or even looked upon, like the holy of holies, or even some French women who, while fellating a male member, will make sure to swallow up every last drop; he understood, too, the medieval sorcerers who would smear it from head to toe, like an elixir of life that summoned evil spirits from the otherworld better than blood. It was one of the reasons that he abstained from masturbation, but if he happened to ejaculate during a dream, he would think in sweet terror how almightily dreadful it must be for a woman, and he would wonder whether she could feel the movement of the male organ inside her suddenly abate and, from it, the hot liquid bursting, rushing, gushing. Truly, one would have to be a degenerate to pull away at that moment and let spill all over the body that living humor that is the *anima mundi*, the quintessence of being, or else, as did some women whom he found particularly odious, to weary all of a sudden, to grow frigid and wince at the ejaculate. He had read somewhere that prostitutes never washed themselves after coition. Oleg had never slept with a single prostitute and took great pride in this as one of his most prized achievements, although not one of his friends believed him. Now he realized just how little he had enjoyed his latest excuse for a love affair, when after the sex, angry at himself, to spite himself, he had rushed to the washbasin to clean his spent member with its dewdrop at the tip . . . Thus, mortifying his passion, Oleg now avoided washing his rod. The filth clung to his hairs and, as he beheld it, he took great pride therein, as though it were a mark of ancient monastic asceticism. Beneath the foreskin there was an accumulation of white matter, which helped the head not to expose itself—something that Oleg could not endure, wondering daily how Jews could go about the streets with the tip of their length unsheathed, and so it was that after an infrequent trip to the bathhouse, where, after a steam, the skin had a tendency to roll back of its own accord, he would constantly dash to the urinal or with his hand in his pocket pull the obstinate skin down over the head.

Tania had climaxed imperceptibly, hiding it from him, and perhaps more than once. In physical terms, she was very much drawn to this heavy, thoroughly chaste and thoroughly sexual Luciferian

Russian man ("with arms bared below the elbow and eyes bluer than ice"), who, despite his crazed mind, never made sexual mistakes, never molested, yet never gave in, slowly, at great length, like unto an endless summer's day, delighting in her flesh . . . "Ah, sweet flesh," Oleg would think . . . Just as it is rare for the obscenity of a naked body to become flesh, so too is it rare for color on canvass to become a hue, for verses to become poetry, for the world to open up and be filled with God's presence, while in a thousand thousand ordinary cases it is but a body without a soul, the naked, obscene crotch of nature.

Oleg failed to grasp how it was that he could never bring himself to rape anyone. His struggle with sex was so desperate that even in his dreams, where all living things roam free, it would continue. No matter how much he desired it, he could never seem to meet Katia in his dreams; things would always get in the way—people, waiters in cafés, a lack of money—and he would never get to sit down next to her at the table where she, completely naked, would be holding court with the Slavophilic company that he found so odious, covered as they were in seaweed and soapsuds. But when at last they did meet, the mere touch of her head was enough to make Oleg release torrents of pleasure, as Proust so chastely put it. Ordinarily, he awoke with his length standing to attention and his body damp with perspiration as a result of the dream, and he could never quite fathom how it was that he had not actually been having sex.

After crawling out of bed naked, Oleg examined his penis curiously in front of the mirror. It looked so enormous, especially when he stood sideways, that he marveled how it ever managed to fit inside a woman. He recalled the narrow, swanlike white stomach of his latest victim . . . It must have reached her midriff . . . He recalled how she had squirmed in delight as he, getting carried away with himself, slid in too deep, and how toward the end she had winced in such exquisite pain when in those final moments he carried on plowing her like snow, unmoving and delicate, grinding down with his tremendous asphyxiator. Oleg's weapon was longer than his palm, and all of a sudden, he felt wildly drawn to the solitary vice. He made several movements up and down while the last cries of censure rent his ears . . . "Succumbing to the solitary vice in the morning means ruining the rest of the day . . . Come on, sleep it off. After all, it'll spoil meditation and make prayer impossible . . . You've amassed all that strength, and suddenly you're staring down the horrifying prospect of total capitulation . . . You won't be able to train at the gym . . ." And as though pricked, Oleg froze, dumbfounded, seeing his rod still in his fist as he stared straight ahead . . . He saw himself narrow-shouldered, pale and soft . . . He envisaged how he would relent and crumple before the gaze of strangers in the street, how they would beat him while he cowered and struggled to break free, to make a run for it . . . Nice try: never again would Oleg lay his hand on his *viris.** His persecution complex had got the better of him. One devil had driven out the other . . .

■ □ ■

When Oleg was happy, healthy, and confident, Tania would not be parted from him for days on end. For weeks her heart refused to be separated, and not for a single moment in the course of a whole evening would the familiar, electrifying circle be broken—the circle of frenzy, guile, and freedom, poking fun at everything and everyone,

---

* Here: penis (*Latin*)

their bestial romps and wrestling, during which they enjoyed especially the feeling of strength in their hands, kneading, crushing,
assailing the other's suntanned flesh, at times losing their head and
biting almost to the point of drawing blood. Sometimes Oleg would
inadvertently throttle Tania almost to the point where she fainted.
But it was rare that Oleg lost his head: if he forgot himself for a
moment and gave free rein to his hands, his broad rib cage, which
contained a malevolent bird beating its wings, would literally crepi-
tate, and, putting on a brave face, he would then smash and fracture
the unruly bone. But suddenly his perspiring head would draw back,
and, like the lion of the apocalypse, raising its head from the flesh
and with its bloody paw opening the book, Oleg would suddenly
pose one of his usual conundrums—and immediately there would
ensue between them one of their distinctive, grim, inscrutable, cabbalistic conversations, set amid the untold splendor of athletic arms,
the sheen of silky chestnut skin, and eyes in which the searing frenzy
of blood would suddenly switch direction, rankling and tormenting the spirit, as it had just coddled and caressed the body.[1] One of
those heavy mythological conversations, full of hidden menace, like
a leaden summer sky—conversations in which they would find their
special peace, their spiritual, bestial happiness, the focus of their
pact, their plot . . . "Listen," Oleg would say all of sudden, pushing
away her shoulder with his fearsome hand, while their legs and loins
remained, like an ancient Greek androgyne, intertwined in a state
of congress. "Do you know what is meant by 'a sexual relationship
with God'?"

During such conversations Oleg's heart would suddenly ice over
and his body cool in a heavy, antique, frescolike expanse of absolute
unreserve, so that as he spoke, Tania would often carry on holding

him by the root of the tree of life, while he, with his strong, cupped hand, would go on pressing, groping at her inner thigh, while their surfeit of health was truly, brilliantly transfigured by the sheer intensity of their heavy, leonine, religious inquisitiveness. Since, as Tania rightly said, neither of them was entirely human, it was humanity that they lacked, and she in particular; she was sooner some magnificent spiritual beast, because she combined the ideal physique with a natural bloodlust for the crystalline music of pure abstract logic, for the metaphysics of the Cabbalah. Thus, too, did Tania roam from the fire and into the flames, from the ice and into the fire, never able, never seeing, never experiencing the golden center of the heart's, the soul's sense of reality, and therefore always restless, tense and hounded by the misplaced fears of one who is, and who vaguely senses that he is, somewhere beyond the limits of reality and, consequently, himself. But Oleg was also possessed of many of these heroic, Herculean, superhuman traits. There was something of an absurd demigod about him; he was half-beast, devoid of the most elementary human moral qualities, indelicate, tactless to the point of naïveté, intellectually ruthless and spiritually immoral, aside, of course, from his cast-iron, irreproachable sexual probity.

"Tania, do you know what is meant by a sexual relationship with God?"

"I know that mine is a jealous God, that He envies my relationship with you."

"You see, here, for instance, a Jew would have to answer differently, despite Jacob's struggle with God, for in the Bible story God clearly sought to enter into a sexual relationship with Jacob. But if a Jew has intercourse with his wife before God, in the presence of God, then he can be sure that every Sabbath night God will be watching what takes place in his alcove, making sure that he smiles when his wife, in her abandon, arches her back into a bridge and lifts her husband from the bed . . .

"The Aryan God, my God, envies a man his wife and a woman her husband, so it is to spite God that an Aryan woman sighs as she stretches out and holds her husband by the root of the tree of life— for the monastery, the act of prayer, and especially the monastic cell is the alcove for congress with God Himself, given that God is always a man, and the soul a woman, who reveals herself, who raises herself toward God, Belus, the sun, the creator of the world . . ."[2]

"Yes, I understand. That is why, for me at least, physical love is both a call to God and deliverance from Him, a kind of equality with Him, the opportunity to look Him straight and unflinchingly in the eye, reliant on Him for nothing, and to speak to Him calmly, defiantly, face to face . . ."

A zealot and a skeptic, a born mystic and a mystifier, a schismatic and a tireless devourer of books, Oleg knew how gradually to retreat, as he spoke, into the fiery mist of half-intelligible, fanciful words . . . After which they woke with a jolt, combed their hair, straightened out their clothes and, like naked dogs, stole into the kitchen on the hunt, searching, sniffing, thieving, eating with their bare hands; with faces happy and mouths full, they returned, smoked, lost all sense of time, played the gramophone, and suddenly, unexpectedly cast together in a dance, stopped, sinking their lips into each other. (Oleg especially loved to kiss Tania's gritted teeth behind her soft parted lips, that white enamel wall behind the soft, hot barrier, which Marcus the Gnostic described as God's stricture, σταυρός, and once again this fascinated him, born cabbalist that he was.)[3] Again, they found themselves in a frenzy of kisses, with the taste of blood on bitten lips. In Oleg's hands, Tania's body turned from a heavy mass into nothing; he bound and spread her arms, squeezing her shoulders until they cracked. To him, who did not know his own strength, she seemed suddenly lighter, more impetuous, almost fragile, imbued with a sweet and fierce-flowing nervous energy; she threw back her head in an almost cataleptic fit, but already it was the simplest thing for Oleg to crush her resistance, and he delighted in tormenting her, like so many kings of Babylon, who with their bare hands had strangled leopards that could easily have mauled any ordinary man—for Tania was uncommonly strong for a woman, and Oleg recalled how once, at a party, she had almost tripped over an inebriated and unconscious Alla in the hallway and, with phenomenal ease, lifted her up and carried her through the length of the flat and into the bedroom.

■ □ ■

Often, basking in the afterglow of their glorious nakedness, Tania and Oleg would argue, curse each other, dream, fight, and philosophize. These were happy days. Tania's parents had gone off somewhere, and her sister had been sent abroad, out of sight, for having failed her exams so miserably. The apartment was empty, and Tania roamed it as she had once done the beach, wearing the same blue skirt with big mother-of-pearl buttons down the side, every movement of which revealed from top to bottom her finely sculpted thigh, knee, and leg. Her breasts were held up by a sash, and between them and a belt her boyish, tanned stomach, in all its wild chastity, voluptuousness, candor, and secrecy, was totally visible. In her savage way, Tania flirted with Oleg as she used to—with her every step and every movement—so that he, as though being struck in the face, often blinked and turned away, such was the dazzling indecency and perfection of her accidentally exposed body. Her body was a thing of rapture, fervor, tenderness, and humor, a kind of miraculous restitution of rights, Oleg's rehabilitation, a return to the weight, luxury, and majesty for which he had been fashioned and which he so tragically lacked, to the aristocratic decorum of deliberate gestures and words for which he so yearned—for one hardly ever encountered it among the poor and wretched, in the Métro, in the cafés, in the street, where everyone bears the mark of manifest, crushing reserve, nurtured since infancy, the inhibition of their movements and gestures, humility, a constant sense of urgency, the constraints of work and a lack of free time, the absence of travel, silence, music and books. Oleg was a fallen man, a has-been, a degenerate, and to him, success with women meant the restitution of his rights, rehabilitation, the patent of nobility. For men judge men from without, even if they are not remotely homosexual, without which phenomenon they would be unable even to apperceive male beauty or exalted physical splendor; yet they too, for reasons unknown, occasionally bend, humbling themselves before certain, particularly successful representatives of their sex. Whereas women, in spite of themselves, are candid, innately impelled toward candor, unable to conceal their admiration, and often restore a degenerate man to his rightful place.

■ □ ■

Katia had been gone only a day, but already, after his meeting with Bezobrazoff, Oleg was left doubting everything: her, his love, almost even her very existence—so powerful were Tania's charms, which sooner hinged on old neuroses and terrors that had outlasted love. The hotel on the boulevard Raspail, which had temporarily broken ranks with the other buildings and blazed with agonizing significance, quickly returned and resumed its neighborly solidarity. Oleg even fancied dropping by to see the owner, who, too, had suddenly diminished in stature, once again having become a mere person, a Frenchman, a nobody. Now a fortnight had passed since Katia's departure, and, with the fleetness of a fairy tale, winter had begun to make up for lost time. Overnight it covered its tracks and heaped on snow—and already Tania's brisk little animal tracks went running across the white surface.

Bemused, having exchanged the smoldering intensity of one love for another, Oleg wondered whether he had not perhaps got things mixed up, like the drunkard at a bar who fails to clock that his neighbor has changed and blithely carries on spouting his nonsense. At any rate, Christmas itself, with all its diabolical, feverish activity, was upon them.

Oleg and Tania began their debauch . . . There were times when Oleg lost consciousness for what seemed like a whole month. His consciousness and memory would fade until they no longer held the reins on life's sequence of events, only on pieces of it, agonizing fragments, just as at the cinema, when, in order to emphasize the chaos and impetuosity of the action, the director fleetingly shows scenes of carnage or a ballroom from an extreme angle or upside down . . . Theirs were the coarse, perspiring, wearied faces of gypsies . . . "Aïda, aï-da . . ." All day long, that eternal refrain, like a belch that had stuck between their teeth . . . Then there were the wild, impassioned kisses, the spread legs . . . the hotels, the fistfuls of money, the hopeless separations, the preparations, the shaving, the hurrying, the tedium, the heavy fat back and incoherent babbling: "Darling, darling, my sweet..." Losing their heads, on the brink of actually having sex, they would flounder, fumble, grope and groan, rub their organs, and, with beating hearts, part, anxious and excited, but yet to consummate their love... Then they would goad one another, fume in exasperation, get dressed and step out into the stairwell, begrudging all the money that they were about to spend.

Before long Oleg gave up, gave way, gave in. Now, in his bewilderment, he ceased to doubt, and, as he continued to expend his happiness, he found himself all of a sudden perfectly sure that this was when things would begin to happen; he tried to convince, and in the end did convince, himself of this, although from the very outset his heart had calmly, sorrowfully, autumnally, too pitifully, without fear or intoxication, opened up to Tania... Of course I love her... No? But of course I do...

The days flew by. Oleg would squander his dole money immediately, a fact for which Tania would always berate him. He would go hungry until he received the next lot and have to borrow and scrounge in the meantime. But still, he threw himself, head and soul, into that last, desperate battle, that argument, that struggle with the inexorably darkening day, the evening of their love. Soon enough, Katia began to seem like just another episode of his relationship with Tania, just as a month previously Tania had seemed like a mistake, from the agony of which Katia had emerged like a vision of life itself... Blind and uncomprehending, Oleg had forsaken Katia, his all-too-brief but fully fledged, precious happiness, for a searing though doomed protective tenderness. Katia had spoiled his days with Tania once and for all, draining them of color, almost making a mockery of them, like a brawl between drunken suitors in a church . . . Likewise Tania, dazzling Oleg with her unnecessary largesse, had spoiled his hours spent with Katia. Each monster had neutralized the other. And Oleg, believing that this was it, that here he had finally embarked on life, now went off striding toward the bitterest, most poisonous kind of Bezobrazoffism . . . But none of this he knew back then. All his kindness, all his humane, feminine soul now rushed to save Tania's love, for Tania did indeed love him. With a kind of dreary abandon, she opened her dresser and bureau and took out her letters and diaries, showing him every last one. Only a year ago, the chance to steal a glance at these would have been enough to bring on a heart attack . . . But now . . . When Oleg first brought home her diary and opened it late one night, when all the secret sordidness, all the wild truth of those days lived by the sea unfurled before him, his head started spinning, and his stomach began to churn from the shock and surprise. Reading, and all the while setting it down, unable to go on reading another line, smoking, and even excitedly pacing back and forth along the concrete platform in front of his building, Oleg learned fantastic things, both true and unimaginably lewd. Namely, he learned that Tania had been ready to love him then, had waited, wanted, been ready to love him the moment that he showed up. Unable to hide her excitement, she had gone tearing out of the cottage and for a long time wandered in circles high up in the mountains; and only with great difficulty, having mustered her stonelike inner dispassion, did she return home . . . He learned that the entirety of his guilt had consisted in the fact of his having showed his hand too soon, having become embarrassed, having lost his independence and that cruel, unloving cheeriness, which, with the atavistic tendencies of Russian women, Tania valued so. And now, the miraculous change that had taken place within him (you've become just like Apollon—only, if he were a living person and not some diabolical actor), all the cheerfulness, the humor, the vulgarity, the independence, the way he had of striking up a tune, humming along and whistling, forgetting everything else in the world, which, now that Katia was gone, had reappeared—it was easy to imagine that all this was but a simple return to his natural state from the profound humiliation of love, the simple consequence of his having loved her less and less. Such a remarkable, mature man—and to have debased himself like that, to have cried and kissed her feet . . . "No, he's no knight in shining armor, fierce and firm in love. He's a woman with a beard," read Oleg later on, and for the first time, when they met afterward, his eyes shone with brilliant joy, for the record had been set straight. Now Tania just stared at him in wonder and felt, with exquisite intensity, that she was no longer a monster or the subject of curiosity, but just a woman, a girl scarcely able to refrain from running and throwing her arms about him. That day, they sat upstairs in some outrageous, ultramodern, expensive café on the place Saint-Michel, where the red velvet, the cubist squares, and the clientele, with their cardboard shoulders and inane, youthful faces, seemed to have been produced in the same atelier belonging to some avant-garde interior designer. (It was with such anguish, courage, and rich-ness of voice, at the high noon of his thirty years, in the prime of life, strength, responsibility, conceit, and incorrigibility, that Oleg despised this fresh, twenty-year-old, unestablished human vegeta-tion, laying waste to it with his gaze.) But Oleg's strength, suddenly awake, rejoicing, shimmering in his athletic, confident demeanor, in his down-and-out humor and deep, chesty, gypsy voice, was no lon-ger with Tania but against her, for she was already a part of that net-work, that conspiracy, that group of nightmarish characters from a

dream of yesterday, a dream from which he had already awakened—
to courage, dignity, and to freedom. In this triumph of his thirty
years of life, in the luster of the red velvet covering these clownish
divans, Tania ought to have read not a love of her and not the beginning of their life together, but her demise and a newfound love of the
world, a love that was visible, assured, and unsparing, one in which
she could no longer have any place.

"Why won't you take me with you, lead me away into your icy
Bezobrazoffism?" she said, not realizing that her love and Bezobrazoff were two absurdly incompatible, impossible concepts. If only
Oleg had not met so steely, so impetuous another man, one as merciless as death, as light of foot and with wings of glass—the very
embodiment of freedom, fullness, incorruptibility, and wit, who like
a falcon, like fate itself, preyed on every living thing, brimming all
the while with the unspent, monstrously intense electricity of life . . .

■ □ ■

Spring set in slowly, inflicting terrific pain. Little by little, unbidden in their toil, the trees arrayed themselves in a fine mist of
green, and suddenly, during those cold non-days—neither winter,
nor autumn—the sky laid bare its azure splendor, so bright that
it seemed artificial, so limpid that one doubted its very existence.
Everything was at once so immeasurably far away, and yet so near
that the minutest of details could be distinguished. In the blink
of an eye, the eternal Impressionist exhibition that the streets of
Paris are when shrouded in kaleidoscopic fog had been replaced
by Spain and Italy, by Fra Beato Angelico.[4] The motor cars all had
a freshly painted look about them; figures dressed in rags were

cleaning windows and, having achieved an extraordinary shine and finding themselves at the very top of their double ladder, now gazed upon themselves in their self-made mirror; horses, cats, dogs, old people, consumptives who in spite of all expectations had survived the winter, fat policemen, curly-haired students who were over-wrought by matters of sex, wandered the streets like flowers-errant. But to Oleg, who had adopted his new role in all earnestness, spring offended the eyes and the heart, for none of it gratified him, none of it helped him to embark on life's path from that deathly but so lived-in ascetic-cum-writer's niche of his . . . He had to work. He simply *had* to go out and work. But what could he do? He tried to learn the streets by rote, but that took up so little time; he wrote, he read Hartmann in the library, and cunningly though unconsciously left the streets for later . . . No, he simply had to take these new days seriously, and without a moment's delay—diving headlong into the freezing water, if only to vanquish his morbid fear of those in charge. In Montparnasse he ran into an acquaintance, a taxi driver and professional striker. "Come on, Oleg, let's go and sell some newspapers!"—"All right, just let me run home first to make myself up as a proletarian."—"Oh, but you've already got that delinquent look about you . . ."

■ □ ■

Once more into the hell of sorrows. Torment has cast off from the material world and is now arguing for the impossibility of itself . . . Words of fate, of fame . . . Frailty . . .

The ground of indescribable, infernal one-liners. Witnesses for the separation: (1) the tree on which hung and from which fell the last yellowed leaf, Adam's skull with crossbones at his feet; (2) the street, swept clean by the wind in the early hours, as sleek as the back of Leviathan; (3) the signs hanging over the shuttered shops, the fitful cold of night.

The deafness of the wind, although it desperately howled. The emptiness of happiness, although it undoubtedly existed. The fate of a hand, which shall inevitably unclench and release a memory from its palm. Thus does evening end in night, and night in the last, unbearably empty, unbearably sorrowful hours before dawn, when the cafés close and even the lights of the Métro are extinguished.

The nonsense of sense having melted through one's fingers, like water from a tap, striking, gushing, filling cupped hands, washing everything away, life having scarcely tried to embrace, to enfold, to embody, to encircle the eternal snowy humor of autumn days. "Whither dost thou vanish in these summer hours? Leaving me to respire beneath the sun . . . It shineth, thy sun, and trembleth from the cold . . ."

Deserted streets at night, incorruptible, irreclaimable, unrecognizable, where people have just defended themselves, wrestled wearily, worried habitually for a life weary of living, when that life has already burst beneath them with the desperate sound of decaying canvas, when everything has already ended with the creaking of a door being closed and the sound of footsteps slowly retreating, soon to fall silent. Once again, the watered-down humor of autumn's delirium and a windmill has reigned over everything, and the night sea, before all others, has forgotten, forgotten happiness.

Worlds have passed by beneath this place. Worlds have rushed by with the terrible clamor of their fiery music. But what does this place remember, this place where so many native Hamlets, having bid farewell to their beloveds, have lit a cigarette with a sense of relief by the very glass of that front door? Nothing at all: the street was just the street along which yesterday's newspaper flew, slowly flapping its torn wings. All this was, was, was, and yet this deathly place remembers none of it—the juncture of four corners and a thousand destinies . . .

The fatigue of steel; a stone unable to retain its solidity; water unable to flow; fire unable to burn. The sudden ephemerality of a world that has let slip its own reality. "How's that? Do we not yet live?" Snow covers snow—and where is the former, and where the latter, God no longer recalls . . .

The degree to which the heart melts is measured by the irretrievability of its previous form . . . The hand unclenches and lets go an empty life, only to be choked by the anguish of terrific absence. Having endeavored vainly to be irreversible, everything revulsively reverts to the cool fabrications of memory . . . Farewell, farewell!

"What can the wind have to howl about?" Oleg wondered, feigning ignorance or a loss of hearing. The anguish of spring was uncommonly tumultuous and absurd that year. It was almost mystically impossible to find work. Humiliated, Oleg envied every last worker who returned from bondage, watching malevolently, subserviently, before turning his back on them, unable to understand anything.

■ □ ■

With all his tales of what newspaper hawkers earned, Tcherepahodoff managed to turn Oleg's heart, which, as it happened, was rather easily accomplished, continuing as it did in its innermost recesses to sleep, to yawn, to think, all on that same right or left side.

Oleg dressed as though for a masquerade ball. Should he take his gloves? Might his hands not freeze? No, a real newspaper hawker doesn't wear gloves, he puts up with it, you son of a bitch. Having arrived, however, Oleg saw a morose-looking crowd of has-beens lingering quietly by a little window deep in the narrow rue du Croissant; they were all waiting for the first edition, referred to as the "fourth," the "afternoon," and the "little-read". His heart sank. An old man, who with his scruffy hair looked every bit the troglodyte, informed him: "*Il y a des mecs qui, leur journée finie, viennent ici prendre le pain aux malheureux.*"* Everybody indulged the beggars with especial civility, though, and soon enough, after much elbowing, Oleg found himself out in the street with a stack of newspapers that he had not yet learned to handle. Adolescents ran past him energetically, proclaiming in loud voices: "*Paris-Soir, tous les détails!*"† He, too, must shout. His first attempt, so excruciatingly strange and not a little terrifying, escaped his throat.

Too loud? Too quiet? He could not yet tell, but his bastard legs carried him to the Grands Boulevards all the same. There, his embarrassment became unbearable: not knowing where to look, he turned as red as a crab, as though he were standing there without breeches . . .⁵ No, he could bear it no longer. He was ready to abandon his stack and run off to Montparnasse. Fortunately, however, he was distracted by his first buyer. Oleg bowed to him ineptly and forgot to give him any change, for which the buyer, with embarrassment and contempt, had to prompt him . . .

■ □ ■

---

* There are some guys who come here after work just to take bread from the poor. (*French*)
† *Paris-Soir!* Read all about it! (*French*)

Hazrie, caucoulia, haque-bis, bique-à-bassis, siganie, ouracarouca, cour-
abassara, bousca-bousca, oucasse, sagosse . . .[6] *"Paris-Soir! . . . Quatrième*
édition!"* God in Heaven, there are still thirty copies left to shift . . .
I could do without this . . . Time is pressing on . . . I could do without
that too . . . Will I manage to get rid of them all in time to stand in
line for the late edition? I wonder . . . *Ouque-bas, ouque-bas, brassina,*
palitesraque, brassignamouque . . . Now if Stalin had just been killed,
or if it were the end of the world, then I'd really earn some money . . .
I could do without that, too . . .

America swamped by sea, ten million dead . . . Social revolution in
Germany . . . Second Coming in Montparnasse . . . Hey, you dropped
your money . . . Idiot, don't take all day about it . . . Dilettante . . .
Ouque-bas, ouque-bas . . . Another fifteen to go . . .

No, nobody was buying. Absolutely no one wanted his fourth
edition. Unless, of course, the Jews, his beloved Jews . . . The Jews
nested in the arcades on the far side of the boulevard de Strasbourg.
But he found not a single buyer there—only the dust and despair of
boutiques newly decorated in the cubist style. The sorrow of a spring
day as it passed in vain and slowly strode through the glass ceiling
toward sunset. People snapped their fingers at him in that Orien-
tal way. Mastering his role, Oleg looked away as he dispensed their
change and, in a sing-song voice, as though in a terrible hurry, pro-
claimed his cantilena: *"Tous les détails du ministère!"*† Another flurry
of activity and five more copies were gone . . . The street again. Oleg
ventured into a café. This was not a usual haunt of his, but the enormous cashier nodded her assent. Hard luck: he was met with looks

---

* *Paris-Soir!* Fourth edition! (*French*)
† All the latest on the ministry! (*French*)

of only sympathy and scorn. In another café, a man, having waited and waited and worn himself out, having spent his nerves waiting for someone, beckoned him over with friendly relief. In a third, some drunkards hurled abuse at him:

"*Alors, on fait du commerce?*"*

"*Non, mais laisse-le, tu vois bien que ça commence à faire autre chose,*"† some drunken old crone said, pounding her fists on the table. But the real boon was the parking lot, where the private chauffeurs loitered, bloating from inactivity . . . He sold the last two to a gloomy band of policemen that he found waiting sinisterly in a side alley. Now he was walking on air, jingling with small change as he went, exhausted and satisfied, scanning his surroundings . . . But no sooner had he come out at Richelieu–Drouot than a thronging, jostling crowd of youths on the sidewalk caught his eye. They were arguing in hushed tones, hesitating, reluctant to part.

"*Alors, on remet ça?*"‡

"*Attends, ça va barder tout à l'heure.*"**

Oleg was loath to go and fetch new papers. At any rate, he was too late and much too worked up. He wanted to join the crowd, to elbow his way in and listen. As always, whenever he was exhilarated, he imagined that he had at his disposal a whole infinity of strength; all he wanted was to keep moving, to keep talking, to keep wisecracking without ever letting up . . . But then, all of a sudden, his legs filled with lead, he felt a pang in the pit of his stomach and had to sit down and rest awhile on a bench. No, Oleg was not cut out to be a newspaper hawker . . .[7]

---

* Are you selling something? (*French*)
† Don't talk to him. You can just tell that he'll start something. (*French*)
‡ Shall we have another go at it? (*French*)
** Wait, it'll kick off soon. (*French*)

09

O leg spent three days in the underworld, dead to friends and spring alike. The infernal parfumerie was situated in a dilapidated single-story villa near the Porte de Clignancourt, where Oleg was set to work now at the back of the house, now in the cellar. His first day was a bright scarlet, the second sooner pink, the third white, cloying and unreal. The first day was the most arduous of them all, however . . . As soon as Oleg, cringing before the owner, had crossed that fatal line separating the free man, the friend, the acquaintance, from the slave, the convict, the day-laborer, he no longer knew how to behave and would laugh unprofessionally, irritating the contemptuous and sullen Jewish failure to whom this stinking fragrance business belonged. He was put on the landing by the back steps, which gave onto a little yard that was full of bottles. Sacks of raw materials for powder stood under a canopy, and there were yellow and red strips stretched out across the ground. He found himself standing in front of a board that had been placed in the corner of two balustrades, atop which, like red sugar loafs, rested several glossy, sweet-smelling blocks of freshly cooled lipstick. Cutting it into long slabs seemed fun at first, almost like a game, so that when the owner silently appeared over Oleg's shoulder, he spat out his first words of reproach, telling him to look sharp and slice more efficiently. The slivers that he cut were then placed into a marble press, from within the walls of which, slowly and reluctantly, the scented crimson mass would re-emerge, oozing out and pausing frequently, because Oleg had to keep stopping all the time . . . The first twenty minutes were easy, despite the handle being unwieldy and hellishly stiff, but soon enough a sharp pain in Oleg's shoulder forced him to stop.

Sweat streamed off him, and gradually he removed all his clothes. The ubiquitous red clay, indelible by ingenious design, adhered to everything. At times, especially in the presence of the owner, who himself, his teeth gnashing and his eyes glinting through his round spectacles, would crank the handle with all the bitter resentment that a Jewish inventor can muster (one whose wife had been left an invalid following an unsuccessful abortion), Oleg would turn it for a good five or ten minutes, puffing away victoriously. The owner would vanish, smacking his lips, but when he returned, he would find Oleg in a state of exhaustion, sitting on the stool with his head slumped. Yet the real hell began only after lunch . . . Wearing his gloves, Oleg ate ravenously as he wandered aimlessly about the streets; he ate with his bright carmine-stained hands which no black soap on earth could whiten. Pale and besmeared with pigment, he ate at the neighboring flea market,[1] examining with feigned indifference the breathtaking chaos of antique objects, and in his face, strained, triumphant, tortured, the face of a schoolboy returning after an excruciating exam, every other worker that he encountered, each one wearing the navy-blue jacket that was his uniform, could see right away that Oleg was just a dilettante, an intellectual, a has-been, and, having realized this, they would turn away in disappointment, or else in sympathetic disdain. After greedily stuffing himself with whatever he could lay his hands on—some cheese, some grapes, some overripe bananas—Oleg loitered there a little while longer to read his *Paris-Midi*. He returned to the workshop ahead of time and, sitting on the stairs, very nearly dozed off in the sun, until an authoritative bark brought him back to reality—one that for him was less real than all his dreams. There, in the leaden drowsiness of unchewed, undigested nourishment, Oleg came to know a truly Babylonian torment, chained as he was to a sticky iron handle that set in motion marble rollers, which seemed to him like cyclopean millstones. His heart was beating heavily and without cease, spinning lights rushed before his eyes, while his legs bowed from unbearable fatigue. Yet he had to keep on cranking the handle, cranking it without ever letting up, for the bald and perspiring parfumier, embittered by his barren and idle wife, would keep score with his own practiced, well-seasoned manufacture, angrily snatching the handle from Oleg's hands and, in the wild fury of a misunderstood genius ("I spent ten years searching for the formula for this lipstick—ten years!—and it includes no fewer than fifty ingredients!" the parfumier had said, and, widening his eyes in mock-astonishment, Oleg had repeated sycophantically, "Fifty ingredients!"), turning it without pausing for breath, the bright folds of his laboratory coat flapping about. With that, he would run off in arrogant triumph, having destroyed Oleg . . . The hours dragged out humiliatingly. Applying himself to this instrument of torture, Oleg held it now in front, now from behind, now with his right hand, now with his left, but still the crimson, artificially scented stick of crushed, pigmented mixture would emerge from under the six marble rollers with that same reluctance. He managed, however, to process the whole lot by evening. But then came yet another misfortune: clumsily, blunderingly, he let red peelings scatter all over floor and had to spend a foul eternity, crawling about on all fours, scraping and cleaning the worn-out linoleum . . . For the first time in his life, Oleg fell asleep on the Métro. The conductor threw him out at the end of the line, and so he had to buy another ticket home. At last, unconscious of everything around him, without eating and without even bothering to undress, he collapsed directly onto his sunken divan, experiencing a heavenly bliss.

Orpheus's second day in the underworld was easier, as it so happened. To begin with, he was put to work in the basement, far from the owner's gaze, where he got talking to the packer, a meek, long-suffering lady in spectacles, who was a former believer and used to attend church, but now had no time for anything of the kind and on Sundays would either sleep or spend the whole day doing laundry. Only of a Saturday evening would she countenance even a visit to the cinema.

"Just how long have you been working here?" he asked.

"It'll be almost a year now."

"And you aren't tired of it yet?"

"No, you get used to it one way or another, and life just flies by in its eternal haste, like a dream . . ."

Once again Oleg was reminded of Freud's words: that every living thing seeks death, unable to withstand the torment of its own good fortune, seeks to expend itself in sex, work, or intemperance. With a look of reproach, he turned away from her meekness, as from the recent sight of a young man masturbating in an underpass. But surely she would have died from hunger? . . . I didn't die from hunger . . . But it's harder for a woman to live in poverty . . . For a man it's more

shameful . . . To work, to forget, to be forgotten, to be reconciled, to be freed of debt, to be . . . Like blood let from veins, like castration, forfeiting, forgoing, we live on life's remains, but just how much does remain—a trip to the cinema, a nap before lunch, a lie-in on a Sunday morning? . . . You ought to be ashamed . . . Be poor, beg, sleep in the street, fight for your life's breath . . . Serve time in jail, join a monastery, go on the dole . . . Spare me. Why not exhaust ourselves with work, with sex, ridding, unburdening ourselves of life in some dark corner? Good riddance, I say . . . Serves us right, *bande de châtrés* . . .*
Oh, I'd shoot dead all that meekness and saintliness for the sake of the poor . . . And good riddance . . .

Oleg spent the whole day stamping and pressing blush—"making compacts," as the parfumerie's reverend mother put it in her revoltingly meek, businesslike way. He would fill the molds and pack them down using the palm of his hand, then, with an aristocratic gesture that was soon mastered, he would quickly twist and untwist the steel press. The work carried on in a sort of frenzy, a delirium, the mindlessness of an unrelenting, monotonous dance—so, thought Oleg, time passes more quickly when you're intoxicated by a rhythmic haste that absorbs the spirit. He took a break in the cloakroom, where he would go to hide in his jacket all the perfumed riches that he had stolen for Tania: powder, cold cream, brilliantine, defective lip pencils—everything that out of sheer devilry and class hatred he would bear, with beating heart, past that genius of a chemist as he lay asleep on the divan by the open door . . . The day passed by in a stupefying flurry of activity, but soon enough he found himself once again out on the street with sixty francs in his pocket—money that

---

* bunch of castrates (*French*)

he had obtained with such difficulty, for the owner, even as he was preparing to pay out, seemed to dawdle, subject to a curious bout of nerves, struggling with himself, as if to part with his shekels caused him physical pain. This day, although having been without physical or moral affliction, without the humiliating need to say something from time to time just to maintain one's dignity, had passed without note, as though it had dropped out of life, as though it had been a dream. Drained almost entirely of strength, Oleg fell asleep once again as he rode the Métro, his hirsute head nodding, slumbering, while he stockpiled all his tales of Herculean labor for the following day, so as to prove, with money in his hands, just how seriously he was taking Tania.

The third day passed in a white mist of nauseatingly scented powder. Oleg spent the whole morning in a whitewashed storeroom lit by a bright electric lamp, turning a drum that declumped the powder. White clouds came flying out of the cracks in the machine, lingering in the air like a sweet, cloying veil that covered positively everything: hair, lips, eyelashes . . . As he turned the drum, he even found a way to read, with one hand and one eye, a little Franz von Baader,[2] but this was terribly dangerous and slowed time down, shattering the rhythmic inertia with work. But toward evening, having stolen yet another clutch of lip pencils, exhausted by the unaccustomed work and as white as a clown, he found himself outside once again. In a blush-colored blaze, the wind quickly descended on Montmartre . . . Every now and then a bell would peal with an astonishing crystalline sound. People were rushing about, bantering with one another and buying their evening papers. Many were heading to the city center, where for two days already there had been demonstrations and brawling in the streets because of some colossal financial scandal . . .[3]

Oleg was walking on air, with the resounding lightness of overexertion, which gave way to an unnatural nervous excitement as he fingered the broad twenty-franc coins in his pocket. He wanted to spend it all, to duck into a shop or a drinking establishment. He was rich and wearily, anxiously, evangelically happy, a fact made all the sweeter by his fatigue . . .

Slowly, among the spring lights of the heavens and the earth, Oleg descended from Montmartre, stopping in front of shop windows, sympathizing with the cyclist who was drenched by a passing truck and who cursed wearily, merrily and with a strange joviality. He stopped also to listen to the drunken arguments of the Saturday workers sitting at the bar . . .

■ □ ■

What a joy it is to have money, after all . . . Now I can go in and devour all these pastries . . . The sky hasn't been snuffed out yet, and the streets are still ablaze with light . . . Where can they all be hurrying? . . . They're hurrying along to kiss one another . . . to sleep, to curse . . . to the cinema, to life . . . I'm glad to be among them today. Everything is so bright that it assails my eyes. But that doesn't bode well: what if I have a sudden, terrible bout of weakness, drowsiness, anguish . . . If it carries on like this, I'll be able to buy myself a radio . . . Ah, the radio, what a marvelous invention. You just sit there and wind it up, and immediately you're transported to every end of the earth . . . Ensconced in an armchair, with Tania on my knees, listening to some jazz or some Schumann, then switching it off and at night, in the chaos of the atelier (for we *must* rent an atelier), in the bright spotlight of a lowered lamp, working, reading, writing,

writing, writing . . . Bliss. And there, beyond the ring of light, in the penumbra, on the divan, Tania's heavy, golden, radiant body . . . Yes! All night long the light will burn, we will argue, quarrel, and kiss amid the sleeping world, like two kings. Why, of course! . . . I'll go and take a look, perhaps there'll be fighting in the streets again today . . . Just be careful, lest they deport you . . . Yes, yes, but with my boxer's mug and my cap down over my eyes . . . Let's take a look in the mirror . . . Well, well . . . Bags under your eyes, a black vest and no shirt, that desperate look of embarrassment . . . Just how is it that women fall for you? Really, you look like a miner, a pimp, a sailor . . . Aha, there go the police . . . All such handsome, strapping fellows. How I'd like to go up to them and, with all due deference, kiss their scarlet cheeks . . . Yes! . . . Right in the middle of the street, like that February in Moscow, when, with a red ribbon on my realist's cap, I still dreamed of joining the militia—but they wouldn't take me . . . All my life I've been denied entry . . . First by my parents, then by the Bolsheviks, now by these illiterate émigré degenerates . . . Soft snow underfoot, that February slush, then "Farewell, school!" . . . Still, how good it was, how great to run off, to give up everything, to escape on the back of a cart down those Ukrainian roads, where once . . . Show yourself, apartment, reveal yourself across the wide expanse of time . . . A prison, cursed, crepuscular, eternal, everything covered in white sheets . . . The music lessons are all I recall . . . and the window ledges . . . In Rostov, among the lousy wounded, I discovered Nietzsche . . . In a boat on the River Don, between heaven and earth, untaught, finding it impossible to read . . . each phrase like a shot at point-blank range, a thousand thoughts, without the strength to carry on, better to row, to swim, to spend days on end walking on the moon with dirty feet . . . But those sunrises, those mornings amid the dazzling freshness of autumn . . . I'd fall asleep in the library and wake, in astonishment, to find that sweet smell of books, the rosy glint of their covers, but still I hadn't the strength to read . . . And all this in the midst of directives . . . military marches along the boulevard . . . exhortations to maintain law and order, denials that the city was under threat . . . So then, just one more evacuation and all this becomes a dream, a tedious, lumbering fantasy, while the reality is Nietzsche, Schopenhauer, and a narrow-shouldered superman, drunk on the light and his own impending doom, in the crystal mountains of Sils Maria.[4] Careful now, you're in the fray . . . Assume an independent, carefree, absent look . . . They're saying it's none of my business. I can't hear with this cap over my ears—what are they shouting? They're shouting to protect their happiness, their brute, golden, bullish happiness . . . *Vive Chiappe!* . . .* Careful now, don't get cocky, otherwise you'll never make it out of here . . . If only I could shout too . . . Ah! But shout what exactly . . . Chiappe's actually a decent guy. He's never bothered the likes of us . . . Ah! *mais tu n'y es pas,*† that's no ideology. Give it to him, lady, there's nowhere to move . . . Quick, let's get out of here . . . Damn it . . . (*In a side street, trying to catch his breath . . .*) He really got what was coming to him . . . The blood got in his eyes, blinding him, and all from a baton . . . Are they advancing again? . . . I'm so tired. And they can tell I'm a foreigner . . . I'm so terribly tired.

■ □ ■

---

* Long live Chiappe! (*French*)
† but that isn't the point (*French*)

At times, the roar of the crowd became overwhelming. Electrified suddenly, Oleg cried out and, forgetting himself, even came to the rescue of somebody (a policeman knocked off his bicycle by the crowd). He was drunk at another man's feast, but not on wine—there, among volcanoes, oceans, geysers of searing blood, all with the magnificence of intoxicated gallantry playing on excited faces . . . *Eh bien . . . faut plusieurs fortes poignées n'ayant rien volé . . . Puis mettre tous les étrangers à la porte et travailler la main dans la main . . . Pas vrai, mon pote? . . . Rapport au prolétariat . . .** and so on and so forth. Anxious and fearful, Oleg ran back and forth, like a woodchip carried by the crowd, jumping over flowerbeds and parapets, becoming entangled in a bush on the Champs-Elysées, before suddenly finding himself face to face once again with the night, in the emptiness of a side street, in the loathsome silence of spring slowly setting in.

■ □ ■

There it is at last. Weariness. Real, sudden, unbearable weariness. How am I going to extricate myself from this mob of foreigners; another moment longer and I'll stop pretending altogether, maybe I'll even start screaming in Russian . . . They're marching and shouting . . . A revolution in ironed trousers. Not for a lack of food, oh no, but because they want more, they want abundance, plenty; not for bread but for butter, for their pagan pleasures, for motor cars by the sea, suntanned skin in white linens, for radios on a winter's evening. Not just for life, but for happiness too, for the ancient grandeur of

---

* Well, for starters we need more muscle, guys who haven't stolen anything . . . Then we need to kick out all the foreigners and work hand in hand . . . Isn't that right, my friend? . . . As for the proletariat . . . (*French*)

unequal estimation, for superiority, inequality, inaccessibility, snob-
bery, while you, an apocalyptic louse, can beat it . . . No, none of this
has anything to do with you . . . They march, filled with indignation,
sensitive to losses and disorder, like radio antennae, but you didn't
care, your parents didn't care . . . Let the cook have her day, let her
reign awhile . . . Reveal yourself across the wide expanse of time, then
disappear, disappear, apartment of mine . . . From their perspective,
there's no alternative: good morning, Your Honor, there's Dobro-
liouboff crossing the street, go and dust his coat for him, a little
harder now, don't take all day about it . . . They were ashamed of the
police, ashamed of money, family, ashamed of living and defending
themselves . . . They were Christians, as it happened . . . Limp glands
or Christianity . . . or was Christianity itself a kind of relaxing of the
genitals . . . My Kingdom is not of this world . . . But all the same,
why not take a stand? . . . Fifty thousand officers in Moscow during
those October days, all in their quarters, and six hundred junkers in
the street . . . Were they afraid? . . . No, even on the front they hadn't
been afraid . . . So why on earth would they fight for apartments,
just to piss away the purity of their souls? They hadn't yet hit upon
fascism—only a white dream with one of Tolstoy's commandments
in their pocket. They were beaten because they didn't fancy organiz-
ing a systematic, mass terror in the rear and instead, hysterically, just
like petty criminals, shot the men one by one, driving them mad,
incapable of instilling fear . . . Whereas fascism is a systematic terror, an iron grip, a firm belief in one's own animal right . . . I wonder,
though, what will come of the Bolsheviks. After all, there is nobody
left to free, to save . . . The old world has been finished off, and, if only
for the sake of those executed millions, I just wish that something
would come of it . . . Ah, they'll learn . . . The first tractor will not

work... The third and fourth will wind up in a ditch... And only by the tenth will they succeed in plowing up Russia, if goodwill, youth, and unlimited prospects remain. But then, the Russian people can be so cruel... Was it not the tsar himself who terrorized the Jews and burned the schismatics? For is the tsar not the people, the people in a crown? Has the Tartar not always terrorized and burned the people of Russia, ripping their bellies open in delight, particularly those of women?... I myself know, for I am Tartar, chekist, policeman, fanatic, rapist... I am both tsar and regicide. I've tied women's skirts above their heads and set them running about the village... I've languished in jails, found sanctuary in hermitages... I've murdered doctors, buried myself alive in the earth, torched barns, sung with gypsies, painted icons and, *entre nous*, there is no such thing as individuality, it's all for sake of ease, scant at that, but within me, everyone and everything—that is, no, not everyone and everything, but all the people and all of Russia—yearn, talk, smoke, pray, grovel, and steal lip pencils... But here everything is foreign to me. I am like unto a dirty root torn out of the earth, a tramp, a spectator, a great glass eye on two and a half legs.

■ □ ■

Crazed, exhausted, not quite himself, Oleg paid Tania a visit. Now he wanted to hide away in her pale-blue room, to revive himself, to rest his morals before falling asleep. To nestle, to nuzzle, to snuggle up to her so that in his field of vision there should be nothing other than her hot tawny shoulder, her face, her body. Triumphant, but inwardly ready to burst into tears, clutching to reality and decency with the very last of his strength, Oleg took the lift to the fifth floor and, as he did so, imagined how he would sit down in the chair in a new, serious way, without playing games, without fawning or larking nervously and theatrically about, and how at last he would master the rhythm of that perfectly adult, equally divided life, in which it was possible to spend a whole day with a loved one in silence yet still not to lose spiritual contact with them, never ceasing to converse with one's eyes, gestures, and the expression on one's face. The peace, the repose of beings having forsaken their heavens voluntarily: that is the noble splendor of a life dominated by the sun.

He pondered all this, but in fact, after his first encounter with the remorseless struggle for existence, he wanted nothing more than to feel a soft, cold maternal hand touch his face. Comfort and repose . . . He felt like crying.

But as soon as he entered the room, he sensed with horror that he would have to force himself to laugh and joke all evening. He found Tania's cousin Gulja, a sweet, approachable creature with dyed hair, sprawled out with a cigarette on the divan, her enormous, kind, dewy eyes aglitter . . . Later, Tania would remark that Oleg had not mentioned his state of exhaustion. And, sure enough, he managed to put on a brave face and show off, recounting the fighting in the street, full of exaggeration, but all the while expecting, crying out for Tania to guess, to realize, to ask him to stop and catch his breath, whereupon he would have been relieved and only too glad to fall silent, to rest awhile, perhaps even to revive a little. But Tania, like any healthy individual for whom exuberance or its absence corresponds exactly to energy or fatigue, like anybody who knows nothing of the wild, excruciating exultation of sheer overwork, could tell none of this from Oleg's monotonously, hysterically raised voice. And since their threesome was a flop, she made the unfortunate suggestion of an outing to Montparnasse . . . Once again obeying, not daring, not able to resist, Oleg found himself sitting in the midst of a crowd whose words struck at his strained, frayed nerves, much as the sound of laughter and commotion assails an insomniac as he tosses and turns in his bed. Everything was cutting, tormenting, destroying him, and now, in a frenzy of morbid loquaciousness, he was made again to tell of his exploits, about which he lied shamelessly, weary and oblivious to the contradictions in his tale. Once again he had surrendered to her clumsy, inattentive love, although all evening he had felt, he had known that he ought to put up fight, that he would never forget this excruciating ordeal, nor that his love, from spite, exhaustion, and hunger, was about to slit its throat in this solitary confinement. As though in a drunken fog, in a terrible listlessness and enslavement of the will, Oleg got up to go to another bar with them, but all of a sudden, losing spirit and the ability to speak, he slumped back down like a wax figure, a corpse, a carcass, a log. He laughed softly, altered in the face, haunted and aged, so much that even Tania eventually noticed and sat down beside him, clumsily attempting to ask him what the matter was. So deep was his resentment, however, that in response he only sneered, pouting sullenly and rocking in time to the music like an imbecile. For a second, the terror of something irreparable clenched her drunken heart. She tried dragging him up to dance, but he refused. Confused and vaguely sensing that she had gone too far, she stood up, and, without saying goodbye to the others, she and Oleg set out into the rain.

In the street, upset and resentful, having long since passed his breaking point, Oleg carried on with his spiteful, hostile silence, having already slipped into the solitary, arsenic-bitter delight of self-pity. "That's right, go and throw it all away . . ." Now, sensing the pointlessness of questions, distressed to the point of heartache, gripped by the panic that something irreparable had happened, womanishly, foolishly, like a seal trying to play the piano, Tania was looking for a way out. Suddenly she stopped in the middle of the street, and all the money that Oleg had received for his labors, pitiful though it was, disappeared into the palm of a sleepy and disgruntled hotel maid, whom Oleg, expiring with regret for the vanishing money, for *his* money as she bore it off downstairs, could not bring himself to tip. In the room, which assaulted Oleg with the diabolical vulgarity of its scarlet checkered wallpaper, with all the unfathomable metaphysical humiliation of the hotel's nothing and nobody, they both, breathing heavily from all the wine that they had consumed, lay down on the bed without bothering to remove their shoes. Then something quite unimaginable and unbearable began, something that was so desperately and painfully apparent to Oleg.

After the nervous ascent, the weariness, the sorrow, the fury, after nobody's having helped or understood him yet again, after having to manage on his own strength, that deathly clarity, that merciless optical definition of complete emptiness suddenly retuned to Oleg... His and Tania's bodies seemed to him like two corpses in an anatomical theater, and he could hear their crazed, drunken conversation from across the room. For, barely alive though he was, urged on by the time-honored atavism of male vanity, Oleg tried to conform, tried to stir himself, to make a show of befitting passion, although at that very moment he wanted nothing more than to go home, to lie down on the divan with his face to the wall, to drink a cup of tea and read the *Latest News*. For the first time, his body seemed to obey, yielding to this grossly unnatural game, but then all of a sudden it renounced this obedience and the game entirely. Because, you see, Oleg's body did not comply with any localized arousal. "He's such a strange man," Tania had observed in her diary. "He gets aroused by laughter, happiness, conversations, even by his own tears." And indeed, Oleg's desire to kiss, to caress, to touch, and to have sex was born of some mysterious game of fortuitous, musical collusion, irrespective whether tragic or comic. He recalled how he had been so struck by Leo Savinkoff's remarkable lines: "The straw did rustle underfoot. You turned to me, my dove: 'We'll build ourselves two houses: one right here, one high above.' " Oleg never knew exactly which of these was to be built first, but he did know that he needed both of them. That way, like an athletic angel trying out new wings, his life could make the journey from heaven to earth and from earth back up to heaven with dizzying speed. And so it was that a beautifully worded phrase, a correctly, realistically, delicately expressed abstract feeling, could elicit in him momentary gratitude, and the spark of excitement that followed would suddenly, instantaneously grow into a wild desire for kisses and physical possession, whereas vulgarity and stupidity would provoke physical alienation. And so, while he was, as it were, inherently made for it, he almost never managed to live with someone physically without his heart's being clouded by that same wild impetuousness that was so thoroughly characteristic of him. How well he understood the ancient melancholic who wrote: *omne anima post coitum triste est.*[5] For as soon as the balance was disturbed, as soon as the physical outweighed the moral by even a single grain on the apothecary's scales, a knife would twist in his heart. How many times had he cursed himself, spat in disgust, growled with impotent rancor, unable to be absolved or calmed by a brief kiss, despising

---

* Every soul is sad after sex. (*Latin*)

himself for the fact that his own savage atavistic pride would make him hold someone's palm in his own for an extra minute or prolong a kiss a moment more, although all the while his internal fire alarm, his tocsin, was ringing, warning him that all this was unnecessary, that it was too much, that it would burn him . . . Hence, he always knew when to stop, and yet never did, not from passion, no, but from some humiliating sense of sexual decorum. That night especially, his soul, striking against the ice of life so painfully and with such force, ricocheting like a billiard ball, suddenly soared high up into the icy Apollonian firmament, so high in fact that it disappeared for hours, talking and laughing with God, before gradually returning, thawing back to life—but Tania understood none of this. And, like an animal, believing in the intoxicating, sexual magic of the forest, she spent a long while gesticulating with her eyes closed in the perfect emptiness of his icy vision. If only she had known how foolish she looked from the 330,000-foot altitude of Oleg's wrath . . .

Deliberately saying nothing, Oleg sat perfectly still atop a table, from which, as though from Mont Blanc, he looked down, despising Tania's heavy, graceless body. She was getting dressed in front of the mirror, shamelessly and with a childlike innocence, without any attempt at modesty, still persevering, still half-wittedly flirting, just as she had done back then in the south, when he had babbled on, lost his head and gestured comically and to no avail, like an ocean wave breaking noisily and pointlessly upon the rocks. He gazed down from the table upon a whole world of love, from the height of his angelic disgust on a whole world now made disgusting, lost forever, without any remorse . . .

This is what I loved . . . The very thing, a mound of healthy, sun-kissed flesh dressing itself coquettishly in front of a mirror—still without a dress, held together by all that grossly elaborate feminine rigging: a girdle for the stockings, a contraption for the breasts—and all tattered, threadbare, mended, uncomfortably, unconscionably, unwearably worn.

It took a long while before Tania noticed, before she spotted, beneath the feigned look of tenderness that began on the very surface of his eyes, another one, rarely shown, calm, cruel, diurnal, emerging from the very depths of those pupils, which were now so mercilessly and unflinchingly trained on her. All of a sudden, their eyes met in the mirror. Oleg had no time to check himself, and the blow was so powerful that Tania, in the classical pose of Susanna before the Elders, covering her temptations with her palms, turned to Oleg with a look of surprised bewilderment.[6] There was something absurd about her, like a statue that had been dressed up in a threadbare *dessous.** And although Oleg averted his gaze momentarily, his curious stillness persisted.

Notwithstanding his complete lack of character in matters of the heart, this was in fact a typically and dangerously aristocratic trait of his ("The lower you bow, the higher you rise . . ."), the ability to bolt out of bed instantly amid a fierce cold and to grow, fiercely, frigidly, three heads taller, to turn suddenly from a monkey, a tapir, a bear, a crocodile into a deer, a tiger, a hawk.

Oleg continued to say nothing, but now Tania spoke. She mumbled, tripping desperately over her words while she anxiously, haphazardly, hastily, hurriedly set about trying to fix her golden thatch of hair, which was flying out in all directions.

---

* underwear (*French*)

Oleg made no accusations, no arguments, as he tried to fob her off with a morose half-smile. Helplessly, shamelessly, having lost all sense of proportion, Tania's malaise was now thrashing about in his quizzical ears, just as he had once prattled on, vainly and gratuitously, in front of her. And this is what I loved for so long . . .

A terrible, icy, unearthly, angelic rancor filled his heart . . . "Why didn't you say something? . . ." Was she really that obtuse? Dragging a corpse to a bar like that . . . When all's said and done, how slow she is, how stupid, how ploddingly unimaginative, how like an animal . . . How little she has of that limpid mountain air, that Luciferian veneer, that unattainability. A child-bearing cow, then, a Don Juan with a cow's udder . . . Oh, to smack her a couple of times right in that fat face of hers . . . No, Oleg, the time for that, too, has passed. The urge to strike and argue is no more . . . Like those dull-witted, angelic animals, like cherubim, those cows with wings, she simply does not see, hear, or seek out that ever-present pain . . . Let her fall into another man's cruel arms; he'll show her what for . . . No, Oleg, she won't even notice her own despair, she'll grow fat, she'll grow as dumb as livestock, get married to some canny flaxen-haired youth who understands all of this and knows how to behave; she'll give birth, wake up and embark on life, like a she-wolf, a heifer, a mare, knee-deep in dung, in life . . . No matter how you try, you'll never pull, never dig, never uproot her from it. Even now, her roots go a good five yards down into the earth . . . Having lived her life above the abyss so naively, like a sacred cow, never having felt giddy or lightheaded, she'll suddenly slip, one fine evening when she's older, into such deathly despair that she'll outdrink all the seasoned drinkers, or else will never know her own despair, never dare to understand it, and will grind to a halt, growing fatter still among cards, books,

charities, and all that contemptible, swinish, pig-penned life. But as
for you, Oleg... Go now, like a planet torn form the sun's gravity, and
soar upon that dizzying path of wilderness and doom, of legendary
superhuman mortality, on the streets, driven mad by the speed, the
emptiness, the freedom... For it is good to flirt and be high-handed
with the fairer sex while your locks tumble down and there is still a
ringing in your ears from all that unruly blood, but when the bandit's
fervor begins to pale and unravel, who then will have need of you,
a bald-headed superman in worn-out shoes, like Christ walking on
the water... But she would have warmed, eclipsed the unbearable
world, like a statue, a monument to freedom, slavery, dreams, sweet
nothingness... But then no, you don't marry your own mother, do
you, you narrow-shouldered weakling with an Oedipus complex?
How strange her body was—jaundiced, cumbersome, so like an
animal... What was it exactly that I loved about it? After all, it had
so few secret passages, and not one of them interesting... All this
makes the heart pine, makes it throb, makes it pound ardently and
sweetly. My dumbbell cannot do that... It just lies at home under the
divan, my heavy, taciturn, metallic friend, my cool, steadfast Bactrian
of iron, my ship of the desert, of life, of sin, of boredom... If only I
no longer had to dress, to shave, to rush off somewhere and spend
money, no longer got aroused or humiliated myself as I stole past the
doorman... Enough! Enough of these legs, these thighs, this ginger
hair that smells of hay, the insults, the tears, the terror... Enough,
enough... Now out into the street, into the rain, to freedom, to your
unknown brethren as they walk by, each of them like you, having
suffered and wept, having abased himself and therefore ardently, bitterly understanding you as he rushes into the abyss of time on worn-
out heels, and therefore a hundred times better than she... Yes, I'm

a degenerate, a sycophant, a lapdog, a lavatory graffitist, but I'm also a Christian. Hear that, you beast? A Christian . . . And so on and so forth in that same vein, with a furious, blunt, naïve, mechanical disgust for this sexual being that was driving his psyche. It was as plainly unjust now as it had been back then in the south, when Oleg had marveled at another such blind mechanism, one that idolized and convinced Tania of her extraordinary, occult virtues, known only to Oleg . . . She had been strange and unattainable even then, but now she was strange still and loathsomely dull . . . And as soon as the door slammed shut with its familiar metallic grunt—once so deafening and heart-rending, now scarcely noticed—Oleg filled to brim with great, ferocious, icy pride and made his way to Montparnasse . . . The exhaustion had vanished. The entire world was swathed in night, and night dwelt within his heart . . .

■ □ ■

With each step, something soft, warm, and pitiable broke inside him. Work? . . . Me, work? . . . Can it be that hippogriffs, unicorns, and leviathans work? . . . And sure enough, a cruel and wicked sense of exaltation re-entered his heart. The nervous fatigue, the deplorable, nervous fatigue of melancholy, evaporated. He breathed deeply and squared his shoulders, and his steps regained a certain bounce . . . Now the occasional nighthawk passing by would look at Oleg with a strange estimation and even avert his gaze upon meeting those severe eyes made wide by the delight of the nocturnal desert, whereas only that evening everybody in the Métro had turned away from him in disgust . . . No, you're not cut out for Christianity . . . There's still too much fiery, icy, Luciferian blood inside you, an astral chill that, like unto iron in the freezing cold, burns like fire. After grimly combing his hair in a street mirror, Oleg found himself at the doors of the Café Napoli, standing tall and handsome, savagely, tearfully delighting in the bright artificial glare of the red neon lights. But just as he was about to step inside, with much laughter and drunken embraces, a whole brassy, beggarly, elegant throng—his band of poetic souls— descended upon him.

There was Katia, Gulja, Alla, Okolichine, Ouvaroff, and Lola Hayes, that elegant, slender-armed, imperious, impetuous, black-eyed temptress, whose chiseled Arab nose swept high over everything. Now Oleg found himself reveling in the night, the speed, the particular coquettishness of people riding in a motor car, in the particular combination of good nature and haughtiness with which they surveyed pedestrians. He joked with Okolichine leisurely, confidently, with the studied immobility of a sponger whose manners recall those of a learned soldier, and even his voice changed. He sunk lower, grew calmer, slower, more sober, more acerbic, relishing the weight of his heavy paw as it rested assuredly on the sleek maroon side of the vehicle, while up ahead, on the other side of the broad windscreen, a whole jolly world was gesticulating mutely, shouting something to them but receiving no answer, and pulling faces in the half-light of the car.

How pleasant it was to participate, to partake, to be accepted by this brazen, melancholy company as one of their own, to speed along in a motor car, to joke and to philosophize with an air of superiority. At times darkened by artificial sorrow (but only insofar as the fashion dictated), at others positively beaming with those dazzling white teeth of his (repaired for free by a Russian lady-dentist, a patron of émigré poetry) . . . It was as if he were being aided by heaven knows what good fortune, confidence, and station in life. And indeed, he was fortunate, for he held fortune in contempt; his was the athletic madness of sheer arrogance, arrogance that mocked life, station, and assurance. "They like you because you play to their basest instincts," Tania had once told him through gritted teeth, partly out of jealousy, since she herself had never quite succeeded in ingratiating herself with them. And of a truth, Oleg had here several never-consummated flirtations, for when he disappeared, cloud-like, into his own wilderness, where he would cast off his worldly identity with all its graces, he would forget them entirely, and it seemed that if were he to meet Alla or Gulja in the path of his blazing, beetle-browed march to the library, he would not greet them, nor would he be quite understandably embarrassed, like an ancient mythological creature exposed in its own divinity. But aside from the latest literary gossip and the newly discovered luster of his teeth, he almost instantly unearthed, strange though it may seem, a genuine liking for Gulja and Lola Hayes; in his half-inebriated, half-sober head, he knew well how to insert himself into a half-cut woman's heart. He laughed and made excuses: "I didn't vanish anywhere," "I was thinking about you the whole time . . ." But unbeknownst to all these café-dwellers, his laughter obscured the sobering shadow of a rocky alpine landscape, and several of the company, vaguely sensing a wolf in sheep's clothing, half envying him, half disgusted by him, watched his head of unruly locks with the characteristic sorrow of retired angels, doubting him and admiring his dissimulation. He could be openly rude, but then, in the blink of an eye, you would find him dancing, holding Lola close and even kissing her perfumed temple—right there, where with all the midnight dreariness of his soul he still knew how to experience, how to appreciate something amorally, in a purely musical way, but he also lacked for nothing, loved nobody, and, as a consequence, could not relate well; for as soon as love, which is to say life itself, seeps out, like blood, then, he knew only too well, you can bid farewell to a gay old time, for love's sole law, far harsher than the Lynch law, is: "learn to inflict pain at any cost." He knew how to place himself beyond the reach of authority and dependency, beyond that eternal, undying, awe-inspiring rancor and strife that lovers share . . . And as he merrily, grimly, insolently kissed the ladies' hands, literally standing on ceremony and forcing everyone else to stand, he was forever scandalizing everyone and forever being forgiven by Alik, who as dawn approached, when the glow of morning cast its azure blight upon their faces, turned suddenly to some dark-eyed ascetic statue, with whom matters had grown serious . . . He truly knew how to live on the very brink of depredation and moral prostitution without ever crossing the line, rescued eternally by stipends, loans, and his government allowance. A professional beggar, an eau-de-cologned hermit without a single adventure to his name, at times it seemed to him that he had genuinely been cursed by fate, that he was destined never to find work or a path in life. But beyond the invisible wall of his peripatetic monastic cell, an unselfish and frugal angel in the person of Fiodoroff, that dole-subsisting pen-pusher, would never leave him without a prison ration of lentils and cheap seasonal eggs on the table. "But to what end is she protecting me?" Oleg mused, at a loss as he examined his mighty arms in the mirror. "After all, all this rustic, masculine beauty will fade." And suddenly it struck him: it was so ridiculously apparent that God loved him, envied him his heavy blood too much to leave him to his own devices. God has chosen you from among the most beautiful in His monastic harem, and is that not the source of this unprecedented, downright puckish display of manhood, arguing with those you love?

As the nocturnal cold of the spring air fanned Oleg's burning face, the American motor car traveled at a terrific speed, whistling past lights, lights, lights. At the crossroads, the cafés seemed toylike, and the people in them simple automatons, doomed to their wretched lots. With a look of instinctive, jealous respect, one by one they met Oleg's cool, malicious eyes, which had grown suddenly impertinent, to the point of angelic serenity.

After passing Les Invalides, the bridge, the river, the Champs-Elysées, after skirting around the Arc de Triomphe with a squeal of the breaks, the car accelerated down the avenue Foch; the hour was late, and the police were nowhere to be seen. At the Porte Dauphine, the steel mount very nearly sped right into a tree; for a moment, the headlights brightly illumined a bench and some flowerbeds, and then row upon row of naked trees in the Bois de Boulogne began to emerge fantastically from the darkness, rushing with tremendous speed toward the white beams before vanishing again behind them. In order to miss a passing car, Lola had to cut the headlamps; lit by a beam of oncoming light, they went hurtling past, squeezing their eyes tightly shut, before the road flashed up ahead once again. And high above there were stars—enormous spring stars . . .

The car stopped, and while the well-oiled lot conferred among themselves, a nightingale began to sing mysteriously and drearily somewhere nearby; it droned, thundered, and chirped out its aria before falling silent again. But soon the car set off again, and once more trees began to rush past.

In the end, everyone got out at the Pont de Suresnes, and, calling to one another in the dark, they picked their way through the wet grass as far as the embankment. They crossed a gangplank over the black water and onto a darkened barge, a former floating restaurant, where there appeared to be no signs of life. But no sooner had they piled downstairs than the twanging strains of a gramophone greeted them.

A vast saloon with plush sofas lining the walls was bathed in the dusky gold of candlelight; people were dancing, and in the back of the room, behind a crude makeshift bar, flat Mongolian faces were pouring red wine.

Oleg lingered with his well-heeled company for a moment or two, but then he abandoned them, and drunkenness ensued at the bar.

■ □ ■

Darkness; all the lights are out, and up above the river's murk a gypsy voice goes ringing out: "Shall e'er we meet again? How quickly, with a weight so sweet, the wine flowed through my veins, how fleeting was the happiness, how desolate the day."

"With tripping dance, with rhythm quick, are woes forgot till morning come. Who art thou, tender friend of chance? How cold thy lips, and numb. Not daring, hesitating now, above the water's mirror face, another leans, a burning cheek now resting on its temple. And having overcome again the cold of life with heavy wine, the soul departs on heavy waves of wine and sorrow, love, and life."

But who is that you're kissing, Oleg? Was it not boredom that you just kissed so impatiently, to the point of boorishness? Why is it that the music, the darkness, the fragrance of hair, the dim glimmer of candles have merged again into a single, mute, heavy, happy ocean, an ocean toward which you drift unawares, fearlessly, having suddenly renounced fear itself, dashingly, desperately? And just who is this that you have in your embrace, who is it that you're embracing with your heavy arms, holding gently, firmly to you? Why yes, it's Katia . . . Wake up, Oleg. Why yes, it truly is Katia, wearing an argent jacket, resting her shiny, perfumed head on your shoulder. Katia, where have you come from? Are you really alive? Can it be that you still breathe, sing and dance? . . . Doesn't everything that we stop loving die, doesn't it disappear from the face of the earth, like dreams in waking? . . . Katia, Katia, whence have you come? . . . From Copenhagen . . . Whither are you going? . . . Onward, Oleg, onward, where life, another life, a new life is beginning . . . Forget those bygone days . . . Oleg forgot those bygone days. And all the more sweetly, in a new and unfamiliar way, her body, soft and warm, drew closer, pressing itself against him, at the mercy of some unknown regret, the enchantment of what can never be put aright. Oleg and Katia floated there for an instant, drifting from life's shore into a dark sea of gypsy music.

Days of sorrow rushed by, like the innumerable shadows cast by a flurry of snowflakes. Once more they had met in the abyss, the cold abyss of dreams and worldly cares. Rush and ring, O music, amid the noise; the air fills with lugubrious song, and for a brief moment happiness will chance to come. O Katia, Katia, our happiness is gone . . . Why, Oleg? No, certainly not gone yet! . . . Try your best to follow me . . . See, more will come of it than you yourself expect . . .

Oleg laughed. To be sure, something would come of it . . . They all wanted so desperately for something to come of their relationships, while all he wanted was to escape them . . . God in Heaven, who still believed in such happiness this late in the day, this late in the autumn of delusions . . . Hadn't all this vanished long ago, like those wooden booths suddenly taken in the night from the spot where only yesterday there stood a traveling fair? . . . What happiness can there yet be, when life, that seascape full of chirring pine trees, is suddenly shown to have concealed the rocky, iron chaos of a hermit's apocalyptic wilderness? Which is to say, his, Oleg's wilderness, that unwelcoming, cherished, smoke-filled cloister . . . He and Bezobrazoff, once again, without kin, without name, outside of history, alone in the world . . . Thérèse in a monastery . . . Averroes up in the sky . . .[7] Who could still be thinking of happiness, when the end of Oleg's world had already begun, when almost nothing now was left of the earth upon which Oleg, having sprouted a beard, had dreamed, plowed, smoked, relaxed on the doorstep, played with children, and in the evening, by a the light of kerosine lamp, had read to Tania his great unwanted works . . . An entire world of ancient bucolic nobility . . . Hadn't it vanished without trace already? Hadn't oblivion's blizzard gone swirling endlessly, everlastingly over the iron rails, the iron trees, the iron souls . . . Everything was snowy, everything was hopeless; who yet spared a thought for happiness? . . . Drunk, intoxicated by the music, never for a moment did Oleg forget the incandescent snowy wind of loneliness, the wilderness and sin. Something was now telling him to spin around, to cry, to kiss, to scrap, for the road ahead was long, infinite, without beginning and without end, from stars to stars. Joke, sing, kiss whomever you like, appreciating no one, growing fond of no one, respecting no one . . . Appreciating no one, valuing and respecting no one, Oleg grew more and more inebriated, hauling at Katia indecently, barging into people, broadening out his shoulders . . .

He grew cocky, drew attention to himself, and caused a terrible scene with his overfamiliarity. Katia offered no resistance, but she vanished somewhere after the dance ended, leaving Oleg looking for her for a long time. Later on, she emerged from the crowd, dancing with a short, swarthy man, whose face was energetic and Spanish-seeming. As soon as they had finished, Oleg made his way over to her, but, spotting him in fright, she once again went spinning in the sallow arms of this foreigner, this wild, illiterate, gifted singer and all-round decent chap. Blind fury began to stir in Oleg's heart, blind fury and ill intent—an especially tempting combination, since the gypsy was small and, in all likelihood, exhausted by sleepless nights . . . "Nice try, kiddo . . . You're too much of a coward to have eyes for a white Russian filly like this," Oleg repeated menacingly, biting his thick lips which were encrusted with the savor of cheap red wine. After losing sight of them again, he elbowed his way to the bar and there, for a whole half-hour, he launched into a sportsman's turgid, pitiful bluster, for both of the river's inhabitants—the waiter and the caretaker of this floating establishment—were stony faced, sinewy melancholics, veterans of Russian sport from the days of Sanitas and the Hercules club . . .[8] Oleg knew a thing or two, but when it came to other people, his answers were hit-and-miss: "Yes, you don't say, yes, of course, I know . . . We used to train together at Rassing . . ." Gradually he transformed into a Russian club champion, then into the émigré record-holder for the four-hundred-meter dash, and after that into a sports journalist. He lied, but not so much as to be caught out, for he mixed truth with falsehood . . .

Then suddenly he recollected himself and, by now utterly drunk, rushed off to find Katia, shoving people out of the way. He came across her soon enough, but she immediately announced, after looking him over, that she no longer cared to dance . . . Bewildered by this, Oleg retreated to the gramophone, when all of a sudden Katia—merry, drunk, flushed, and all the more grotesquely beautiful for being in the gypsy's embrace—sailed past him, laughing loudly and turning her back, ignoring him. Oleg's eyes met the piercing charcoal pupils of the horse thief, while the latter, in the frenzy of success, deliberately, provocatively, rudely triumphing over all this brawn, like a sober David over a drunken Goliath, said to him in passing: "Play it again, won't you? You saw how well we danced together."

Oleg's intoxicated blood rushed to his head . . . Just wait till I get my hands on him! "No, wait . . . I'll show you, pharaoh's tribe, just what I think of your smiling, elegant company. I'll show you just how much I need friends with a car, the literary patrons of Montparnasse. You think you've got the better of me? . . ." Suddenly, from his state of complete apathy, Oleg launched into blunt, savage, absolute action, lunging at and grabbing this Wallachian horse doctor by the collar, tearing him away from Katia with great felicity and, with all his might, punching him, sending him flying to the ground . . . Toppling over from his gnomelike height, the gypsy broke something as he landed; immediately there was a commotion and an outcry, the familiar, merry atmosphere of scandal, which, like a powerful drug, pushed Oleg over the edge. How he adored those precious seconds when a scandal was growing, maturing, becoming inevitable. How he loved the fear and delight, the determination to break the chains of human kindness, propriety, and respectability, the resolve to break away and burst in on all that is ancient, wild, cruel, and dreadful . . . Oleg was still shaking. A feeling of enormous pleasure was coursing through his arm: the still vivid sensation of another person's body and how, like an object, like a bag, a kettlebell, it had yielded and given way. And how often after a fight he loved to caress that aching and worthy hand of his . . . Having recovered from the initial shock and fright, the gypsy, now clinging to his honor, tried to launch himself at Oleg like a child, like a savage; held back by the crowd, he snatched theatrically at the empty pocket where he kept his gun, while Oleg taunted him rudely, cruelly, mercilessly, hurling some final words of profanity at him and finding one last, wild pleasure in transgressing life's rules of propriety. Then, like a wild animal, Oleg liberated himself from everything and everyone.

■ □ ■

Playing to the crowd, spouting off, peacocking, making a show of his own magnanimity, Oleg donned his jacket while rebukes and remonstrations rained down on him . . . The fresh air cooled his face . . . No sooner had he climbed up on deck than the muffled noise of the interrupted festivities disappeared entirely, and now in its place reigned the undisturbed tranquility of this desolate spot, the serenity of wastelands and backwaters. Day was breaking. The river, still beneath moving skies, glistened with a misty gray cobalt. Slowly through the dust of rain, distant bridges and the opposing bank, sluices, chimney stacks, and squat factory buildings came into view. Day was breaking with the vast, tranquil, unswerving generosity of its clear-eyed, dispassionate natural strength. Even before that spark of ferocious insanity (directed at Tania, of course, for, without even knowing it, it was she whom he had struck, thrown to the ground, and publicly disgraced), down below, through the heavy fog of alcohol, Oleg had noticed that the barge's low square windows had turned blue, without asking anyone, without concerning themselves with anyone, and the lights of the distant shore, having been completely extinguished, now glimmered in pale yellowish strips, mingling with the reflected glow of the dawn. The rain was barely noticeable and so fine that it did not fall so much as it was blown through the dusk of morning; it chilled the body and his intoxicated ardor suddenly shrank, creeping down to the tips, to the very extremities of his limbs, freeing his strangely clear head entirely . . . Through Oleg's energetic crimson face, which suddenly crumbled, melting in fatigue, like snow in water, another one surfaced, one that had never totally disappeared, the face of youth and helpless tenderness that had given Thérèse such a devastating shock . . . Now the memory of the day, which had been too long, too tortuous, awash with a thousand desperate outbursts of excitement and dejection, fire and fear, overflowed, spilled and floated downstream, breaking away from him. Everything that went together with Oleg, the seer of this dream, the hallucination and its hero, left his heart, like one long ice floe of shocks and waste. His soul had died and risen again, so that, were it not for the tremendous fatigue that he felt, it might have seemed as though he had read it all in a book—as after a full day of sweaty, stifling summer reading, when, with head disheveled, he would suddenly rouse himself from one of Dostoevsky's novels, and for a few seconds he would be unable to tell what time it really was, whether he had eaten, and what yet remained for him to do. Thus do memories, clumping together in groups, worlds, départements, divisions, thus do they cast off together from the shore. No sooner does the individual in those days, unable to withstand the shock, fall apart, or simply, abruptly change his course, than life goes off to seek new a new calling, breaking away not gradually, but all at once from this world of service with everything that is important, terrifying, and absurd in it, to go and abide with its melancholy comrades in misfortune and, moreover, with a special, temporary, professional personality, a mask. Just as after the last, irreparable argument and parting, the house, the street, all the acquaintances of a loved one, all the places where you went on a date, they all cast off, headed for the cold sea, so now, in a mere moment, Oleg's heart renounced his weary identity, and the cold essence of Monsieur Nonentity slowly emerged through the rain, like a distant shore though the last shadows of night.

Weak after the latest crazed outburst of nervous masculinity, suddenly haggard with shoulders slumped, he made his way across the bridge, unsteady on his feet . . . A well-oiled group of factory hands, their voices raise in Negro song, pinned him against the parapet, and one of them, with a cap worn at an improbably jaunty angle, so much that it was almost invisible behind his shock of hair, gaily, merrily, malevolently, threatened him: "*Alors, tu n'y vois pas clair, citoyen andouillard?*"* Oleg did not even respond; it did not even occur to him to respond, for he was, in a sense, enjoying himself.

By now the cold had calmed his soul, driven out the effects of alcohol and chilled his body. He turned up his collar and huddled from the rain . . . Standing in the shelter, he had to wait a long while for the tram. The bright, white day assailed his eyes. Figures flushed from the cold would greet each other amicably as they entered, exchanging a few incidental though always well-chosen words. The tram was running late. Desperate to warm himself, Oleg stood next to the door jamb, drifting farther and farther away, sinking. Everything that had happened over the course of that long spring seemed dead, distant, safe, and amazingly serene. Finally, like a warm carriage, trundling and shuddering, the tram rolled up, and at long last, ensconcing himself in a corner, Oleg dragged himself home.

---

* Can't you see straight, you prat? (*French*)

10

Slash and scrape, O aquiline nights, at the glow and radiance of fallen lights. The icy drowse, the dream of slumber's gauge. Learn not to live, but to revive, to thrive, to grow alive to life, to deprive the silent of the clarion's rays. There will be days like this, days much too long, too unembraceable for memory, which will become lost in their midst, as in a forest . . . Too much had happened in a single day, there had been too much unrest, too much joy, too many arguments, tears, humiliations, and triumphs. With glass in its nose, with a ringing in its ears, the soul had at last crawled as far as the shore of night and lain down to rest upon it, covering itself with a blanket, like the lid of a coffin, and closing its eyes. The heavy dawn was resting its head of azure upon the spring sky. Day was breaking as Oleg made his way homeward. They both of them went about their own dreary business. The day grew reluctantly bluer, while Oleg scratched at his strained crotch and through the fog tried to fall asleep in waking. But still, despite himself, he watched the world go by from a tabletop, wearily, satedly, hungrily, impassively. The day dawned brighter and brighter, but Oleg hid from it behind heavy eyelids. Even there, though, the day caught up with him and assailed his eyes. The first tram rolled by, ablaze with the fires of virtue, twilight, the easy conscience of those who work, freshened by water and sleep. Like a drunkard, Oleg scratched himself and rued, madly, bitterly, humiliatingly rued all the money that he had frittered away . . . He should have spent it on eggs, oranges, ice cream, and chocolate. How tenderly he yet loved himself, soothed and ensconced himself, in religion's rays. "And yet there is still something about you, something rotten, among the flowers of paradise," Bezobrazoff had once told him. And so the day was victorious, while Oleg capitulated, cowering from it, scuttling off, like a diseased crab, into nightmarish dreams.

Once again Oleg stirred from a whole year of blistering new torments, finding himself alert to a radiant cold, and this awakening blended perfectly with the onset of sleep; willingly, blithely, he let the dream go, releasing it from his hands and almost from his memory. Now it seemed as if he never had intended to provide himself with a family, an apartment, children. "*Je ne travaillerai jamais*"*—he would repeat Rimbaud's phrase, which had struck him so, as though fired at point-blank range.[1]

Oleg had the sense that God both feared him, appalled by his gallantry, and loved him as he was now, with an entirely different kind of love, one that was terrible and passionate, and not with the protective and peaceable one with which he had loved Oleg the married, the bearded, the reconciled to life, the mild-mannered and silent, the safe. No, it was the paladin, the celibate, the hermit, the prophet, the Lucifer that God loved in him, just as a great potentate loves the proudest, most beautiful maidens of his tribe, marking them out

---

* I shall never work. (*French*)

for his harem and for a long time struggling stubbornly with their metaphysical willfulness. He sensed a thunderous, steely cloud of divine jealousy over him, persecuting him, like Israel in the desert. Like the swan persecuting Leda, like the bull seducing Europa, like the golden cloud descending on Danaë.[2] Forsaking once again the wide and sweeping road, he embarked upon the rocky path of asceticism, chosenness, loneliness. His step was light on the scorching pavement; one minute more and he would cry out and start running toward God . . .

You thought, Oleg, that at last you could do without God, that you could repose yourself from His insatiable demands; but lo, it is He who has done without you . . . Behold, Nature is about to embark upon her sorrowful, short-lived summer glory, while you have been sleeping and, with a heavy head awash with the warm water of slumber, have been dreaming of a worldly, full-blooded, full-bearded life. Oleg, once again you have offended God; you have tried living without Him and have hit the ground face first— heavily, foolishly, like a clown. When at last you awoke from the pain, you looked around and saw that the trees were already in full bloom and spreading out their bright, plentiful new foliage . . . It is summer in the city, and here you are again, face to face with God, reluctantly, like a child who, wishing to hide from the Eiffel Tower behind a flowering bush in the Trocadéro gardens, takes another turn around the shrub and is instantly overtaken by the monstrous wrought-iron dancer taking up the entire sky. You try not to notice, but it hurts to look at the white sky and a heavy, sudoral sultriness weighs on your heart. Again, you find yourself on the open sea, in the open air, under an open sky covered with white clouds, in the intolerable, inexorable sight of God and sin. And you haven't the strength not to believe, haven't the strength to doubt, to despair cheerfully in a cloud of tobacco smoke, to settle your nerves with a daytrip to the cinema. The entire horizon is blindingly taken up by God, and in every minute detail, in every perspiring creature, again He is there. Your vision grows dim, and there is no shade to be found anywhere, for there is no home of one's own, but only history, eternity, apocalypse; there is no soul, no identity, no "I," no mine, but only, stretching from heaven to earth, the fiery waterfall of worldly existence, of becoming, of disappearing, where Katia and Tania and Apollon and I are but shadows, faces, and mysterious figures.

Why was it that you finally awoke from Katia and Tania, from that fairy-tale epic? Could you not go on living, could you no longer stand life? Or was it the result of weakness? . . . No, secretly you remained indifferent to everything, like a hand that cannot be crushed because it relents and folds in someone else's, only then to take up its original form again once the grip is loosed. That is why, in order to live, one must have faith and not condemn oneself for living, not run from God into materiality, but bear God in this waking life, carrying out and cementing everything through Him. But you: as soon as you envy, as soon as you hear words of sympathy, you give up at once your toilsome service and take to mocking God. "You see," you would say to Him, "how miserly, how uncommunicative, how tedious and severe You are . . . Just look, how much warmer, more tender, more attentive than You is this beast . . . This beast has replaced You." Having cast out his innate, customary harshness, Oleg melted, softened, numbed amid the empty pleasure of an eternal, everlasting holiday, the tender indulgences of mutual admiration, flirtatious, rustic witticisms, cigarettes, bananas, confections, cinemas, and kisses . . . He knew how to love only in falling away from God, incognito, as it were, and the love would pass like a drunken night as soon as the cool hangover of insult and resentment chilled the dawn air. He knew not how to admit God into his love, and he laughed greatly when people would tell him that in the peasant huts of Old Believers, the woman would draw a black curtain over the icon before having sex.[3] Yes, how remote it is from blessed congress by the light of a menorah on a blessed Sabbath night, with the reading of a special prayer during *viris introductio* . . .* He knew not how to love piously, strictly, austerely, sharing his God slowly with a beloved. No, he sooner ran from God when in love, and, as he returned to Him, cursed his flight as a shameful weakness and a most grave offense, the bitter aftertaste of obsequious neglect and cringing stealth, like that of elders with spoiled children. Confusion, bewilderment, and deceit lingered on in the hearts in which his disheveled countenance had lived awhile . . . "It's the Pole in him, such a gentle and reserved nature," Tania would later say, before lapsing into a heavy silence as she took a long and sorrowful look at the past.

■ □ ■

Oleg had slept for two days straight, and so on the morning of the third, having slept disgracefully long, to the point of pain in his head and in his heart, to the point of lassitude throughout his entire body, he awoke well before the sun and, lying there naked on the divan, listened with a rare sense of surprise and perplexity to the crowing

---

* penetration (*Latin*)

of a cockerel and birdsong . . . "How can it be that there are so many of them in the city?" he wondered as he rubbed his aching shoulders. Outside he could hear the jaunty rhythms of footfall. Sunday morning had begun early for the cyclists, excursionists, and other artists of the feet who had already found time to shave and walk down to the municipal shower with a comb and a sliver of soap in their back pocket; it is too late now for those who decided to carry on dozing, basking in the idleness of a week worked off, to walk down to the market and return with a whole flowering garden in their new oilcloth bag. And he too—for himself, for God—fancied washing and dressing himself, and neatly, slowly combing his clean, wet head. "Unlike you, I cannot conceive of loneliness and so am forced to live obtusely, foolishly, in eternal anticipation of some rendezvous, and in eternal loathing of myself for the fact," Tania had once written to Oleg . . . "Do you think it is easy?" he smiled, satisfied and sorrowful as he registered her hatred. And so, Oleg was now alone once again. Alone and face to face with the searing white sky of loneliness. And from the moment he woke, he would have to recommence his battle with ennui. "Be stronger, harsher, colder," he would tell himself. "*Sois dur, dur, dur,*"* he would whisper through gritted teeth as he lifted a cast-iron kettlebell and squeezed out of his soul, as though from a freshly laundered shirt, the muddy water of sorrow. Be insensitive, be hard, be a stone dressed in a lounge suit, dare at last to take on that stony finality, the irrevocable design of things.

Venturing out with a light tread, with all his muscles tensed, on tiptoes, Oleg found that everything was already bright, quiet, and

---

* Be tough, tough, tough. (*French*)

uniform in that summertime, Sunday way, and he recalled the lines
written by his god:

A quatre heures du matin, l'été,
Le sommeil d'amour dure encore.
Lentement l'aube évapore
Le parfum des soirs fêtés.[*,4]

Almost everybody was still asleep, happily asleep, having finished
work and borne their money off to a savings bank, or to a bar, asleep
behind closed shutters, behind closed eyelids, deep in the depths of
vivid and meaningless early-morning dreams of sun-dappled eros.
Crumpled bedsheets gathered at their feet, their legs outspread, their
swollen organs exposed. But now, in the weary stupor of summer
slumber, they came together in sweet, irrevocable congress, spilling
that hot, quick-flowing liquid as they sweated and kissed each other
gratefully, before suddenly growing limp and lying down again on
the bed to rest for another brief hour and a half.

Alone amid the silence, purity, and brilliance of a summer's day
being born, Oleg wandered aimlessly and without compunction,
gazing up at the boundless azure of the sky. Young trees were shimmering brightly in the sun. No longer the chestnuts of those bygone
Bezobrazoff days, under which Oleg's youth had cowered from the
rain and eaten ice cream with eyes wide with wonder (ice-cream
eyes). In that torrid year of 1934, Paris had arrayed itself in the fashionable growth of poplars (for its Maupassantesque chestnuts had

---

[*] At four o'clock on a summer's morning, / the sleep of love still lasts. / Slowly the first light
evaporates / the perfume of festive nights. (*French*)

suddenly withered all at once, asphyxiated by the reeking clouds of gasoline), and above them, across the tall viaduct, glided the brand-new locomotive of the metropolitan, turning at full pelt, its green lizard's side gleaming in the sun; meanwhile, standing on the other side of the viaduct, sharply silhouetted by the azure, were little houses and villas whose palisades abutted the towering vertical edifice of a gray skyscraper, the top of which was, to the right, level with the tall billowing chimney of a prewar factory.

His shoulders squared, baked by the sun, Oleg walked beneath the viaduct, between the light and dark columns, like a masonic novice between Yakîn and Boaz.[5] He stepped into a tobacconist's and, while the owner was trying to find his change, he gazed from the counter at the sunny reflections of a still-empty café, where the freshly washed floor, covered in crimson linoleum, was casting a festive and serene damask light back up at the ceiling. Past the observatory and the hospitals, Oleg began to encounter those first Sunday pedestrians, and so commenced a happy, innocent, endlessly fascinating summer's duel with their glances.

■ □ ■

Everything in Oleg's life was weighed according to what he dubbed poverty or luxury, absolutely everything, save for the poverty and luxury of money. Despite himself, however, poverty still seemed shameful, whereas luxury was noble, natural, divine . . . Poverty was a sin, retribution, impotence, whereas luxury was like unto a kingdom in which everything reflects, extends, embodies the slightest flutter of the Almighty's eyelashes. Nevertheless, Oleg stoically, heroically managed to realize his life, setting it free in spite of the poverty, the constraints and the obscurity of his underground lot. Having received no education, he wrested one, his posterior growing numb from sitting on uncomfortable benches, from well-thumbed, miserably lit library books. Being anemic and emaciated, through abstinence and the drudgery of daily wrestling with iron weights, he wrung from life cupola-shaped shoulder muscles and an iron grip. Being ill-favored in looks and unsure of himself, through diabolical solitude, all-knowingness, and the valor of his asceticism, he acquired that bright, wolflike ocular mechanism that inclined, that subjugated (often to his amazement) female heads so radiant with youth and beauty. For Oleg, like all ascetics, was uncommonly attractive—and his ugliness, his rudeness, and his assuredness only heightened his charisma. Life had denied him everything, and so he had created everything for himself, reigning and enjoying himself now among the invisible fruits of his fifteen-year labors; thus, in conversation, he would calmly and artfully radiate the universality of his knowledge, which amazed his audience as much as did the ease with which, while sitting on a divan, he could lift and toy with a thirty-kilo kettlebell, or a chair that he could hold horizontally by its back, while he laughed at the bleak, lifeless, non-ascetic, mawkish, faithless Christianity of the Parisian émigré poets. "Death is one of God's perfect accomplishments, *un des luxes de Dieu,** and perhaps His most dazzling, for the artist does not suffer to hold in his hand a single thing that is atrophied, broken, early spent. God is the luxury that is the saints' joyous reward, but so too is He the unique genius of hell's torments for sinners. He is both the brilliance of the flame and the fury of destruction rained down on everything that has betrayed

---

* one of God's luxuries (*French*)

life; He is the sacred dawn silence of a soul calmed at night by the acceptance that love is perfect joy." Poverty alone seemed to him irreligious, undivine, shameful. The poverty of health and temperament, the frailty of sexual dissipation. The poverty of an idle mind. The poverty of cold, inimical blood. "And he that hath not, from him shall be taken even that which he hath," he often liked to quote Paul.[6] Deeming the taint of sexual dissipation to be more shameful than oblivion and death: "O death, thou miracle of Divine artistic integrity, what would become of us if He did not have the courage to deprive of life all these sexual deviants, these café writers without purpose or pride?"

Thus, one against all, on the sunny side of the street, Oleg performed his impeccable rhythmic dance. Before the azure ark that was the morning sky, rolling up the sleeves of his vest to the point of obscenity, he walked aimlessly with an uncommonly jolly, proud expression on his dull, misshapen, suntanned Slavic face, battling the astonished passersby with his eyes, for here, in this act, concluded his recompense, his pain and ugliness, the crumbling mountain, the delusion of grandeur from which he plunged, exhausted after having behaved in the most despicable of ways, headlong down into the blue ravine of a persecution complex. As a lion at a bull, Oleg threw himself from his seventh-story height at the dejected souls of the students in Saint-Michel, degraded by the ennui of summer. Yet his victory failed to light up the sky, to set his breath free, to lighten his step; rather, it tied him painfully, ineluctably to those passersby, and, having squandered, frittered away his nervous energy, having wearied prematurely and lost his grip on reality, he suddenly diminished in height, blackened in the face to the point of unrecognizability, and looked around pathetically, abjectly, cringing with a lost expression.

The natural reaction of a nature that constantly strove to restore balance, his persecution mania bent him double, after which Oleg paid ten times over for all his diabolical adventures. Having incautiously, imprudently broken his natural "democratic" isolation—beyond which, as though under a glass ceiling, every soul goes about its own business peaceably, judging, mocking, taunting others with looks alone—Oleg crawled along, trying at times to hide behind his hands, judged by all, humiliated, tormented pathologically, nervously, at the mercy of each and every passerby. The desire to wield power turned into servitude and self-effacement—and thus his whole life would he roam from insolence to obsequiousness, from boorishness to flattery, lavishing affections on one-half of his acquaintances while pouring scorn on the other. But that was a thing of the past now. Taught by a thousand horrors, Oleg, on this serene Sunday in April, walked not among the people, but apart from them, a thousand miles away from opinion and thralldom, repeating to himself as he went: "*Sois, dur, dur, dur* . . . The sin of asceticism has isolated you, and you no longer know anything of these lives, whereas each of them, over the towering wall of your ignorance, is Christ Himself in patent-leather shoes. But you do not see this, for you cannot see past the shoes . . . You are shackled by the pitch darkness of sin, you walk as a blind man among a thousand searchlights, before the chaos of angels and elephants of the Apocalypse. Seek not, therefore, to reward anybody with what he may deserve. You are not a worker, and there is no need to play the learned Bolshevik, *il ne faut pas accepter ce rôle,** the one offered you by this burly digger in navy trousers; you are neither a Catholic nor an artist, neither a poet nor a writer, for all these are

---

* you must not accept this role (*French*)

but surrogates for your ascesis; you are a religious one-of-a-kind, but your religiosity is demonic and cursed, *tu es un damné, un monstre, un hors-la-loi, grandiose et archaïque, mais prends ton parti de toi-même et gravis ton chemin avec une folle obstination de semihumain.*[*] Do not attack and do not retaliate, do not do violence and do not incur it, dance your destiny with absolute precision and serenity, fated only unto yourself, understood only by yourself, for better, for worse." And so Oleg donned his jacket in order to cover up his muscularity and pass unnoticed through the crowded place.

■ □ ■

Speeding past him, spinning as though on a merry-go-round, motor cars skirted the Arc de Triomphe, while high above a dazzling fleet of clouds sailed by more slowly, radiantly, majestically, as the young new poplars stretched up to meet them, rustling in the spring sunlight. Oleg was sitting to the right of his dignified friend, the unknown soldier, and they both of them kept their counsel: Oleg, staring at life as it gaily and noisily rushed by; the latter, toppling back into a black-winged abyss of peace and eternal justice. Some young foreigners dismounted bicycles fitted with luggage racks and photographed the arc and the two of them as they competed in immobility with the stone bas-reliefs. He loved to sit there, exhausted, basking in his long, steady perambulation which followed the asphalt and his ideas in tandem—from his pitiful, aching regret at Katia's departure, to his absolute stoic acceptance of his fate. Get close, he would tell

---

[*] you are damned, a monster, an outlaw, spectacular and archaic, but make peace with yourself and tread your own path, with all the desperate obstinacy of a half-man (*French*)

himself, take on the form of your fate, just as lips take on that of the bronze statue that they kiss. Having divined your fate, mimic it alone, learn from it alone. You, unknown soldier of Russian mysticism, inscribe your occult-black revelations, rewrite them on a typewriter and, having made of your ream a neat stack, place it on the steps by the front door and let the spring wind scatter them, bearing them away and, perhaps, carrying a few pages to future souls and times, while you, athletic author of an unpublished apocalypse, rejoice in your fate. You are one of those who have been cast aside, who continue to grow stubbornly like grain under snow, who will perhaps be deemed worthy to enter the ark of a new world flood—a world war. An ark that is now being built in Montparnasse; but should the flood come too late, you shall perish. But this too you shall bear with equanimity, just as you have accepted and borne the loss of your happiness and that of your works, which languish in absentia . . . Wait and gather up the sun's energy; perhaps you too shall be poisoned with gases, and only after death, in other worlds, in such familiar worlds of dazzling dreams and nightmares, all your pent-up golden strength will ignite and explode . . . This life . . . Its meaning lies in recompense . . . When you look at yourself, do you not see that you too set out with an utter lack of respect for the opinions of others, with an instinctive disregard for the freedom of others, with religious intolerance, with spiritual cruelty? In previous lives or in the body of your forefathers, you yourself banished, carried out executions because of creed and burned manuscripts; because of blinding spiritual hatred, you held yourself to be revenger, judge, fate, and now, forced by destitution into a monastery, you find yourself once again fettered in your cloistered cell of unprintability and obscurity . . . Your time shall come only when a completely destroyed world has to be built anew, for man concerns himself with the spirit reluctantly and as a last resort, and only through despair can he be turned toward the Divine and His mediums, or else everything will be postponed until the life to come. Think only: "Would your spirit have endured another fate, another life, one based not on the blind rejection of incarnation, manifestation, realization, not on hand-outs, unprintability, poverty, and emigration, but on fame, happiness, money, and power? . . . Is it not too early for you to think about this, you who so often in the blink of an eye have betrayed your golden city for a single quiver of rose-bright lips, for the slick radiance of a beautiful, perfumed head? Were it not for the revolution, you would now be, at thirty-one years of age, an old, dissolute, unloved, clapped-out writer, and there would be nothing intense, nothing ascetic or electric, nothing pleasing to God about you . . . The spirit, like an electrically charged thundercloud, would not soar eternally above your wilderness, above your desert lair, where the body is stripped of its bones. Take heart, you big, shaggy lion . . . They will pay, your enemies, that great affliction of sterile decadence, for their contempt for this dazzlingly sublime tempest of the spirit, which has passed by so close to them, as close to the barren wilderness as did other tempests—Léon Bloy, Ernest Hello, Charles Péguy . . .[7] Yes, that is how it has to be, and you are one of them, one of those who have been walled up alive. At opposite ends of the sky, two stars are burning over your solitary cell: the star of suicide and the star of asceticism—and that is your path, the path of the strongest and bravest—of Epictetus, Ramon Llull, Martinez de Pasqually, and all these dazzling, chaste paragons of incorruptibility . . ."[8]

Oleg grew wearier and wearier; alarmed and anxious, his thoughts became muddled and began to take on ever more mythological, cloudy outlines. With his chin slumped on top of his powerful hand, he stared blankly at the cars sweeping past, distinguishing little that he saw, when all of a sudden, the familiar, almost hateful, but so wonderfully calm voice of Bezobrazoff asked him:

"Well then, did you manage the journey homeward from heaven?"

"No, Apollon, I didn't . . . The earth wouldn't have me."

"So, then, you are going back to heaven?"

"No, Apollon, neither to heaven nor to the earth, but to great poverty, the arrant silence of absolute night . . . Remember Saint Jean de la Croix. On a dark night, O happiness, O joy, noticed by none, my soul went forth from my house, O happiness, O joy, to meet my . . . betrothed."[9]

"Well, never mind about all that . . . So we're friends? . . ."

"Yes, Apollon, once again in the paradise of friends . . ."[10]

■ □ ■

1934–1935

NOTES

1

1. **Jean Paul** is the pen name of the German writer Johann Paul Friedrich Richter (1763–1825). Though the author belonged formally to the Romantic movement, much of his writing prefigures the modernist experiments of the late nineteenth and early twentieth centuries. His invention of the "polymeter," an unrhymed rhythmic prose poem contained within a paragraph, stands out among his formal innovations that seem to have resonated with Poplavsky. The epigraph itself is a misquotation of a line from a polymeter titled "Das Menschen-Hertz" (The heart of man), which appears in Jean Paul's satirical novel *Dr Katzenbergers Badreise* (Dr Katzenberger's journey to a spa, 1809), whose eponymous hero, akin to Bezobrazoff, is a detached observer of the phenomenal world in all its grotesquery. The original line reads: "*Mir träumte, ich sei unnennbar selig, aber ohne Gestalten, und ohne Alles, und ohne Ich, und die Wonne war selber das Ich*" (I dreamt that I was indescribably happy, but without form, and without anything, and without Me, and that the ecstasy was itself Me).

2. The "previous act" refers to the novel *Apollon Bezobrazoff*, which Poplavsky worked on between 1926 and 1932, publishing only a handful of fragments before his death. Six years intervene between the events of *Apollon Bezobrazoff*, which take place over a period of fifteen months in 1925–1926, and those of *Homeward from Heaven*, which begins in the summer of 1932 and ends in that of 1934.

3. The *Paris-Midi* was a midday newspaper in daily circulation between 1911 and 1944. It enjoyed wide popularity and catered principally to a working readership at a time when two-hour lunch breaks were still common. Here, its "mass appeal" is presented in juxtaposition with the intellectual esotery of the German philosopher Johann Gottlieb Fichte's (1762–1814) *Grundlage der gesammten Wissenschaftslehre* (*Foundations of the Science of Knowledge*, 1794–1795). Such stark contrasts are characteristic of Bezobrazoff's personality, as indicated by his name, which

invokes at once the god of form and that which is *bez obraza*, "without aspect," "without form."

4. The typescript of the novel includes the following omitted passage, which was crossed out by Poplavsky during subsequent revisions:

> Reader! Place your hand to your precious organ and, holding thus your fate in your hand, hear my sordid words, which, like pages of a Russian newspaper amid a raging storm, fly up from the earth to the sky . . . For the beginning of every dark tale is to be found in the heavens. From on high, as a tree grows down into the earth, man's fate is writ backwards, from right to left. Back to front it speaks, and at times even sings, all because some snub-nosed hero chooses his faith, while that faith has really chosen him, much as the rain chooses a field, on a whim, so as to drench him, to daze and derange him, to weigh him down like a cloak awash with water, and in the end to cheer him during the utmost dissolution of his summertime disgrace, for no one is master over his own appearance, just as day is not master over the sky's dazzling azure (for the day is itself the consequence of that azure), nor evening over the ubiquitous amber of twilight (for the twilight gives life to the evening, and that life lingers atop the crest of a hill, over there, where past the bend in the highway a brand-new yellow advertisement extols the ubiquitous Shell corporation), nor night over darkness, for darkness is both its flesh and its fate, just like my carnal abstinence from fate, which began—who knows how or where—in the fading light of that first and desperate hope for pity.
>
> Abstinence from fate . . . Yes, the lives of the living are an unbroken, unwearying congress with the air, the white road, with the radiant purity of glass and music, with God.

5. In the years after the Bolshevik Revolution, Russian émigré charities such as the Zemgor, the Red Cross, and several scouting associations bought up then-cheap plots of land along the coast of the French Riviera, building on them summer holiday camps for émigré children and youths. These ventures bolstered the already-strong Russian contingent in the Alpes-Maritimes, particularly in the environs of Nice, where many Russians had lived since prerevolutionary times, and where many now came to recuperate and to work on the numerous agricultural colonies in Provence. The Riviera setting of the opening chapters is based on Poplavsky's visits to Natalia Stolyarova in 1932 and 1934. Recalling these days in later life, she wrote:

> In that distant summer of 1932, there was a marvelous and, at the time, pristine little spot called La Favière, which was populated almost exclusively by Russians. High on a ledge overhanging the sea, there stood a little cottage called "Lou Bastidoun," which by some miracle has been preserved to this very day

in the town, now unrecognizable after half a century. That summer, as they do now, Russians were staying there. In and around it, the fates of many collided and entwined.

(Natalia Stolyarova, "Instead of an Introduction")

6. While the writer and poet **Katherine Mansfield** (1888–1923) did live for a time in the Bandol, where she had gone to escape the English winter, she in fact died at Avon, near Fontainebleau. A consumptive, she spent the last years of her life undergoing treatment by a number of Russian émigrés, including the physician Ivan Manoukhin (1882–1958) and the mysticist Georges Gurdjieff (1866?–1949), at whose Institute for the Harmonious Development of Man she eventually met her end.

7. The "castle of water" seen by Oleg and Bezobrazoff at the connecting station is really a calque of the French *château d'eau*, denoting, more prosaically, a water tower.

2

1. Another reference to the "previous act" (see chap. 1, note 2). Thérèse is the young Franco-Russian heroine of *Apollon Bezobrazoff*, who at the novel's end leaves the group of Russian émigrés to join a Carmelite monastery.

2. The typescript of the novel includes the following omitted dream passage, which combines surrealist imagery with *chastushki*, popular song, biblical paraphrase, and even a corruption of lines drawn from Pushkin's *Eugene Onegin*. Poplavsky appears, however, to have marked it for deletion during later revisions.

APOLLON: What are we going to gorge ourselves on today?

OLEG: We could pick some grapes. They'll leave something out for us after lunch.

CHRIST IN HADES: I am the vine, and my father is the vintner, but we cannot steal.

THE APOLLO OF DELPHI (*naked, in a starched collar*): Lies, all lies! . . . The Devil stole him and carried him to the temple roof, he carried God, like a pair of pleated trousers. It's lies, all lies! (*An orchestra plays "On the Hills of Manchuria."*)

CHRIST IN HADES: Like Lazarus—who resultantly had to die twice, of course—they will, at best, be fed on crumbs from the table of a slovenly angel . . . Why, though? When in hell they could be full up and drunk on fire and sorrow. (*A colossal cloud of smoke; for a moment a chorus of sinners can be heard singing "Let the Grave Punish Me . . ." And again Christ hums along and whistles wearily, barely audibly, as he reads the newspapers of yesteryear.*)

THE APOLLO OF PARIS: Well, how about a swim, to drive the bastard out, not to put too fine a point on it?

OLEG: I'm bored of swimming. I'd much have rather a game of cards or steal those apes' canoe. (*In the middle of the day, the sky slowly darkens. The water turns into some heinous blue gelée full of tin cans and the forest seems packed with greasy, well-thumbed issues of the Latest News, while beyond them on the horizon, like red clouds, enormous genitals appear.*)

CHORUS OF GENITALS: Winter! . . . The peasant triumphantly inaugurates the track downwind. Feeling the snow on his red paws, he hurries to lay a brick . . . (*An unfathomable sorrow clenches his heart, while cigarette butts, pages of physics textbooks, and lumps of barracks walls painted gray-green rain down from the sky. Then gradually everything is blanketed with snow, and from under it the enormous red angel from the previous act mumbles, while he tosses and turns in a dream.*) David took a harp and played with his hand. To jack in the john isn't all so grand. The Jews, they are a grubby race; what of Jonah's needs in those three days?! (*Slowly, a military band flies low over Lubyanka Square, playing Mozart's Requiem; some animals, buildings, and worlds, poorly adapted to anything, open their eyes and look around in fear, with no idea where they are; again the orchestra plays "On the Hills of Manchuria." Wincing from the smoke,* CHRIST IN HADES *finishes a cigarette, while above him, in a dark-blue halo, a haughty woman of antique build talks to herself.*)

HAUGHTY WOMAN: The Creator chose love, for good is good not because the Creator loves it, but because it is good . . .

HAUGHTY WOMAN'S PRIVATE PART (*in a beautiful, melodious voice*): Love lulled the Creator to sleep, for good is good not because it is good, but because He drank himself sick on sweet wine . . . And so, let the grave punish me . . .

APOLLON (*morosely*): It's all a bit bleak here . . . Do you think we can make it back to Paris without any money?

OLEG: The sea's making such a strange sound—heaving and crashing as though to rebuke the shore, while there are splotches of sunlight skimming over the mountains, illuminating and forgetting everything as they go.

CHRIST IN HADES: But what is above is a reflection of what is beneath, amen . . . Thus, it follows that Don Aminado is also reflected in the seventh heaven . . .

SATYRS (*in caves and silk hose*): Glory to the sailor Christopher Columbus . . . who discovered America for its vast expanses.

MOTHERS IN THE UNDERWORLD: There's nothing to be done. We're open . . .

3. At various points in these opening chapters, Poplavsky names the holiday resort on the Riviera variously as **La Favière** and Saint-Tropez. While both locations did host Russian holiday colonies, it is likely that the erroneous references to La Favière are remnants from earlier drafts of the novel, which were aligned

more closely with historical reality and events from Poplavsky's own life (see Introduction).

4. **Konstantin Leontiev** (1831–91) was a philosopher and religious thinker, as well as an incisive literary critic. His anti-Western ideas had an undisputable influence on the development of Eurasianism and Scythianism.

5. **Jules Laforgue** (1860–87) was a Franco-Uruguayan poet, best known for his masterpiece of Symbolist verse *L'Imitation de Notre-Dame la Lune* (The imitation of our lady the moon, 1886). He was a favorite of Poplavsky's and even appears as the dedicatee of some of the author's own verses. **Marcel Proust** (1871–1922) exerted an almost unparalleled influence on the younger generation of Russian émigré writers, most notably Gaito Gazdanov (1903–1971) and Yuri Felsen (1894–1943). The text of Poplavsky's most famous pronouncement on Proust, "O Pruste i Dzhoise" (On Proust and Joyce), has not survived; however, it is clear from other sources that Poplavsky disagreed with Proust on a number of aesthetic grounds. Poplavsky argued, for instance, that Proust's surfeit of reasoning transformed his novels into "essays," and that "between Joyce and Proust there is the same distance as there is between the pain caused by a burn and a narrative about it."

6. **Gilgamesh** was the mythopoeic ruler of the ancient Sumerian city state of Uruk, whose reign, described in the ancient Mesopotamian poem *The Epic of Gilgamesh*, is believed to have occurred at some point between the twenty-eighth and twenty-fifth centuries BCE. While the wall-building at Uruk and the oppression of the populace are now known to be distinct elements in the epic narrative, they were conflated by early commentators in Poplavsky's day due to lacunae in the source text.

3

1. **Paul Eluard** (1895–1952) was a French Surrealist poet. The epigraph is taken from his poem "Tous les droits" (All rights), which was included in the collection *La Vie immédiate* (The immediate life, 1932).

2. A pun on the French *O mer* ("O sea") and *amour* ("love"). In Poplavsky's original, the pun turns on the corresponding Russian and Latin equivalents.

3. The *Latest News* (also known as *Poslednie novosti* in Russian and as *Les Dernières Nouvelles* in French) was the leading Russian émigré daily in France. It was published in Paris from 1920 to 1940.

4. One of the most instantly recognizable tangos in the popular repertoire, "Jalousie" (Jealousy) is a so-called "gypsy" tango, written by the Danish composer Jacob Gade in 1925. An arrangement with lyrics by Winifred May was recorded and released in 1932, the year of Oleg's summer trip to the Riviera.

5. The motif hummed by Oleg is likely the opening bars of the bridal chorus "Treulich geführt…" (Faithfully guided…), which begins third act of Richard Wagner's opera *Lohengrin* (1850) and whose theme has become one of the most recognizable wedding processionals in the Western world.

6. An oblique reference to Poplavsky's fourth collection of poetry, *V venke iz voska* (In a wreath of wax), which was published posthumously in Paris in 1938.

7. In ancient Greek mythology, the ferryman Charon conveyed souls across the river Acheron, which divided the world of the living from that of the dead. Here, Poplavsky has confused the Acheron for the Lethe, another of the five rivers in the Greek underworld of Hades.

8. The line is a misquotation of lyrics from the *chanson* "Complainte" (Lament), which was written by the director Julien Duvivier for his 1933 film adaptation of George Simenon's novel *La Tête d'un homme* (1931):

Et j'ai cherché le visage	And I looked for the face
De l'amour que j'ai rêvé	Of the love that I dreamt
Dans chaque être de passage	In every passer-by
Et je ne l'ai pas trouvé	And I did not find it
[…]	[…]
Dans la foule qui me roule	In the crowd that envelops me
Seule comme en un linceul	Alone, as though in a shroud,
Poursuivant le néant	Pursuing the emptiness
D'amours sans lendemain	Of loves without tomorrow
Sans caresse, sans tendresse	Without caress, without tenderness
J'ai vécu mon destin	I lived out my destiny
Et la nuit m'envahit	And the night engulfs me
Tout est brume, tout est gris.	All is mist, all is grey.

The *chanson*, which is used in the film to punctuate the protagonist's disillusionment with fantasy, was performed and later recorded by the actress and singer Marie-Louise Damien (1889–1978), better known by her stage name "Damia." The name of the bar that Oleg has just visited when he sings these lines may also, in addition to its Chekhovian overtones, be an indirect reference to the singer, one of whose most famous songs was "Les Goélands" ("The Seagulls").

4

1. The epigraph is a slight misquotation of a line from **Maupassant's** *Sur l'eau* (*Afloat*, 1888), a poetic and digressive account of a boating trip taken along the Côte d'Azur. Here, the word *femmes* (women) has been substituted for the original *formes* (figures, manners).

2. The boulevard **Saint-Michel** is one of two major thoroughfares in Paris's Latin Quarter (the other being the boulevard Saint-Germain) and demarcates the boundary between the fifth and sixth arrondissements.

3. Poplavsky reworked the ending of this section several times. It originally read: "Dear reader, but of course you won't understand any of this, because you're a lazy swine, and you can sod off."

4. In the 1930s, lighting was affixed to the upper stage of the **Eiffel Tower**, showing moving clockfaces and a thermometer that reached from the top of the second stage all the way to the cupola. As is standard in Europe, the temperature is given in degrees Celsius.

5. The **Pont de Passy** was renamed in 1948 and is known nowadays as the Pont de Bir-Hakeim.

6. The typescript includes the following deleted line: "For me, Maupassant and syphilis are one and the same. Syphilis is a terrible, mystical word, invisible and ever-present. If I were to find out that one of my friends had syphilis, I should be unable to shake his hand and would just look at him, burning with horror, curiosity, and perhaps even a certain respect."

7. **Jack London** (born John Griffith Chaney, 1876–1916) was an American author and journalist, who enjoyed tremendous international success in his day. In part because of his socialist views, London's works were especially popular in Soviet Russia, where he was the second-most published non-Soviet author after Hans Christian Andersen.

8. Several of Poplavsky's contemporaries—Roman Gul, Yuri Terapiano, Vladimir Varshavsky, Vasily Yanovsky, to name only a few—wrote about the **Rotonde**, the **Napoli**, the **Dôme**, and other Parisian cafés that were the purlieus of so many young émigré poets, writers, and artists. As Andrei Sedykh recalled in his memoir *Distant, Near* (1962), "It was a long time ago, in the twenties. We would roam about Paris for days on end in search of work, and then in the evenings we would gather at the Rotonde, which at the time was still a cheap, grubby, dingy café. The Rotonde was our sanctuary, our club, and kaleidoscope. All the world would pass by, and you could survey that world as you sat quietly and stirred your twenty-centime café au lait." In Montparnasse there were various cafés that served the emigration's many cliques and literary circles: the group "Cherez" met at the Café de Port-Royal; the members of "Gatarapak" and "Palata Poetov" congregated at the Café Chaméléon; the Sélect was the spot of choice for Georgy Adamovich, Alexander Ginger, and Anna Prismanova, while the more discreet Napoli was a favorite of Yuri Felsen's and Nina Berberova's. In his early days in Paris, Poplavsky would meet his friends, the artists Konstantin Tereshkovich, Mikhail Larionov, Victor Barthe, and Sergei Karsky, almost daily at the Rotonde, a stone's throw from the Académie de la Grande Chaumière, where Poplavsky studied between 1921 and 1922.

9. In all likelihood, the prototype for the character **Tchernosvitoff** was the artist and writer Serge Charchoune (1888–1975), whose biography and appearance broadly

accord with those laid out here by Poplavsky. Charchoune had in fact lived in Spain for a time before settling in Paris and is known to have styled himself as "the first Russian Dadaist" (and later Surrealist). By contrast, **Okolichine**, the "Jewish lord without a farthing in his pocket," bears a marked resemblance in both character and demeanor to the writer Yuri Felsen.

10. The **Cabaret aux Fleurs** was a genuine establishment on the rue du Montparnasse and is mentioned in the diaries and letters of several writers of the era, including Anaïs Nin and Claude Mauriac. In a letter of 1935 to the émigrée artist Ida Karskaya (1905–1990), Natalia Stolyarova, by then having returned to the Soviet Union, wrote: "Moscow is such a big city, noisier than Paris, faster-paced and busier. People, students—they all work so much more than they do in Paris, but then they have a better time of it too. After a few nights here, it makes me laugh and galls me to think of the Cabaret aux Fleurs."

11. Derived from the Ancient Greek μέτοικος, a term denoting a foreign resident in Classical Athens, this Gallicized variant was officially adopted by the Académie française in 1927 and already carried a somewhat pejorative meaning. Oleg's use of the term to describe the French is humorously subversive and indicative of his primarily Russian milieu.

5

1. Although having been attributed previously to the French poet Guillaume Apollinaire (1880–1918), the exact source of these lines is unclear; they are likelier a pastiche by Poplavsky in the style of the poet. These measures also appear in Poplavsky's diary, in the entry for June 20, 1935, when Poplavsky was at work on the novel. The concluding line of the French text reads: "*Et encore une fois je fais connaissance avec le désespoir, je devrais déjà y être habitué*" (And again I made the acquaintance of despair; I ought to be used to it by now).

2. The line first appears in Poplavsky's poem "Morella I", written in November 1929, and later again, in a slightly altered version, in a diary entry from December of that same year.

3. Both Imperial Russia and the Soviet Union practiced a system of political and **administrative exile**, whereby individuals, groups, and entire nationalities were deported and forcibly resettled across the length and breadth of the state's vast territory. This manner of determining people's fates was referred to with various official euphemisms including, in Soviet times, "administrative exile," which alluded to the "administrative" (i.e. extrajudicial) manner of decision-making on the part of executive bodies.

4. The line is a quotation from Arthur Rimbaud's poem "Chanson de la plus haute tour" ("Song of the Highest Tower," 1872).

5. In all likelihood, the figure mentioned to in Oleg's dream is the notorious embezzler Serge Alexandre **Stavisky** (*sic*), a naturalized Ukrainian Jew, who in 1933 found himself at the center of a major financial scandal in France that became known as the Stavisky Affair. His death in January 1934 was officially recorded as suicide but widely rumored to have been orchestrated by the French government and the police. Details of his involvement with so many ministers of state led to the resignation of the socialist prime minister Camille Chautemps, whose successor Edouard Daladier immediately dismissed the prefect of police, Jean Chiappe, a figure notorious for his right-wing sympathies. In retaliation, the fascist league organized a demonstration on the night of February 6, during which fifteen demonstrators were shot by the police and some 2,000 people were injured in the course of the riots. These events form the historical basis for some of the scenes in chapters VIII and IX.

6. Founded in 1440 by King Henry VI, **Eton** College is one of England's oldest and most prestigious schools. At no point in its history has it accepted female pupils.

7. According to biblical texts, **Jachin** and **Boaz** were the names given, respectively, to the right and left bronze pillars that stood at the entrance to the first Temple in Jerusalem. (As so often with Poplavsky, the transliteration of these names is filtered through French.) In classical Hebrew, the name Jachin (יָכִין, *yakin*) means "he shall establish," while Boaz (בֹּעַז, *bo ʿaz*) means "in it [is] strength." Poplavsky appears to invoke the two pillars here for their many interpretations in the Jewish mystical tradition, according to one of which they are seen to represent and elucidate, being both distinct and separate, contrary and complementary in appearance, the relationship between man and woman.

8. Andrei **Rublev** (*c.*1360–1428) was one of the greatest medieval painters of Russian Orthodox icons and frescoes. Here, the sophistication of Rublev's artistry is contrasted against the *lubok*, a type of woodcut print that originated in the seventeenth century and is characterized by a simple folk style and typically bright colors.

6

1. From 1855 until 1938, Paris was served by an extensive tramway system, which predated the Métro by almost half a century and, at its height, consisted of more than 120 lines. In the 1930s, however, the oil and automotive industries began lobbying the Paris Police Prefecture to remove tram tracks in order to make way for motor cars, eventually resulting in their total removal. The No. 82 tram that Oleg recalls originally ran from Vitry to Châtelet via the place d'Italie; after successive shortenings of the line, however, it finally disappeared in 1933.

2. Literally meaning "iceworks," **Glacière** is a Métro station in Paris's thirteenth arrondissement, so called because prior to the advent of the electric refrigerator, ice was collected in the area from the ponds of the Bièvre River during the winter and stored for the summer in wells built for the purpose. The Russian canteen mentioned is likely the "Socialist Revolutionary" one on rue de la Glacière, recalled by Ilya Ehrenburg in his memoirs:

> I remember two canteens: the Socialist Revolutionary one in the rue de la Glacière (it was called that because some Socialist Revolutionaries, relatives of the owners of "Vysotsky's Tea," donated money for feeding the émigrés), and the non-party one in the rue Pascal. Both were cheap, dirty and crowded with nasty food. The waiter shouted to the cook: "*Un borshch et bitochki avec kasha!*" A red-haired S.R. woman repeated hysterically that unless they gave her a battle mission she would kill herself. Grisha, a Bolshevik, was outraged: passing the Café d'Harcourt he had seen Martov sitting inside—that's how opportunists go to pieces!
>
> (Ilya Ehrenburg, *People and Life, 1891–1921*,
> tr. Anna Bostock and Yvonne Kapp)

For the last nine years of his life, Poplavsky himself lived not far from this canteen, at 22 rue Barrault, between Glacière and the place d'Italie. The address, in the thirteenth arrondissement, was the Citroën "pavilion," built by the émigré architect "Kaganovich" in 1925 on top of the Garage Barrault roof. The complex consisted of a series of small Alsace-style apartments, intended for the firm's (predominantly Russian) taxi drivers.

3. The year 1925 refers to that "legendary time," depicted in the novel *Apollon Bezobrazoff*, when Oleg's former incarnation fell under the spell of the eponymous character. The year also marked significant changes in Poplavsky's own life, for it was then that he, having formerly lived "in the paradise of friends," began to distance himself from them in the hope of winning broader artistic acclaim, "exchanging his soul" time and again, as Oleg does in these paragraphs.

4. This last phrase is a quotation drawn from the lyrics of the Russian folk ballad "Mogila" (The grave), written and composed by Yakov Prigozhy (1840–1920).

5. The jota is a Spanish folk dance, originating in Aragon.

6. Mikhail **Zoshchenko** (1894–1958) was a Soviet writer and satirist. His characters, who so often stand on the fringes of Soviet society, are notable in linguistic terms for their many stylistic infelicities, overloaded flights of metaphor, tortured cliché, and misapplied bureaucratese.

7. Poplavsky did indeed manage to achieve this desire: before his death, he collected and edited a selection of poems written in the years 1922–1924, which eventually constituted the posthumous collection *V venke iz vozka* (In a wreath of wax).

8. Karl Robert Eduard von **Hartmann** (1862–1906) was a German idealist philosopher, whose reputation was established with the publication of *Philosophie des Unbewussten* (**Philosophy of the Unconscious**) in 1869. Hartmann was one of several philosophers to be singled out for criticism in Vladimir Lenin's *Materializm i empiriokrititsizm* (*Materialism and Empirio-Criticism*, 1909).

9. One of Paris's smallest Russian Orthodox churches, the Church of the Three Holy Hierarchs was completed at 5 **rue Pétel** in 1931 and consecrated that Easter. Its catacomblike interior was embellished by the émigré icon painters Leonid Ouspensky (1902–1987) and Grigory Krug (1907/8–1969).

10. The typescript contains the following passage, which was crossed out, apparently by Poplavsky during the last round of revisions:

> Oleg did not much care for the Grossmans. Nikolai Grossman was a myopic and uncommonly proud man with ginger hair, an old classmate of Oleg's from his days at the art academy, but he was unsuccessful and reclusive. He had been the first of them to take French citizenship, and now he locked himself away from them all, living on his seventh floor and on his lifelong dole money. But since the Grossmans lived in the environs of Montparnasse itself, Oleg, in the sublime boredom of his wanderings, would occasionally find himself in front of their very building and could not resist calling on them to have a bite to eat. For Grossman's morbid amour propre found expression in, among other things, his unusual, emphatic hospitality, although each visit resulted in some vague spat between them, since Grossman was nervously disinclined toward Russians and, as far as he was concerned, Oleg was a typical specimen of Russian recklessness, the kind before whom he felt he could make a great show of his spiteful, well-mannered alienation, pricking Oleg each time and involuntarily provoking him to rudeness. That was why, for example, Oleg could never forgive Grossman for never visiting him at home, nor himself for continuing to call on Grossman in spite of it all—and this Russian–Jewish ordeal of unhealthy vanity lasted for a very long time indeed.

11. A reference to Ludwig van Beethoven's (1770–1827) Symphony No. 3 (1804), also known as the "*Sinfonia Eroica*" or "Heroic Symphony."

12. Titled more fully *Prélude à l'après-midi d'un faune* (Prelude to the afternoon of a faun), this short symphonic poem was composed by Claude Debussy (1862–1918) in 1894 and constitutes a musical response to Stéphane Mallarmé's (1842–1898) highly sensual, dreamlike eclogue "L'Après-midi d'un faune" (1876).

13. Hermès was a popular brand of typewriter, manufactured by the Swiss company E. Paillard & Co. from 1921.

7

1. Like Oleg, Poplavsky was, to all intents, too young to participate in the Russian Civil War (1917–1922), although his youth did not spare him the experience of its effects. In the summer of 1918, he and his father left Moscow for the Russian south, splitting up the family. In March the following year, they left Russia for Constantinople, but returned in July after the White forces reached Kharkov. Thereafter, Poplavsky and his father endured the hardship and peril of the rapidly changing situation, moving in a very short period from Novorossiysk to Yekaterinodar to Rostov-on-Don, from which in 1920 they would eventually be evacuated for a second time to Constantinople, first taking refuge in the house of the Armenian patriarch on the island of Prinkipos (present-day Büyükada) before settling in the Turkish quarter of Beşiktaş. While Poplavsky's tender years largely preserved him from any direct experience of warfare, some other émigré writers such as Gaito Gazdanov, who was Poplavsky's coeval, did nevertheless join Baron Wrangel's Volunteer Army out of a desire "to know what war was."

2. A reference to the émigré poet **Boris** Zakovich (1907–1995). The name given in the Russian text is "Pusya," which, as Vasily Yanovsky attests, was Poplavsky's term of endearment for this "friend, disciple, and slave." Poplavsky dedicated his second volume of poetry to him.

3. Literally meaning "the city of the emperor," **Tsargrad** is the old Slavonic name for Constantinople. The toponym is most likely a calque derived from one of the city's many honorary appellations in Greek.

4. One of Mikhail **Lermontov's** (1814–41) Hussar poems, "Ulansha" ("**The Uhlan girl**") is a barracks ballad that recounts the gang rape of the titular figure, which leaves her bruised, bitten, and largely unrecognizable as the company departs the following morning. The poem reputedly enjoyed tremendous popularity among cadets and officers of the day.

5. The *Great Lives of Saints*, also known as the *Cheti-Minei* and the *Menaion Reader*, is one of the most significant liturgical works of Slavonic literature. Compiled by Saint Dmitri of Rostov (1651–1709), the work constitutes a record of the saints' lives, arranged by month.

6. "O Heavenly King" is a prayer in the Eastern Orthodox tradition, commonly used to invoke the Holy Spirit at the beginning of religious services: "O Heavenly King, Comforter, Spirit of Truth, present in all places and filling all things, treasury of good things and giver of life: come; take Your abode in us; cleanse us of every stain, and save our souls, O Good one."

7. **Isadora Duncan** (1877–1927) was an American dancer who won fame in Europe and the Soviet Union especially. The sometime muse of Antoine Bourdelle and Auguste Rodin, Duncan was also married for a brief time to the Russian poet Sergei Esenin. She died tragically and famously in the south of France when her

long, flowing silk scarf became entangled in the spoked wheel and axle of the cabriolet in which she was riding, pulling her from the open vehicle and breaking her neck.

8. Here, Poplavsky refers to a **panopticon** not in the carceral Benthamian sense of the term, but rather in a now-archaic usage that denotes a museum of waxwork figures.

9. From the early days of his youth right until his untimely death at the age of thirty-two, Poplavsky experimented widely with recreational drugs, including hashish, **cocaine**, and heroin. Having been introduced to drug use by his sister, the decadent poet and noted cocainist Natalia Poplavskaya, the author recalled, even at the age of fifteen:

> We would go, you and I, and sniff cocaine in church,
> The painted eyes of the icons would smile,
> The candlelight would grow brighter, then fade,
> And at times, a series of visions would pass . . .

Like Poplavsky, Natalia also met a tragic end. She left émigré Paris at some point in the 1920s, to seek "the ultimate high," as Simon Karlinsky put it. The search took her to Madagascar, Africa, India, and finally to Shanghai, where she died of pneumonia, apparently the result of time spent in the city's many opium dens.

10. The department store **Aux Trois Quartiers** was one of Paris's oldest and most luxurious. Founded in 1829 on the boulevard de la Madeleine in the eighth arrondissement, the store was reconstructed in the modernist style by the architect Louis Faure-Dujarric in 1932.

11. Figuring in Homer's *Odyssey*, **Laërtes** was king of Ithaca and father to Odysseus. The lines here refer to the myth of the **cattle** of Helios, known also as the "oxen of the Sun," as related in Book XII of the *Odyssey*. (Poplavsky's conflation of Apollo and Helios is consistent with interpretations from the Hellenistic period onward; however, in Homeric literature, they were treated as distinct deities.) According to the legend, Helios was said to have seven herds of oxen and seven flocks of sheep, each numbering fifty head. Described as handsome, wide-browed, fat, and straight-horned, these immortal cattle were guarded by his daughters, Phaëthusa and Lampetië, and it was widely known that harm done to any of these beasts would incur the wrath of the god. While stranded on the Isle of Helios by a storm sent by Poseidon, Odysseus's men, under the encouragement of Eurylochus, drove off and sacrificed the best of his cattle in an attempt to leave the island. Hearing of this, Helios ordered the gods to take vengeance on Odysseus's men, threatening that if atonement were not made, he would take the sun to Hades and shine it among the dead. Before long, the gods showed signs and wonders to Odysseus's men: the hides began to creep, the flesh, both roasted and raw, bellowed upon the spits and there was a lowing as though of cattle. For six days the men feasted upon the kine of Helios, and on the seventh day Zeus smote their ship with a bolt of lightning, killing all the men but for Odysseus.

12. Situated eleven miles northwest of Athens, **Eleusis** was an ancient town in West Attica and was the original site of the cult of Demeter, goddess of harvest and agriculture.

13. The founder and first ruler of the ancient city of Thebes, **Cadmus** had four daughters with his wife, the goddess Harmonia.

14. *The Imitation of Christ* (*De Imitatione Christi*) is a fifteenth-century devotional text composed in four books. Originally written in Latin, it is ascribed to the German monk and mystic Thomas à Kempis (*c.*1380–1471).

15. **Diana**, goddess of the hunt, is the Roman equivalent of Artemis, the twin of Apollo, whose temple at **Ephesus** was held to be one of the seven wonders of the ancient world. Images and cult statues of the Ephesian Artemis are noted for their particularly distinctive form, with a tapering, pillarlike term, outstretched arms, and mural crown.

8

1. A reference to the **Lion** of Judah as it is described in the Book of Revelation: "And one of the elders saith unto me, Weep not: behold, the Lion of the tribe of Juda, the Root of David, hath prevailed to open the book, and to loose the seven seals thereof. And I beheld, and, lo, in the midst of the throne and of the four beasts, and in the midst of the elders, stood a Lamb as it had been slain, having seven horns and seven eyes, which are the seven Spirits of God sent forth into all the earth" (5:5–6).

2. Meaning "lord" or "master," and hence also denoting God, **Belus** is the Latinized form of the classical Greek epithet βῆλος, which itself derives from the Hebrew בַּעַל (*ba 'al*).

3. Likely a reference to **Marcus**, the founder of an early Christian Gnostic sect that flourished at Lyons from the second to the fourth centuries AD. Known almost exclusively through a long polemic in Irenaeus's theological treatise *Adversus Haereses* (Against Heresies), Marcosian doctrine is especially notable in the context of Poplavsky's writing for its contention that knowledge is the product of a divine revelation of the body:

> Moreover, the Tetrad, explaining these things to him more fully, said: I wish to show thee Aletheia (Truth) herself; for I have brought her down from the dwellings above, that thou mayest see her without a veil, and understand her beauty—that thou mayest also hear her speaking, and admire her wisdom. Behold, then, her head on high, *Alpha* and *Omega*; her neck, *Beta* and *Psi*; her shoulders with her hands, *Gamma* and *Chi*; her breast, *Delta* and *Phi*; her diaphragm, *Epsilon* and *Upsilon*; her back, *Zeta* and *Tau*; her belly, *Eta* and *Sigma*; her thighs, *Theta* and *Rho*; her knees, *Iota* and *Pi*; her legs, *Kappa* and *Omicron*; her ankles, *Lambda* and *Xi*; her feet, *Mu* and *Nu*. Such is the body

of Truth, according to this magician, such the figure of the element, such the character of the letter. And he calls this element Anthropos (Man), and says that is the fountain of all speech, and the beginning of all sound, and the expression of all that is unspeakable, and the mouth of the silent Sige. This indeed is the body of Truth. But do thou, elevating the thoughts of thy mind on high, listen from the mouth of Truth to the self-begotten Word, who is also the dispenser of the bounty of the Father.

(*Against Heresies*, 1.XIV.iii, tr. Philip Schaff)

4. **Fra Angelico** (*c*.1395–1455) was an Italian painter of the early Renaissance. Described by Vasari in his *Lives of the Artists* (1550) as having "a talent so rare and so perfect," he earned his reputation primarily for the series of frescoes that he made for the friary of San Marco in Florence. He was given the epithet "Il Beato" (The Blessed) on account of the heavenly beauty and harmony of his works.

5. Aside from its literal implications, the description of Oleg as being "**without breeches**" is of course also a calque of *sans-culottes*, a French term originating in the eighteenth century and denoting the lower classes. The image of embarrassment is intensified when we recall that Oleg does not in fact wear any underwear.

6. Evoking the cries of newspaper hawkers and the sounds of the Paris streets impressionistically, these nonsense words recall Poplavsky's early *zaum* or "beyonsense" poetry written during the period of Russian Dadaism.

7. The typescript continues with the following deleted fragment, parts of which are reworked later in Chapter IX:

> From time to time, some emphatically polite policemen proclaimed loudly but respectfully, "*Messieurs, pas d'attroupements*," but as soon as Oleg neared the Opéra, a group of ruddy, rowdy, narrow-shouldered students marched past him, clearly mustering their courage and chanting: "*A bas les voleurs . . . Vive Chiappe!*" And so it carried on until evening, the cries growing then fading away, until darkness fell and the streetlamps lit up over the crowded streets. Carried in all directions, crushed by the protestors, Oleg would occasionally find himself right beside the police. He watched as the crowd taunted and hauled at one of them, stealing his helmet and his bicycle, which immediately ended up on a streetlamp. Suddenly imbued with their sense of patriotic feelings, Oleg now imagined himself to be his savior and began shouting over and over, "*Laissez-le, laissez-le!*" eventually helping him force his way into a tobacconist's. But suddenly Oleg was carried by the crowd to the police cordon, where he instantly lost all understanding of why he was there. Nobody touched him, although the tired and angry policemen, their eyes filled with blood and red wine, brandished their truncheons over his head . . . That was when he made a run for it, straight into an alleyway, where the shouts and confusion of the crowd barely [. . .]

9

1. The flea market where Oleg strolls during his midday break is likely, given the geography, to be Les Puces de Saint-Ouen, one of Paris's oldest and largest flea markets, situated near the Porte de Clignancourt.

2. Born Benedikt Franz Xaver Baader, Franz von Baader (1765–1841) was a German Catholic philosopher, theologian, and physician. Much of von Baader's idiosyncratic philosophy is difficult to interpret, expressed as it is in aphorisms, mystical symbols, and analogies; however, his work is essentially a form of theosophy, which, combining with his theories on physiology and anthropology, gave rise to a number of treatises on gender and, more specifically, androgyny (he speculated that man was originally an androgynous being).

3. See chap. 5, note 5.

4. A small Alpine village in the canton of Graubünden in southeastern Switzerland, Sils Maria is where Friedrich Nietzsche spent several summers during the 1880s.

5. Encapsulating the ancient belief that the expenditure of vitality diminishes the spirit, the line is a paranomastic corruption of one attributed to the Greek physician Galen (129–c.210 AD): *triste est omne animal post coitum, præter mulierem gallumque* (all animals are sad after sex, save for women and the rooster).

6. In the Roman Catholic and Orthodox churches, the story of Susanna and the Elders is included as an addition to the Book of Daniel. According to the text, the fair wife Susanna, having sent away her attendants while she bathes in her garden, is clandestinely observed by two lecherous elders, who proceed to blackmail her, threatening to claim that she was meeting a young man unless she agrees to have sexual relations with them. The episode is the subject of paintings by many renowned artists, including Lorenzo Lotto, Guido Reni, Van Dyck, Rubens, Tintoretto, Rembrandt, Tiepolo, and Artemisia Gentileschi.

7. Rather than his namesake of historical renown, this Averroes is a character who appears in the novel *Apollon Bezobrazoff*:

> I recollect sitting in the "Rotonde" with the medieval philosophy expert whom Apollon Bezobrazov had christened Averroes, the one who employed him. Averroes was an extraordinarily odd person, with a life story nothing short of fantastic. But for a long time now we had considered only the fantastic to be natural. First Averroes had been a rabbi, then a doctor, then a stockbroker, a contractor for various governments, a builder, the owner of a gun factory, and a student again, this time in a department of theology. Then he almost became a monk, was a resident of a psychiatric institution for a while, and finally, acting upon a gloomy fantasy of his, he became the owner of the flower store and studio where they painted flowers in unnatural colors and bred loathsome tropical species.
>
> (*Apollon Bezobrazov*, tr. John Kopper)

8. In late-nineteenth-century Imperial Russia, "heavy athletics" acquired a respectable image and was popularized in the form of wrestling and weightlifting clubs. Among the most famous of these, the **Hercules** club was founded by the professional wrestler Ivan Lebedev in St. Petersburg in 1896; it was quickly followed by the equally famous **Sanitas**, both of which offered a program of physical development through wrestling, gymnastics, and body building. Similar clubs sprang up across the empire.

10

1. The words, though often attributed to Arthur Rimbaud, were in fact spoken by a young Louis Aragon at a conference in Madrid in 1925. The line, in full, was: *"Je ne travaillerai jamais, mes mains sont pures"* (I shall never work, my hands are immaculate).

2. A reference to three of Zeus's metamorphoses: firstly, as a swan, which rapes the Spartan queen **Leda**; second, as a bull, which seduces and abducts the Phoenician princess **Europa**; third, as a cloud of golden rain, which impregnates the Argive princess **Danaë**.

3. In the history of the Russian Orthodox Church, so-called **Old Believers** are those who clung to the liturgical and ritual practices of the Church as they stood before the reforms enacted by Patriarch Nikon of Moscow between 1652 and 1666. Rejecting Nikon's reforms, the Old Believers held that the official Church had fallen into the hands of the Antichrist.

4. The lines are misquoted from Arthur Rimbaud's poem "Bonne pensée du matin" (Pleasant thought for the morning, 1872).

5. One cabbalistic tradition holds that **Jachin and Boaz** symbolize two of the three pillars belonging to the Tree of Life. According to this interpretation, the two bronze pillars represent, respectively, strength and wisdom; the third, which will stand between them, represents harmony, and is embodied by the individual passing through the portal. It has been recorded that replicas of these pillars are situated at the entrance to the lodge room in some Masonic lodges and serve a similar symbolic role in initiation rites.

6. While Poplavsky implies an attribution of this line to Paul the Apostle, the words are in fact a paraphrase of Jesus's teaching to his disciples as set down in the Gospel according to Mark (4:25). They also reoccur in slightly altered form in the Gospel according to Matthew: "But whosoever hath not, from him shall be taken away even that he hath" (13:12).

7. **Léon Bloy** (1846–1917) was a French novelist, essayist, and diarist, whose works are noted particularly for their stark stylistic combination of vulgar and exalted elements. His historical biographies (on figures including Napoleon and Joan of Arc) are striking for their attempts to uncover the true meaning of their heroes'

fates. **Ernest Hello** (1828–1885) was a French Roman Catholic writer, philosopher, and theologian with mystical tendencies, perhaps best remembered for his *Physionomies de saints* (Physiognomies of saints, 1875). He is mentioned in Joris-Karl Huysmans's novel *Là-bas* (The Damned, 1891): "The real psychologist of the century . . . is not their Stendhal but the astonishing Hello, whose inexpungible unpopularity beggars belief." **Charles Péguy** (1873–1914) was a French poet, essayist, and publicist, whose philosophy encompasses a mélange of socialism, nationalism, and Roman Catholicism. Péguy wrought a considerable influence on several twentieth-century thinkers and writers, including Graham Greene, who in *The Lawless Roads* (1939) described Péguy as "challenging God in the cause of the damned."

8. **Epictetus** (*c.*50–135 AD) is held to be one of the most important philosophers of the Stoic school. Born in the Kingdom of Majorca, **Ramon Llull** (*c.*1232–*c.*1315) was a troubadour in his youth, but later devoted his life to philosophy and theology. A mathematician, polymath, logician, and mystic, his more than three hundred works are informed by the confluence of three cultures: Christianity, Islam, and Judaism. Jacques de Livron Joachim de la Tour de la Casa **Martinez de Pasqually** (1727(?)–1774) was a theosophist of uncertain origin, renowned in his day as a miracle worker. His elaborate doctrine emerged under the influence of Gnosticism, and he is regarded as the originator of Martinism.

9. **Saint John of the Cross** (1542–1591) was a Spanish Catholic priest and mystic and a Carmelite friar, whose poetry and studies of the soul stand among the greatest works of all Spanish literature. Here, Oleg refers to his most famous of works, the poem commonly known in English as *The Dark Night of the Soul*, which narrates the soul's journey to a mystical union with God.

10. Having ended the novel on this final note of friendship, Poplavsky fittingly inscribed on the verso of the edited typescript's last folio a list of those friends with whom he intended to share his completed opus: "To give to read: 1) Lida [Lidia Chervinskaya] 2) Kostitsky 3) Pusya [Boris Zakovich] 4) [Serge] Charchoune 5) Sonia 6) Sofia 7) [Georgy] Adamovich 8) Dina [Tatishcheva] 9) Nikolai [Tatishchev] 10) G[eorgy] Ivanov 11) [Yuri] Felsen 12) [Vasily] Yanovsky 13) Ol. Lv. 14) Frid 15) Olya."

R

CPSIA information can be obtained
at www.ICGtesting.com
Printed in the USA
JSHW020009270623
43787JS00003B/19

9 780231 199315